Hitting the Goal Line

CHICAGO DARK KNIGHTS BOOK 3

JOCELYNE SOTO

Hitting the
GOAL LINE
CHICAGO DARK KNIGHTS BOOK 3
JOCELYNE SOTO

From the age of five, I knew one thing;
Blake Jacobi was going to be in my life for a very long time.
For years, he was my protector, my best friend, my shoulder to
cry on. I even followed him to Chicago when he got picked up
by an NHL team.
Then lines got blurred and we landed in each other's beds, but
we were able to push feelings aside and not let a few little slips
ruin our friendship.
At least, that's what I keep telling myself.
Somewhere along the line, I fell in love with my best friend, and
as much as I want to tell him, I can't. All out of fear of losing
him.
So I hold in those words and try to lose myself in relationships
that I really shouldn't be in. But my efforts start to feel as if they
are for nothing when Blake lands himself in a jail cell.
All because of me.
Now those words that I've been wanting to tell him, may never
see the light of day.
Because after the night that we just had, I might have lost Blake
for good.

PLAYLIST

Little Do You Know - Alex & Sierra
Jealous (with Ella Mai) - Kiana Ledé
Nonsense - Sabrina Carpenter
To Be So Lonely - Harry Styles
Cruel Summer - Taylor Swift
I miss you, I'm sorry - Gracie Abrams
Best Friend - Rex Orange County
Dress - Taylor Swift
Anything 4 u - LANY
Friends - Ed Sheeran
Feelings - Lauv
You Are In Love (Taylor's Version) - Taylor Swift

DISCLAIMER

Hitting The Goal Line takes place before, during and after Skating The Blue Line and Passing The Red Line. Reading in order is not necessary.

To readers that have been waiting for Blake and Sophia, thank you for sticking by my side while I figured out their story.

AUTHOR'S NOTE

Please be advised that this book does touch upon heavier subjects, such as domestic violence. If this is not something that you are comfortable with, please do not read.
Thank you.

PROLOGUE
BLAKE

THERE'S a chance that I've lost her.

Those years of memories, of happiness, of loving her, could all be gone.

If I did lose her and everything that made us us, is gone, all it took was one punch. One broken jaw. A single call to the police, and all that we've had, all that we have built throughout the years of friendship, has been thrown into the toilet. Flushed away to never be seen again.

I might have ruined what we had, and now there's a possibility that we will never be the same. We will never be as close as we were. She will never look at me the same way. She'll most likely never again give me the smile I love so much. Not after what I did this morning.

The way that she looked at me may now be ruined, and it's all my fucking fault.

And all because I didn't tell her sooner.

All because I thought that she would always be with me, be at my side, and be mine in some capacity, no matter what. Fear may not have let me make her my everything, but at the very least I would have my best friend.

All I had to do so this never happened, was to tell the girl who has been in my life since I was five, three little words. Words I've wanted to say to her for a long time and actually meant. Words that would have changed everything.

But I didn't.

Now here I am sitting in a jail cell, with thoughts that I've lost her forever circling through my head.

All I had to say was, "I love you," when she was in my bed, when my team won the Cup, when we had dinner every night, before she met that fucking asshole, and we wouldn't be in this mess.

We would be at home, and she would be in my arms, and I would be kissing her body, marking it as mine once and for all, for nobody else to ever touch again.

But I'm an idiot. An asshole who was just trying to protect her and wasn't listening when she screamed at me to stop.

There's a chance that because of my actions, she will never talk to me again. That she will take his side and never look back.

There's a chance I've lost her for good.

And I have nobody to blame for it but myself.

CHAPTER ONE

SOPHIA

Present day

THIS WAS SUPPOSED to be the week I finally did it.

After weeks of feeling scared and trying to find the courage to leave, I was finally going to do it. I was finally going to leave the guy who has made me fearful of even talking to my best friend, and then I was going to go home and do the one thing that I've been running from for years.

I was going to end things with the man who has isolated me from everything I am and was going to finally tell the man who has owned every part of my heart for as long as I could remember that I wanted to be with him. That I loved him. That I was in love with him. That I didn't want to lose him, lose us.

Everything was all planned out. On both sides. I knew what I was going to say, I knew what I was going to do, and everything was going how I wanted it to, until it didn't.

I never expected to fly to San Francisco on a whim. I never expected for the breakup conversation to go the way it did. I never expected to be put in a literal corner with no place to go, no place to run, and for Blake, the man who has been my everything since I was five, to be thrown in a jail cell because of it.

I tried to stop it. I tried to calm him down so that he wouldn't get hurt, but nothing worked. He saw what I was going through, and he just flipped, and he did everything he could to take care of me like he has been doing all of our lives.

He was taking care of me, but when shit got tough, I wasn't able to do the same for him.

But that was Sophia a few hours ago. Sophia now is going to try everything she can to take care of him. To protect him and make sure that his life, his career, isn't ruined.

Squaring my shoulders and taking a deep breath, I walk into the San Francisco Central Police Station, where I was told Blake was going to be brought for processing and head to the front desk.

The place is busy. So busy there's a line of people, at least ten people deep, all waiting to be helped by the officers at the front desk. Not only are there a ton of people, but the phones are ringing nonstop, waiting for someone to answer.

I stand in line for about ten minutes, and when I eventually make it up to the front, the two officers behind the desk are busy with the phones.

One of them even holds up a finger for me to wait some more. So I do, and the whole time I try my hardest to keep my heartbeat at a steady pace. Trying but failing.

It takes another five minutes before one of the officers becomes available, and as soon as she is done with the phone call, she waves me over. As I approach the desk, she gives me a look of concern.

"Can I help you?" she asks, her eyes shifting to my cheek.

I haven't checked, but I'm sure there's already a bruise forming, if it hasn't already. There's probably also bruises forming on my ribs and thigh, too. I wonder what the officer's face would look like if she saw those.

Taking a deep breath, I answer the officer's question.

"Yes, I'm wondering if I can get information on someone who was brought in. The officers who responded to the call said I could come down here and get more information as to when he could possibly be released." I try to keep my voice even, but it cracks in a few spots.

"Can I get the individual's name?" the officer asks, giving me a small smile.

"Blake Jacobi," I say to her, hoping that the officer isn't a hockey fan or that the last name Jacobi doesn't sound familiar. Since we are in San Francisco, it is a toss-up. This officer could know of either one of the Jacobi brothers. As much as I love Blake's brother, we don't need star power to interfere with this. Or any star power, for that matter. We can't have this being national news, at least not until I let our families know what is going on.

"Relation?"

"Um." What do I say? If I say best friend, they won't take me seriously, and if I say anything besides significant other, there is a chance I won't get any information whatsoever. The only option I have here is to lie through my teeth. "He's my boyfriend."

The officer nods. "Do you by any chance have a picture of the two of you together? People come in here and lie to get information all the time."

"Um yeah. Let me pull one up."

Do other police stations ask for those types of pictures as proof that you are who you say you are? Or does she recognize the name, and she just wants to make sure I'm not a crazed fan?

Who knows, but thankfully, I have plenty of pictures of Blake and me throughout the years.

With shaky hands, I pull up a picture of us from Christmas two years ago and show it to her.

She gives me another nod and types something in her computer before responding. "It looks like he's in booking and will be calling this place home for the night."

The night? It's not even noon.

"What? Why? The officers who arrested him said he could be out of here in a few hours." This can't be happening. Things are literally going from bad to worse to actual hell right before my eyes.

"Yes, but that was before the other party decided to press charges," the officer informs me, and I instantly get the urge to punch something.

"Charges? What charges? It was self-defense. Blake was defending me and himself. If anyone should be pressing charges, it is me."

"Do you want to?" She raises her eyebrows at me, looking over at my cheek again, while she gets her notepad ready just in case I decide to say something.

I open my mouth to tell her yes, but nothing comes out.

Everything that has happened so far starts rushing through my body, and it feels like it's going to take over and destroy everything.

Pressing charges should be something I don't even have to stop and consider. I was physically hurt by someone in my life, and when someone else stepped in to help me, they got hurt, too. I should press charges against the bastard. I *need* to do it. Not only for my safety but for Blake's. So if I know that, why am I hesitating to tell this officer that yes, I want to file all the necessary paperwork to get this man, who has possibly hurt other women before me, out of my life and to take away his chance to ever do it again? He should be in the holding cell, not Blake. He should be the one who is facing whatever charges are getting thrown at Blake for what happened today and be put away for a long time.

But what if I say yes, and everything backfires? What if I tell this officer yes, tell her everything I've been through, and nothing comes from it? What if Blake ends up hating me for landing myself in this situation and landing him in a jail cell?

So many what-ifs are running through my mind with one simple question. I don't know what the correct answer is anymore.

I do know one thing, though. I need to get Blake out from where he is and apologize a million times over.

"If I say yes, will Blake be released?" I ask, hoping that maybe she will take pity on me and do so anyway.

She looks at me for a long minute before eventually letting out a sigh. "Unfortunately, it doesn't work that way. Because official charges have been filed against your boyfriend, he has to stand in front of a judge. But if you are pressing charges against the other person, there is a chance of him being released with no penalty, more so if you have evidence."

Evidence.

I have evidence. I was going to show it to the officers when they were arresting Blake, but so much happened in so little time that it completely slipped my mind.

Now I can use it. If I want to help Blake and not ruin his hockey career, I have to use it. I have to do what is absolutely necessary to take care of him, to protect him, like he has done countless times before for me.

Because I love him, in more ways than I comprehend.

Like I did when I walked into the station, I square my shoulders and give the officer a nod. "Then I would like to press charges, and I have evidence."

The officer gives me a small smile as if to tell me that she is proud of me.

"Go ahead and take a seat. I will go get another officer to take your statement."

I give her a curt nod and follow orders.

As I wait for the other officer to come talk to me, I touch the locket around my neck to calm me down, but as I sit here, I can't help to wonder how we got here.

How did almost eighteen years of friendship, a friendship filled with laughs, hard times and memories, get us to this point?

My mind goes through every single memory we have built together to find the turning point.

Part 1

CHAPTER TWO

SOPHIA

Five years old

I LOOK out at the ice and move behind Mommy. It looks cold out there and slippery. I already broke my arm once while I was playing on ice. I don't want to do it again.

"Sophie, it's okay. It's just like the skating rink we went to when we went to visit Grandma and Grandpa, remember?" my mom tells me, pushing back my curls.

"It doesn't look like the one with Grandma and Grandpa," I tell her, hiding deeper behind her as someone bangs against the wall. This place is bigger, and it has a lot more people than the ice rink Grandma and Grandpa took us to.

"This one is just bigger," my mommy says, moving so I'm no longer standing behind her and so she could now be the same height as me. She gives me a smile that Daddy says looks like mine. "Are you scared of going out there?"

I give her a nod.

"Because of your arm?"

I give her another nod.

"You weren't scared when you and Daddy went skating two

weeks ago. What happened between then and now?" she says, smiling at the mention of my daddy.

Tears start falling from my eyes. "He's not here."

"You don't want to go out there because your daddy isn't here?" Mommy asks, giving me another smile, but this one looks sad.

I nod. "He said he would be here, but he's not. What if I have to go to the hospital again? He won't be able to find us."

"Oh, Sophia," Mommy says, wiping the tears from my face. "Daddy will always find us, mi amor. And he is going to be here. He is just going to be a little late. But he will be here before you finish."

"How do you know?" I ask, feeling my mouth shake as I ask the question.

"Because he told me. Now how about we get your skates on, and then you can join the rest of the kids out on the ice, okay?" She holds up my white skates that I wear all the time, shaking them a bit in the process.

I narrow my eyes at my skates, remembering everything that happened the last time I had them on when Daddy wasn't with me.

We were with Grandma and Grandpa, and I wanted to play on the frozen lake they have. I grabbed my skates and put them on and went out to the lake. I was having fun until I fell on the ice and hurt my arm. My mommy and grandma came running outside when I started to scream, and I started to cry when Mommy yelled at me for going out to the lake without her.

She took me to the doctor, and after they put me in a big machine, the doctors said that my arm was broken in two places.

It really hurt, and I had to wear a cast for six weeks. I told Mommy I never wanted to go skating again, but Daddy said that I should give it another try because I loved it a lot. So because he was there, I did.

But now I'm scared, and I don't want to go out there without him. But I also don't want to disappoint Mommy, so I give her another nod.

"Good," she says, giving me a smile that isn't sad and walks me over to the bench and makes me sit so she can help me put on my skates.

Mommy doesn't usually put on my skates—that is Daddy's job—but I'm not going to tell her I don't want her to do it. It will hurt your feelings.

"I think I got it," Mommy says to herself as she ties the laces and then looks up at me. "How do they feel?"

"Okay," I say, my voice not very big.

"Okay?" Her pretty eyebrows shoot up. "Are they too tight? Or lose?"

I don't want to hurt Mommy's feelings, but my skates are too loose, and I don't want to fall again.

"They are too loose." I wiggle my feet for her to see.

"Crap," she says under her breath and then quickly looks up at me. "Don't repeat that."

I giggle, and Mommy smiles and tries to tie my skates again.

She does it for a long time, but the more she tries, the more it looks like she can't figure it out.

"Can I help?" a voice that sounds like my age says from next to us. I turn, and I see a boy who looks around my age and my height, standing there with skates on.

How does he know how to tie skates?

Mommy looks at the boy in surprise and gives him a smile. "Do you know how?" she asks him.

He nods. "I've been skating since I was two. My brother taught me."

"Oh, okay." Mommy looks from the little boy to me, before she gives him a nod. "Give it a try. If you've been doing it since you were two, you must be an expert." The little boy gives her another nod and comes over to stand in front of me and starts tying my shoe.

He's in the middle of untying Mommy's work when a lady appears behind him.

"Blake, what are you doing?" she asks him.

I look up at the lady and notice that she looks like the boy tying my shoe. She must be his mommy.

Blake answers his mom. "I'm helping tie her skates."

"Honey, you haven't learned yourself. What makes you think you can do it for someone else?" the lady asks him, placing her hand on her hips.

"Because Hunter taught me," he says, still tying the laces together.

The lady rolls her eyes, and I let out a giggle. "Your brother can't even wear clean socks. He's not in any position to teach you how to tie your skates."

"He ties his cleats."

"I tie his cleats, just like I tie your skates. Now move over, so I can tie her skates properly so that she doesn't fall and break a bone," the lady tells Blake, and he just looks up at her and lets out a sigh.

He gets up and comes to sit next to me.

"Hi," he says, holding out his hand.

I look at his hand, and then look up at my mommy.

"You're supposed to shake it, baby."

I knew that.

Giving her a nod I understand, I place my hand in Blake's hand and shake it. "Hi."

"I'm Blake. What's your name?"

"I'm Sophia. Thank you for trying to tie my skates. My mommy didn't know how either."

"Hey," my mom yells out, giving me a smile like she can't believe I called her out.

I just give her a shrug.

"Are you okay with me tying her skates?" Blake's mommy asks my mommy.

"Oh yes, please. Sorry, my husband is the hockey player and usually does the skate tying. Of course he's not here the one time he is needed," my mommy tells her, sounding a bit crazy.

"No need to apologize. I'm happy to help."

While Blake's mommy ties my skates and talks to my mommy, I look over at the boy next to me and find him already looking at me.

"What?" I ask him, wondering if I have boogers sticking out my nose.

"Your dad is a hockey player?" he asks, smiling.

I lift my shoulders and drop them. "I guess. I've only seen him play a few times, but he does skate a lot."

"That's cool. I want to be a hockey player one day," he says, almost jumping up and down on the bench.

"Why?"

"Because it's the best sport ever. My brother plays football, but I hate football. I want to play hockey."

"Then you better learn how to tie your skates because your mommy can't be tying them all the time. Especially when you're bigger," I say, raising my eyebrow at him, just like Mommy does to Daddy when she talks sometimes.

"You better learn, too," Blake yells out.

"Why? I'm not going to be playing hockey."

"Because you're going to be my friend, and my friend needs to learn how to tie her skates. I won't be able to do it forever."

"You can't even do it now!" I say through a giggle, but that giggle stops when I hear my mom and Blake's mom laugh.

The both of us look at our moms wondering why they are laughing.

"I think that you two are going to be really good friends," his mom says, and my mom nods in agreement.

Blake and I just look at each other and shrug.

"I'm going to go skate," Blake announces, getting up from the bench and holds out a hand for me to take. "Are you coming?"

He wants me to go on the ice with him.

I look over at Mommy, and she gives me a smile. "Go ahead, mi amor. I will wait for you here."

"Okay," I say, but I don't know if it was to answer Blake or my mom.

I take Blake's hand, and we walk over to the ice.

"You won't let me fall, right?" I ask as we step on the ice.

"Don't worry. I'll protect you."

And I believe him.

CHAPTER THREE

BLAKE

Ten years old

I SKATE over to the boards during my warm-up, and I try to look for him, but he's nowhere in sight. Not in the seats that are right behind that glass and definitely not where Mom, Hunter, and Jainie are sitting.

Maybe he's out at the concession stand getting something to drink.

Doubt it.

This happens every single game, every single practice. Every single time he says he is going to be there, yet he never is. I don't know why I even believe him anymore.

Oh, I know why. Because he can go to Hunter's games and practices, but he can never make mine. I don't have to ask him to know who his favorite son is.

I can't help but wonder if he doesn't come to my games because I'm not at the high school level like Hunter or because he really is picking favorites.

Favorites, of course it's favorites.

"Blake! Finish your warm-up!" Coach Martinez yells in my direction from the team box.

I look over at my coach and have the thought I've had more than a few times since I landed on his team.

I wish he were my dad.

Sophia, his daughter and my best friend, is so damn lucky to have him as her dad. He never misses anything and always puts his kid first. Not like Roy Jacobi, where he only cares about one kid and his job.

He cares about you.

If he cared, he would be here right now.

"Jacobi!" Coach Martinez yells out again, and this time I follow orders and continue with my warm-up.

Today we are playing against the Ducks, and if we win, we will be able to move up in the bracket and be one step closer to winning our league championship.

As I finish up my warm-up, I notice that someone has joined my mom and siblings, but it's not my dad like I'd hoped. It's Sophia.

Her mom must have dropped her off because she never misses one of my games. Well, she never misses one of her dad's games, but I like to think that she is also here for me. I have been her best friend forever for five years now. That's worth attending every single game over. I attend all her soccer games, so that should mean something. She sees me looking in her direction, so she sends me a wave, and I wave back right before skating over to the bench.

Coach has me playing goalie today to see how well I do in the position and to see if I like it.

I already know how I like it—I don't—but because I respect Coach Martinez, I do what he tells me to do. And maybe playing this position every so often will help me out in the long run.

Fingers crossed.

For right now, I have to put my dislike for the position aside and play my best game ever.

I doubt that will happen, though, because as the game starts, I look out to where my mom is and see that my dad is still not here. He's not coming. I knew that was going to happen, so I don't know why I'm disappointed.

I try to put the anger I feel about my dad not being here into the game and try to stop every single puck that comes my direction. The operative word being try. One of the centers from the Ducks is able to get the puck past me and then, somehow, so does one of the left wingers.

Ultimately, we end up losing, and the loss just adds on to my bad mood.

First my dad, then the game. I just want to go home, play video games, and not think about hockey for a very long time. And I will be able to do that, since we didn't win, which means the hockey season is now over.

Maybe I should listen to my brother and give football a try. Maybe then that would make my dad come to one of my games.

"Hold up, mijo," Coach Martinez says to me as I make my way out of the locker room.

I give him a nod and hold back as my other teammates leave, and I wait for Coach to head out.

"You did good, kid," Coach tells me as we walk down the hallway heading out to the ice, both of us with hockey bags in hand.

I shrug. "I let two pucks get past me, and we lost."

"Yeah, but you blocked eighty percent of the shots tonight. It's better than the last time you played goalie." He is trying to cheer me up.

This is the thing that I like about Coach, he always sees the best in every player, and he doesn't just yell about what we are doing wrong all the time.

"I guess. Can I just play one position next season?" I ask, giving him the same look that Sophia gives him when she wants him to take us for ice cream.

Coach laughs and messes up my hair. "No. Good try with the eyes, though. I see my kid is rubbing off on you. Speaking of my kid, are you coming home with us, or are you heading home with your mom?"

Ever since Sophia and I met when we were five, we've been attached at the hip. Those are my mom's words not mine. It's not really a lie. We bonded that day, and every day after that, we would wait for each other before we got on the ice. Our moms ended up setting up playdates to get us together outside of the rink, and now we don't ever go a day without seeing each other. We even go to the same school and have sleepovers all the time. So me going home with Coach isn't weird.

I shake my head. "I'm going with my mom. She said we were going to have dinner with my dad, but since he didn't come to my game, I don't know if that is still going to happen."

Coach gives me a nod, staying quiet when I mention my dad.

My dad is definitely a sore subject for a lot of people. My mom, Coach Martinez, my brother. I've even heard Coach Martinez talk to his wife, Maya, a few times about how he doesn't really like my dad, and he doesn't understand how he can promise me something and not follow through. I've heard more than a few words come out of Coach's mouth when it comes to my dad. Since I'm not supposed to be hearing those conversations, I don't say anything about them. I just keep my mouth shut.

"Well, if you come over this weekend, we'll make sure you

get pizza with pineapple on it." Coach tells me, a smile on his face as he tries to make me feel better. It does a little.

"I'll hold you to it, Coach," I say as we both walk through the doors that lead to the ice.

When we make it to the stands, I see my mom and siblings standing there with Sophia.

"Honey, you did so well," my mom says, giving me a kiss on the cheek.

"Thanks, Mom," I say, because if I argue with her, she's just going to continue to tell me the opposite.

The six of us all start walking out of the arena, and as we do, Sophia comes to walk next to me.

"You sucked today," my best friend tells me, and I can't help but to laugh.

Only Sophia is going to tell me how it is.

"I did. I told your dad not to put me at goalie ever again," I say rolling my eyes at her.

"Yeah, he's not going to listen," she says as we make it to our parents' cars. "See you tomorrow at school?" she says, as if I ever miss a day of school.

I give her a nod. "Yeah, I'll be the one with your breakfast sandwich," I say. My mom always sends me with two breakfasts. One for me, and one for Sophia.

"I'll be there with your lunch," she says before throwing me a wave and getting into her dad's truck.

I slide into the back of my mom's car and help my sister buckle her seat belt, while Hunter gets in the driver seat since he got his driver's license last month.

The car ride is silent, well it is for me. Jainie is watching some video on her tablet, and Mom is too busy yelling at my brother about everything he is doing wrong the whole way home.

I spend the car ride just thinking about the game and if there are ways I can get my dad to go to one of them.

When we get home, I notice that my dad's car is in the driveway.

Part of me is angry that he was able to make it home early but not come to my game, but the fact that he is even home is taking some of that anger away.

I guess we are going to dinner after all.

Once Hunter parks the car in the driveway, I get out of the car quickly, grabbing my hockey bag before my mom yells at me and running into the house to see my dad.

He's in the living room, sitting on the couch watching something on his phone.

"Dad," I say, trying to get his attention, and when he turns to me, I smile. "Guess what position Coach Martinez had me playing tonight?"

My dad puts his phone down on the coffee table and turns to face me, giving me a smile, one that doesn't really reach his eyes. "What position?" he asks, actually sounding interested in what I have to say.

"Goalie. The other team was able to get two pucks past me, and we lost, but Coach said that I did good. That I blocked eighty percent of the shots."

My dad reaches over and pats me on the shoulder. "That's great, buddy." He gives me another smile before he looks over my shoulder. "Hunt, how was practice? Did you get a good workout in this morning?"

I turn to look at my brother, who is walking into the living room and beelines it to the recliner. "Practice was good. Coach said that come next year, I'm probably going to start, so I have to work extra hard this summer to make sure that happens."

My brother is currently in his sophomore year of high school, and football is his life. Everything and anything he does, it has to be football related. Sometimes I wonder if he plays because he likes it or because our dad wants him to play.

I also wonder if I should give up hockey altogether and just play football instead. Maybe then my dad will come to my games.

"I know a camp that we can get you into. Keep you busy all summer long," Dad says, giving him a nod, me and my game completely forgotten now. His attention is now on Hunter. Dad doesn't even turn to look at Jainie when she comes and gives him a hug.

"Roy, I thought that we were going to meet at the restaurant," Mom says, walking into the living room, but staying by the entryway.

Dad turns slightly to look over at Mom. "I thought that we would just have dinner here. Make things easier."

Mom doesn't look happy about this. "We had a plan."

"Well plans change. Let's have dinner here."

"Fine, but we are going to talk to the kids first, and then we will see about dinner," Mom lets out, crossing her arms across her chest. She doesn't look all that happy.

"Whatever you want," Dad answers, rolling his eyes when he turns away from her.

Mom grunts, and I look over at my brother to silently ask if he has any answers as to what is going on, but he looks as confused as I feel.

"Talk to us about what?" Hunter asks, looking from Mom to Dad. I do the same.

Mom looks at us three kids, and eventually she lets out a sigh before coming to sit on the couch right next to me. She takes me and Jainie in her arms as she answers Hunter's question.

A sad smile spreads across my mom's face, and right away I know that whatever is going to come out of her mouth is going to be bad. She only smiles like that when something bad happens.

"We wanted to talk to you guys about your father and I getting a divorce."

"Divorce?" both Hunter and I ask at the same time.

I may be ten, but I know what that word means. A few of my friends at school and on the team have told me that their parents are divorced. That they are no longer married and that their parents now live in separate houses.

At first, I thought it was cool, but now that I'm seeing how sad my mom looks as she talks about it, I don't feel like that anymore.

"You guys are thinking about getting a divorce?" Hunter asks, leaning forward in his seat looking worried.

"Not thinking about it, doing it. We are getting a divorce," my dad responds, his voice clipped like when he yells at Jainie and me for being too loud.

"What does divorce mean?" Jainie asks, looking up at our mom. She's only six. She doesn't know what any of this means.

"It means that Mommy and Daddy aren't going to be married any more or living in the same house," Mom explains, and I can see in my siblings' faces that they don't know how to feel about this.

I do. I'm glad, which I know is a bad thing to say or even think. But my parents fight a lot. Every time us kids go to bed, they start screaming at each other about one thing or another. Dad is never home, and Mom doesn't look happy at all even if she is always smiling.

I may not understand the whole definition of divorce, but even at ten, I know this is what's best for our family.

"I'm going to be moving to Billings, and I'm taking Hunter with me," Dad announces.

Everyone turns to look at my dad.

"What?" both Mom and Hunter say at the same time. I guess this was news to both of them.

My eyes start to prickle.

Why is he taking Hunter? And why only him?

Do Jainie and I not matter?

Apparently not, because if we did, he wouldn't have announced that Hunter was moving with him the way that he did.

I don't think we ever mattered. Not like Hunter.

I'm not allowed to say curse words out loud, but I am allowed to think them. Fuck my dad. Taking one kid is absolutely bullshit.

Not wanting to hear any more of this conversation, I turn to look at my mom, who looks like she is about to erupt like a volcano.

"Can I go get the mail, please?" I ask.

She takes her eyes off my dad and looks over at me, scrunching her eyebrows in the process. Our mailbox is at the end of the driveway, but she never lets me go out there when it's already starting to get dark out. From the look in her eyes, though, she can see that I need an escape, so she gives me a nod. Because we both know that I'm not really going to get the mail.

"Yeah, honey. Go right ahead," she says, just as a small tear escapes from her eye. She's probably seeing the anger on my face that is there because of my dad. Not because of the divorce, but because he's choosing Hunter.

I don't like seeing my mom cry, and I have a feeling that she is going to be doing a lot of that tonight.

I walk out of the house as soon as Mom tells Hunter to take Jainie upstairs and slam the door shut as soon as the arguing starts.

Without thinking, I grab my bike from where it lays on the

grass in the front yard and start peddling until I'm a mile away from here.

By the time I reach where I want to go, I'm out of breath, but I don't care. I just need my best friend.

I drop my bike by the grass like I always do and run to the front door, hoping someone is home since no cars are parked in the driveway.

Thankfully, Sophia's mom answers the door, looking surprised to see me.

"Blake," she says, looking over my head to see if someone is with me. "What are you doing here?" She places a hand on my shoulder and walks me inside the house, closing the door behind me.

"I didn't want to be at home. My parents just told us they are getting a divorce. Can I have dinner with you tonight?"

"Oh honey," Sophia's mom says, giving me the same sad smile my mom did. "Of course. Go up to Sophia's room. She's doing homework. I'll call you down when it's ready."

"Thank you, Mrs. Martinez," I say, quickly hugging her before running upstairs to Sophia's room.

When I walk in, Sophia is laying on her bed reading a book and not doing homework like her mom said she was. When she sees me, she jumps up, like I was a ghost or something.

"What are you doing here?" she asks, sitting up on her bed, totally forgetting about her book.

"I'm having dinner with you," I tell her, going over and sitting on the floor in front of her bed.

"Why?" she asks, lying back down and wrapping her arms around my head like she always does.

"Because my parents are getting a divorce, and they are arguing about Hunter going to live with Dad in Billings." I sound angry, and I am. At my dad, at Hunter, at everyone.

"Oh," she says, tightening her arms.

"Yeah."

We stay silent for a little bit, just listening to the music playing downstairs as Sophia's mom makes dinner.

Eventually I break the silence, by asking Sophie a question that I've been wondering about.

"Soph," I start.

"Yeah?"

"You'll love me if I continue to play hockey, right? You won't leave me, like my dad is?"

Sophia doesn't say anything for a long time. She just tightens her arms around me even more, and I feel something wet fall against my cheek.

She's crying. Just like with my mom, I hate it when she cries.

"I will be by your side and love you for always and always. Hockey or no hockey."

A ten-year-old girl loves me more than my dad does.

CHAPTER FOUR

SOPHIA

Fifteen years old

"SOPHIA, c'mon. We don't have all day," my mom says from the other side of the curtain, waiting for me to come out in the fourth dress of the day.

I look at myself in the mirror, and I make a face. When the lady that owns the shop was helping me put it on, it looked pretty. Now I look like I'm wearing one of those dresses that would be worn by Marie Antoinette or someone. Not a single inch of skin is showing, besides my face and hands.

"Sophia!" my mom yells out, sounding a bit annoyed. I would be, too, if my daughter was supposed to come out five minutes ago but just spent her time looking at herself in the mirror.

"I guess it's time to get tortured," I mumble under my breath and slide the curtain open to reveal myself to my parents and Blake.

My mom's eyes go wide instantly, my dad just nods in appreciation, and Blake looks like he's holding in a laugh.

I don't have to ask how they feel about the dress, I can see it in their faces, but the question spills out anyway.

"So, what do you think?" I ask as I get situated on the platform in front of a group of mirrors.

This dress is so much worse looking at it from all of these angles.

"Who picked this dress?" my mom asks with a fake smile on her face so she doesn't offend anyone.

"Your husband," I grumble, pulling at the neck. It's so damn itchy.

Through the mirror, I see my mom turn to my dad and give him the death glare.

"What? It's a cute dress. I like it. Covers things up," my dad responds, and my mom shakes her head at him.

"She looks like an ugly-ass cupcake," Blake says, finally letting out the laugh he has been holding in.

"I do not!" I argue, but who am I kidding? He's right, I do look like an ugly-ass cupcake. A puffy one at that. But that still doesn't stop me from narrowing my eyes and giving him the same look my mom is.

When he sees the way my mom is looking at him, Blake controls himself and starts clearing his throat.

Eventually my mom turns back to look at me. "How do you feel about it?"

I could lie and tell her that I love it and make my dad happy. But if I do that, he may actually buy this dress and make me actually wear it for my quince. I'm going to want to burn every single picture.

I cringe a little as I answer my mom. "I'm going with Blake on this."

"The kid has no style whatsoever," my dad grumbles, acting all butt hurt about it.

Blake stands up from his chair and sticks out his tongue at my dad. I swear, Blake is the son my parents never wanted.

"I have better style than you, old man," he throws out as he walks to one of the racks filled with pink dresses.

Blake makes a face and shakes his head before quickly moving on to the next rack. My best friend knows me so well.

I go back into the dressing room and quickly get out of the cupcake dress. Thank God I decided to dress down today, in bike shorts and one of Blake's hoodies I stole last year, because getting undressed and redressed again would be a nightmare.

Quinceañera dress shopping is already a nightmare.

After getting dressed, I leave the dressing room and go find Blake in the sea of dress racks.

I find him in the orange section and instantly make a face. I don't want to wear an orange dress. Please don't let him pick out an orange dress.

Thankfully, though, he is not looking at the dresses, but instead his phone.

"Setting up a hot date back home or something?" I ask when I approach him.

Blake and I are officially in that stage where we are seeing the opposite sex differently. We've both started dating, him more than me, and so far I'm finding it not as fun as a lot of people said it would be. Blake, on the other hand, loves it. He loves that all the girls are flocking to him, hoping he will ask them out. He never does, but he still loves the attention.

He looks up at me and shakes my head. "It's Hunter."

I feel my eyes go wide at the mention of his brother's name. For the last almost six years, they haven't been close at all. After their parents divorced, Hunter went to go live with their dad in Billings, and Blake and Jainie stayed with their mom. Blake absolutely hated everything about the situation, his dad and brother included.

For a few years, Blake and his sister were going to Billings one weekend a month, but that only went on until Blake started high school, and now he doesn't go at all. Just Jainie does. I find it interesting and weird he stopped going when his brother moved to California for college, but I don't say anything. Maybe subconsciously, Blake wanted to repair his relationship with his brother, but when he went to California, he stopped wanting to try.

The two of them don't really talk a whole lot now as it is, maybe a quick text checking in once every few weeks. If I remember correctly, the last check in was maybe two weeks ago, so I'm finding it weird he is texting him now.

"Does he know you are in California?" I ask, going over to one of the racks to distract myself a bit.

"Yeah, I told him. He was going to drive down from Seaside, but his coach called a second practice before they played Oregon, so he wasn't able to."

I'm speechless. Hunter actually made plans to visit Blake?

I honestly can't remember the last time he made any type of plans to visit one of his siblings when it wasn't a holiday.

"Have you guys been talking for a while?" I ask.

If Hunter knew Blake was going to come dress shopping in Los Angeles with me and made plans for it, it makes it seem like they have, and that's news to me.

Blake always tells me everything. Why wouldn't he tell me about this?

He gives me a nod as he pockets his phone. "Yeah, just for a few weeks, though. He texted a little bit ago, to check in, and we just continued talking."

"Just like that?" I ask, feeling a certain way about it.

I like Hunter, I do, but I saw the hurt in Blake every time his father picked Hunter over him and more so when his dad chose

Hunter to move with him but not his other two kids. I don't want them to get close and then see Blake go through that hurt again.

"Yeah, he said he realized the fucked-up situation that we were put in and how he added to it, and he wants to make it better. So we are trying to make it better."

"Why didn't you tell me?" I ask, feeling a little hurt he would hide something like this from me. This is big. Trying to repair his relationship with his brother is big, and we tell each other big things.

He shrugs. "You've had a lot going on with soccer and this party. I didn't want to add more to it. I was going to tell you eventually. Oh, which reminds me. I have to give your Christmas gift early. Or do you just want me to wait for your party?"

I look over at him with confusion. "Why would you have to give it to me early?"

"Because we're going to California for Christmas," he says, like it's not a big deal we aren't going to be spending Christmas together for the first time since we were five.

"You are?" This is news to me. Again.

"Yeah, Hunter has a bowl game a few days after, so he and Mom thought it would be best for us to spend Christmas here. Stay for the game and then fly back with plenty of time for your party."

"Oh."

"Don't do that," Blake says, wrapping his arm around my neck and rubbing his fist against the top of my head, messing up my hair.

"Don't do what?" I ask, after I escape his hold.

"Don't make a face. It's one Christmas, Soph. We've spent every other holiday together, we can spend one apart." He's right, but it will still be weird to not have him over at our house for Christmas Eve and not go to his house on Christmas Day. But like he said, it's just one holiday. I can handle one holiday.

"Whatever. Just know that I'm jealous you are going to have a sunny Christmas, and I will probably get snowed in."

"I'll take you with me next time," he offers, throwing me a wink.

"You better," I say with a laugh and turn back to the dresses. "What do you think about this one?" I ask, holding up a lavender dress.

He makes a face.

"No shades of purple, but I do like that dark green color over there." He points behind me, and when I turn around, I see a rack full of dark green, and I automatically fall in love with the color.

"I like that," I say, turning back and throwing him a smile. He gives me a smile, one that gets bigger when I wave a hand out to the rack. "Take your pick."

Without hesitation, he goes over there and starts sifting through the dresses.

"Remind me again why aren't we looking for your quince dress in Montana. Why the hell did we have to come to California?"

I shrug. "There isn't a whole lot of choice when it comes to these types of dresses in Montana, especially with the time crunch. Mom said we might find something here, and I think she's right."

A few months ago, my abuela came to visit us and asked my parents why I wasn't having a quinceañera. She went into this big thing about how I was her only granddaughter and how I should really have one.

My dad shook his head the whole time, telling his own mom no, but since Mom and I never have gone to a true quince, we overruled Dad and agreed with Abuela that I should have one. The man grumbled and grumbled and eventually gave in. But he only agreed to it sometime in November and told us we had until the end of the year to plan and throw the party because he didn't want us to go crazy with it.

Little did he know that planning a party like this is going to get crazy. Especially when it comes to the dress. We are keeping it small in terms of guests and my court, with Blake being the one and only escort, so he's good in that regard.

"Why do you need a quince anyway? Your birthday was months ago, and you're closer to sixteen than you are to fifteen."

I give him a shrug. "I thought it was a good idea. Every girl wants to be the center of attention for a day, you know?"

"Like you aren't already," he snorts.

"I'm not," I argue, because it's true, I'm not. Who gives me attention besides my parents, Blake, and the small group of friends I have?

There's a reason I hate dating, and it has nothing to do with the type of guys who are out there. It's because none of the guys I'm interested in are interested in me.

"Soph, the guys at our school would kill for a chance to take you out," he says, rolling his eyes at me.

"No, they wouldn't." He's blowing smoke out of his ass.

"Yeah, they would."

"Then why don't they ask me out?" Because if they would kill for a chance to be with me, I would be aware of it, not hearing it from Blake.

"Because of me. They think we're together."

"They what?!" I say a little too loudly for the dress store.

I look around to see if anybody heard me, but there isn't anyone near me and Blake.

"They think we're together. That's why they don't ask you out, but trust me they want to," Blake tells me, but I can't help but notice that he sounds mad. No way he feels that way. I must be hearing things that aren't there.

"Why would they think that?" I give Blake a confused look.

"Why do you think?" he says through a chuckle. "We're together all the time. I drive you to school, we eat dinner and breakfast at each other's houses, we still have sleepovers, and we go to every single one of each other's games."

When he puts it that way...

I guess doing all that does make it seem to the outside world like we're together when we're not. I've never even looked at Blake in that way. Hell, I didn't really notice boys until a year ago. No way was I going to notice if my best friend is cute or not.

As he looks through the dark green dresses, I look at him. Like really look at him.

He is cute, especially with his dirty blond curls sticking out of the baseball cap he is sporting, and he's tall and definitely has the body of an athlete since he plays hockey like he needs it to breathe. I can definitely see why girls fawn over him, and maybe if things were different, and I didn't spend years smelling his hockey bag, I might feel the same way, but no. There aren't any butterflies when I look at Blake. Maybe it will change when we get older, but I really hope it doesn't because I really like the friendship we have.

"I guess I can see it," I say, coming up next to him and looking through the dresses he has already passed. "Maybe we can start telling people that things aren't like that between us."

"Maybe," he says, not even looking at me. All his concentration is on the dresses. "I still think this is a lot," he states, coming back to the conversation about why I'm having this quince.

"My dad did offer a trip to Cancun to an all-inclusive resort, but I chose the party."

Blake slowly turns his face to look at me, his eyes wide and his mouth open. "We could be having the time of our lives in Mexico, and you choose to have a party? What the fuck? Who does that? That warrants getting your best friend card revoked."

"Who said anything about you being invited?" I shove him.

"Pshh, please. Your parents love me more than they love you. Of course I am invited." He shoves me back. I'm not going to argue with that. They do love him, even if my dad wants to choke him every so often. He calls him the son he never wanted.

"Whatever. Pick a dress already. I'm starving."

We've been at this for hours now. This is our second stop of the day, and I don't know how much longer I can survive off the French toast I had for breakfast this morning.

Blake continues down the line of dresses, and after about a minute, he stops at one and inspects every inch of it.

He looks from the dress to me and then back, and eventually he gives me a smirk and starts pulling the dress off the rack.

"This is it," he announces proudly.

I roll my eyes and give him a smile at the same time. "Finally."

We head back to the dressing room where my dad is falling asleep in his chair, and my mom is talking to the owner of the shop about all the accessories they offer.

When my mom sees us, she slaps my dad awake, and she and the lady head into the dressing room with me to help me into the dark green dress.

My mom lets out a gasp when she finishes zipping me up, and when I hear it, I know that this is it.

This is the dress.

I don't even have to look in the mirror to know it. But I turn anyway, to give myself that confirmation.

Slowly, I look at myself in the mirror, and the second I do, I can't help but to smile when I see my reflection.

I look so beautiful, even without a single ounce of makeup or without my hair done.

"This is it," I tell my mom, and she gives me a nod.

"Yeah, I think so, too," she says, giving me a big smile. "He did good."

I nod in agreement. "He did really good."

CHAPTER FIVE

BLAKE

I'M GOING to be honest. Spending Christmas in California with Hunter sounded like the worst thing in the whole fucking world.

We're supposed to love our siblings and want to spend all the time with them we can, but when you don't know them or talk to them all that often, and at times they remind you of your asshole father, it's a bit hard to show the love.

When Mom brought it up, I got mad. Going to California would ruin my Christmas tradition of spending Christmas Eve with Sophia and her parents. Not only that, but if we went, that meant that not only were we going to spend one day with Hunter but a whole four days. I honestly can't remember when I've spent more than three days with him. When he comes to visit us, he stays at most two days, but most of the time he gets there Saturday morning and leaves twenty-four hours later. I didn't want to spend four days with the guy, especially if he was going to talk to me like Roy does. Sure, we were talking more and more, and he had even made plans to visit me in California while I was there with Sophia, but interacting with him on the phone and in person are two different things.

But Mom and Jainie were excited about going, even my stepdad, Daniel, my mom's new husband, was encouraging, so I couldn't say no.

I grumbled the whole flight to California, and when we arrived at Hunter's apartment, I tried my hardest to act like the broody teenager that I am, but that only lasted a few hours.

Things shifted when I started to see how he was being with Jainie and Mom, and how he really meant it when he told me he wanted to make things better. The act I was putting on quickly went out the door.

For four days, I had my brother back. The person who looked out for me when I was a kid, the one who taught me how to tie my shoes and went to all of my games before he moved away, was back in my life, and I couldn't have been more grateful for it.

Sure, there are still a few bumps in our relationship we need to fix, but we'll get there. Hopefully.

"Hunter, tell me about Selena," Mom states from the back seat of Hunter's truck as he drives us to the airport.

I laugh.

Last night after Hunter's bowl game, the guy ditched us. He said he had to deal with something, but in reality, he was meeting up with a girl. I guess he fucked up with her a few weeks ago, and she showed up at his game in hopes that they could kiss and make up.

Given the hickey the asshole has on his neck, I would say they did just that.

At breakfast, Mom had asked him where he had gone, since he didn't get back to the hotel until about five in the morning, and instead of lying that he went out to party or something, he told mom about the new girl in his life.

"I told you all about her at breakfast," he says, getting on yet another freeway. Driving in California is so damn confusing.

"Telling me that her name is Selena, that she's twenty-two, and that she goes to Cal U, isn't telling me all about her. How did you two meet?"

The way Hunter gets all red is very telling.

He clears his throat a few times before answering Mom. "We had a class together last semester."

I hold in a laugh because with the way he's acting, they definitely didn't meet in class, but I keep my mouth shut.

"And do you really like this girl?" Jainie throws out, adding to Mom's interrogation.

The girl is only eleven, but she knows how to bust someone's balls when she feels like it.

I turn slightly to look at my brother and see him smiling like a total dweeb. Damn, I've never seen him smile like that. Has he always had that smile, or is this Selena girl the only one who has been able to pull it out?

"Yeah, Jain. I really like this girl."

I have to be going crazy because I swear I see his eyes fucking twinkle.

"Oh shit," I voice out loud without meaning to.

"What?" my mom asks, leaning forward in her seat to see why I called out. Might as well give my brother some shit.

"Your oldest son is in love," I say, and as soon as I do, a punch lands on my shoulder.

"Hunter!" Mom yells out.

"What the fuck was that for?"

"Blake!" Now Mom is yelling at me.

"What? He's the one who punched me. And while he's driving, I might add," I say, rubbing my shoulder but still with a smirk on my face.

"You instigated it," Mom throws back, pulling my ear in the process. "And don't curse. Now, Hunter, are you in love with this girl?"

My brother quickly looks over at me, giving me a death glare for giving mom more ammo to talk about his love life, but he should have known that specific question was coming.

His face continues to turn red as he answers mom's question. "I think it's too soon to tell, but I do see it going in that direction."

"Aw, I love that. I can't wait to meet her," Mom says, and if I turn around right now, I'm sure that I will find her with her hand on her chest and a lovey dovey look on her face. "I am going to meet her, right?"

"Yes, Mom. You'll meet her."

"Good. Blake, take note from your brother, and don't settle down with someone until you're in college. Maybe even wait until after you graduate."

I shrug as I watch Hunter take the exit to the airport. "I don't plan on settling down until after I get drafted, maybe not until I sign my NHL contract and have a few years under my belt."

"Big words coming from a sophomore in high school. At least Hunter is in college and already has draft papers. What makes you think you are even going to get drafted or that the NHL will want you?" Jainie, unwarrantedly, adds to the conversation.

I turn around to narrow my eyes at her. If I was closer, I would pull her hair.

"Watch. I'm going to do it and leave you with your mouth wide open with no room to talk," I say to her, sticking my tongue out in the process.

I'm about to sit back in my seat when I look over at my mom and see that she has tears in her eyes and a smile on her face.

"What's wrong?" I ask her, starting to feel a little worried.

Jainie looks over at Mom, too, scooting over to take her hand.

"Nothing," Mom says, shaking her head, wiping away tears,

but still she somehow has a smile on her face. "It's just been so long since I've had the three of you like this. Fighting and sounding happy. I've missed it."

We go silent as Hunter pulls into the parking garage, and we continue to stay that way well after he finds a parking spot. Eventually he breaks the silence.

"I'm sorry, Ma," he says, turning around in his seat and looking at our mom before reaching out and taking her hand in his.

"Oh, honey, no. This isn't your fault," Mom reassures him, reaching over and patting his cheek.

"It kind of is. If I hadn't moved with Dad, you would be having moments like this all the time. Not just on random occasions or when I finally realized that moving away so that I could concentrate on football was a dick move that probably hurt you more than you will ever admit."

I would never tell him this, but he is right. It is kind of his fault he's not as close to me and Jainie as he used to be and that Mom cries the majority of the time, she talks to him on the phone. If he hadn't moved with Dad, four hours away from us, we wouldn't be sitting in an airport parking garage pouring our fucking hearts out.

Step one is admitting you were in the wrong. So, I guess we're going in the right direction.

"Hunter, you moving with your dad was the best decision for you. Like Jainie said, you have draft papers ready for you to fill out. If you would have stayed with me, there's a possibility that you wouldn't even be playing right now. But look at you, your team just won a bowl game, and you have a shot at making a name for yourself in a few months. Have there been hard moments? Sure. Do I wish you were closer to your siblings than what the current state is? Of course, I do. But honey, you were just a kid. Me crying as I watch you guys laugh and actually acting like siblings isn't your fault, so get it out of your head that it is."

Hunter tries to smile at Mom, but it doesn't quite reach his eyes.

So, I decide to lighten the mood a little bit.

"I'm okay with blaming Dad for all the bad stuff, if you guys are."

The second words leave my mouth, the three of them laugh, and the tension that was developing in the car starts to disappear.

"I'm down for that," Hunter says, smiling at the three of us.

"You two are too much." Mom starts shaking her head, but we all know that she wants to agree with me. "Alright, let's go. I don't want to miss our flight."

Within minutes, we are all out of the car with our luggage and are making our way down to the terminal.

When we get to the check-in desk, Mom and Jainie go over and print out our boarding passes. While they do that, I decide to shoot Sophia a quick text telling her that we are on our way home.

Since her party is during one of the busiest times of the year for travel, she was nervous we wouldn't make it. That our flight would get canceled, or that there would be a blizzard or something that would keep us out of Montana. She has sent me so many damn screenshots about flight cancelations and weather conditions these last four days that I actually thought about blocking her. I kept telling her that she has nothing to worry about, but the girl won't believe me until I'm standing in front of her wearing a damn three-piece suit at her party.

"You texting your girlfriend or something?" Hunter asks as we wait off to the side for Mom and Jainie.

I shake my head, pocketing my phone. "No, it's Sophia.

She's freaking out because she thinks that we won't make it back in time for her party."

"And you're trying to calm her down," he says, more as a statement of fact than a question.

"Yup, that's what best friends are for."

"You ever think about making her more than just your best friend?" my brother asks, raising an eyebrow at me.

I look at him like he's crazy. "Why would I do that?"

Hunter shrugs. "She's a pretty girl. You're not a bad looking guy. Given your history and how well you know each other, I think you two would be great together in that way."

"She's my best friend."

"She can be your best friend and your girlfriend at the same time," he tells me. Who knew that a twenty-one-year-old could be so wise?

"I'm not her type," I argue, trying to find anything that would stop this conversation.

"But is she yours?" Hunter asks, and as much as I want to come up with an answer, I can't.

If Soph wasn't my best friend, and we hadn't been in each other's lives since we were five, I would have asked out in a heartbeat. She's pretty, smart, so damn funny, and most definitely my type. I never really saw her in that way until last year when we went to a party together, and for some reason, I just started looking at her differently.

I found my best friend to be the prettiest girl I had ever seen, and as much as I wanted, or should I say want, to tell her, I could never find the words. Thinking about it now, I still can't find the words to tell my best friend that I find her pretty. She'll probably laugh in my face and quickly change the subject.

Hunter takes my silence as a yes and gives my shoulder a pat. "You should tell her, man. Because if you don't, she might slip through your fingers."

I want to tell him that he has no idea what he is talking about. That I don't find Sophia attractive at all, but that would be a complete lie.

The whole flight home, though, I can't help but wonder about what my brother said.

What if I do tell her, and she slips through my fingers anyway? What happens then? Do I lose the one person who has meant something to me for so long?

I don't know, but one thing that I do know is that it is not a risk that I'm willing to take.

CHAPTER SIX

SOPHIA

THE PARTY IS in full swing, and I feel like I need to take a breather.

Being the center of attention is a lot harder than I thought it would be, and I don't know how I feel about it.

What I do know is that I need water and at least a ten-minute break away from everyone.

Going into hiding is a little hard, especially with the size of dress I'm wearing, but somehow I'm able to grab a bottle of water and head out of the ballroom of the hotel where my quince is without anyone noticing.

I can still hear the music blasting as I walk out to the small courtyard the hotel has just outside the ballroom. I'm actually a little surprised other guests aren't out here getting some fresh air, too, but that just means I get the place all to myself.

Opening up the water, I take a big gulp and let out a sigh of relief when the coldness hits my throat. It feels like I haven't had any water in days, when in reality, it's only been a few hours.

I chug the water down until the bottle is empty, and once it's finished, I take a few minutes to look up at the dark sky filled with stars.

It's surprising the sky is actually clear tonight. I wasn't expecting it. Some snow fell a few days ago, and I thought that it was going to continue to fall through today, but I'm glad it didn't. Otherwise, it would be too cold to be out here without a jacket, but right now it feels perfect.

I'm so busy looking up at the stars that I don't notice that someone has joined me outside until I feel something land on my shoulders.

Looking up, I find Blake right next to me, placing his suit jacket around my bare shoulders.

He must have seen me leave the party and followed me out.

I smile up at my best friend. "Thank you," I say, taking the jacket even though I'm not cold.

"Figured you got peopled out when I didn't see you come back, so I thought I would come check on you."

"Aww, so thoughtful." I say, the sarcasm bleeding through my smile.

"Yeah, whatever." He takes a seat next to me and looks up at the sky. "I thought it was going to snow."

I let out a laugh. "I was just thinking that before you interrupted me."

"I guess that's why we're best friends, huh?" he asks, keeping his eyes up.

For some reason, the way he says that doesn't sit right with me. I don't know why, but it just feels like he was trying to say something else. Like maybe we shouldn't be best friends, but I may be reading too much into it. I might still be a little bit hurt that he didn't tell me about him talking to his brother, even though that happened almost a month ago.

I bump his shoulder with mine. "And you are never getting rid of me. I hope you know that."

I mean the words as a joke, but I still feel the need to drive that thought through his head just in case he's starting to feel differently about our friendship. And if he is, I hope he tells me.

"Never. My life would be a snooze fest without you." He grabs my face and shifts it slightly so that he can place a hard kiss against my cheek. Something that I used to do to him when we were kids whenever we said bye.

"Gross," I say, repeating the same thing that he would tell me whenever I did it.

Blakes laughs. "You ready for your Christmas gift?" he asks, pulling out a small box out of his pants pocket and twirling it in his hands.

Every year we get each other a Christmas gift.

At first it was just something small, like a stuffed animal or a book or a CD, but over the last two years, it's been bigger things like shoes and hats or whatever our allowances will allow.

He told me in California that he wanted to give me my gift early, since he wasn't going to be here for the actual holiday, but I told him last week to just wait until he got back.

"I thought we were going to exchange gifts tomorrow?" I ask because that's what we had planned. We were going to have a small Christmas celebration for just the two of us, with movies, leftovers, and gifts.

He gives me a shrug. "I figure you should open at least one gift at your birthday party."

Because my birthday had already passed, my mom said it was best to make my quince "no gifts." I've been handed cards, but that's about it.

"I can open it tomorrow," I say, feeling bad that I don't have his gift with me so he can open one, too.

"Just open it, Soph," he says, holding out the box for me to take.

It takes me a second, but I eventually take it and don't hesitate opening it.

Nestled in all the tissue is a gold locket necklace.

It's dark outside, but the locket still shines in the minimal light that there is.

"Oh my god, this is so pretty." I take it out and place it in the palm of my hand so that I can look at all the details more closely.

"You should open it," he says, bumping my shoulder.

I do what he says, unlatching the two parts to look at what's inside.

Both sides have a picture of the two of us. One from around the time when first we met and we claimed each other as friends. It's actually the first picture we took together.

I was in the process of learning an axel, and after falling so many times, I was finally able to land one. It was the happiest day for little Sophia. When we were leaving, Blake, who was finishing his hockey practice, came running up to me excitedly, telling me how it was so cool that I was able to land the jump. It was small, but it was mighty.

My mom took this picture of us as we so happily talked about how I was able to jump so high. Because a few inches off the ground was so high for a five-year-old.

I didn't know Mom had taken the picture until she showed it to me a few years ago. It became one of my favorites. One I didn't know that Blake even had.

"How did you get this picture?" I ask, feeling tears form in my eyes at the sentiment behind this gift.

"I fought your mom for it. That lady can be vicious when she wants to be. She didn't want to give it to me. I think her exact words were 'I'm not giving something so priceless to the boy who doesn't even wash his hands.' For the record, I wash my hands."

I laugh, looking up at him. "Not all the time." He grunts at my comment, probably calling bullshit in his mind. "I'm guessing she finally caved and handed the picture over?"

He shakes his head. "Nope, she showed it to me, and I took a picture. So, it's a picture of a picture. Which I guess is better because I don't want your mom to murder me because I had to cut up the original so that it would fit in the tiny circle."

I laugh, because while my mom won't attack him with a knife, she will give him the death glare every single time that she sees him for the next month or so.

"Did you see the other picture?" he asks, nodding toward the locket.

I was so preoccupied with the one side that I actually didn't pay attention to the other. You would think that a picture so close to the other would be hard to miss.

Moving my eyes to the other picture, I see that it's a more recent one. One from my actual birthday a few months ago.

I didn't want to do anything big, so my mom made a small dinner at our house and ordered a banana cake from my favorite bakery. It was just me, my parents, and Blake. Mom got a little picture happy that night and took pictures of everything.

The picture staring back at me is one of me and Blake smiling at the camera with faces covered in cake and frosting after a cake fight my dad had started.

Both pictures capture our friendship perfectly.

"I love it," I say, wiping away a tear and smiling up at Blake.

"If you love it, why are you crying?" he asks, his voice filled with concern.

"Because this gift is everything, and my Christmas gift to you is complete shit." And it is. How do you compare tickets to a hockey game to a locket with pictures that mean the world?

"I'm sure I'll like it."

"I know you'll like it, but it doesn't have the sentimental value that this does," I argue. Sure, mine will be fun, but it's not something he will remember forever.

"Soph, anything you give me has sentimental value. Because

it came from you. That's all that matters," Blake tells me, a smile on his face and his blue eyes shining in the moonlight.

I look at my best friend for a few seconds, and I can't help but wonder when he started to look so much older than his actual fifteen years of life. The more that I look at him, the more I feel the sensation of butterflies fluttering around my stomach. A sensation that has never been there for Blake until this very moment.

"Whatever you say," I say, trying not to think about the butterflies and holding up the necklace to him. "Help me put it on, will ya?"

He takes the necklace, and I turn my body so that my back is to his front. As the cold metal slides along my neck, I can't help but hold my breath as his fingers glide against my skin.

Never have I done that when Blake has touched me before. Never have I held my breath, and never have I had butterflies. What makes this time different?

Maybe it's that this necklace means the world to me, and I'm afraid to lose it. Maybe it's the sentimental value of it.

Maybe...

"There," Blake says as soon as the necklace is secure.

I turn back to face him, and without any hesitation, I lean up and place a kiss on his cheek like I have done a million times before, but this time, it feels different. A hell of a lot different.

"Thank you. I love it."

"Good because I had to do Jainie's chores for two whole-ass months to get it."

I let out a laugh and fall in love with my gift even more. Knowing what he had to do to get this for me makes it all that more special.

I will forever hold this locket as close to my heart as possible.

Will I be holding onto the butterflies just as long, though? That is the question.

CHAPTER SEVEN

BLAKE

18 years old

I LOOK at my phone as it rings and try my best to ignore it.

The person who's calling only remembers my number when it becomes convenient for them, not when they actually want to talk to me or even to see how I am doing.

And the ironic part is, if I had gotten this call three months ago, or even a month ago, I would have answered it in a heartbeat. Because three months ago it would have been a celebratory call for signing my letter of intent for Montana State. A call a month ago would have been to apologize for missing one of the most important days of my life. But the call I'm getting right now is a little too late and definitely has some motive behind it. Especially given what's happening tomorrow night.

The call ends, and as soon as it does, I pick up my phone and dial my brother.

There's a slight chance that he's already on his flight to Montana from California to be here for tomorrow, but that's a risk I'm willing to take.

Thankfully the call is answered after three rings.

"Hi, Blake," a female voice answers, and as soon as I hear the voice I relax a little bit. Selena, my brother's girlfriend of three years, is one of my favorite women in the world, and I'm more than happy to talk to her instead of my brother any day.

"Hey, Lennie," I say, calling her the nickname Hunter has for her, all while a smile spreads over my face. "Is my brother around?"

"Nope," she answers, sounding annoyed. "He forgot his wallet at home so he went to go get it."

"I'm guessing that you guys were already at the airport when he realized he didn't have it." I theorize.

I swear I can hear her nodding from the other side. "We were at security. I wonder how a man who flies so damn much forgets what he needs to actually fly because this isn't the first time."

"And you have his phone because?"

"Because he panicked and threw all his shit at me so that I could look through it, while he looked on the floor and checked with security just in case he dropped it, and someone turned it in. But then he remembered that we put an Air Tag in it because again, this has happened more than once, and saw that he left it at home. He took my phone to track it, which makes no sense, since he could have used his phone, but who am I to argue with him?"

I'm not a relationship type of guy. The girls I've dated have mostly just been to pass the time and to have a little fun. Not a single one of them has been anything serious, nothing more than a few months. According to my mom, the most serious relationship that I've had is with hockey and Sophia. And I plan to keep it that way. But I'm not going to lie, having a relationship like the one Hunter and Selena have would be great.

Maybe once I'm settled in the NHL, I will put in the effort to have something like they do.

"Can you have him call me back when he gets back to the airport?" I ask her.

Ever since we went out to California for Christmas three years ago, Hunter and my relationship has improved big time. We talk a few times a week, and he has come home a lot more often in the last three years than he did the five years before. When he got drafted into the NFL by the San Francisco Gold, I thought for sure that the guy who put football before everything else would be back and forget about his family all over again. I couldn't have been more wrong.

When deciding on whether I should enter the draft this year or not, he was there for me, giving me advice and walking me through every single thought process. He told me that at one point he was contemplating not even entering the NFL draft because he didn't know why he was playing football anymore. He went down the rabbit hole of how, for a time, it was no longer fun to play anymore because of all the pressure our dad was putting on him to choose the right team. And how he didn't want to play because of the money but instead because he loved it.

It was during those conversations that I learned just how strained his relationship with our dad had gotten and that he hated that Jainie and I weren't getting treated the same way he was.

And here I thought that Hunter had the easier end of the deal when it came to Roy Jacobi.

"Yeah, I can tell him. What's up?" Selena asks, not because she wants to intrude in my business but because she genuinely wants to see if there is anything she can do to help.

I let out a sigh and tell her, "Dad keeps calling."

As I say the words, the beep indicating that I have another call coming in, sounds in my ear. I pull the phone back a bit, and sure enough, it's the same person who was calling earlier. My dad.

"And you don't want to answer or talk to him so you want your brother to intervene." Selena concludes, like this is something I call about all the time.

Do I? I don't think so.

"Yeah, pretty much," I say, letting out a sigh.

"And I'm going to go take a wild guess that the call you have on the other line is him."

I nod as if she were in front of me. "He's been calling all day. He didn't call for graduation, or hell, even my birthday, but yet he calls today. The day before—"

"You see if you will get drafted into the NHL," Selena finishes for me.

For a whole year, I debated whether or not I was going to join the draft this year or hold off for another year. I saw the benefits of waiting another year—I could get faster and better— but so much could happen in that time that I wasn't sure if I wanted to risk it. After talking it over with my mom and my stepdad, Hunter and Selena, Sophia, and her dad, I decided to enter.

If I didn't get drafted this year, I still had a few more chances.

But Isaac, Sophia's dad, and the man who has not only been my coach since I was a little kid, but who has always been like a father to me, and helped raise me and mold me into the almost man that I am today, said I was ready. That I am a sure-fire pick this time around.

I didn't believe him. I still don't, but I'm not going to tell him that because he has already threatened to disown me if I mention any shit about not getting drafted to him.

Either way, I entered. And now I just have to wait and see if

I get drafted and hopefully become an NHL player when I leave Montana State.

"Can I ask you a question, Len?" I ask, leaning back in my desk chair, practically testing its limits.

"Anything."

"Do you really think I'm good enough to get drafted?" I ask, feeling like I need someone who doesn't see me play all the time to give me their honest opinion on whether or not I have a future in hockey. I've asked Sophia countless times, but she's biased as hell.

"I've only seen you play a handful of times. I don't know if that gives me the power to answer a question like that."

"Try?" I urge, massaging the space between my eyebrows, trying my best to remember that manifestation shit Soph has been learning lately.

"Fine," she says but then pauses for a few seconds. "Yeah, I think you're good enough, and I'm not saying that because I'm your brother's girlfriend. I'm saying that because I may have only seen you play a few times, but those few times, it seemed like you belonged out on the ice. You made your stick an extension of you, and if I'm being honest, not a lot of the players out there did that."

Since I was a kid, Coach has always drilled into my head that my stick is more than a piece of wood. That I needed to treat it as if it was a part of my person and that I needed to protect it at all costs. My stick gets hurt, I get hurt. I guess if Selena, who I'm sure isn't even a hockey fan, noticed something like that, scouts and teams will, too.

"Sophia and her dad think that I'm a sure-fire choice," I say, feeling a bit more confident in my decision to join the draft than I did a few seconds ago.

"I would believe them."

Yeah, I would, too. They are the two people who know me best.

I stay silent, not responding to Selena, just trying to digest everything.

"Look, a lot could happen in the next twenty-four hours. How about you distract yourself a little bit and go into tomorrow with a clear head?" Selena suggests after a few minutes of me not saying anything.

"And how would you suggest I distract myself?" The only way I can think of is with hockey, but it's late, and the rink is already closed.

"I don't know, you're eighteen, go to a party or something. Grab Sophia, and go to a movie. Just do something to not think about the what-ifs that can come with tomorrow or your dad calling you because he now wants to be in your life because of it."

I don't have to even think about it to know that she is right. Hunter wouldn't have been this damn wise.

"Don't tell your boyfriend, but I like you better than him."

"I know you do. Now, go do what I say," she orders, and by the sound of her voice, I know she has a smile on her face.

"Aye aye, captain. See you tomorrow."

We end the call, and I don't waste any time dialing Sophia's number. If I'm going to go get distracted, she's coming along.

The phone rings once before she answers.

"I just put a face mask on, so this better be good," she grumbles.

I'm about to get my ass chewed out, but I don't care.

"Get dressed, we're going to a party."

Ten minutes later, I'm in Sophia's parents' living room waiting for her to finish getting ready for the party. One of my buddies from the team is throwing a going-away party before he heads down to Florida for school, so I figure that would be the perfect distraction.

I hear shoes coming down the stairs and let out a sigh of relief.

"Fuck. Finally," I say in the direction of the stairs.

Sophia usually doesn't take very long to get ready, but tonight she took her sweet-ass time.

I walk over, and when I see her on the last step, I see why she took forever.

Her light brown hair is in curls, and her face glows with the makeup she is wearing.

I keep my eyes on hers as long as I possibly can, but they decided to move on their own, down the rest of her body.

I've known Sophia for thirteen years of my life. I've seen her in everything from sweats to a damn bikini, but never in a damn black miniskirt that looks like it's barely hanging on and a crop top that shows more skin than it covers.

As I watch her as she slides on her shoes so we can leave, I can only think about one thing. My best friend has always been gorgeous to me. My type and fucking gorgeous, but I've never had the guts to tell her. Not when we were fifteen, not now. Some days, her beauty, both inside and out, is all I can think of.

Right now, though, all I can think is that my best friend is hot as fuck, and there is no way in hell that tonight is going to be a distraction like I had planned.

It's going to be fucking torture.

CHAPTER EIGHT

SOPHIA

IN ALL THE years I've known Blake, never have I felt self-conscious around him. I could wear anything and everything in the world and feel like the most confident girl around.

That is, until tonight.

When he called earlier and said that we were going to a party, I saw it as an opportunity to dress out of my comfort zone. I had been planning for a moment like this since high school graduation a month ago. I'm going to be a college freshman soon, in a whole different environment than high school. It was time to up my game in the whole wardrobe department.

I've been spending the last few weeks curating the perfect closet, and tonight was the first night I had the opportunity to show off my new clothes.

But now, I'm second guessing myself big time.

As we drive to the party being put on by Landon, one of Blake's teammates, Blake continues to throw quick glances my way.

What does he keep looking at?

"Everything okay?" I finally ask, shifting in the passenger seat.

Blake doesn't look at me as he answers. "Yeah, why wouldn't it be?"

I try to read his profile, but I'm not getting anything besides him possibly being irritated. At what, I have no idea.

He was fine back at the house. I wonder what happened between when he got there and now that caused his mood shift. I know I haven't said or done anything.

Maybe he's just freaking out about tomorrow, or maybe it's his dad. I know he has been calling nonstop today because Blake mentioned it when I talked to him before dinner, so maybe he's irritated with that and not with me.

"Because you keep looking over like you're checking if I've disappeared or not," I admit, shifting again when he turns to look at me, this time a lot longer than just for a quick second like he has been.

"I'm not looking at you that way," he answers, and I notice his hand wrap around the steering wheel of his truck a little tighter.

"Whatever you say." I decide to drop it, not wanting to go through all the back and forth.

We go back to being silent, something that I'm usually comfortable with, but for some reason tonight, it feels awkward.

The awkward silence lasts a few minutes until Blake breaks it.

"Is that skirt new?" he asks, after clearing his throat.

"My skirt?" I ask, confused. He never talks about clothes with me, unless it's about a piece of clothing I stole from his closet, or I'm straight up asking for his opinion. "Yeah, I bought it a few weeks ago."

Does he not like it?

And if he didn't, why does it matter? I don't dress for him. Maybe I did for a bit after my quince because there might have been a time when I had a crush on my best friend, but since nothing came out of said crush, I stopped.

"Why?" he asks, pulling me out of my thoughts and back to the present.

"Why, what? Why did I buy the skirt?" I ask, feeling so damn confused by all of this.

He gives me a nod, keeping his eyes on the road and his hand still tightly wrapped around the steering wheel. "Yeah, why did you buy it?"

I tilt my head to the side. "Because I like it?"

Where the hell is this conversation going?

"You don't think it's a little short?" he suggests, quickly looking at me again before looking away just as quickly.

"No, I don't. It comes to my fingertips," I argue.

Even if it was short, why does he care? It's not like half the girls he has dated over the years haven't worn the same thing. I never heard him complain about them.

"Definitely doesn't go to your fingertips when you're sitting down," he grumbles under his breath, thinking that I wouldn't have been able to hear him over the roar of the truck, but I certainly did.

"Do you have a problem with what I'm wearing, Jacobi? Because if you do, just come out and say it." I brought out the Jacobi card. I only call him by his last name when I'm trying to tell him he is acting like a pompous hockey player. It feels like tonight is going to be one of those times.

He gives me a shrug, his knuckles almost white. "I just think that you could have worn something else."

"Like what?" I ask, shifting in my seat so that my whole body is facing him.

"Something that covered your body a lot more," he says, giving me a pointed look.

"You sound like my dad." I roll my eyes at him. I can't believe we are even having this conversation. He hasn't had a problem with how I dressed before. Why is tonight different?

"I'm actually surprised he let you leave the house like that. If you were my—"

"Your what? If I was your what, what would you do?"

His jaw starts to tick, and his knuckles go from being white to absolutely transparent. "If you were my sister," he says the word through clenched teeth, "I would have told you to go back upstairs and change."

Sister.

If I was his sister. Because that's all I will ever be to him. A sister or his best friend. This is something I've known for years, so I don't know why I'm so bothered by it now.

Yeah, you do. Because that crush you had on him a few years ago is still deep in you, and you don't want to let it go.

There is a slight chance my subconscious is right, but just because it's right doesn't mean I'm actually going to do anything about it. Do I still have a crush on him? As much as I want to tell myself that I don't, I know it would be a lie. It's just now, it's buried deep, and there's no way am I going to let it see the light of day. If I do, it might ruin what we've built these last thirteen years.

We're going to go to the same college, possibly going to spend even more time together since we will be in the same dorm. I can't let a crush ruin all of what we have.

"Well, thank God I'm not Jainie because I sure as hell don't need you policing what I wear." I move my body back to face the front of that car.

Blake lets out what sounds like a growl, which means that if he wasn't irritated with me before, he sure is now.

"Why are you changing the way you dress? Are you trying

to impress a guy or something?" he asks, reaching over and pulling at my hair.

It's funny how three years ago I did dress for a guy, for him, but he didn't even notice and now that I don't even want to impress him, he's noticing.

Stop lying to yourself. You are trying to impress him.

"I'm not trying to impress anyone," I say, but I don't know if I'm telling myself or him. "I just wanted to get new clothes. In case you missed it, I'm eighteen and about to go to college. I can dress however I want."

"Whatever. But if some asshole starts to get handsy or begs you to go home with him, don't come crying to me."

My mouth legit drops. No fucking way he just said that to me.

"Are you telling me I'm dressed like a slut?" I ask, absolutely dumbfounded.

He jerks his head toward me, looking angry. "The word slut didn't come out of my mouth."

"No, but it sure as hell sounded like it wanted to," I say through clenched teeth, starting to feel tears form in my eyes.

Blake and I fight like any other friends, but this feels like a lot more than just your stereotypical best friend fight. This feels completely different, on a different level.

The truck jerks to a stop, and when I look around, I see that we're at Landon's house already.

I honestly don't want to be here anymore.

"Have fun at the party," I say, opening my door. "I'm walking home."

Blake grabs my hand, pulling me back into the cab of the truck before my foot can even touch the ground.

"You're not walking home dressed like that. You wouldn't be walking home even if you weren't," he says, his jaw tight.

"Watch me." I yank my arm out of his grip and jump out of

the truck. If my parents were home, I would be calling them right now, but they decided to have a date night. And because I don't want to interrupt them, walking is my solution.

I hear a door slam behind me, and within seconds, Blake is pulling me to a stop.

He turns my body to face him, and I see that he is just as pissed as I feel.

"Look, I'm sorry, okay? I didn't mean for it to come out that way. My head isn't in the right place."

"So? Don't take out on me," I say, shoving him away and crossing my arms when I take a step back. I don't miss his eyes looking down at my chest when I do.

No way in hell he just did that. I must be imagining things.

"I know," he says, letting out a sigh. "Look, if you really want to go home, I'll take you. But with everything going on tomorrow, I really need a distraction, have a little fun, and as much as I know you probably hate me right now, I want you to stay. You're choice, though. You want to leave, we'll leave."

I look at the boy in front of me. In less than twenty-four hours, his life could change for the better. He might get drafted and go to Montana State knowing there's an NHL contract waiting for him when he's done. That's huge.

He's put in a lot of work to get this point, and he deserves to have fun tonight and get drafted tomorrow. No matter what he deserves, though, he has no right to talk to me the way he did in the truck.

That should be reason enough to leave, yet I find myself wanting to concede.

I flip-flop for about a minute on whether or not I should stay or leave. After looking into his icy blues one last time, I finally decide.

"I'll stay, but I don't feel like being around you right now. So, give me some space."

He gives me a nod. "As long as you are here and not walking home alone in the fucking dark, I'm okay with that."

I give him a curt nod and walk around him to head into the house.

If I'm going to get through the night, I'm going to need a drink.

CHAPTER NINE

BLAKE

THIS IS the last time I take advice from Lennie.

I don't care that one day she might be my sister-in-law, or that she is one of my favorite females on the planet, or that she is sweet and quiet and shit. She sucks at giving advice.

If I hadn't listened to her, I would have found distraction by calling Sophia over so we could binge watch whatever reality show she wanted and pig out on pizza. But no, I had to listen to Lennie and go out to party, and now the night has turned into absolute shit, and I'm blaming it on her.

Her and the damn skirt Sophia is wearing.

From the second Sophia came down the stairs at her parents' house to now, my eyes have stayed on her. I've watched the way she moves, the way she bends over, the way she laughs with other people who aren't me. I've also been watching all the guys who have been staring at her all damn night, looking at her and licking their lips as if she was a lollipop, and they couldn't wait to suck on her.

All my attention has been on her all damn night, and every part of me hates it. Not because Sophia doesn't warrant my attention. She does, but she's my best friend, I have no right to look at her the way I have tonight. I have no right to have thoughts about what she might be wearing under that skirt of hers. I have no right to picture the type of bra she has on because whatever it is makes her tits look absolutely perfect.

She's my best friend. She has been at my side since I was five. She deserves to have someone at her side who will be there for her, to take care of her and protect her, not someone who is trying really hard not to have a fantasy about her naked body in the middle of a party.

Are these thoughts new? As much as I want to say yes, I would be lying to myself.

Thoughts about being with Sophia in a way that isn't solely a friendship have definitely come up more times than I can count over the last three years.

Even while I was with other girls, thoughts of Sophia have been ever-present. Thoughts of how she would feel under me. Of how she would sound moaning out my name, or even how she would look if she were to wrap her full lips around my cock. Thoughts that are definitely making me out to be a horrible friend.

But sexual thoughts aren't the only thing that pop into my mind when it comes to her. I also think about what she might say if I told her I wanted to make her mine. I think about what it would be like to be in a relationship with her, to hold her hand, or just go to sleep with her right next to me day in and day out. I think about how us being friends would make us the best partners for each other. Just like my brother said when I was fifteen.

They're just thoughts, though. Thoughts and never actions or spoken words.

Because even though I've known this girl, this woman, my entire life, I'm terrified of being with her. I don't want to hurt her. I don't want her to hate me. I sure as hell don't want to lose her. So instead of growing some balls and telling my best friend that I've been attracted to her for fucking years and want to try at possibly having a future together, I hold everything in as tightly as possible. All so I don't fuck it up.

Maybe she feels the same way.

I doubt it, but hey, I could be wrong. Unless she tells me, I won't know otherwise.

I try not to let my mind drift back to Sophia by drinking my fourth beer of the night. Good thing Hunter and Selena are flying in because no way would I be able to call my mom or my stepdad to come pick us up.

The beer I'm drinking is fucking gross, but it's the only thing Landon was able to get his hands on, so it will do. As long as I don't think about Sophia and sliding my hand under her skirt, I'm fucking golden.

A few of the guys come over to where I've decided to chill for the night and talk about the draft. They're all excited that one of their own has decided to go for the professional route. As much as I want to join in on their excitement, I can't. Yeah, it's cool and all, but there is a big chance things won't work out how they think they will.

They all start talking about how they plan to meet up tomorrow to watch the draft, and I'm about to add something about them possibly coming to my house if they want to, but I see something in my periphery that draws my attention away.

Turning slightly, I check to see what it was, and the second I do, my jaw starts to tick. Sophia is walking with some guy toward the kitchen, and from the looks of things, she doesn't look all that happy to be anywhere near him.

I try to see who the guy she's with is, but I can't get a good look at his face with this stupid-ass lighting. Whoever it is, she wants to be as far away from him as possible.

I take my eyes off Sophia and the douchebag mystery guy for a second and look around for her friends. When we got here, she instantly found some of her girlfriends and went straight to them, leaving me to hang out with my teammates if I wanted. I didn't. I wanted to hang out with her, but she said she needed space from me, so I gave it to her.

But now she is with some rando, and her friends are nowhere in sight.

I turn back to look at Sophia and her new friend for a little bit longer, watching how the two of them interact and how she tries her hardest to step out of his reach whenever his hand is only a few inches away. She starts looking around, like she is looking for someone, but when she doesn't see who she is looking for, an expression of defeat covers her beautiful face.

I know for a fact that she isn't looking for her friends. She's looking for me, and because I'm basically hiding in the shadows, she can't see me.

Everything in me is saying that I should go over and rescue her from this dude, but she said she wanted space. If I go over there and interrupt their interaction, there is a chance that she will end up even angrier with me than she already is.

So, I keep my distance but keep my eyes on her. I watch her all that I can, but when the fucker guides her toward the basement, I throw out caring about giving her space and follow after them.

Sophia has come with me to other parties at this house on multiple occasions, so she knows the basement is mostly used for playing video games. She also knows even though there are people playing video games, people tend to use the dark parts of the room to fool around.

It doesn't matter how many people may be down there, there are always at least two couples hidden in plain sight making out or going to third base. She has never gone down there willingly.

I don't care who this fucker is, he's going to meet my fist for taking her down there.

As soon as I step onto the stairs to head down, I smell the weed that is probably making its rounds.

Thank fuck, I'm not going to get drug tested tomorrow because no way would I be passing it after this.

I make my way down the basement stairs, and the second my feet are on solid ground, I look for her everywhere I can.

There are not a whole lot of people down here, so I'm able to find her quickly, and when I do, I see fucking red.

The douche has her pushed up against the wall in one of the dark corners the basement has, and from what I can see, she is trying to push him away. From the way her mouth is moving, she's telling him no, but the asshole doesn't budge.

He's about to wish he had.

I stalk over there, catching Sophia's gaze when I'm about a foot away. The way she looks relieved to see me is everything I need to pull the fucker away from her and get between them.

As soon as I come face to face with the fucker, I recognize him as one of the guys on the football team who thinks he's the god of all gods.

"Don't you fucking know that when someone pushes you away and tells you no, that's the universal sign to back the fuck up." I place my hands on this fucker's chest and shove him away.

"Stay out of it, Jacobi. This has nothing to do with you. Me and the pretty girl were just talking," Miller, the football douchebag, says, shoving me back just like I did to him.

I brace my body as much as I can, not wanting to hurt Sophia. The guy has two inches and about twenty pounds of muscle on me, one wrong move, and not only am I going to be falling to the ground, so is Sophia with my weight suffocating her.

"This does have something to do with me," I say, straightening out my body. "She's with me. So, if you want to stick your dick somewhere it doesn't fucking belong, I suggest you go look somewhere else."

"If this was your piece of ass, you should have just said that, Jacobi. I would have backed off." Miller grins, like all this is a joke.

Instead of red, I'm seeing blood.

There is no hesitation in bringing my arm back and letting my fist meet the asshole's jaw.

Sophia lets out a scream behind me, but even that isn't enough to pull me out of my rage. I hit the bastard two more times before he is able to get a few punches in. I feel someone pulling at me, and I hear Sophia's voice yelling at me to stop, but I don't.

The fight continues until someone much bigger than Sophia is able to pull the two of us apart.

Not a single face registers, but one.

Sophia steps into my line of sight, her face filled with concern as she places her hands on my cheeks and looks at the damage that no doubt covers my face.

If I get drafted tomorrow, Mom can say goodbye to getting a good picture to post on her social media.

CHAPTER TEN

BLAKE

A COLD LIQUID lands on my face, and I can't help but to hiss and flinch away from it.

"Stay still," Sophia orders as she dabs a piece of gauze on the apparent cut I have on my face, courtesy of Miller.

As soon as the fight was over, Sophia dragged me out of that basement and that house as fast as she could. According to her, she didn't want me to start another fight. I kindly reminded her that I didn't start a fight, the fucker who was hitting on her crossed a line, and I simply taught him a lesson.

She didn't like that very much, so she took my keys from me and shoved me into the passenger seat of my truck. Apparently I was the only one drinking at the party, because she was stone cold sober. At least one of us was. I don't want to know how bad my face would have looked if she was drunk and wasn't able to push away Miller's advances.

Now, I'm sitting in her bathroom in her parents' house, and she is trying to clean up my face as best she can.

"Where are your parents?" I ask, as she spreads some type of ointment above my eyebrow.

Her face is full of concentration as if she were a nurse or

something. She even sticks out her tongue just a bit as she does it.

"On their date night in Belgrade," she says, reaching for a butterfly Band-Aid.

"They coming home tonight?" I ask, because if they are, I would rather leave before they get here. I don't need to hear a lecture from her dad about fighting. If my mom doesn't rip me a new one, he will.

Sophia stops what she is doing and looks me straight in the eye. "Do you really think I would have brought you here, looking like this, if they were? You would have gotten yelled at for fighting and I would have gotten yelled at because I let you get in a fight." She slaps the Band-Aid on my face to drive home her point.

"You didn't let me fight," I say, taking in every single inch of her face.

"No, but I was the cause of it." As she finishes her sentence, her bottom lip quivers as if she is about to cry.

Would she be crying because I got into a fight because of her? Or would it be because of how bad the situation could have gotten if I didn't follow them down when I did?

"You didn't cause shit, Soph. That asshole did. I saw you trying to get away from him. I saw you push him away and tell him no. You weren't the cause of it. He was."

She just nods and finishes up cleaning up my face. Five minutes later, she backs away to look over her handy work.

"There. Hopefully there won't be a whole lot of bruising tomorrow. If there is, I'll just do your makeup or something," she says, more to herself than to me.

"It's fine. Mom is going to see it anyway when I get home."

She gives me another nod and starts cleaning up the first-aid kit that is spread out all over the bathroom counter.

I stay seated where I am, on the closed toilet, and just watch her. This night has turned into absolute shit, and I know for a fact there isn't any way to salvage it.

As she throws away the Band-Aid wrappers, I reach out and take her hand in mine and turn her body to face me so I can look into her light brown eyes that match her light brown hair.

"I'm sorry, Sophie," I start, using the nickname I used a lot when we first met, and rub my thumb against the back of her hand. "I'm sorry for what I said in the car. I'm sorry about the fight. You could have gotten hurt, and I didn't even think. I'm so, so damn sorry, Soph."

She looks down at me, her bottom lip between her teeth and tears still forming in her eyes. I know she is holding them in for me because I have told her that I hate seeing her cry, especially if I'm the cause of it. But right now, I want more than anything to see a tear run down her face because then maybe she will talk to me and accept my apologies.

"You were right, though," she says, intertwining her fingers with mine and holding on tight. "Some asshole did start getting handsy and begging me to go home with him. I guess that should be a sign to get rid of this skirt."

Fuck. I made her blame herself by making a stupid comment.

Without thinking, I find myself explaining my words.

"Do you want to know why I told you that?" The words come out before I can even think about it.

"Because it's slutty. I get it." She pulls her hand out of mine, and she starts walking out of the small bathroom, but again, I reach out and stop her.

"No. That wasn't it, and you know it," I say a little louder than I intended.

"Then why would you say that then?" She turns to face me fully, determination in her eyes.

"Because I was pissed other guys were going to see you in

it!" I yell out in frustration. "I wanted to take you back home and make you change because I wanted to be the only person who saw you dressed like this."

Sophia looks at me stunned. Her eyes are wide, and her mouth is open, as if she heard my words but hasn't comprehended them yet.

"What are you saying?" she asks, her voice small, almost as if she is afraid to speak or even breathe.

I close the distance between us and look down at her. "I'm saying I wanted you to be wearing that skirt for me and only for me."

A small gasp leaves her lips, and I raise a hand up to her face and cup her cheek ever so gently.

"The second you came down the stairs, it was as if I couldn't think about anything other than you. And you stayed on my mind all damn night. I wasn't even having fun because all I wanted to do was go to you and be close to you, but I didn't because you wanted space."

The tears that she was holding in earlier finally escape, but I catch them with my thumb before they are able to roll down her face.

"You're still drunk. You don't mean anything you're saying." She shakes her head, making my hand fall as she takes a step away from me.

"I'm completely sober, and I mean every single word." I need to shut up before I do or say anything stupid because right now it feels like I'm about to.

She continues to shake your head. "No, you don't. There's no way in hell you were thinking about me all night or were even affected by my skirt. There's no way you've ever thought about me like that, ever."

"I can show you." Shut up, Blake. Just shut up.

"How? How are you going to show me?"

I don't think, I don't hesitate, I don't stop. I close the distance between us, take her face between my hands, and kiss her.

All my thoughts about the night, about the fight, about the draft tomorrow disappear the second my lips meet hers.

For a second, I do think about pulling away because I have no right to be kissing her, but then I feel her kissing me back, and any thought of pulling away goes right out the window.

I let my tongue slide along her bottom lip, not expecting anything whatsoever, but my girl opens up for me and lets my tongue slide against hers.

For years, I've wondered what it would be like to kiss this girl, how it would feel to have my tongue slide against hers. Now that I'm experiencing it, it feels like the best thing in the world. Kissing Sophia feels nothing like it has with any other girl. With her, it feels right.

After what feels like just a few seconds of kissing her, I start to feel like I may be overwhelming her, so I pull away slightly. My hands are still on her face, and my mouth is still inches away from hers. I just need to know if she is okay with what is happening or if she wants me to stop.

Her eyes are still closed as I rest my forehead against hers. Her breath is coming out in pants as it mixes with mine.

I want to keep going, but I need to know she's okay.

"I'm sorry," I tell her again. This time for the kiss.

Her eyes pop open. "Why are you apologizing?" she asks, her voice low and husky.

"I had no right to kiss you." And I didn't. She didn't give me permission, I just pounced. It's basically the same thing Miller was trying to do earlier.

"But I kissed you back." She reaches up and gently touches her lips with her fingertips.

"Did you want to?" I ask, just to torture myself.

Her doe eyes look up at me. They are full of wonder, and I want to get lost in them. I want to get lost in everything this girl is.

She doesn't say a single word for the longest time, but then she nods her head and as soon as she does, it's as if I can breathe again.

I give her a smile and move my hands away from her face, down to her waist.

"Do you want me to continue showing you that you do in fact affect me?" I ask her, bringing her body even closer than mine, as if I'm not already all over her.

Her eyes shine at the question, and the way her head nods yes tells me she is just as eager as I am.

My hands mold themselves to her waist, right before I lift her off her feet and walk us out of the bathroom and across the hallway to her room.

CHAPTER ELEVEN

BLAKE

I'VE BEEN in her room more times than I can count.

During my parents' divorce, it was my safe space, my escape. We've watched movies in here. We've had more than a hundred sleepovers in here. We've been through so much shit together in this room, and through all of it, I never thought that I would be walking in here, with Sophia in my arms, while I burn up with anticipation to kiss her again.

I lay her on her bed, and I quickly climb on top of her, hovering my weight over her so that I don't hurt her.

"Are you okay?" I ask her, noticing the worry that has suddenly appeared in her eyes. I brush her hair out of her face, trying to see if I can calm her down, but I have no idea if it's working.

She takes her bottom lip between her teeth, and the worry in her eyes grows even more.

"I'm a little scared," she admits.

I try to pull away from her, but she wraps her legs around my waist to hold me in place.

"We don't have to do anything. We can stop things right here, right now," I offer.

I would never pressure Sophia to do something she wasn't comfortable with. Sure, when we were five, I pushed her to get on the ice when we first met, but this is different.

"I want to," she says, letting out a breath. "I just..." she stops as if she needs time to think about what she wants to say. "Promise me, that whatever happens here tonight, it won't ruin us. I can't lose my best friend."

My eyes stay on hers as I give her my promise. "I promise that whatever happens between us tonight won't ruin us. I can't lose my best friend either."

It's supposed to be a promise, but in reality, I know it's a lie. A lie that burns my tongue. Because this will in fact ruin our friendship beyond repair. After tonight no matter what we do, no matter if we just kiss or go further than that, our relationship will change. For the better or for the worse, it will change. Whether we want it to or not, our friendship has already changed. With just one simple kiss, it has changed. There's no going back now.

From the look in her eyes, her mind is going in the same direction mine is, but that doesn't stop her from sliding her hands into my hair and bringing my face down to hers.

This time, instead of me taking something that I wanted, it's Sophia taking something she wants. Her lips move in such a hungry way that I'm desperate to give her everything she wants.

I know I'm not her first kiss. She went on about how horrible that was when it happened, but this is her first, or should I say second, kiss with me, and I want it to be a fucking memorable one. I want this to be her most memorable kiss ever, and a selfish part of me wants it to be her favorite and best one, too.

Our tongues slide together, tasting what the other has to offer, and I'm not going to lie, it feels so damn good.

I have the girl I've thought about constantly in ways I

shouldn't have, under me, and her mouth is fucking perfection. Soft and warm.

As my mouth dances with hers, I shift just slightly so I can place a hand on her hip and let it slip up and down her body in a soft caress. I'm bold enough to make it under her shirt, and the way Sophia lets out a hum drives me so crazy, I start thinking up different things I can do to get that sound out of her again.

I pull my mouth away from hers and move it to her neck to place kisses against the exposed skin. The perfume she wears is burning into my brain so that I can smell it every damn day.

"Can I touch you?" I ask, keeping my hand on her ribs and not any further up.

"Please," she pants out, arching her back in the process.

My hand moves up her torso until it's just under her bra. I let my palm glide over the material, desperately wanting to have skin on skin contact with her. But this may be the one and only time I have her like this, so I'm going to take my time and appreciate every single inch of the beauty that is Sophia.

I move my mouth down her neck until I reach her chest. Earlier, I hated this shirt she is wearing, but now I'm loving it so damn much.

Feeling the need to see more of Sophia, I sit up, straddling her body and place my hands on the edge of her shirt. I look at her, with a silent question in my eyes, and with a nod, she gives me the permission to take her shirt off.

The second the small crop top is off her, my mouth starts to water at the sight before me. Her tits are wrapped in a black lace bra that barely covers her, and the locket I gave her for Christmas three years ago sits perfectly between the two mounds.

I love that she never takes off something I gave her. That she is always wearing it, even when she goes out on dates. It's as if she is always holding a part of me close to her heart.

"You're so fucking pretty," I say to her, letting my finger run along her exposed skin.

"You're biased," she answers but arches her body into my touch.

"Maybe I am, but I've been wanting to tell you that for years because it's true. You are so damn pretty, sometimes I can't fucking take it," I tell her because, why not? She has every right to know how much I think about her outside of being my best friend.

"Really?" she asks, almost bewildered that I would say such a thing.

"Yes, really." I move my finger away from her breasts and down to her stomach until I reach the waistband of her skirt. Goose bumps cover her skin as I move my finger along the material and seeing them is making me harder than it should.

Seeing how I'm affecting her just by touching her makes me wonder how she would react if and when I put my lips somewhere besides her mouth. Will the goose bumps spread all over? Will she blush? And if she does, how deep will it go? Will it cover her whole body?

Fuck, I really need to control myself and my thoughts because the way this is going, I'm bound to do something stupid and regretful, and right now I don't want to regret a single thing.

Sophia leans up on her elbows, her brown hair cascading down her back, and she reaches out to touch my shirt-covered chest. I swear I feel her touch burning through the fabric, marking me with every single motion she makes.

"I've wondered sometimes if you ever saw me the way you see other girls," she starts, her eyes on her fingers. "I've wondered if you ever thought of me in the same way you thought about them. If I was as pretty, if I was as special. Sometimes I would tell myself that I wasn't because of how you would introduce me to people, or how you looked at me versus how you looked at them. But then there were times when I questioned if I was wrong in thinking that because you would put me before them or because I knew you in a way they never would."

She finally looks up at me, and as soon as she does, I take her face between my hands again.

"You shouldn't compare yourself to a single girl I've dated. You are prettier than they will ever be and a hell of a lot more special." I place my mouth against her once more and savor her taste.

I feel her hands move down my chest until they reach the hem of my shirt. Only then do I pull away from her and slide my shirt off as fast as I possibly can.

The second my shirt is off, I shift so I'm no longer straddling her. With my body parallel to hers, I start kissing her again. First her mouth, then I move down to her neck, then down to her breasts. I pull down the lace and take one in my mouth, sucking and grabbing on to her as if she were my favorite dessert. I take her dusty rose-colored nipple in my mouth and let out a groan as it hardens against my tongue.

I do the same to the other side, but I don't spend a whole lot of time admiring how good her tits feel in my mouth and hands. I have other things I want to do to this girl.

Moving, I kiss my way down her stomach until I reach the waistband of her skirt. I plant kisses along the edge of the fabric, from hip to hip, while Sophia opens her legs a bit wider for me to settle between them.

Her skirt has bunched up just at the top of her mound, and I'm rewarded with a sight of black panties that match her bra. Her pussy is right there, and I can't fucking wait to taste her.

I palm her, my fingers caressing her through the lacy fabric, while one of her sweet moans fills my ears. Feeling the need to taste her, I look up and silently ask her for permission. Again, she gives me a nod, this time attached with a smile.

No time is wasted as I shift further down the bed and position myself right at her pussy. I can smell her heat, and I know without even tasting her, she is going to be the best thing that will ever be on my tongue.

I kiss her inner thigh, pushing her skirt up until she is fully uncovered and swipe my tongue across my lips.

Slowly, I make my way to her core, shifting her panties to the side and swiping my tongue against her.

I was right. She is the best thing that has ever been on my tongue. One swipe, and I want more.

So I go for it. I take what I want, and in the process, I have Sophia withering under me, her hands in my hair and my name on her lips.

I'm barely touching her, and she is ready to come for me.

Wanting to give her what she needs, I pull out everything that I have. I take her clit in my mouth and suck as hard as I can.

"Blake, oh my god," Sophia pants, while she grinds her pussy against my face, trying to get the friction that she needs.

"You taste so damn good, Soph," I say against her, my fingers teasing her entrance.

"I don't think I can handle more of what you are doing," she moans out when my fingers slide into her wet, hot pussy.

"You can, and you will. Come for me, baby. Let me taste you. Fuck, I want to taste you and have you in my mind forever."

"I've never..." she starts but stops, and I don't have to look up at her to know that she's blushing from what she was about to say.

"You never come on a guy's tongue before?" I finish, not relenting the motion of my fingers.

I look up and find Sophia looking down at me, shaking her head.

"No," she answers shyly.

"Good. I get to be your first," I say, placing a kiss on her clit before giving her a smirk. "Now, coat my tongue and scream as you do it."

I replace my fingers with my mouth and devour her as if she were my last meal.

Her hands make their way deeper into my hair, and she pulls so damn hard that it's almost painful, but fuck does it feel good.

My name comes out of her mouth in a chant, and I have to stop grinding my cock against her mattress because hearing her scream out like that is so damn hot, I'm on the verge of embarrassing myself.

I slide my tongue into her entrance and pinch her clit with my thumb and forefinger, and that is all it takes for her to unravel for me.

Her sweet release coats my tongue in the best fucking way. I can't help the smirk that forms on my face as I take it all.

My tongue gently slides against her folds as she comes down from her high.

"Fuck," she lets out, absolutely breathless. "Is an orgasm supposed to make you see black spots?" she asks.

I don't know if she meant that to be a rhetorical question or not, but either way, it doesn't stop me from getting pissed off. I know for a fact she has dated a few guys these last few years. Sure I don't know how far she went with them, and I really don't want to know, but one of them has to have made her come, right?

Or were they just stupid and didn't pay attention in health class or biology when the fucking clit was pointed out to them?

Fuckers.

If I didn't hate them already for even breathing the same air as Sophia, I sure as hell would hate them now.

I'm so much in my head about Sophia's comment that I don't feel her shift under me until her hands are on my chest, and she pushes me back enough that we switch spots. I end up on my back with Sophia on top of me.

"Let me make you feel good, too," she says, sliding her body down mine, until she comes face to face with the waistband of my jeans.

The image of my dick sliding between her lips shines bright in my mind, and as much as I want that image to come true, I can't. I'd much rather make whatever this night is turning into about her and showing her just how special she is to me.

So I stop her.

"No," I say, sliding a finger under her chin and making her look up at me.

"What?" she says, sitting up, hurt filling her eyes.

She thinks that I'm turning her down.

"No, I don't want to suck me off," I say as gently as possible.

"Why? Do you think that I can't do it? Because I can," she responds, and an image of her sucking someone else off invades my mind.

I hate that she might have done that with someone else, and as much as I want to erase the image from my head, I stand my ground.

"It has nothing to do with whether I think you can do it or not. I would love for you to wrap that pretty mouth around me, but if you do it right now, I don't know how long I'm going to last. And if that is the case, I would rather do something else."

Her eyes shift, and for a second, she looks scared.

"What?" I ask, sitting up so that I can cup her cheek.

"I," she starts but then pauses, bowing her head like she's ashamed about something. "I've never done more."

Our virginities have never been something we've talked about.

Actually, we haven't talked about sex in general.

So hearing she is still a virgin is news to me. I thought she still was, but I could have been wrong.

Hearing her say those words, though, makes me want to pound my chest. Not because there is a possibility of her giving me something that is important to her, but because she didn't hand it over to some fucker who was undeserving of it and would have just added it to his list of conquests.

"Neither have I," I tell her, revealing the one thing I haven't told her, and I tell her almost everything.

Given her expression, my little piece of news takes her by surprise.

"What? That can't be right. Every single girl you've dated has told me otherwise," she says, giving me a confused look.

I roll my eyes. I think I know why they would tell her that because they wanted to make Sophia jealous, but I keep that thought to myself.

"All lies. The furthest I've gone is third base."

"How is that possible?" she asks, shaking her head. "You date a new girl every month."

Not *every* month, but that's a moot point.

I shrug. "None of them felt right."

"If you're lying to me right now, so I give you my virginity, I swear to God I will never talk to you again," she lets out, sounding like she's ready to cry and punch me at the same time.

I slide my hand down her neck until I reach her chest and place my hand over her heart. Taking her hand, I place it in the same location on my chest.

"I swear on my heart and on yours, I'm not lying to you."

And I'm not. None of the girls I've been with have felt right. At one point I tried to view sex as just that, sex, but it felt wrong for some reason. It felt wrong to use the girls I dated, to cross something off a list of things to do before college. Sure, I've done other things but never have gone all the way.

Right now, with Sophia, though, it feels different. It doesn't feel like I'm just crossing something off a list. It feels like it's more. Like it's life-changing.

Sophia leans down and places a kiss on my lips. Sealing my words. Our bodies fall back, and we continue to kiss until we are both panting and needing more.

We move on to the next part of our night in what feels like slow motion. Both of us just trying to take in the moment.

I watch her as she gets rid of her bra and the skirt that started all of this. When she is in just her underwear, she grabs my hand and places it on the lace, letting me push the material down until she is in front me wearing nothing but my locket.

She gives me a shy smile, and tries to cover herself up, but I stop her, telling her that I want to see all of her.

When I start getting rid of my clothes, or at least what's left of them, her eyes follow every single one of my movements.

Her eyes go wide when my cock springs out of my briefs, but when she licks her lips, I can't help but let out a groan as my dick aches to be touched by her. I'm rock solid, and it's all because of my best friend.

Like our kiss a few minutes ago, we come together slowly and start exploring each other's bodies as eagerly as we can.

I kiss every single inch of Sophia's body, wanting to savor this moment, taking my time but also being fast and quick because the anticipation of having her is becoming too damn much.

Through more kissing, we end up how we started—with her on her back and me hovering over her.

The only time I break away from her is to grab a condom from my wallet and slide it on. Thank God I listened to my brother and started carrying one a few months ago and changing it out every few weeks.

Once I'm back in bed, her legs are spread wide, and I settle between them, ready to slide into her.

Like everything else tonight, I take my time, sliding into her tight pussy one inch at time. My eyes stay on her face the whole time, ready to pull away if she needs me to.

Eventually I'm fully in her, and she lets out a groan as if she's in pain.

I start pulling out, but she wraps her legs around my waist, keeping me in place.

"Give me a second," she pants out, shifting her body a bit, getting comfortable.

"Take however long you need," I say, as I lean down and whisper in her ear.

I feel her breath against my face and her hand against my back. It's calming, but I don't know who she is trying to calm, me or herself.

A kiss lands on the corner of my mouth, and her heel pushes against my ass.

"Okay, you can move. I think I can handle it," she says, right before giving me another kiss.

"You tell me when you need me to stop, okay?" I say to her, pressing my face against her neck and giving her a small bite just behind her ear.

"I will."

All it takes is those two little words, and I start to move. I start off slowly, so that she can get used to it, and then pick up speed when she digs her nails into my back.

I pick up the pace and start fucking Sophia harder and harder. Our pants and moans fill the room, and it feels like the both of us are on the brink of explosion.

Sliding into her feels so fucking right that I don't want to stop doing it.

I pound into her, and when she moans out my name, it just drives me even crazier.

"I need you to get to the edge, Soph. I need you to come before I do. Please, I need you to give me everything you've got."

She shakes her head against her pillow. "I don't know if I can."

"You can, baby. You can. Your pussy is wrapped so tightly around me, I can feel how ready you are. Come, Sophia." I place my fingers against her clit and start drawing small circles with my thumb to get her closer to the brink.

"Blake, oh my god. Yes," she moans out, her eyes closing and her head getting thrown back.

I feel her tighten around me even more, so I continue to pound into her and rubbing circles against her clit.

Her pussy is pulsating around me, and when I slam into her one more time, she lets go.

"Oh my god! Oh my god!" she screams out, her release taking over.

Not being able to hold back anymore, I take the image of her coming around my cock just now and let go in my own release.

I grunt into her neck, releasing everything I have into the condom.

Now I know what Sophia meant by seeing black spots when experiencing an orgasm. What we just did was fucking intense, and black spots cloud my vision because of it.

Feeling like I'm probably crushing her, I finally move my body off hers and lie next to her, taking in the moment.

It takes me a second to realize what just happened.

I just had sex with my best friend.

I just had sex with Sophia, and there is no going back.

Holy shit.
What did we just do?

CHAPTER TWELVE

SOPHIA

FOR SOME REASON, I'm jerked awake.

My eyes pop open, and it takes me a second to take in my surroundings and figure out what might have woken me up, but it's just me in my room, in my bed.

It must have been a dream I don't remember.

I roll over to my side, and right away I'm met with a whiff of the cologne Blake started wearing on his eighteenth birthday. That was the day he said that he was an adult now, and he could wear adult shit and smell nice. That memory makes me roll my eyes because it triggers another one where he dragged me to every single department store the mall closest to us had to offer, so he could find his signature scent. He was able to find it six hours later, and now he wears it all the time.

As I continue smelling it, though, all the memories from last night start to flow back.

For a second, I was thinking it was a dream, but the more I smell his cologne on my pillow, something that is rarely there, no matter how many times he's been in my room, the more the things that happened last night become clearer.

We had sex.

We made out, touched each other's bodies, we kissed like it was our first and last make-out session, and we had sex.

I saw my best friend naked, and he saw me naked. And he slid not only his fingers and tongue into me, but also his dick.

I had sex with Blake Jacobi, and I have no idea how to feel about that.

Last night was something that will definitely stay with me for a long time, and I mean that in a good way. He made me feel all sorts of things, and as much as I want to regret the actual action of it, I don't. Blake put in the effort to make our first time feel special.

What I do regret is everything that comes after it.

I have no idea where we stand right now. Even though he promised me that us getting together wasn't going to ruin us, it feels like it did. Even if it's just a small bit, it definitely changed something in our friendship. What, I'm not exactly sure.

It's not like he's here for me to ask him.

Since I hear the shower running, I know he's still in the house, but not here next to me.

I have so many questions that I have half a mind to get out of bed and run into the bathroom just to get answers.

Are we still friends?

Are we more?

Are we nothing at all?

Whatever those answers may be, I know we absolutely need to talk about this, and no way are we going to be able to sweep this under the rug.

I hear the shower turn off, so I decide it's best to get out of bed and get dressed. As much as I want to have his eyes roaming my naked body again, I don't know how much good it would do, especially if we are going to talk. So covering up is for the best.

I'm sitting up on my bed, wrapped up in my blanket and wearing one of his hockey T-shirts I took from him one day after swimming, when he walks in. His hair is wet, but he is completely dressed in a pair of sweats and a T-shirt.

He spends so much time here that my parents let him leave clothes in our extra bedroom. There have been a handful of times where he has come over for dinner after hockey practice and ended up showering here. So it made sense to give him a place to leave some clothes. That's where he must have gotten what he is wearing now.

Blake walks in the room and looks over at me, giving me a small smile. "Hey."

"Hi," I say, my voice small.

I'm not really sure how I should be acting right now.

He lets out a sigh and walks over to take a seat on the edge of the bed. I take in his profile as he sits with his elbows on his knees, not saying anything, and that's when I notice not only is his face bruised from the fight, but that he also has a hickey on his neck. A hickey that I put there.

Great.

Now we have to figure out a way to hide not only the bruises but also the damn hickey.

"How are you feeling?" Blake breaks the silence, and my hickey-filled thoughts start to flow away.

I could lie and tell him that I'm good, that everything is peachy, but I don't think that I can. So I go with the truth.

"Confused," I tell him, bringing my knees up to my chest and wrapping my arms around them.

He gives me a nod, like he knows exactly how I'm feeling.

"Yeah, last night definitely messed with my mind a little bit, too," he says, sounding defeated.

Does he sound defeated because he knows this is the end of our friendship? I don't know if I can handle losing him in any capacity. We're about to enter the college chapter of our lives, and I don't know if I can do that alone. I want him at my side.

As much as I want the answer to that question, I need an answer to a different one. "Do you regret what we did?"

He looks over at me, his eyebrows bunching up at my question, and his eyes searching mine. Eventually, he shakes his head. "No, I don't. Do you?"

I take a deep breath. "Not the action of it, no. I'm happy you were my first. It's just everything that comes afterward I'm feeling like I will regret."

Blake nods in understanding. "I get that. Like where do we go from here? Are we still friends, or are we more of a thing?"

"Yeah, I don't want what happened last night to be the reason I lose my best friend," I say, my voice breaking a bit in the process.

"It won't. You won't lose me," he says, coming closer to me and placing a hand on mine.

"We had sex, Blake. That changes things."

"It doesn't have to." He squeezes my hand, and I try my hardest not to get lost in his icy blues.

"So, how do you suggest we handle this then?" I ask because I can't come up with anything.

My best friend looks at me for a solid minute. He doesn't say anything. He doesn't even open his mouth so that words could come out. He just looks at me.

I see the conflict in his eyes. I see that he is battling with himself on this. He is trying to find the right thing to say because he also knows the promise he made last night was a lie. We both know it.

"We don't have to do anything. We can let this be one night where we both needed each other, where we wanted to feel closer to one another. We can just have this one night and go back to how things were before yesterday. We don't have to ruin anything. We don't have to make it more. We can just let it be and continue with how we were going."

"Just like that?"

"Just like that."

It sounds so simple, not doing anything.

Like we can just forget it and move on and still act like our normal selves.

As I sit here on the bed that we had sex in a few hours ago and feel the ache between my legs, I realize something. I'm in love with Blake, and I probably have been for years. Since I was fifteen when he gave me my locket. My crush on him is more than a crush. It always has been, and it always will be.

Last night meant the absolute world to me, and I don't want to forget it. I want to remember it for years to come. It's my favorite night we've had together.

And as much as I want to tell him that we *can* do something, that we *can* see where this thing between us could go, that we both have an attraction to each other and think the other is special beyond belief, I can't.

If things don't work out between us, I will lose him for sure, and I will never be able to handle that. If I lose him as my friend, I will never be able to talk to him again. I will never be able to cheer him on at his hockey games. I will never be able to be there for him when he needs me, when his dad decides to insert himself in his life again. I will lose all of those things and more.

I don't want that. I don't want any of that.

So I give him a nod.

"Okay," I say, feeling my heart break as I do. "Let's not do anything."

My chest feels like it wants to rip me from the inside out, but I ignore it.

This is for the best.

Even if it hurts me, I will rather have Blake in my life in this capacity than not at all.

"Okay," Blake says, giving my hand a squeeze.

We sit like that for a few minutes. In silence and looking at each other, possibly trying to figure out what the other is thinking. We could ask, but I think that we both need a few minutes where we don't share what we are currently feeling.

Eventually, we head downstairs and start looking around the kitchen for something to eat.

In a few hours, the day is going to become even bigger than it already is. Blake may get drafted today, and it will change his life forever. So I try to put all my concentration on that instead of our conversation up in my bedroom or our night together.

As we're eating cereal at the kitchen table, the door to the mudroom opens up, and my parents walk in. They're all smiles, but my dad's smile quickly disappears when he notices Blake and the bruising on his face.

"What the actual fuck happened to your face?!" he roars out.

The three of them start talking about last night and how Blake having bruises for his draft night is unacceptable.

I just listen to everything they have to say, not contributing whatsoever as I put way too much concentration on my cereal.

As they talk about the fight, all I can think is that I have to find a way to mend my broken heart when it shouldn't be broken in the first place.

CHAPTER THIRTEEN

BLAKE

WITH THE FIRST *selection of the second round of the NHL draft, the Chicago Dark Knights are proud to select Blake Jacobi.*

Those words still ring loud in my mind even though I heard them almost a month ago. Never did I think that I was going to hear those words, and yet, I did, and I still can't wrap my head around it.

Chicago. I was drafted into the NHL by the Chicago Dark Knights. Holy crap.

Earlier this year, when I submitted the necessary paperwork to enter the draft, I had decided I wouldn't be flying to wherever the draft was being held. This year's draft was in Nashville, and I didn't see the point in flying all the way there with my family, all so that I wouldn't get picked. More so because I knew I wasn't going in the first round.

So I decided to watch from home and give the NHL four numbers—mine, my mom's, my brother's, and Isaac's.

If I didn't answer, I would have rather heard the news from one of them.

Me, my family, Sophia, and her parents, plus a few of my coaches and teammates, all gathered at my mom's house for the two-day event. Because I knew I wasn't going in the first round, nerves weren't running high during day one. Day two was tough, though. I'm not going to lie. Before round two even started, I had already puked three times, locking myself in the bathroom.

The only person who was brave enough to come in there with me while I emptied out my stomach was Sophia. She came into the small, cramped room and sat on the floor with me, my head on her lap, and she brushed my hair back in such a calming way.

I fucking loved her for it. Especially since our night together was still fresh. I saw the hurt in her eyes when I suggested we do nothing when it came to our night together, but I pushed it down so I wouldn't ruin our friendship even more.

Being close to her in the bathroom like that felt good, and it helped bring down my nerves.

When it was time, Hunter came to get us, and we sat in front of the TV patiently waiting for round two to start.

I had a feeling the Knights were going to draft me. My meeting with them had gone well, and my agent was optimistic, so was Sophia's dad. Chicago was my dream team, and I would have been bummed if I was picked by someone else. But I didn't want to get my hopes up. Chicago had the first pick in the second round, but things could have gone in so many damn directions.

My mind goes back to that day.

"Who has the first pick this round?" Selena asks from where she was sitting on Hunter's lap. I was sitting on the floor with Jainie and Sophia on either side of me, while our parents sat behind us on the couch.

"Chicago," me, Sophia, Mom, and Isaac answer her at the same time.

My brother's girlfriend looks over at me and gives me a smile.

One that is small, but warm and reassuring. "Is this what you've been waiting for?" she asks.

I don't give her any words, I just nod my answer.

"Okay, then. Let's hope that Chicago has their shit together," she says, causing a small smile to form on my lips.

We all look up at the huge-ass TV that was mounted on the wall by my stepdad, ready for round two to start. My hands are getting more sweaty with each passing second.

I didn't realize I was sort of rocking back and forth until Sophia took my hand in hers, calming me down again.

Looking over at her, I find her watching me, her smile just as warm and reassuring as Selena's, but her smile has an extra level of comfort.

"You got this. They would be stupid not to pick you," she tells me, and all I want to do is get lost in her again and never come back up for air. I was wrong to tell her we should put our one night together behind us and act like nothing is different. Everything is different. If it weren't, I wouldn't be thinking about getting lost in her body.

"Of course they would be stupid. Those fuckers wouldn't know what hit them if they pass up on Blake. They'll be crying their sorry asses to sleep," her dad says from where he sits behind me.

"Isaac." His wife reprimands him, and I don't have to turn around to see that she probably slapped him on the arm. The way he yelps tells me everything I need to know, causing a laugh to escape my lips.

"What? It's true," he answers, and when I turn around to look at him, he gives me a smile.

This man is more of a father to me than my own and sees all the potential I have. I want to get drafted because it's something I've dreamed of since I was a little kid, but I also want to get drafted for him. I wouldn't be the player I am today if it wasn't *for him. I want to be able to show him that all his hard work has paid off. I want to be able to make him proud.*

The music starts, and the announcers start talking on the screen, while everyone in the room goes quiet. Both Sophia and Jainie take one of my hands, and I feel a hand on my shoulder, but I don't turn to see who it is. I already know.

The Dark Knights are announced as the first pick of the second round, and all the air leaves my lungs. This is either it, or not. Whatever it may be, I'm definitely not fucking ready.

Someone from the team steps up to the microphone and gives the camera a smile.

"With the first selection of the second round of the NHL draft, the Chicago Dark Knights are proud to select Blake Jacobi."

Twenty-two words, and my life fucking changed forever.

I can't help but smile as I remember all the excitement that burst through the room the second my name was announced. That smile starts to disappear slightly when I remember all the calls from my dad still waiting to be returned, but I push that aside.

That day was fucking amazing, and I'm not going to let thoughts of my dad tarnish it.

A month later and I'm in Chicago to meet the team. I'm not signing on to the Knights right away. I'm still going to attend Montana State and play for them for a few years, keeping my fingers crossed I don't get hurt, but the team invited all their draft picks to the city to give them a warm welcome.

And all of this seriously feels like big boy shit.

Especially since this is also the first time that I've traveled all by myself. Usually if I fly somewhere, either my mom, my sister, or Sophia is with me. This time because school had just started for Jainie, my mom decided it was best for her and my sister to stay behind. Hunter couldn't come with me because his own season was about to start, and he couldn't get away.

As for Sophia, she used the excuse of packing for school to get out of coming with me. We are set to move in next week, and according to her, she hasn't packed a single thing.

That's a lie, and I know it. The girl is an absolute planner and probably started packing everything that she wanted to take to her dorm the second she accepted her admissions offer.

She most likely didn't want to come with me because of what happened the night of the party. Because she didn't want us to be in a situation where we would be likely to cross the line again.

Things between us have been awkward at best this last month, and coming with me could have complicated things even more. So, when she made up the packing excuse, I understood where she was coming from. It doesn't mean that her refusal to come with me doesn't sting, though.

I want to share this experience with her, and if I hadn't said what I did, she would probably be here in Chicago with me as more than my best friend. But this is for the best, for both of us, and I'm sticking to that. No matter how much the organ in my chest is telling me it disagrees.

"So, Blake. What did your mom feed you and your brother growing up because apparently that woman has the secret power of raising pro athletes," one of the Knights, I think his name is Simon, asks me from across the table at the welcome dinner.

This welcome dinner is at some swanky restaurant that is close to the team's arena, and I honestly don't think I've had a more expensive dinner. The food is good, not going to lie, but the prices sure as hell made my eyes pop out a little bit. I had to take a picture of it and send it to Sophia. Not only to show her how crazy the prices are but also to give her a glimpse of the food she could have been eating right now.

I go back to Simon's question.

When I got drafted, everyone went crazy when they found out that an NFL quarterback's brother got drafted by Chicago. It was like everyone's minds were blown over the fact that Hunter even had a brother, but even more so that he, too, would be a pro athlete one day.

It's freaking insane.

Since I'm sure this isn't the first time I'm going to answer this question, I decide to mess with the guy.

"Raw eggs, broccoli, turkey meat, cheese, and carrots all blended into a smoothie. It's absolutely disgusting, but the woman wanted pro athletes for children, so she forced it down our throats. My brother still drinks it every day."

The way Simon's face drops is fucking hilarious. He actually believes me.

When I finally laugh at his expression, he is able to compose himself and finally put it together that I was joking.

"Good one, Jacobi," the team captain, Sydney, says from next to me, slapping a hand on my shoulder. "He was actually contemplating making the smoothie to try it out."

"No, I wasn't," Simon counters, shaking his head at his team captain.

"Don't deny it," one of the team's forwards, Liam Crawford, throws out, pointing his fork at Simon. "We all saw your face. You were planning out your next grocery run."

"Fuck off." Simon throws a napkin in Liam's direction, and the table erupts with laughter. This group of guys is fucking amazing. Hopefully they're still like this when I sign on to the team.

"Did you guys hear we got a new acquisition this morning?" someone asks from the other side of the table, his name not coming to my head.

"Who?" Sydney asks, taking a bite of his food.

"Christian Rodriguez, the guy from San Jose," the guy answers, giving Sydney a nod.

I recognize the name. Rodriguez is all about speed and sure as hell knows how to keep players from scoring. The guy is going to be fucking fantastic playing for a team like Chicago. There's no doubt about that.

The guys continue to talk about how ecstatic they are about Rodriguez joining the Knights. Since I don't have much to contribute to the conversation, I just lean back and savor every moment of tonight.

I never thought I would get drafted, yet here I am, and it feels like I'm on top of the world.

After dinner, we order dessert, and I take another picture and send it to Sophia. She responds with a crying emoji at the picture of the piece of cheesecake I sent her way, and I can't help but smile.

With time, we're going to go back to how things were before we hooked up. I just have to be patient with it.

Once everyone is finished eating their small pieces of dessert, someone suggests we go back to the arena to give the draftees a tour of the team facility. We all agree, and once the bill is taken care of, we all start walking over there.

I've been to the arena twice—once when I came to talk to the team about them potentially drafting me and another for a game with Sophia and her dad. He knew I wanted to play for Chicago, so he brought us to a game to show me what could be in my future. That game was fucking amazing, and it was added to the list of things Isaac has done for me that I can never repay him for.

So as we walk to the arena, I'm fucking pumped. I just don't let it show because I want the Knights who are here to think I'm cool and not just some kid.

As soon as we are close to the arena, I take another picture and send it off.

"You sending pictures to your girlfriend?" Liam asks, as we cross the street, all the other guys ahead of us.

I turn to him and give him a confused look before he nods at the phone in my hand that is open to the camera app.

"Oh, uh, no. Not my girlfriend. I mean she is a girl, and she is my friend, but she's my best friend. Has been since I was five," I say, stumbling a bit and telling him more than necessary.

Liam laughs. "What's her name?"

"Sophia," I answer, a little bit too quickly, feeling my face get all red for no reason.

He gives me a nod. "And do you always get all flustered when you talk about Sophia?" he asks, basically calling me out.

I'm pretty sure my face is just getting redder.

I clear my throat a few times before answering him. "I don't get flustered." Liam gives me a pointed look that tells me that he doesn't believe me. "I don't."

No way in hell am I about to tell a possible future teammate that I've slept with my best friend and have developed deeper fillings for her than what I had before.

"Whatever you say, Jacobi. But can I say one more thing?"

"What?"

"If I were you, and I looked at my phone all goofy like that whenever I texted my best friend, who happens to be a girl and a friend, I would lock it down. That way I could have my girlfriend and best friend all rolled up in one," Liam says, giving me a shrug and just continues walking, leaving me there in the middle of the sidewalk speechless.

That's the same thing Hunter told me when I was fifteen.

Is that the go-to piece of advice from athletes?

It's not a bad, or even a wrong, piece of advice. It's actually pretty solid, and if I wasn't scared, I would follow through with it in a heartbeat. But there's a lot to consider, a lot of what-ifs. As much as I want to consider everything and walk myself through every what-if, I can't.

I hate it so damn much, but staying best friends is what's best for both of us.

It takes a few seconds, but I'm able to collect myself and catch up to Liam. "It's not like that between me and her," I say to him, my tongue burning the same way it did when I promised Sophia that nothing was going to ruin us.

"Okay," he says, giving me a nod, but I'm not sure he's accepting my words as a good enough excuse. "When you finally come to play with us, I can't wait to meet your friend who also is a girl."

The fucker is laughing at me, and when I narrow my eyes at him, he just chuckles and walks across the street to the arena.

I want to say something else, but the second I take a good look at the building in front of me, all thoughts of responding to Liam go out the window.

Fuck.

It all just became more real.

I take a second to admire the arena, but then follow the guys in when a security guard named Gus opens the door for us. The other guy who was drafted by the team and I are left in awe as the group of guys who took us to dinner show us around and give us a little history lesson on the place.

They take us everywhere, eventually ending up in the locker room.

It's one thing seeing all of this on a TV screen or in pictures, but seeing it in person is fucking mind-blowing.

For a second, I start to think I shouldn't be here, that maybe I'm not meant for all of this, but then I see it.

In the locker room, the guys have a surprise set up for us. A surprise that includes a section for both of us, our last names at the top, merch laid out in front, and a jersey with our last names on the back hanging inside.

"Holy shit," I say, approaching my section and grabbing the jersey.

"Hopefully, you were thinking about sticking with number ten," Liam says, coming up next to me as I admire my jersey. My first official Dark Knights jersey.

I'm not able to respond, I just give him a nod.

I've been number ten since day one. No reason to change it now. It has meaning to it. Because of my brother and because of Sophia. The fact that I think about her every time I see the number should be a mind-twister, but it isn't. That's just how things have always been.

I look down at the jersey in my hands and smile.

This is it.

I fucking made it, and I'm here to fucking stay.

CHAPTER FOURTEEN

SOPHIA

Twenty years old

"C'MON, Jacobi! You need to learn how to hit the puck into the actual net!" I slam my hand against the armrest of my seat, feeling frustrated as Blake and the rest of the Montana State hockey team play against the University of Vermont. They are in the third period, and Montana State is down by one.

My dad laughs from where he sits next to me. I'm glad one of us isn't pissed off our team is losing.

"Nomas es un juego, Sophia," he tells me right before he pops a few pieces of popcorn into his mouth.

It's just a game. He's been telling me that for years, but no matter the game, or the score, I always get a little crazy. Especially when I'm cheering for Blake.

"I know," I say, letting out a sigh. "But they're so damn close to the conference championships and the Frozen Four, they can't be screwing up right now."

"They'll be fine," my dad says, bringing the popcorn back up to his mouth and sliding the remaining kernels in.

"Maybe you can do a few extra sessions with Blake," I

suggest, already pulling Blake's schedule up in my head and trying to see if he has extra time to spare.

He has time in the morning. He might be able to pull it off. I would just have to convince him to get up earlier.

It will be hard, but doable.

Besides, he likes working with my dad. He's been doing it for years, and he even told me a few weeks ago that he wanted to ask him if he would be willing to write up a workout for him. He just hasn't had the time to ask. This is me making that happen.

My dad side-eyes me. "I don't think he needs extra sessions."

"He just hit a slap shot into the glass. He definitely needs something." I point in the direction of the ice. No doubt that shot is going to end up on social media somehow. My guess is that one of the many jersey chasers this school has is going to upload it by the morning.

"I saw that," he nods, looking back toward the ice, probably noticing things the everyday fan won't, but that comes with being a former player.

My dad grew up in Seattle and spent the majority of his childhood playing hockey. He had a dream to go pro, and he was heading in that direction until he got hurt around the time that I was born. That injury ended his hockey career. So when we moved to Montana, and I started taking figure skating lessons at the rink where I met Blake, he decided that he wanted to try his hand at coaching. He's pretty good at it if I do say so myself. Aside from Blake, he's had two other players get drafted by the NHL, one is off playing in Europe, and a handful of them are playing at the college level.

Isaac Martinez is good at what he does, and I honestly think he can go a lot further than coaching kids in Montana, but he will never try. He's too happy where he is.

"Blakie looks distracted," he states, as his eyes move with the game. "Did he break up with his girlfriend or something?"

My jaw locks at the word girlfriend.

For the past seven months, Blake has been with this girl from the cheer team, and I wish he would break up with her. Not because I want him to be with me or anything, but because she is such a bitch.

Don't get me wrong, in the beginning, this girl was so sweet and kind that even I had a crush on her. I spent hours picturing the awesome friendship the two of us could have had if she and Blake went the distance. But maybe three or so months ago, things switched in her or something. She became a complete bitch, throwing me the stink eye every time she sees me.

And I'm pretty sure she blocks me on his phone a few times a week because his phone calls and texts come through to me, but he apparently never sees any of my calls or text messages if he happens to be with her. I don't think he has put two and two together on that one, though.

I understand she is trying to put boundaries between me and her boyfriend, but I'm not going to steal him. Yes, we were together once, and yes, occasionally I get reminded I have feelings for my best friend, but I don't do anything about said feelings. I stay in my lane, and Blake stays in his. At this point in our lives, we are strictly friends, nothing else, no matter how much it hurts. But that is life.

His girlfriend, Gwen, apparently doesn't see that and finds it weird at just how close Blake and I are. Something that she has told Blake.

I've tried to give them space, I tried to not talk to the man for a few days at a time. No calls, no texts, no nothing, but every time I do that, he shows up at my door wanting to know what's wrong. And every time, I make up an excuse because I can't find it in me to tell him that his girlfriend is a bitch and a half.

"Nope," I say, putting a little bit too much emphasis on the p. "They are still very much together." My eyes move down to where Gwen is sitting with her friends. All of them wearing a number on their back and done up to absolute perfection.

"Then why else would he be distracted?" Dad looks at me like I always have the answers when it comes to Blake.

He's lucky I actually do have the answers this time because ever since we came to Montana State, hell, ever since we spent the night together, that hasn't been the case.

I look at the ice for a long minute contemplating if I want to share with my dad what Blake shared with me. Eventually I decided to share. It's my dad. Blake would want me to tell my dad.

I turn in my seat and look at him. "This stays between us because he hasn't even talked to his mom about it."

My dad gives me a nod. Looking at his face, he probably thinks that I'm about to tell him something bad. It's the opposite actually.

"He wants to graduate early, or drop out if he has to, to start the process of signing with the Knights next season." I can't help but smile a little as I say the words.

Blake has done so much to get to this point, he's just a few steps away from everything paying off. Sure, dropping out of school to do it isn't the brightest idea, but maybe years from now, he can come back and get his degree.

"Three-year rookie contract?" my dad asks, raising his eyebrows at me.

I nod. "Yeah, as soon as he's done with the hockey season, he wants to call his agent and see what they can do."

My dad gives me a nod. "I'm guessing he probably swore you to secrecy, so why are you telling me this and not him?"

Why indeed.

I have no reason to be doing this. No reason to go against the best friend swear that Blake and I have. No reason to go to my dad and ask him if he would pick up extra training sessions with

Blake. No reason other than he's my best friend. I want him to be able to achieve his dreams, so I'm going to do everything I can to help with that.

"Because he would do the same for me. If I wanted to achieve something, he would do everything in his power to help me get there. So this is me helping." And it's true. No matter if our friendship is strained or not, he would do everything he could to watch me succeed.

"I'll think about it."

He'll think about it?

"Dad, he's like your second kid. You used to get up at five in the morning to drag him out of bed and make sure he was getting ice time. What is there to think about?"

"Maybe I have things to do and don't have time to deal with a pain in the ass kid. Especially if he has a loud best friend screaming at him whenever he does something wrong."

I let out a gasp. "I'm not loud, and I don't scream at him when he does something wrong." The man has the audacity to raise an eyebrow at me, calling my bluff. "I give him suggestions, that's it."

He lets out a laugh. "Reminds me of your mom when she was your age. She would come to all of my games and threaten everyone on the ice if they ever got too close to me. Seriously thought she was going to end up in the trash a few times."

I smile as he goes down memory lane.

My parents had me young. They were still teenagers when my mom found out she was pregnant, and even though they tell me that it was tough, they made it work.

"I'm definitely not as bad as Mom. That's for sure."

Dad lets out another laugh, and we go back to watching the game for a few minutes. During that time, I yell out a few more suggestions toward the ice.

As soon as the final buzzer sounds out, calling the game

with Montana State losing by two, my dad finally says something.

"I'll talk to him and see if he wants to put together a few more sessions. It wouldn't hurt. He mostly needs to tweak the basics and get out of his own head. Concentrate on finishing up the season as best he can and then he can think about the NHL."

I give him a smile. "He'll appreciate that."

He gives me a nod, and as we make our way out of our seats and out of the school arena, he wraps his arm around me like he has always done since I was a little girl.

"How about you? You doing okay? With the nursing program and Theo and stuff?" my dad asks, as we make it to the front of the arena. He asks those questions as if I didn't talk to him a few days ago when I went home for dinner and told him about all of that.

Either way, I humor him and give him a nod. "Yeah, I'm doing okay. I am finding my flow with nursing. It's hard, but I'm liking it. Like really liking it."

Coming into Montana State, I didn't know what I wanted to do—what I wanted to major in, what I saw myself doing in five years, or even what I wanted to learn. So for my first year here, I just concentrated on getting my general education requirements out of the way. Going into this year, I sat down and thought about what I wanted to study, and out of everything, I kept going back to nursing. That's the one thing that called my heart, so I decided to go for it. It's intense, but I'm happy with my choice.

"Good, and the boy?" he asks, making a face at the mention of my boyfriend.

Like Blake, I've been seeing someone for the last year or so.

I met Theo in my psychology class last year, and we hit it off. At first we would only hang out to do class assignments together, but then it turned into coffee dates and dinner, and before I knew it, he was asking me to be his girlfriend. He's kind and sweet, but lately it feels like we're forcing a relationship and just going through the motions of being together, while not actually being together. I don't even think I've seen him this week or talked to him all that much.

I hate to admit it, but it might be time to end it. This type of situation isn't good for either of us.

But I don't tell my dad that. "He's good. He's a little bummed he couldn't make it to the game today and see you."

It should feel wrong just how easily lies about my boyfriend roll off my tongue.

"I'll catch him next time."

For the next fifteen minutes or so, Dad and I wait outside of the arena for Blake. It's a tradition that whenever one of our parents comes to one of his games, we go grab a bite to eat afterward.

But when Blake comes out with Gwen attached to his arm, I know there's a chance that isn't going to be happening.

More so when Blake looks away from Gwen and gives me a smile when he sees my dad standing next to me. The girl hates it when he even speaks to me, so him smiling in my direction probably has her wishing she had lasers to shoot out of her eyes and annihilate me.

"Coach," Blake says, untangling himself from Gwen and running over to my dad and wrapping him in a hug.

Blake has grown a lot since starting college. He's over six foot two, and last week he mentioned he was weighing in at over two-twenty. The boy I met all those years ago is all muscle now, and the only thing boyish about him is his dirty blond curls on top of his head.

"Out of all the games, you had to come today?" Blake asks when he finally lets my dad go.

Dad gives him a shrug and a smile. "I wanted to come see Vermont kick your ass," he answers before turning to the girl who has reattached herself to Blake. Does she always have to be touching him? "Hi, Gwen. How are you?"

"I'm good, Mr. Martinez. I'm so glad you were able to make it to the game. I know how much it means to Blakie."

I hate that she calls him Blakie. I called him that when we're five, and it has stuck through the years. She has no right using it.

Also, how is it that she can be sweet to my dad but not to me?

"Wouldn't have missed it. Are you guys ready to grab something to eat?" My dad looks at the three of us, and when Blake and Gwen give him a nod, I know I have to make a decision.

I either go to eat with them and deal with Gwen throwing daggers at me the whole time for even thinking about interacting with my dad and her boyfriend. Or I don't go at all.

Given the stares I've already gotten in the last five minutes, I know what I need to do. Dad and Blake aren't going to like it, but I feel like I have to, especially if I want to continue to push my feelings for Blake to the side and see him happy.

And I think Gwen makes him happy. If she didn't, he wouldn't be with her. Right?

"Actually," I say, already cringing as I start talking. "I have something to do for my biology class. I've been putting it off, and it's crunch time. You guys go. I'll join you next time."

I want to cry. I want to spend time with Dad and Blake, but I would rather put my sanity first than deal with a cross Gwen.

"Are you sure?" Dad asks, giving me a confused look because I never turn down food. Blake is looking at me the same way.

Gwen, on the other hand, is smiling.

I give them a nod. "Yeah, I'm sure. Go, catch up."

Dad looks at Blake, and they have a silent conversation, like they are both trying to figure out what is happening with me.

Eventually one of them shakes their head, while the other lets out a sigh, and they look back toward me.

"If you say so," Dad says, wrapping his arms around me.

"I'll order you something and bring it back to your place," Blake offers, also wrapping his arms around me once my dad lets me go.

Something that his girlfriend dislikes so damn much.

I want to say fuck her and go, but I rather not stir up shit between them.

"You don't have to," I tell Blake, detangling myself from him quickly.

He gives me an eye roll. "I want to."

All I can do is give him a small smile.

"Have fun. I'll see you later," I tell them as I back away and start walking toward my dorm.

I hate this, but it's for the best.

Those four words continue to repeat in my head the whole time I walk over to the dorms, trying to convince myself they are true.

Even if I know they are not.

CHAPTER FIFTEEN

BLAKE

SOMETHING IS UP WITH SOPHIA. It's been going on for a while, and I've been telling myself not to get involved, but today finally pushed me.

The girl that loves to eat and is a total daddy's girl, but she turned down a meal with her father. The second she said she wasn't going with us to get food, the red flags started to flash like crazy. I let whatever is going on with her go on for too long, and now I need to know what is happening with her.

I feel like she's been icing me out. I thought things were back to being good between us after our night together two years ago, but now it feels like we're back to square one. Barely talking, barely seeing each other, barely hanging out.

This is going to stop today.

"I don't know why you're insisting on bringing her food. She said you didn't have to," Gwen says as we leave the parking lot of the restaurant we just ate at, adjusting the bag of food that is currently sitting on her lap.

Having a meal with just Isaac and Gwen was a little awkward. It was mostly me and him talking and Gwen trying to insert herself here and there. When I tried to include her in the conversation, she wouldn't say much, at most it was a word or two. It made me wonder why she was there at all.

I wouldn't have invited her, since she never goes to eat with me whenever my parents are in town, but for some reason she tagged along today. For a second, I thought she might have done it because she thought Sophia was going to go, but when she backed out and Gwen stayed, that thought went out the door.

"Because knowing Sophia, she's hungry right about now. She has to eat. We were just at a restaurant. Why not take her food?" It's not that complicated to understand, I want to add, but I don't.

"Her dad could have taken her the food," Gwen adds, annoyance clear in her voice.

I try my hardest not to roll my eyes at her. "Yeah, but her dad was going home, and I'm already going to the same damn building. It doesn't take much for me to walk up two floors and deliver food to her."

When we first came to Montana State, Sophia and I both got assigned to the same dormitory. When our first year ended, we talked about possibly finding somewhere else to live because living in the dorms was not for us. We found a building a few minutes off campus that had two vacancies. We threw around the idea of living together, but ultimately decided not to. Things still felt fresh between us from the summer before. And I think we both knew if we did move in together then, something might happen between us, and we couldn't go down that path again.

So we talked to a few friends and now just live in the same building, but different apartments.

"I just think it's too much. She can order something herself and have it delivered by someone else. Why do you have to take her something?" Gwen asks, the annoyance growing stronger and stronger.

She's not the only one getting annoyed here.

"Because she's my best friend. She would have done the same thing for me if I hadn't gone," I answer, trying to keep myself controlled, so I don't blow up on her for acting like a brat. "What's with you today?"

Has she always acted this way toward Sophia, or is today just a special day?

I look over just in time to see Gwen give me a shrug. "I just think you are doing too much for her. Like I get she's your best friend and everything, but you don't need to take care of her twenty-four-seven. She's a big girl."

"I know that," I say as I turn the truck to head toward the school.

"Do you? Because it's always Sophia this, Sophia that. Everything is always about Sophia. She texts you all the time, and if she isn't texting, she's calling. As your girlfriend, it's pretty annoying when I have to compete with another girl to get your attention. I swear, it's like she's in love with you or something." Gwen lets out a huff, as if she has been holding all that in for a long time, and she's finally getting it all out.

Is she seeing something that I'm not? Because it's been a long time since Sophia spent all day texting me and calling me. I honestly can't remember the last time she called me, and we talked on the phone for hours. It's been a few weeks, that's for sure. Yes, we spend time together, and yeah, I do things for her, but nothing over the top. Sophia would do the same thing for me. It's nothing special.

Soph and I are close. There is no difference between my relationship with Sophia and Gwen's relationship with her sorority sisters.

"Do you have a problem with her and I being friends?" I ask, probably already knowing the answer to the question but needing confirmation of it either way.

Gwen stays quiet, keeping her eyes on the outside and not turning to look at me at all.

I guess that's my confirmation because if there wasn't a problem, she would have said something.

Given where I want to take my career in the next few weeks, I don't have the time to deal with the fact my girlfriend hates my best friend.

"Alright then," I say, making a turn up ahead that will take us to Gwen's sorority house and not my apartment building.

"Where are we going?" she asks, breaking her silence. When I pull up to the sorority house, she gives me a look like she doesn't know what is happening.

She knows, she just wants me to say it.

"I'm bringing you home," I say as I put the truck in park.

"Why? I thought we were going to hang out tonight." She sticks out her lip and gives me puppy dog eyes.

Any other night, I would have gone with her act. I would have felt bad and gone back to my place, but I'm not up to that right now. Not when I want to find out what is going on with Sophia, and Gwen has started to piss me off with her dislike of my best friend.

"I'm not feeling it tonight," I answer, not giving her much else.

"You mean, you are choosing her over me," Gwen concludes, giving me an eye roll.

"I didn't say that, but it's clear you don't want to see her, so I'm dropping you off, and then I am going to take her the food I bought her."

"And then do what? Spend the night with her?" Gwen spits out, getting angrier by the second.

She can't honestly believe that I'm going to cheat on her with Sophia. Yes, we've slept together, but Gwen doesn't know about that. But just because that happened, it doesn't mean we are doing it every chance we get. It's not like that between the two of us. Even if things were like that, I'm not a cheater, and I will never be.

I feel my jaw tic as I answer her question. "No. I'm not going to spend the night with her. I don't know what I'm going to do, but I do know that I need space from you tonight. So get out of the car, leave the food, and go inside."

Gwen looks at me with daggers shooting out of her eyes. I can see the anger fuming all over her facial expression, and I'm sure if we were in a different world, smoke would be coming from her ears, too.

"Whatever. Have fun with the little hussy," she lets out, pushing the passenger door open and dropping the bag of food on the passenger seat.

I'm about to say something to her, but she slams the door behind her and storms into the sorority house.

I really need to reevaluate my love life, because fuck, this is too much.

The whole time Gwen and I have been together, I've seen Sophia be nothing but respectful to Gwen and my relationship with her. There is no fucking reason why my girlfriend should be acting this way. I want to tell her that Sophia was here before she was, and she will be here after she leaves, but I don't want to piss her off even more, even if it is the truth.

Letting out a sigh, I start up the truck again and head over to Sophia's and my apartment building.

Hopefully she's done with her biology stuff because I feel like talking. About what's going on with her, check in on her because it feels like I haven't done that in a while, and possibly get advice about my relationship. So many things.

It takes me five minutes to get from the sorority house to the apartment building.

With the food in hand, I make my way upstairs, and instead

of stopping at my place really quick, I head straight up to Sophia's.

With no thought about the time whatsoever, I pound on the door. It's not until Sophia opens the door all wide-eyed, that I remember it's late, and her roommates could be sleeping.

"What are you doing here?" she asks me, opening the door some more to let me in. It doesn't go unnoticed how she checks behind me to see if someone is potentially with me before closing the door.

One hundred percent she is checking to see if Gwen is with me.

Have I been in a cloud or something that I haven't noticed my girlfriend and best friend are not getting along? I fucking need to get my shit together and fix this situation.

I hold up the food I got her. "I said I was going to bring you food."

"Oh," she says, looking at the bag. "I didn't think you were actually going to do that."

"I always do that," I say, holding out the bag for her to take. "You want it, or not?"

She doesn't even hesitate taking the bag from me and heading over to the kitchen to start eating. I knew she was hungry.

A few minutes after she starts eating, I break the small bit of silence we were in.

"Your dad asked me if I wanted to meet up a few times a week to get a few extra workouts in. Work on the basics and such," I say to her, trying to take her attention away from her food.

"Are you going to do it?" she asks, not looking up.

I don't have to ask to know she talked to him about me wanting to possibly leave school early so that I can sign with the Knights. If it was to help me out, Soph would break our best friend swear ten times over, and I would do the same for her.

I was going to bring up some possible training sessions to her dad the next time I saw him because even though I don't need them, it wouldn't hurt to get back to the basics for a little bit. Sophia knew that, and I can't be mad at her for beating me to the punch. I'm appreciative.

"Yeah, if I want that three-year contract, I'm going to need all the help that I could get."

"Good."

"Thank you for telling him," I say to her, throwing her a smile to show her my appreciation.

She gives me a smile back. "You would do the same for me."

For the next few minutes, Sophia eats her food, and I try my hardest to let my phone distract me as she does, but I keep thinking about something that Gwen said, and I can't keep my mouth shut anymore.

"Can I ask you something?" I ask when she is almost done.

She gives me a nod. "Go for it."

"Why don't you text me all the time anymore?" I ask, curiously.

I watch Sophia, and I see her facial expression shift a bit, but then she quickly tries to mask it.

She finishes up her food and goes to toss the to-go box in the trash. "I text you like twenty times a day. You're the one who doesn't respond."

"I respond to every single thing that you send," I retort because it's the truth. I respond to every single one of her texts, maybe not right away, but I respond.

Sophia looks up at me, and for a split second, her eyes look sad. She opens her mouth to say something, but then she quickly closes it. Like she wants to say something, but at the same time doesn't.

"What?" I ask, desperate for her to tell me what the hell is going on.

She shakes her head, not wanting to answer. "Nothing. You're right. I don't text you as often. I must have been thinking of before when I said I text you twenty times a day."

"Bullshit. You were about to say something else. What was it?" My patience is thinning here.

My best friend looks over at me, like she is silently asking me to drop this, but I stand my ground.

Eventually she lets out a sigh and grabs her phone from where it sits on the kitchen counter. She does something on it for a few seconds before handing the device over to me.

It takes me a second to realize that I'm looking at the message thread between the two of us. Confused as to why she is showing me this, I start to scroll through our conversations and notice that the majority of the time, she is talking to herself with not a single reply from me to be seen.

I finally put together what's going on when I see a message she had sent, asking if she had been blocked again.

Not even when I was pissed off at Sophia over something stupid have I blocked her. Not even after our night together.

Pulling out my own phone, I go and check my block list and sure enough, Sophia is at the top of the list.

"What the fuck?" I ask myself more than anything. There is only one person who could have done it, and that is my girlfriend. "How long has this been going on?" I ask Sophia, unblocking her number and changing my passcode.

I look at Sophia for an answer, and she gives me a shrug. "A few months."

"Why didn't you say anything?" I ask, feeling anger moving through my body.

It's one thing to not like the fact my best friend is a girl, it's a whole other thing to cut her out of my life without fucking consulting me.

Again, she gives me a shrug. "What was I going to say? For all I knew, you didn't want to talk to me, or you wanted space. I didn't know she was actually blocking me. I thought about it, sure, but I didn't have any proof that she was actually doing it."

"I wouldn't have given a fuck. You could have come to me, and I would have taken care of it."

"You're happy with her, Blake. I wasn't going to get in the middle of that. So I didn't say anything, no matter how many dirty looks she throws in my direction."

I understand that to an outsider, my relationship with Sophia is a bit much. But if I'm going to be with someone, they have to accept our friendship. And if they don't, I would rather they come to me, so we can discuss it, not make decisions for me.

I'm about to tell her I'm not happy, that things with Gwen have mostly been to pass the time, but the words get trapped in my mouth when a knock sounds through the apartment.

Sophia gives me a small smile and goes to answer it. By the way that she greets the person, I'm going to take a wild guess and say her boyfriend is here.

So much for talking all of this out.

"Oh, hey, Blake," her boyfriend, Theo, says when he walks into the apartment and sees me in the small kitchen.

"Hey, man. How's it going?" I greet him, nodding in his direction.

"Nothing much, just thought I would come by and hang out with my girl for a little bit."

His girl.

Why does that irritate me?

Maybe because she deserves someone better than Theo.

Someone like you?

Nope. Sophia deserves someone better than me, too.

"I'll get out of your guys' hair then," I say, offering both of them a smile, not wanting to leave but also not wanting to intrude on their night.

"Are you sure?" Sophia asks, wringing her hands together. I don't miss the way Theo looks over at her when she asks the question. I wonder if that is the same look that Gwen gives me when it comes to Sophia, and I just haven't noticed it.

"Yeah, I'm sure," I answer her and wave to both of them.

"Don't do anything stupid, okay?" she says, giving me a pointed look, and it takes me a second to realize that she is talking about not doing anything stupid in regard to my relationship with Gwen.

"No promises. I'll see you later, okay?"

She gives me a nod as I open the door and let her spend some time with her boyfriend.

I stand in the hallway for a little bit, and without thinking about it, I pull out my phone and send one text.

I'm sorry, but we're done.

Five words—that's all it takes to end a relationship.

If my significant other can't accept Sophia, then they don't deserve to stay in my life.

Sophia is here to stay.

CHAPTER SIXTEEN

SOPHIA

I TAKE a minute or two to sit on my bed and contemplate what I want to wear out tonight. For the first time in weeks, I finally have a night where I don't have to study, worry about getting work done for a class to get ahead, or attend a hockey game since the season is officially over.

I have one full night completely free, and I want to go out and act my age for once.

My roommates were talking about one of the bars in town having a band tonight, so they were going to go and have some drinks. They invited me to go with them, and when Theo told me he was going to go, too, I decided it would be good to have a little fun and join them. I'm not allowed to drink just yet, but I can still go.

Maybe I can also use tonight to get reacquainted with my boyfriend after basically giving him the cold shoulder for the last month or so.

It's not that I wanted to give him the cold shoulder. I did try to be a good girlfriend, but things would come up here and there, so I haven't been the girlfriend that he has been needing.

I've definitely canceled on him more this last month than I have during our whole one-year relationship.

In retrospect, I should have broken up with him a while ago. I even came close to doing it one night, but I got scared about hurting his feelings. I'm still scared to do it. This is my first serious relationship, and even though my feelings for him aren't as strong as I had hoped, I still care about him, and I don't want to see him get hurt.

But even if I don't break up with him, I'm still hurting him by not being present. So I'm going to take tonight and decide what to do. Maybe by the end of the night, I'll be able to figure it out.

I just have to decide what to wear.

This is one of those times where I could use Blake to help me pick out what to wear. Just like he did with my quince dress and more than a handful of times since then.

I didn't want to call him for this, but it feels like it's necessary since I've been sitting here for about an hour and still haven't made a choice.

Letting out a sigh, I pick up my phone and call him. At least I know he's going to pick up since the whole blocking thing ended when he broke up with Gwen a few weeks ago.

The phone rings three times before he picks up.

"What's up, Soph?" he says instead of a greeting.

"Are you home?" I ask, getting straight to the point.

He makes a weird noise. "I'm not. Why?"

"Oh." Where is he? "No reason. I just needed you to help me with something," I say, trying to remember if he told me if he was going out tonight, but I come up blank.

"I can try to help over the phone," he suggests just as someone calls out his name.

He's with a girl?

Of course, he is. He's single now. Where else would he be?

"No, it's fine." I say, shaking my head even though he can't see it. "Have fun wherever you are." I start pulling the phone away from my ear and let my thumb hover over the small red button.

"Sophia," he calls out loudly, right as my thumb moves down to push the button, stopping me.

Why am I acting this way? He has a right to date. He's single, he can see and be with any girl he wants.

You already know the answer to that question.

I push that thought to the side and bring the phone back up to my ear.

"Sophia, tell me what you need," he says, his voice stern but still filled with care and kindness.

I let out a sigh. "I need help picking out something to wear. Lucky's is having a band tonight, and I want to go. I just don't know what I should wear. I figured you'd be able to help me."

"You want me to help you pick out clothes? Me?" he asks, a laugh bubbling out as he speaks.

I nod even though he can't see. "It's more like I need your opinion, but yes."

"You have two girl roommates. Why the hell would you want me to help you out with this?" he asks, bewildered.

That is a good question. One I definitely don't have the answer to.

"Maybe I wanted to hang out with my best friend," I respond, not having another answer.

He lets out a laugh. "We'll hang out tomorrow. Besides, I have a surprise."

My outfit is now completely forgotten. "Surprise? What kind of surprise?" I ask.

If he's about to surprise me with his new girlfriend, I don't know if I will be able to handle it.

"A good one, I promise," he says, and I picture him smiling as he says the words, which causes me to smile, too.

"It better be."

He lets out another laugh, and for a few seconds it feels like we're back in high school, and nothing has gotten in the way of our friendship.

"Wear whatever you want, Soph. You'll look pretty in everything."

My mind instantly goes to that night almost two years ago.

You're so fucking pretty.

He had said those words as he was straddling my half-naked body and hearing him say the word pretty now is making my whole body feel hot.

I need to end this call before I say something that I won't be able to take back.

"Okay," I say, after clearing my throat. "I'll see what I can find. Have fun doing whatever it is you're doing."

"I will. Have fun at the bar."

We end the call, and for a solid minute I just sat there, wrapped up in my own mind.

My feelings for Blake are something I've been trying to push down for years. Every so often, I try to convince myself that it's just a crush, and I only feel like it's more because of everything that has happened between us. I told myself that when he was dating Gwen. I told myself that when he dated other girls. Hell, I told myself that when I realized that Theo and I probably aren't going anywhere.

At eighteen, I realized I was in love with him, but to this day, he still doesn't know because I'm too scared of what could come of it if I say those three little words out loud. That love is still very much there, no matter how hard I try to push it down, no matter how much I try to build a relationship with someone else. I'm in love with Blake Jacobi, and there is a chance I will always be.

I need to figure out a way to rein in these emotions because in the end, if I never tell him, I'm going to get hurt, and the only one to blame is going to be me.

A text message from my roommate, Claire, pops up on my screen, telling me they are at the bar, and Theo is there.

Great. My boyfriend is at the bar waiting for me, and here I am spending my time thinking about someone else.

I should use that piece of information to do what I've been wanting to do for some time. Break up with Theo.

There's a chance he's going to end up hurt, but I would rather hurt him by breaking up with him than continue hurting him because I'm emotionally cheating on him by thinking about Blake.

I get dressed with no second thought about what I'm wearing and head down to the bar.

LUCKY'S IS ABSOLUTELY PACKED by the time I get there.

As someone who doesn't come to the bar very often, since I'm a few months shy of my twenty-first birthday, it becomes overwhelming very quickly. But I power through it and try to find my friends.

Claire had texted me earlier to tell me they had a table, since they had gotten here early, so I send her a text back telling her that I'm here, hoping that she will direct me on where to go.

A minute after sending the text, Claire pops up next to me,

with a big smile on her face. "You made it!" she yells out, wrapping me in a big hug.

"I told you I would," I say, letting out a little laugh at her excitement.

"I know, but this isn't your scene. C'mon, let's get you something to drink." She grabs my hand and drags me deeper into the bar until we arrive at a table filled with our friends.

For a good hour, I have a good time. The whole table is filled with drinks and laughs, and it makes me so happy that I decided to come out tonight. I haven't hung out with my friends like this in a while, and I really needed it.

After a few drinks, I realize that I haven't seen Theo. Claire had told me he was here, and he told me himself that he was coming, but I have yet to lay eyes on him.

"Hey," I call out to Dana, my other roommate. "Have you seen Theo?"

She looks over my shoulder as if to look for him, but she shakes her head. "Not since before you got here."

I give her a nod. I hope he's still here because I don't know if I will be brave enough to have the conversation I need to have with him if I leave the bar.

"I'm going to go look for him," I yell toward her, so she can hear me over all the music and the people talking.

She gives me a nod and turns back to talk to our friends.

My body sways a little bit as I get up and start walking around. Claire and Dana snuck me a drink or two, so I'm not drunk, but I'm definitely tipsy. Exactly how I want to be to have this conversation with Theo, if I find him.

As I walk around the bar, I notice a group of his friends in the back corner by where the band is setting up. I look at all of their faces, but still don't see Theo, so I decide to approach the table in hopes they know where he is.

"Hey, guys," I say to the table, waving at each of them.

I've hung out with these guys more times than I can count, and they have always been sweet to me. They have also acted like older brothers a time or two, so you would think that approaching them is a fine idea. But by the look on their faces, it isn't.

Each and every person sitting at the table in front me looks absolutely terrified to see me.

Okay, then.

"Have you guys seen Theo? He said that he would be here," I ask, giving them a smile, hoping that they will stop looking at me like I'm wielding a knife and about to attack them.

Not a single one of them answers. They just look at each other and then look back at me, like they don't know what to say.

They always have something to say. They're frat boys—something stupid is always coming out of their mouths.

After about a minute, one of them breaks the silence.

"I think he went to the bathroom," he says, giving me a smile that doesn't reach his eyes.

Okay, why are they acting so weird?

Completely done with this interaction, I give them all a nod and walk away from the table and head in the direction of the bathrooms.

I make it down the hallway, and because nobody is waiting for the bathroom, I lean against the wall and wait for Theo to hopefully come out soon. With my luck, he has already walked out and is back at the table with his friends.

I stand there for a good minute or two, before I start thinking about just walking back to the table with my friends, when one of the bathroom doors opens.

At first, I think it's just a random guy who frantically opened the door, but then it clicks in my head that it's Theo.

Not only did he open the door frantically, but everything

about his facial expression looks like he just saw a ghost. His eyes are wide, his mouth is popped open, and his skin looks pale.

I'm about to ask him if he's sick, but then I see a flash of blond behind him.

The bathrooms at Lucky's are single stalls so there's no reason for someone else to be in the bathroom with him. Unless...

Unless he took someone in there with him.

My eyes stay on the figure behind him, and when it turns ever so slightly to hide behind Theo's body, that's when I see that the figure is actually a pretty blonde.

Tears start to form in my eyes as I let them travel down the length of my boyfriend's body. His clothes are all out of place, and his jeans are popped open, with the zipper down.

It looks like Theo was having a little fun in the bathroom with a girl who isn't me.

"Sophia," he says, coming out of the bathroom fully and closing the distance between us.

I sidestep him, not wanting to be touched by him.

"You're cheating on me?" I ask, my voice shaking in the process. Here I was thinking I was hurting him by being distant, when in reality it was him doing the hurting all along.

"I can explain," he says, reaching for me again, and again I step out of his reach.

"What's to explain? You were just in a bathroom, at a bar I might add, fucking some girl. There's nothing to explain. The picture is loud and clear," I say, a small tear escaping the corner of my eye. I don't even move to wipe it away.

As I stand there in front of him, Theo's face shifts. He goes from being apologetic to full-on mad.

"You're one to talk."

"What is that supposed to mean?" I ask, feeling my blood start to boil.

"It means the reason I was in the bathroom fucking some girl is because you were going behind my back and fucking Jacobi." He punches the wall right next to my head, causing me to jump a little.

"What are you talking about? I'm not sleeping with Blake," I yell out. He can't blame his indiscretions on me.

"Sure, you are. I see the way you look at him. You two are always together. How many times have I walked in on you two all alone in your apartment? Don't fucking deny it. I know you're fucking him." He almost spits the words out at me.

"Just because you may think that I look at him a certain way or because we're always together, doesn't mean shit. I'm not sleeping with Blake. Whether you want to believe me or not, that's the fucking truth." More tears flow down my face. I may not have cheated physically, but I may have done it emotionally. But what Theo did is crossing the damn line. I look away from him and see the girl he was just with, poking her head out of the bathroom, watching the whole thing. I'm done. "Continue having fun with your side piece. I'm done. We're done."

I walk away from him without a second thought or glance. I head back to the table, but find it empty, guessing that my friends probably went to get more drinks or are out on the dance floor enjoying themselves.

Not wanting to ruin their night, I grabbed my bag and headed out.

Thank God I thought about catching a ride to the bar tonight because no way am I able to drive. Not with the few drinks I snuck in, but also with my emotional state. I feel like bursting into tears, and I don't think I would be able to do that while manning a steering wheel.

Before calling for a car, I dial Blake's number and hope he's finished with whatever he is doing and can come pick me up. But the call doesn't even ring, it goes straight to voicemail.

The perfect ending to a shitty night.

The only one to blame here is me.

If I would have broken up with Theo a long time ago, I would have saved myself all of this heartache.

CHAPTER SEVENTEEN

BLAKE

I HANG up the call with Sophia and turn off my phone before I slide it into the pocket of my jacket. Today is too much of a big day for my phone to go off at random times.

Selena waves me over, and from the look on her face, everything is set. They're probably just waiting on me to start.

"Sorry," I say, walking over to her, wiping my hands against my pants. "I was talking to Sophia."

Lennie smiles at me at the mention of my best friend. "Is she excited you're doing this?" she asks as we walk over to the conference room that is reserved for today.

I shake my head. "She doesn't even know," I answer, bowing my head a little bit.

"You didn't tell your best friend you are about to sign your first professional contract?" she asks, bewildered by it all.

"I want it to be a surprise. We've talked about me doing it after the season ended, but I haven't told her that I've started the process and have been in negotiations."

The hockey season ended for Montana State a few weeks ago. We were one point shy of making it out of regionals, but unfortunately we couldn't pull it off. I was a little butt hurt after the season ended because our team had the potential, but the loss opened up the door for negotiations between me and the Dark Knights. I wanted that rookie contract, and this was the perfect time for me to get it.

Keeping it from Sophia was something I thought about because I didn't want to distract her from her classes. Ever since she started the nursing program, she has been putting everything that she has into school, not swaying even a little, and I didn't want to give her this news and cause her to lose her focus. Keeping her concentrated on school, on the nursing program, was only part of the reason why I didn't tell her, though There's definitely more to it.

More I'm not sure she will go for.

I can't sign an NHL contract and then leave for Chicago without my best friend.

That girl has been with me since I was five years old. She has gone to every single game since we met, everything from youth hockey to high school to college, she has been there for it all. She deserves to be there at the pro level, too.

I wasn't joking when I told her I had a surprise. I just didn't mention that the surprise might also extend to her, too, if she'd let it.

"She's going to choke you to death when she finds out that you did this without her," Lennie answers, shaking her head at me.

"Probably, but she won't stay mad at me forever." We walk into the conference room, and everything becomes all that much bigger.

The Dark Knight's general manager and their head coach, Shawn Anderson, are currently standing a few feet away from the door talking to my agent and my brother. All the while, my mom and Isaac stood on the other side having a silent conversation. Eighty percent of the most important people in my life are here to watch me do this today. The day would have been better if Sophia was here, but hopefully my surprise to her makes her not being here for this all the more worth it.

Everything just got a whole lot more real.

"Blake, are you ready to do this?" Hunter asks from across the room.

I look over at my brother and give him a nod. When I thought of this moment ten years ago, I never would have pictured Hunter here.

Ten years ago, I hated my brother so damn much because he was Dad's favorite. Because he was going to live with him so he could concentrate on football and leave Jainie and I behind. I thought he was a douchebag and a half, and I wanted nothing to do with him.

Now, I can't picture this moment without him. He's been there every step of the way. If I couldn't have Sophia here with me, at least I have him.

I walk over to the table where a stack of papers sits in the middle, and I feel like a little kid at Christmas.

The general manager and Coach Anderson take a seat on one side of the table, and my mom, Isaac, my agent, and Hunter take a seat on the other side, leaving a chair open for me.

This is it.

Taking a seat, it feels like my stomach is going to jump out my body and my hands are going to drown in all the sweat.

I push all of that aside, though, and grab the pen that is in front of me. The second the barrel of the pen lands in my hand, everything else after becomes a blur. I don't know how I do it, but five minutes later, every single line has a signature on it.

"Congratulations, Blake Jacobi. You are officially a Dark Knight. Welcome to Chicago, son."

Holy shit.

I did it.

I just signed my rookie contract. I'm officially in the NHL.

CHAPTER EIGHTEEN

SOPHIA

THE FIRST THING that I do when I get home is let out a sigh of relief that Claire and Dana didn't decide to leave the bar early and beat me back here because now I can have a good cry and not have my roommates questioning me about it.

I throw my bag down on the floor by the door, deciding that I will grab it later, and walk deeper into the apartment, feeling all types of emotions. I'm sad, sure, but I think both anger and frustration are overpowering it.

Am I angry that my relationship with Theo ended? Not really. I'm angry at how it ended and the fact that he thought that I was doing something with Blake behind his back.

Just because we spend a lot of time together doesn't mean there's something going on with him. There isn't, and if there were, I wouldn't be doing it behind my boyfriend's back. If I wanted to be with someone else, I would have ended it with him way before anything else started. I'm not a fucking cheater, no matter how much Theo thinks that I am.

Besides, nothing will ever happen between me and Blake. Not again. No matter how much my heart wants it to or even if

I'm in love with him. I will never say the words out loud to him. I value our friendship too much to listen to that part of me.

I shake my head and walk over to the kitchen. I'm done seeing guys for a while. I don't think I can handle someone else accusing me of cheating on them and then cheating on me in return.

"Fuck Theo and his wandering dick," I grumble and start making myself a sandwich all while tears continue to run down my face. Tears of anger, not sadness.

I contemplate calling Blake again as I sob and eat at the same time, but if he didn't answer the first four times I called him, he's not going to answer the fifth. Whatever his surprise is, it must be big if his phone is turned off.

After my sandwich is gone, I feel like absolute shit. My heart aches, my head hurts, and my eyes are angry with me for crying so much. I decide to go to my room and try to get some sleep. Maybe if I sleep for a few hours this horrible night will disappear from my mind, and I will be able to concentrate on finals.

As I sit on my bed and just let the tears run some more, I hear a pounding coming from the front door. The only person who pounds like that is Blake, and as much as I don't want to see or talk to anyone right now, I get out of bed and sluggishly walk over to the front door.

Sure enough, when I look through the peephole, Blake's curls are front and center.

Not wanting him to see that I'm crying, I back away from the door and start walking back to my room. Maybe if I pretend I'm not here, he'll leave, and I will talk to him tomorrow.

I'm pulled to a stop, though, when he pounds on the door again.

"C'mon, Soph. I know you're home," Blake yells from the other side. "I ran into Theo at the bar. I'm sorry I didn't answer your calls. But open the door, yeah? I have something to tell you, and I don't think I can wait until morning. Please. My news will make up for me not picking up any of your calls, I promise." He bangs his fist against the door again.

I wipe my face as best as I can as I walk back to the front door. If Blake sees I've been crying, there is a chance that he will go crazy.

My efforts to hide my tears go out the door, though, the second I open it, Blake quickly goes from having a bright expression on his face to having one full of concern.

"What happened?" he asks, walking into the apartment, while pushing me back so that he can close the door.

I shrug. "What's your surprise?" I ask with a little bit too much bite in my tone. There's no reason for me to be angry with him since he isn't the one who cheated on me. But for some reason my mind wants to take that anger out on someone, and it looks like Blake is that person.

"I'll tell you as soon as you tell me why you're crying," he says, grabbing my hand and walking me over to the couch.

"Well, if you had answered your phone, you would have known already," I say, throwing myself on the couch and crossing my arms like I'm a child. And honestly, I'm acting like one, too. I can admit that.

"Cut the shit, Sophia," Blake says, coming to sit next to me, looking at me with concern and annoyance. I would be annoyed, too. "Now, tell me what is going with you."

I try to keep the tears at bay, but the second his last word makes it out of his mouth, the tears start flowing again.

Even through my tear-filled eyes, I'm able to see Blake's jaw tick. He hates seeing me cry.

I control myself a bit and wipe my face with the sleeves of my sweater before I answer. "You saw Theo at the bar," I state, as if that is explanation enough as to why I'm a crying mess.

"Yeah, and?" His hands start to ball up to fists on his lap.

"He's there without me because I caught him in the bathroom with some blonde. According to him, he was in the bathroom fucking some girl because I was fucking someone behind his back." Another tear escapes from the corner of my eye, but I catch it before it rolls down my cheek.

I shouldn't be crying over Theo. I was going to end things between us anyway, but it still stings that it had to go down this way. It stings he wasn't man enough to end things with me before he slid his dick into someone else.

"Who does he think you're fucking behind his back?" Blake asks, the tic in his jaw becoming more prominent.

I bite down on my lower lip and look at my best friend.

"You," I answer shyly.

Without a second thought, Blake is off the couch and heading back toward the door. "He's dead. How can he think that? How can he hurt you over something stupid like that?"

A sharp pain shoots through my heart, but I try to ignore it. I guess I'm the only one who thinks about our one night together in some capacity.

"I don't know, but it doesn't matter," I say, following behind him.

"Yes, it does matter," Blake says, stopping a few feet from the door and turning back to face me. "He hurt you, Sophia. He not only cheated on you but accused you of doing it, too."

"I know, but it's done. Over. I'm no longer with him. There's no need for you to go back to the bar and beat the crap out of him."

"But he made you cry." He points it out like it was news to me.

"So? I'll get over it. Just please don't go. I really need my best friend right now," I answer, practically begging for him to listen.

Blake looks me over.

I don't know what he sees, but he gives me a small smile and walks over to me, wrapping his long arms around my body and bringing me in for a hug.

This is what I've been needing. My best friend's arms around me, making things better.

"I'm sorry," he says against my hair.

I nod against his chest, holding his body tighter against mine. "Yeah, me, too."

We stand like that for a bit, eventually breaking apart.

"What's your news?" I say, wiping away the remainder of the tears.

"I can tell you later," he answers, sheepishly sliding his hands into the pockets of his jeans.

"Just tell me now. I need a distraction," I say, letting out a small laugh.

Blake doesn't laugh with me, though. He just stands there and gives me a nod, like he is contemplating how to say what is clearly on his mind.

"Just rip the Band-Aid off, Jacobi." I push, wanting to hear his news already.

"Fine," he pauses for a second, just as a big, beautiful grin spreads across his face. "I signed with the Chicago Dark Knights about three hours ago."

It takes me a second to digest the news.

"You did what?" I ask, feeling a smile spread across my face.

"I signed my first official NHL contract. I'm heading to Chicago."

Not being able to help my excitement, I jump up and down until I eventually throw my body at him.

He's been waiting for this moment since he got drafted. The fact that we were talking about this a few months ago, and now it's actually happening, is insane.

"That's awesome! I'm so excited for you!" I say to him, placing a kiss on his cheek.

"Thanks," he says, and I don't need to pull away from him to know that the grin on his face is somehow bigger. "But there's something else that comes with it, though, and I don't know how you are going to feel about it." He lets out when I'm back on my feet.

"What?" I ask, a huge grin on my face from all the excitement that I'm feeling. All thoughts of Theo and what happened earlier are now completely gone.

"Move to Chicago with me."

A laugh forms in my chest, and I try to keep it in, but I can't. It escapes, and for a solid minute, I'm laughing as if Blake just told me the funniest thing in the world.

My laugh becomes almost uncontrollable, but when I look up and see the hurt in his eyes, it stops completely.

I look him over, my eyebrows shooting up in the process.

Oh my god. He's serious.

Blake wants me to move to Chicago with him, and I just laughed in his face.

This rollercoaster of a night is about to go into hyper speed.

CHAPTER NINETEEN

BLAKE

SOPHIA'S EYES ARE WIDE, like they are about to pop out of her head if I walk over and squeeze her even the slightest.

It isn't the reaction I was expecting, but at least she's not yelling at me for not telling her about signing my contract today. We always said she was going to be right there next to me whenever I did it, but because I wanted it to be a surprise, I took that away from her.

As for asking her to move to Chicago with me, that was something that I've been thinking about for a while. I knew that if I signed, there was no way in hell I would be able to move to a new city without her at my side. Having her move to Chicago is selfish, I know, but when it comes to Sophia, I'm always going to be selfish. I'm going to do everything I can to always have her there with me.

Take going to Montana State for example. I could have gone to any school in the country that had a hockey program, but I chose Montana because she chose Montana to be close to her parents. I don't regret that decision one single bit, and I know I'm not going to regret taking her to Chicago with me either.

My delivery could have been better, though. I should have waited to ask her to move with me, or at the very least, done it when she wasn't emotional from a breakup. Dinner might have been a good option to broach the subject, or even during one of our movie nights, but I got too excited.

After leaving the hotel, with my freshly signed contract in hand, I wanted to come tell her right away. When I turned my phone back on and saw that she had called me four times, right away, I wanted to call her back and tell her, but signing something like an NHL contract isn't news you give over the phone. It's something that you do in person, and that's what I was going to do.

I went to the bar first, since she said that's where she was going to be, but when her friends and Theo, who now that I think of it, looked pissed to see me, told me that she had left, I didn't think anything of it. I just came straight here.

If I had known what had gone down between Sophia and her douchebag boyfriend, I would have slammed his face in. I never liked the fucker. He's a prick who acts like he's the sweetest person in the whole fucking world. Apparently he's the sweetest person who would cheat on his girlfriend. I saw through his fake persona the first day I met him, but I didn't say anything. Sophia liked him, and even if I didn't like it, it looked like the asshole made her happy. So, I didn't say anything, but now I know I should have.

But now the fucker is out of her life, thank fuck for that, and she can now seriously think about moving to Chicago with me.

"So are your eyes popping out of your head your way of saying yes to moving to Chicago with me?" I ask, breaking the silence in the room.

I think I'd rather have her laughing her ass off at my question than have her silent, looking at me like I have two heads.

The question takes Sophia out of her stupor.

She shakes her head as if to clear it and then looks at me straight on.

"You want me to move to Chicago? With you?" she asks, clarifying.

I give her a nod. "Yes."

"Why?"

Is she serious? We always talked about moving wherever I landed.

"Because I want you there with me," I say, closing the distance between us and placing my hands on her shoulders. "We always said that no matter where I land, you would come with me so I wouldn't be alone or get homesick."

She looks up at me, her bottom lip going between her teeth. It takes everything to keep my hands at my side and not reach over to release her lip and soothe it with my thumb.

I've been fighting urges like that ever since we got together almost two years ago. Urges to kiss her, urges to get lost in her body once more. I have so many urges when it comes to Sophia, but I don't act on any of them. We've come so far since that night. I don't want to risk anything. I especially don't want to risk losing her. So I keep those urges at bay as best that I can.

"We did say that, didn't we?" she says, still gnawing on her lip.

"We did. We even talked about it when I got drafted. So why are you freaking you out?"

A piece of hair falls in front of her face and another urge comes rolling through my body. Control yourself, Jacobi.

"I don't know. Maybe because I wasn't mentally preparing to move to Chicago now? I know you talked about signing early, but I didn't think it was actually going to happen, so I didn't plan for it. Besides, we made the majority of those plans when we were kids. I didn't think that they would hold any ground. If I remember correctly, I said that I wanted to be a princess when

I was six. That doesn't mean I'm going to go out and look for an actual prince to marry and make that dream come true." She looks up at me, her eyes wide again.

"What is there to plan?" I ask, ignoring her tangent about being a princess. She's freaking, and I see that as a good sign. Besides, it all seems simple to me.

"Um, school? I can't drop out and just go to Chicago. I have to find a school to transfer to. On top of that, I have to find a place to live. There's so much to plan."

I guess that now is the time to shock her even more.

"I have that covered," I say, giving her a smile.

Instead of smiling back at me or giving me a look that tells me that she is thankful for taking a few things off her plate, she scolds me.

"What do you mean 'you have it covered?'" The way she asks the question reminds me of when both of our moms used to yell at us whenever we walked into the house with mud all over our shoes.

Stepping closer to her, I place my hands on her shoulders and give her a smile. One that I hope is going to work in my favor.

"I put a lot of thought into this," I say, pulling out my phone. "I have a list of schools within the city that have vacancies in their nursing programs and their transfer deadlines." I turn my phone over to her so she can see the list that I found. "And if none of these schools work out, I also have another list for programs in the state of Illinois. All of them are top-rated."

She takes my phone and scrolls through the list. Not only does it have school names, but it also has dates, addresses, emails, everything.

"What does this number next to each school mean?"

Like I said, I thought of everything, including where she was going to live.

"That's the distance from the apartment to the school," I tell her, dropping my hands from her shoulders and taking a step back to protect my body.

"Apartment? What apartment?"

I feel sweat dripping down my face. "The one I found for us to live in."

Word registers in three, two, one...

"I'm sorry, for *us* to live in? What do you mean by *us*?" Her eyebrows go all the way to her hairline.

Out of all the reactions, that one was one I was least expecting. Sophia throws a curveball. I for sure thought that she was going to knee me in the balls first, then ask questions later.

A nervous smile takes over my face. "I mean, I found an apartment for *us* to live in. Like together. You and me."

I thought about this long and hard. It was an internal battle that I dealt with for weeks regarding if it was a good idea for Sophia and me to live together or not. I went through every single pro and con. I even fought myself for thinking up the idea.

Living with Sophia would be a good and a bad thing. Good because I don't have to worry about her living alone in a strange city or her safety at night. As for the bad, well, there are a lot of reasons why living with her would be a bad idea.

The way I feel about her is definitely a problem. I don't know if my body, or fuck, my heart, will be able handle being around her twenty-four-seven. I don't know if I would be able to handle her bringing home a guy and hearing him fuck her in a way I crave.

I know for a fact that I won't be able to handle hearing her laugh day in and day out and not bring her closer to me so that I can make her laugh even more, preferably with my mouth.

It will be pure torture, but I'd rather torture myself and have her close than not have her at all.

I've kept the façade up for two years now. I can keep it up for longer.

How much longer?

I don't know.

Maybe one day I will get to the point where I won't be scared to lose her, and finally I can tell her about the grip she has on my beating heart.

Until then, I'm more than willing to suffer.

Last year we weren't ready to take a step like this, but now I think we are.

"Are you insane?" she asks as she starts to pace the length of her tiny living room.

Probably. I'm probably a little more than insane.

"It makes sense, Soph," I argue, even though she has every right to freak out. "We won't have to tackle being in a new city alone, and we'll both have someone to come home to. We always talked about living together, why not do it now?"

"Because what if…" she starts, but then she pauses as if she is trying to find the right words to say.

"What if what, Soph?" I ask, coming over to her, and stopped pacing.

She looks up at me with sad eyes. "What if we can't handle living with each other, and we end up back in bed together?"

What if.

For two years, I've been thinking about that "what-if," and if I'm being honest with myself, it will be a fucking fantastic what-if.

In the two years since we landed in bed together, this is the first time we are mentioning it out loud. I think about it every time I see her blush or whenever she lets out an involuntary moan when she eats something good. I just don't know if she does the same because again, we don't talk about it.

And in this scenario, even though I might be okay if that

'what-if' happens, she may not be, and if she's not, I'm not going to make her think differently.

"It won't happen," I tell her, my insides churning as the words leave my mouth. "Us ending up back in bed together won't happen unless that is something that we both want. Do you?"

She looks up at me again, her eyes sad as she gives me a shake of her head. "No."

No.

A no straight into my fucking heart.

I push the hurt down before I respond. "Then it won't. We'll make rules or something if that will make you more comfortable. I'll do anything you want me to for that matter. Just please say yes, Soph. Say yes to moving to Chicago with me. Say yes to living together. Because I need you there. I need my best friend through it all. I need *you* there through it all. Please. Or at the very least, tell me that you are going to think about it."

I shouldn't be doing this to her. I shouldn't be taking her out of the school she chose, away from her family and friends, all because I want to chase a dream. I should be man enough to not need her at my side.

But I'm not.

Sophia is quiet for a little bit, her eyes looking down at her hands, and moving around the apartment, possibly contemplating everything.

Looking out the window, I see that it's pitch-black outside, which means it's late. Last time I checked it was close to eleven, so it's probably closer to midnight now. This shouldn't be a decision that she makes this late or after a major breakup. She should sleep on it, and then we can talk.

I'm about to suggest just that when she opens her mouth to speak.

"Okay."

"Okay, what?" I ask, raising an eyebrow at her. "Okay, you're going to think about it? Or okay, you'll move to Chicago with me?"

The way she smiles make my heart skip a fucking beat.

"Okay, I'll move to Chicago with you."

Part 2

CHAPTER TWENTY

SOPHIA

Twenty-Two years old

Eight months from present day

"THERE YOU GO, MR. HENDERSON," I say to the patient I'm helping back into his bed after taking a trip to the bathroom. "Do you need anything else?" I ask.

The man is in his sixties and landed here at the hospital after a motorcycle accident. No family or friends have come to visit, so the nurse who's in charge of us nursing students, told us to take care of him the best we can. To make his stay a little easier, she said.

Mr. Henderson gives me a nod. "Think you can turn the TV on to the sports channel? The Knights are playing in game seven of the Stanley Cup, and I don't want to miss them kicking Florida's ass and them winning. A Chicago team hasn't made it this far in so damn long."

I smile at the man, a bit of pride swarming around in my

chest. "Sure, I'll turn it on, but you do know the game doesn't start for another four hours, right?"

Grabbing the control from the bedside table, I click through the channels until I find the one where I know the hockey game is going to air.

"I know, but I don't want to miss a single thing," he answers.

"I'm with you there," I say, finding the channel and looking back at Mr. Henderson. "Anything else, I can do for you?"

"Yeah, keep the Knights in your thoughts and prayers. They are going to need everything they can get," he says, giving me a dazzling smile I'm sure turned more than a few heads when he was younger.

"Oh, I already got you there," I say to him right before I lift my scrub top and show the old man my Dark Knights long sleeve I am wearing under.

"Atta girl. I knew I liked you for a reason," Mr. Henderson praises, giving me a nod in appreciation.

I let out a laugh. "Enjoy the game," I say to him before walking out.

As I head back to the nurse's station, I check the time on my watch, and I let out a sigh. I was supposed to get off an hour ago, so I would have time to go home, take a nap, shower, and look somewhat presentable before heading to the Dark Knights arena for the pregame festivities.

But of course, when you are a nursing student, nothing ever works out the way you have it planned.

Maybe if I leave in the next thirty minutes, I can still go home and shower, but I might have to skip the nap if I want to do my hair and my makeup, but that's fine. As long as I make it to the game, that's all that matters because out of all the hockey games I can miss, this one is definitely not one of them.

"Weren't you supposed to leave early today?" Linda, the RN in charge of the department, asks as I approach the desk.

I give her a nod as I take a seat at one of the computers. "Yeah, but Cindy had me help her with a catheter insertion, and then Mr. Henderson asked for help to go to the bathroom."

She gives me a nod as she takes a sip of her water. "Yeah, time gets away from you when you are having fun," she throws me a wink because we both know that inserting a catheter is not fun for anyone. "Why don't you head out? No need for you to stay any later."

"Really?" I ask, already reaching for my bag under the desk. I don't know why I'm so excited. I'm already off the clock.

"Yeah, really. Go have a life outside of this place."

"Is that even possible?" I ask through a laugh, but still get everything I need to call it a day.

"Nope, and as soon as you get your nursing degree and your license, you will find out," she tells me, waving me away.

"Thanks, Linda." I wave to her as I start making my way toward the elevators to get out of here.

For the last six months, I've been taking part in nursing clinicals to be able to finish off my degree. I have quite a few hours left to complete, but even then, I couldn't be happier. I'm one step closer with each passing day. Hopefully in a few months, I will be able to wear my stethoscope with pride and officially be a registered nurse.

I never thought I was going to see the light at the end of the tunnel, especially since I transferred into the program, but the transfer was the best thing I could have done. I'm grateful every single day that Blake asked me to move to Chicago with him. If I hadn't, I wouldn't have gotten the opportunities that I'm getting here back home.

Speaking of Blake, I check my watch one more time and let out a sigh of relief when I see I have plenty of time to do what I'd planned, with plenty of time to make it to the game.

Like Mr. Henderson said, this is the first time in years that the Dark Knights have come this close to winning the Cup. And the fact Blake is a part of that team absolutely blows my mind.

I'm so damn proud of him.

Last year was a little rough, since it was his first year, not only with the Knights but also playing at this level, so there were things he still had to learn. I thought this year was going to be the same, but Blake showed up and became an asset to the Knights.

Now here we are hours away from game seven of the Stanley Cup Finals, and it's absolutely mind-blowing.

I walk out of the hospital with a smile on my face and that smile stays in place until I run into something, and I'm falling to the ground.

"Oh shit, I'm so sorry. I didn't see you there," a male voice says, while my vision starts to fill with black spots.

Crap. Did I hit my head? I don't have time for a head injury right now.

"Are you okay?" the voice asks me, just as the person who owns the voice comes into my line of sight.

I'm still seeing spots, but I'm able to make out dark hair and light eyes and a worried face. A handsome, worried face.

"Wh-what?" I ask, trying to find my bearings. I don't think I hit my head, it doesn't hurt, but I can't say the same for my back.

"I asked if you are okay," the handsome, worried face asks, just as a small smile spreads on said face.

"Um," I say, taking a second to take a mental assessment of myself. The only things that hurt are my back and my ass. Thank God. "Yeah, I think so. Just a little winded."

I groan as I try to sit up. I'm definitely going to be feeling it tomorrow. Maybe I'll finally take Blake up on one of those ice baths he's been trying to get me into for years.

"Yeah, my bad," the guy says, offering me a hand to help me off the floor. I decide to take it. It's better to take a stranger's hand than to stay on the ground. "I was in a little bit of a rush to get up to see my grandma so I can make it to the game on time. I wasn't paying attention."

I stretch my back when I'm on my feet, and I can feel the pain shooting down my spine.

A groan escapes me, and the guy makes a face.

"Sorry," he says, giving me a nervous smile.

"You're fine. I was in a hurry, too. I also want to make it to the game on time," I say, giving him a small smile in return.

"An avid Dark Knights fan, or are you being dragged there against your will?" he asks, his smile shifting from a nervous one to a full-blown grin.

"Definitely not the second one," I say with a laugh. "But I am somewhat of a fan. My friend plays for them."

I don't know why I decided to tell this stranger that. Unless I know a person, and they are in my life in some capacity, I wouldn't tell them about Blake and what he does for a living. Why I told this stranger who ran me to the ground is beyond me.

"Really?" The stranger asks, his eyebrows rising and his smile spreading a bit more. "Who?"

I should lie now. I should lie to this handsome man and tell him that my friend is the mascot or something. Mascots are considered players, right? They are part of the team, and they get on the ice sometimes. That might be believable, but I can't seem to let my mouth form the lie so I tell him the truth.

"Blake Jacobi, he's one of the second-year rookies," I say, a proud smile on my face.

"That's awesome. He got his nose broken during game four, right? That hit was nasty."

It was nasty in all aspects. More so for me because I had to pull the gauze out of his nostrils a few days ago, and it was absolutely disgusting, and that is coming from a future nurse who has been cleaning people's butts.

On top of that, Blake is a huge-ass baby. Even more so with his mom being in town so she can attend all the home games this playoff season. He can't move, clean, or cook because his nose is broken. I'm surprised that he has even let his mom and stepdad sleep in his room and not on the couch. He's injured, and the precious baby needs his sleep more than anything. To say that I wasn't shocked when he brought out the air mattress to put in the living room so he could sleep on it would be a complete lie.

"It was. The aftercare has been just as bad, but it will heal," I say to him.

"Is he playing tonight?"

I nod. "As far as I know, he is."

"Good, because the Knights need all the help they can get," the strange man says, his eyes twinkling a bit.

"You're the second person to tell me that today," I say through a chuckle, my mind drifting back to Mr. Henderson for a quick second.

"You're really pretty when you laugh," the strange guy tells me, causing my chuckle to come to a stop. "Sorry," he says, holding up his hands. "I tend to say things out loud without even thinking about them. I didn't mean anything by it."

"So, you didn't mean to say that I'm pretty?" I joke, an eyebrow rising for effect.

The man is taken aback by my response and stumbles with what to say. "No, I mean you're very pretty, fucking gorgeous, I just didn't mean for it to come out when it did." He pauses and then shakes his head before holding out a hand. "Let's start over. Hi, Elijah, the man who should be looking where he is going when entering a hospital. I would like to also state that I do in fact think that you are pretty."

I let out a small giggle and place my hand in his to shake.

"Nice to meet you, Elijah. I'm Sophia. Someone who also should also be looking where they are going, and I would like to also state I was joking with the whole pretty comment."

"A jokester, a hockey fan, and an all-around beauty. My kind of woman," Elijah states, throwing a wink in my direction.

If I wasn't blushing before, I am now.

Our gazes lock for a few seconds, and as much as I don't want to break it, I have to if I want to make it to the game on time.

"I should get going," I say, nodding toward the street.

"Right, I should, too. Maybe if we don't see each other at the game, we can grab a coffee or a drink sometime," he offers, his smile causing butterflies in my stomach.

I smile back. "I would like that."

"Great, let me have your number, and we can set something up."

He pulls out his phone and hands it over to me so I can enter my phone number. The second that I do and hand it back to him, he presses the call button so that I have his number in mine.

"It was nice meeting you, Sophia," Elijah says after everything is all said and done.

"It was nice meeting you, too." I give him a wave and start walking away.

When I'm a block away, my mind finally puts together everything that just happened.

I got a guy's number.

Not only that, but I also felt butterflies, something that I've only felt with one other person, and that has always been Blake. Maybe, just maybe, my crush on my best friend is going away.

And if it is, I should grab the opportunity.

Maybe...

CHAPTER TWENTY-ONE

BLAKE

SOMEONE DESERVES a good kick in the ass. Or a punch in the throat. I'm good with giving them both. Especially to that fucker who decided to punch me in the nose during game four of the Stanley Cup Finals and broke it.

Now, half my face is bruised, and if we win tonight, pictures of me with a broken nose will forever live on. At least they will go well with my draft pictures. There's no doubt in my mind that my mom is going to yell at me every time she sees a picture, even if it wasn't my fault.

"Dude, your nose looks absolutely disgusting," Christian, my teammate and left winger for the Knights, says to me as I try to clean up my nose as best I can before the game. It's still oozing even days after it's been set.

"I know. Imagine how I feel. I almost puked the other day when Sophia was helping me clean it up," I tell him, seeing him gag a little bit in the mirror as I do.

I guess the big, broody asshole has a weakness.

"I still can't believe that Anderson is letting you play. That has to be a hazard or something," Christian throws out, Pulling his jersey over his head.

"I begged him to play. Fuck that two-week bullshit. And after getting him his favorite bottle of scotch, he said yes. Besides, it's game seven of the finals. We need all hands on deck. He would be stupid to not let me off the bench," I say, giving him a smile that he just rolls his eyes at.

"Ass kisser," Christian throws out.

I have my rebuttal on the tip of my tongue when my phone goes off with a text notification. I usually tend to turn off my phone a few hours before a game, but today, I left it on, just in case Hunter needed to reach me.

Liam, our team captain, has a baby on the way, and the baby is literally days away from coming, and instead of his baby mama, Chloe, staying at home and watching the game from the comfort of her own couch, she has decided to come to every single home game this playoff season.

Tonight is no different. So, since my family is here, Liam wants all eyes on her, just in case anything happens. And from the text message I just got from my brother, something is happening.

"Oh, shit," I say out loud, grabbing Christian's attention.

"What?"

I look over at my teammate and decide to tell him. There's no way in hell I'd be able to go a whole game holding this news in.

"I told my brother to tell me when Chloe made it up to the suite," I start to explain.

"Okay, and?"

"And according to him, she's there, but her mom wants her to go to the hospital because apparently she's having contractions."

The way Christian's face transforms is insane. By looking at the guy, you would think that he doesn't give two shits about anyone, but then you tell him news like this, and he comes out to be a total fucking teddy bear.

"Oh, shit," he says, repeating my words from a minute ago.

"Do we tell Liam?" I start to panic. I should be getting in the damn zone to play in one of the most important games of my life, but instead, I'm over here freaking out if I should tell my team captain that his baby might come tonight.

Who the hell put me in charge of this? Why couldn't Christian take care of this? His family is here. They could be sitting up in the suite, informing him about all of this. Why did this have to fall on my hands?

"Dude, why are you freaking out?" Christian asks, taking a step back as if I'm about to explode.

"Because I don't know what to do here."

"We're not going to do anything. If we tell Crawford what your brother told you, not only will he freak out, he will either leave to be with Chloe or play the game and be distracted the whole time. We're screwed with either of those choices."

"So, you want to lie to the guy?" At least it's Christian coming up with this plan and not me.

"Do you want to win tonight?" he asks, raising one of his eyebrows at me.

"Yeah."

"Then we withhold information from the guy. We don't tell him unless it's absolutely necessary. Now get your head on right. We have a game to win," Christian states, clapping me on the shoulder before walking away.

Ninety percent of the time I wouldn't listen to a single thing Christian says, but tonight I'm following his word. Both with what I tell Liam and with getting my head on right. It may be wrong in a few areas, but I'm following it.

After Christian leaves to go do God knows what, I turn my phone off and try to get myself back in the zone. That is after I check in with Liam and tell him that Chloe made it up to the suite we designated for our families.

He seemed to relax a little bit after I told him, which made the decision to not tell him the other little bit of news a lot easier.

As we get closer to the game, the more my head clears. I try to block out all outside noise and everything that comes with a game of this magnitude. This game can go one of two ways.

We lose and people forget that we even played in a game this big, or we win and our names will be engraved in history. Literally.

I try not to think about that, though, as I slide my jersey on and get one step closer to hitting the ice for three solid periods. I try to think about why I decided to play hockey and why I love it so much. I try to think of my support system, and how without them, I wouldn't have even been here. If it wasn't for my mom, Isaac, and even Sophia, I wouldn't be in this locker room right now, about to play in the most important game of my life.

I would be nowhere without my mom and everything she did to make sure I continued to play the sport that I loved. I would be nowhere without Coach Martinez, who taught me everything I know and has treated me more like a son than my own father did.

A father I know for a fact is in the stands tonight, a father who has been in the stands for every game the Knights have played this playoff season. As much as I want to tell myself that he's here to support me, I know it would be a lie. He's here to show his buddies and colleagues he has a pro athlete for a son, one who he is supposedly proud of, just like he did when Hunter played in the Super Bowl. Roy Jacobi only cares about image and money. Nothing else.

He doesn't deserve to be in my thoughts tonight, so I push

everything that has to do with my father to the side and think of what is important.

The second that my skates hit the ice, everything becomes clear.

Why I chose this over anything else.

Why I love it so much.

Why I'm still playing.

Every single doubt I have ever had about playing this sport goes away just like it did when I played in my first NHL game.

The only difference between then and now is that now I know I'm here to stay.

This is my sport, my team, my people, and I'm going to do everything in my power to help get this win.

The second the puck meets my stick, I know that this will be a game worth remembering.

Good or bad, this game will be engraved into my mind with all the other precious memories I have. My night with Sophia being at the very top.

CHAPTER TWENTY-TWO

SOPHIA

THE ENERGY in the suite is chaotic, and it has nothing to do with the fact that the Dark Knights are playing in the last game of the Stanley Cup Finals down on the ice right now.

Oh, no. The energy is crazy because Chloe, Liam's girlfriend, is in labor, and she doesn't want to go to the hospital and miss the rest of the game. If I were her, I wouldn't want to go either. Blake and his teammates are only a few points away from making history. This is too much of a big moment to miss, but she is having a baby, and right now, that's more important. Especially if the baby is saying screw hockey, I'm coming.

"Chloe, ándale. You have to go to the hospital," Chloe's mom says to her as she tugs on her arm to make her get up from her chair.

"But you said that labor takes forever. I can stay and watch the rest of the game," Chloe lets out, but the poor girl doubles over in pain. The hiss that she lets out tells me that she is hurting and really needs to go to the hospital.

"That one was way too close, sweetie. You have to go to the hospital," Lynnette, Liam's mom says as she goes to stand next to Chloe and her mom. Both grandmas look concerned as hell.

"I'm fine," Chloe says to them, but then she hisses again, which tells everyone in the room that she is not fine.

The grandmas shake their heads, and Chloe tries to plead with them by using her eyes to let her stay, but the two women just shake their heads.

Chloe then looks over at her dad for some help, but the man doesn't even look at her, probably for fear of getting on his wife's bad side. Same thing with Liam's dad.

The woman then turns to look at me. At me! She doesn't have to say a single word for me to know she is begging me to help her convince the moms to let her stay.

If I had my nursing license, I would, without a doubt, fight to let her stay. I would be able to keep an eye on her until the game is over and do everything I could to make sure the baby wouldn't be born at a hockey game like I almost was, but the moms look scary. And as much as I want to help, I don't want to get on their bad sides, so I shake my head no. I'm not about to get my head chopped off.

It's decided, after what feels like forever, that it's best to go to the hospital after Chloe asks Hunter and Selena. Her contractions are too close—it's best for her and the baby to go to the hospital.

Almost everyone leaves with Chloe, just leaving me and Patty, Blake's mom, and his stepdad, Daniel, in the suite.

"Your mom texted me and told me they were down in the seats. Why didn't they sit up here?" Patty asks, as the three of us take a seat out in the balcony.

"Because my dad said that he wanted to experience the game like a real fan and not like some high-profile person. That, and he wants to be the first person that Blake sees, win or lose." I swear my dad loves Blake more than he loves me sometimes, which I'm totally fine with.

"Sounds like something that your dad would do," Patty says,

giving me a smile and taking my hand in hers, before putting her attention back on the game.

The buzzer sounds to call the second period, and as the ice is getting cleaned for the third, the energy in the arena is at an all-time high. I've been to a lot of games in my life, but not a single one has ever felt like this.

The energy and atmosphere are on a whole other level.

As the third period starts up, every single person in the place stands up.

The Knights are currently ahead by one, and I'm keeping my fingers crossed it stays that way.

"This is absolutely insane," I say to no one, as my eyes dance with the players on the ice. Every single person who is down there, whether they are wearing a Chicago jersey or a Florida one, is hungry to win the Cup.

"Yes, it is." Patty grips my hand tighter, and I don't blame her. It's a high-stakes game, and the majority of people in the room will be highly disappointed if the game doesn't go how they want it to.

There's a line change, and Blake comes onto the ice to replace one of the right wingers. My eyes follow his every move, and I smile when I see he is doing something that he has been doing since he was a kid. Using his stick as an extension of himself. I know for a fact that my dad is pumping his fist up in the air with pride right now down in the seats.

He body checks a Florida player and is able to take the puck away and send it flying to Liam, who takes a shot at the net, but the puck is stopped by the goalie. That would have been an awesome assist and given the collective groan that sounded through the crowd, I wasn't the only one who thought that.

As Blake goes back to the bench, I feel my phone vibrate in my hand. I had taken it out to take pictures, but I have been so enthralled with the game that I completely forgot to open up my camera.

I look down at the screen, and I see it's a text message from the number that I saved only a few hours ago.

A smile spreads across my face when I see it, and I can't help but to open it right away.

It's a selfie of Elijah as Blake skates by.

Blake looks like the epitome of concentration, while Elijah looks like a total goofball. I love it.

"Who can possibly have you smiling that big?" Patty asks, taking my attention away from my phone.

Feeling like I got caught looking at something that I shouldn't be looking at, I quickly lock my screen and turn to her with a nervous smile on my face.

"Nobody," I answer, feeling a little bit guilty. There's no reason to feel guilty. I'm not doing anything wrong.

"That smile doesn't say nobody," she says, raising her eyebrows at me like I've been caught.

She isn't going to drop it, so I might as well show her.

I quickly unlock my screen and show her the picture that just landed on my phone.

"Oh my god, I love that picture," she says, almost letting out an awww. "Who's the guy?"

I don't have to look up to know that Patty is looking at me with a smile on her face. Instead of looking at her, I try to keep my concentration on the ice.

"Somebody I met a few hours ago," I admit, feeling a blush creep up my cheeks.

"And he already has your number?" Patty questions, and I make the mistake of looking at her. Sure enough, she's smiling. I don't think I've ever seen her smile that big.

"Yeah." I feel my blush get deeper. "We ran into each other, literally, and when we both said that we were coming to the game, he asked me out for coffee and for my number, and since I thought he was cute, I gave it to him."

"Sophia, that's awesome," Patty lets out, wrapping an arm around me.

"It is?" I don't know why, but I always thought that Patty hated whenever I told her I was seeing someone. She always gave me a tight smile, the same one my mom would give when I told her the same thing.

Deep in the back of my mind, I know why they act that way. Both of them are hoping for the day when Blake and I get together. I'm pretty sure they have been hoping for that day since we were teenagers, but it hasn't happened, and with the way things have been going, it never will.

While my heart still beats for Blake, I'm too stubborn to let him know. It's not only me, though. Blake doesn't see me in that light anymore because if he did, he would have said something.

It took him years to tell you that he saw you differently the first time. He might be doing the same thing now.

As much as I want to believe my mind that that is the case here, I don't think that I can.

I've lived with that thought since we moved to Chicago two years ago. Hell, I've probably been thinking that well before then, and I can't continue living with it. It isn't fair to me to hold onto something that isn't there. As much as I don't want to, I have to move on from Blake, no matter how much my heart hates me for it. No matter how much my head tells me that maybe one day, I might get the courage to tell him how I feel, how he makes my heart sing, I can't continue to wait for that one day to possibly happen. We're best friends, we're roommates, and that's probably all we will ever be.

"Sophia." Patty's voice pulls me out of my head. "I want you to be happy. So of course, it's awesome you've found interest in someone. My son may not like it because he has always been protective of you, but this isn't about him. This is about you. And as long as you are happy, I'm happy for you. I will be rooting for you and..."

"Elijah. His name is Elijah," I finish for her.

"Elijah. I like that. Hopefully, it can go somewhere," she says, giving me a wink.

I smile back at her. "Yeah, hopefully."

Our attention is brought back to the game with the buzzer goes off signaling a goal.

My first look is to the ice, and I see the Florida players celebrating. My shoulders sag a little, when I see that the game is now tied, with six minutes left on the clock.

"They can do it," Daniel says, but I don't know if he's saying that just to reassure me and Patty or because he believes it. I really hope that it's the latter.

When the clock hits the five-minute mark, the three of us stand up from our seats like everyone in the crowd and watch the game play out. Never have I been this nervous about a hockey game until today.

The Knights have worked so damn hard for this. They deserve to have their names added to the Cup, but with the way the game is going, I have no idea if it's going to happen.

The last time out of the game is called at the two-minute mark, and the score is still tied.

Hopefully Chloe was able to make it to the hospital in time because I wouldn't want her to miss watching this on TV.

The clock starts up again, and it feels like the whole arena is holding their breath, just waiting for what is about to happen next.

My eyes move from the ice to the clock, back and forth, until there are twenty seconds on the clock, and the Knights start a new play. A play that has Liam passing the puck over to Blake, who then passes it to their teammate Logan.

Logan takes care of the puck for a few seconds before he passes back to Liam. I watch as number twenty-one gets into position and slaps the disk toward the net.

I hold my breath.

One.

Two.

The buzzer sounds through the arena, and it feels like every single person in here starts to scream.

Holy shit, they did it.

The Dark Knights just won the Stanley Cup.

Blake's team just won the Cup.

Holy crap.

I turn to Patty, who is in her husband's arms, with a huge smile on her face and tears running down her face.

She looks over at me and opens her arms for me, and I don't hesitate walking into them.

"Our boy did it. Holy shit, he did it."

All I can do is nod, cry, and smile because the same words are running through my mind.

He did it.

Eventually, we pull apart, wiping the tears away, and start making our way down to the ice.

Thank God for the friends and family passes.

When we get down on the ice, it's so chaotic, but in the best way. Players are all over the place hugging each other and hugging their loved ones. It's a special thing to see.

But my eyes don't stay on the other players for long.

There's one player I'm looking for, and when I see him skating over to me, a huge grin spreads across my face.

When he is a few feet away, his mom is the first to go up to him and hug him as tightly as she can, all the while she peppers kisses all over his face. That woman should be so damn proud of her kids. Each one of them is doing spectacular things.

"I'm so damn proud of you, my baby," Patty says, slapping a few more kisses against Blake's cheeks. Just watching them brings tears to my eyes.

After Patty untangles herself from Blake, Daniel goes up to him and wraps him up in a big bear hug.

When that's done, Blake turns over to me, and the smile he is wearing is enough to make my tears turn into a full-blown sob. A happy sob, but still a sob, nonetheless.

The second Blake wraps his arms tightly around me, I control myself slightly, but tears are still making their way out of my eyes.

"I'm so proud of you," I say into his chest, not caring that he smells like a dirty hockey bag.

He places a kiss against my hair and tightens his hold on me. "I couldn't have done this without you, Soph. Thank you so fucking much for believing in me."

"I will always be by your side, hockey or no hockey, remember?" I say, reaching up and placing a kiss that was meant for his cheek but ended up closer to the corner of his mouth. I didn't even think about doing it, I just did it, but at this moment, I don't care. Not one bit.

"I remember," he says, the smile he is wearing spreading some more. "Love you," he tells me right before placing a kiss on my cheek in return.

This isn't the first time that he has told me that he loves me, and it won't be the last, but a part of me wishes that it was a different kind of I love you that I was hearing. One between lovers, and not one between best friends.

Either way, I smile up at him and repeat the words. "Love you, too."

I love you.

I'm in love with you.

I've loved you for a long time.

So many versions of those three words that I want to say but keep them to myself because they will never be said back in the same manner.

"Let's go find your parents," he says, taking my hand and helping me to the other side of the rink.

All the while my heart aches for reasons he may never comprehend.

CHAPTER TWENTY-THREE

BLAKE

MY BODY IS ABSOLUTELY SOARING.

We just won the Stanley Cup, and all I want to do is climb the tallest building the world has to offer and yell it out for everyone to hear.

It feels so fucking good to be the champs, to be at the top of the world.

After the game, the team had a little champagne celebration in the locker room. Well part of the team. Liam and Christian left as soon as the game was over to head to the hospital. Apparently Hunter took Chloe to the hospital somewhere during the second period, and as soon as the game was over, our team doctors told Christian, and he told Liam. Within seconds, they ran off the ice.

Off the ice, but not out of the arena. Liam apparently jumped in the shower before leaving because he didn't want to smell like cooked rotten cheese. Whatever that means.

The good thing is that he was able to make it in time, and according to the text message that popped up on my phone about an hour ago, he now has a beautiful baby girl named Emma.

Now, it's three in the morning, and the celebration of just winning the Cup has dwindled down a bit.

Me and some of the other guys on the team decided to rent out a restaurant at a hotel close to the arena so we would have somewhere to go after the game. Win or lose, we wanted to at least finish up the season with a good meal and a drink.

Thank fuck we won because that would have been one hell of a depressing meal.

After the celebration at the arena finished, we came to the hotel and partied our little hearts out. Now, hours later, only a few of us are left standing.

My mom and stepdad went back to my apartment to get some sleep, and Sophia's parents and Hunter and Selena went to their respective hotels to get a few hours of shut eye in before they all head back home in a few hours.

That just leaves me, Sophia, Logan, and a few other guys trying to see if we can make it until the sun rises.

"Dude, it's been, what, six hours? And I still can't wrap my head around the fact that we won the freaking Cup," I say to Logan since he's the closest to me, distance-wise.

"Trust me, I can't either. It's fucking crazy," Logan responds before taking a drink of the vodka he has been babying since maybe one in the morning.

Logan and I had somewhat of a rough start when I first came to the Knights. If you can even call it that. Logan isn't much of a talker. He keeps to himself a lot, so when we met, and the most I could get out of him was a grunt, I thought he hated me. It wasn't until the start of this season that he started to open up to me. The grunts turned into actual words. Now we're friends, maybe not best friends, but still friends.

He, Liam, Christian, and I make up a good little group.

"Did your family watch the game?" I had asked him a few days ago if his family was going to make it to game seven, since I hadn't seen them at any other game, and he straight up said no. So, I figured they were going to watch it at home. Wherever home may be, because Logan is tight-lipped about anyone who is related to him.

Logan gives me a shrug. "I haven't asked, but if someone did, it's going to be my brother."

That's something, I guess, but it's still sad as fuck.

"Well, at the very least they will be proud of you," I throw out, taking a drink of my water.

Logan just shrugs and changes the subject by nodding toward Sophia, who is sitting next to me.

"You should go take her home or something," he suggests.

I look over at the girl next to me and find her head is bobbing up and down as she tries to fight off sleep but fails.

I would be, too, if I've been up for almost twenty-four hours. Since she was going to leave the hospital early to attend the game, Sophia went in early. And by early, I mean the girl left our apartment at six in the morning. Way before I was even up.

Thank God I thought ahead and got a room here, just in case too much alcohol was consumed. Now, I don't have to lug her into a car to head across town.

"I have a room upstairs," I say, finishing up my water and getting up.

"Take her up, and just come back down," Logan says, getting a second wind by the way he's finishing up his vodka.

"Nah, if I go up, I'm going to want to fall into bed and never come back down. Might as well call it a night," I answer him, looking down at Sophia trying to figure out how to get her up.

We've been here before, and she is not the least bit helpful when it comes to carrying her while she's asleep.

"Pussy." Logan throws in my direction as I place my arm under Sophia's thighs.

"Fuck off. I will see you in a few hours." I grunt as I lift the girl up and get her settled in my arms hoping I don't drop her. If I do, I will never hear the end of it.

Sophia shifts slightly in my arms, cuddling deeper into my hold and wrapping her arms around my neck as I make my way out of the restaurant.

"I can walk," she lets out, her voice full of sleep. But even as she says the words, she relaxes deeper into my hold.

"Alright, let me put you down then," I tease, bending down ever so slightly so that her feet touch the floor, but she let out a whine.

"I said that I *can* walk, not that I wanted to," she throws out, almost rolling herself into a small ball so that she doesn't touch the ground.

"Whatever you say." I chuckle, hike her up higher in my arms.

As I walk us through the lobby and into the bank of elevators, she's quiet, which makes me think that she has fallen back asleep, but that theory gets thrown out the window once the elevator doors close.

"You did it, Blakie," she whispers, using the nickname from when we were kids.

"What did I do?" I ask her, a grin forming on my lips.

"You won the damn Cup. That's what you did. I'm so damn proud of you," she says, placing a kiss just under my jaw.

In all the time we've been friends, she has only kissed me there once, and that was during our one and only night together. I remember that kiss just like I remember every other kiss she has given me or we have shared.

Her kissing me in that specific spot, has my body reacting in ways it shouldn't, especially when I have her in my arms, pressed up against a part of me that she hasn't felt in years.

My fingers dig into her thighs.

"Are you drunk?" I ask, because even though I haven't had anything alcoholic in a few hours, I still might be, and I could be imagining she's kissing me just under my jaw when she isn't.

"Maybe a little. Are you?" she asks, her fingers moving along the nape of my neck.

"Nope," I say just as the elevator opens on the floor our room is on.

I walk out of the steel box and make my way down the hall. When we get to the door, I finally put Sophia on her feet, and thankfully, she doesn't object this time. Once the door is unlocked, I open it for her and follow her inside.

When I booked the room, I thought that I would be the only one using it, or at the very least, giving it to my parents if they didn't want to head back to the apartment. So, I didn't think when the front desk person said they had a king bed available. I just took it.

Now that Sophia is here with me, I'm kicking myself in the ass for not asking for a room with two beds.

We both take a second to look at the single bed.

I clear my throat and scratch the back of my neck. It suddenly got a little hot in here.

"You take the bed. I'll sleep on the floor," I suggest, feeling awkward.

We've shared a bed before. We've also shared a hotel room, so I don't know why I'm suddenly hot thinking about it now.

I live with the woman. Her bedroom is down the hall from mine. If I've been able to live with her for the past two years, I sure as hell can handle this.

"It's fine, Blake. We can share a bed. We've done it before." She gives me a small smile before looking away. "Do you think I can borrow a shirt or something?" she asks, eyes moving to the duffel by the wardrobe. "I really don't want to sleep in jeans."

Without thinking, I go to my bag and pull out a shirt and hand it to her. She gives me an appreciative smile before heading to the bathroom to change.

"Get it together," I tell myself, as I go back to the bag and pull clothes out for me to sleep in.

We live together. Sharing a bed isn't any different. Besides, it won't even be for one full night. A few short hours aren't going to hurt us.

That's what I keep telling myself up until Sophia comes out of the bathroom, wearing just my shirt. The second she steps through the doorway, the thought of being able to handle a few hours goes out the window.

Sophia wearing my clothes and it affecting me isn't a new thing. I've been getting hard-ons at the vision of her in my clothes for fucking years. It's been one of the constant images that plays in my mind whenever I'm in the shower or in bed, and I need to blow off some steam.

But tonight, winning the Cup and the drinking must be making me hypersensitive to everything Sophia does because not only is my dick getting hard just at the sight of her, but my hands itch to grab her and find out if she's wearing anything underneath my shirt. I'm usually able to control the urges that come with Sophia by putting distance between the two of us, by going to my room or heading to the rink, but that's not going to happen tonight, or this morning, I should say.

"Bathroom is all yours," she says as she climbs into the bed, her hair in a messy bun at the top of her head.

Oh, how I want to reach over and unravel her hair.

She dyed it a few years ago, and it's now this honey blonde that suits her skin tone perfectly, and I just want to dig my nose deep in the strands and take in her smell. If my damn nose wasn't broken, and I was able to fucking smell, I would have done it while I held her.

Without saying a word, I get up from where I was sitting on the bed and head to the bathroom.

I don't take a long time in there—just enough for Sophia to fall back to sleep.

So when I go back to the room, I try to be as quiet as possible, but those efforts are for nothing when I climb into bed and find Sophia wide awake.

"I thought you would be asleep," I say, turning my head to look at her.

"I think the energy from the game is still running through me," she says, a small smile playing on her lips.

"You were dead asleep downstairs," I respond, narrowing my eyes at her.

"Maybe I was faking it so you would carry me home. Key word being home because I didn't know you got a room for tonight."

I shrug against the mattress. "It was an impromptu decision just in case I drank too much."

"Smart man," she says through a chuckle. Hearing it has me wanting to move to her side of the bed so that I can drown in the down while I hover over her.

Sharing a bed is definitely a bad idea.

We lay there in silence for a few minutes, me looking up to the ceiling with my hands on my bare chest, and Sophia lying on her side with her hands under head.

I close my eyes to see if maybe I can get a few hours of sleep, so I don't do anything stupid with Sophia when something lands on my chest.

Opening my eyes, I see Sophia's hand on my chest. I turn to look over at her, and I see that her eyes are on me and another smile is on her lips.

"I know I told you this earlier, but I'm really proud of you.

Not only did you make it to the NHL, but you also now have a Cup win to your name. Those are great accomplishments."

Her fingers start to caress my bare skin, and since I'm not able to take it, I place my hand over hers to stop her movements but to also keep her hand on me.

"Before I saw you and my mom on the ice, I saw my dad. I don't know how he got a pass because I didn't give him one, but he got one, and when I saw him, he said four little words. 'You did good, kid.' That's it. He didn't tell me he was proud or that he loved me or that he was happy to see that I was achieving my dream. He said, 'you did good, kid.' If it was any other time, I would have taken those words and would have told him that it meant a lot to me that he was there. But this was the Cup Finals, Soph. His four little words didn't mean shit, especially not when I needed to hear them when I was growing up. So I just gave him a pat on the back, a smile, and I skated away. The fact you are telling me that you're proud of me, it means the fucking world, Sophie, and I can't thank you enough for giving them to me."

"Always and always," she says, repeating the words she gave me when we were ten years old.

Words that have been true even after all of these years.

Feeling the need to see her face to face, I turn my body to face hers, all the while I keep her hand on my chest.

Back at the arena, when I saw her on the ice, I had the urge to kiss her. I wanted to mark her as mine right there and then, but I held back. Now as the night has dwindled and morning starts to rise, the urge is still there, but now it's at an all-time high.

Fuck it.

"Don't hate me, Soph," I say, holding her hand tighter to my chest.

"Why would I hate you?" she asks, her beautiful eyes full of curiosity.

I don't respond. I just drop her hand and place mine on her face and lean forward, kissing her.

For the first time in four years, I am kissing my best friend, and there is not a single regret rolling through my body.

CHAPTER TWENTY-FOUR

SOPHIA

THE SECOND THAT his lips meet mine, it's like I'm transported into a world where I get to have his mouth on me all the time. A place where I don't have to hold in my feelings for this man. A place where I can openly tell him that I love him and kiss him whenever I want. A place that I never want to walk away from.

I savor every single second of this kiss with Blake, and when his tongue glides along my bottom lip, I open up so that I can get even more of him.

This takes me back to the first kiss we shared, but we're older now, more experienced, which makes the kiss a hundred times better.

I never want this moment to end, but it does when I remember that Blake's nose is broken, and there is a slight chance that he's not breathing. Not only that, one wrong move, and I could hurt him even more.

"I'm sorry," I say, pulling back from him.

"Why are you apologizing? I'm the one who started kissing you, remember?" The hand that is currently cupping my cheek, slowly starts to move up and down my face in soft caresses.

I could get lost in his touch and how his eyes are looking at me right now.

"I know, but I don't want to hurt your nose any more than what it already is," I say, raising my hand up to his face and slowly gliding my fingertips along the bruised skin.

"It's okay. I have a nurse that can take care of me." He throws a smirk in my direction and then leans in again to give me another kiss.

Another kiss shouldn't be happening, we should both stop what we are doing and talk about what is happening between us. Actually, there isn't a should about it. We need to talk about this.

But I can't seem to pull myself away.

I'm getting lost in this man's kiss again, and I can't seem to find it in me to make it stop. So I kiss him back. I kiss him with everything that I have, until our bodies shift, and I end up straddling his body and him under me.

"We shouldn't be doing this," I whisper when he pulls his mouth away from mine just to move it down my neck. His hands also move down my body like they are learning every single one of my curves.

"No, we shouldn't," he whispers as he peppers kisses from one ear to the other.

"We should stop then," I say, almost breathless, as I feel his hands land on my ass and start massaging the muscle. The movements of his hands feel absolutely delicious, especially after the fall I had before the game.

I didn't feel much pain during the game, but it has definitely hit in the last few hours, and the way Blake's hands are getting rid of the knots, feels like perfection.

"Do you want to stop?" Blake asks, shifting slightly so that he is somewhat sitting up and is able to pepper more kisses along my skin. This time pulling down the shirt I'm wearing ever so slightly so that he can reach my collarbone and part of my chest.

"Blake," I say, protesting, but it comes out sounding more like a pant than a protest.

He pulls away just enough for me to see his icy blues staring back at me, almost embedding themselves in my mind for what feels like the first and millionth time. "That isn't a no, Sophia. Do you want to stop? Because if you do, we will. You call the shots here, not me. Tell me to stop, and I will stop kissing you. I will stop touching you. But I need you to say it. Do you want to stop?"

I think about the question for a second or two, but I don't even have to think about it that long. I already know the answer.

"No, I don't want to stop," I answer him, and the way his eyes glow has flutters moving all over my body.

"But you do want to talk about it," he offers, his hands not moving off of my body.

I give him a nod. "We kind of have to."

He gives me a nod in return. "We do," he says, but then he goes silent for a bit before speaking again. "I care about you, Sophia." He starts up again, and I'm able to see all the sincerity in his eyes. "More than you can comprehend. You're one of the best things to ever happen to me, but I don't want to lose you. I don't want to lose my best friend."

"I don't want to lose you either," I respond, giving him the truth about how I feel for once. I don't want to lose him, not now, not ever.

"We can have this." He starts up again. "We can have this moment of weakness with each other, and once we leave this room, we can keep it close to our hearts like we did with our first time. We can have this one moment and not let it ruin us. Just like we promised on our first night together."

I want to break hearing his words. I don't want this to be just another night where we need each other, and we shelve it right next to the night that came before it. I want us to have more than just a moment of weakness. I want us to have it all.

But from the sound of things, Blake doesn't want the same thing. He doesn't see me like I see him, no matter if his lips are moving along my skin right now. He will never love me the same way I love him. I deserve better than just a night of weakness. I deserve better than a single night of feeling loved by the one who owns my heart.

But even knowing that, even hearing what he is saying, I still find myself nodding. Nodding that yes, we can have this. That we can have this moment of weakness.

Even if it will break me and leave him intact.

That way that Blake smiles at me is everything that I need, though. That, and the way he is holding me, and the way he leans back in to kiss me, is all that I need to get through this.

"We can do this," I say between kisses, but I don't know if it's for me or for him.

I don't give myself time to question my words because one minute I'm getting lost in what this man's mouth is doing to me, the next I lose focus of absolutely everything when I feel him getting harder under me.

Since I'm straddling him, I'm in the perfect position to move my hips so I'm able to grind myself against him. The only thing between us is the material of my panties and the material of his basketball shorts. And even then, it's still too much material separating us.

I want to feel him, and I want to feel him everywhere. I want to feel him raw and uncaring.

Feeling bold, and needy, I pull my mouth away from his and kiss down his body like he did our first time together.

"Sophia," he says, almost in frustration, as if to tell me that he wasn't done kissing me yet.

I don't stop what I'm doing, though. I continue to kiss every single inch of his exposed skin and move my way down his torso until I reach the waistband of his shorts.

"Fuck, you look so damn pretty kissing me like that," he lets out, his hand coming up to cup my cheek.

I marvel at his words, so much so that I decide to drag my tongue along his happy trail, and every single one of the ridges of his abs.

This man has the most spectacular body.

I start to push down the waistband of his shorts when one of his hands stops me.

"You don't have to do that," he tells me in a tone filled with so much sincerity. He said the same thing our first night together.

"I want to," I answer, shooting him a smirk and dragging his shorts down.

"I should be making you come right now, not the other way around," he groans when I lick him from hip to hip.

"You will, but I want to take care of you first," I say, pulling the waistband of his briefs down and revealing all of him.

My mouth waters at the sight of his cock. The memories of how good he made me feel when we got together the first time come rushing into my mind. I wanted to take him in my mouth then, but he stopped me. Now I'm going to do what I want.

I look up at Blake and give him a smirk as I palm him. He watches me intensely and continues to watch me as I lower my face and slide his cock between my lips.

The groan he lets out when I give him the tiniest little suck, sends a shiver down my body.

I slide him out of my mouth and run my tongue along the

length of him. From base to tip, I leave no inch of him uncovered.

I have never enjoyed giving blow jobs. It has always felt like something I was forced to do because the guy I was with went down on me. But with Blake, I'm just starting, and I want to feel him swell up in my mouth. I want him to pull on my hair as I suck him off. With him, it's definitely something that I want to do.

I slide my body further down the bed and position myself between his legs and take all of him in my mouth, without a second thought.

My head bobs up and down, coating every single inch of his cock with my saliva.

Blake lets out a groan as I work him, and his hand makes it into my bun, pulling at my strands every time I do something that he enjoys.

"Fuck, Sophia. You're sucking me off so damn good," he says, tightening his grip on my hair.

Loving the praise that he is giving me, I move one of my hands down my own body and touch myself as I continue to suck him off.

His cock swells in my mouth, and at some point, it becomes a little hard to breathe, but I power through, because I'm making him feel good, and that is all that matters right now.

I slide him out of my mouth with a pop, and I can't help but to smirk at how hard I'm making him. I see some pre-cum leaking out of his tip, so I swipe my tongue against it, loving the taste of him.

"Are you touching yourself, Sophia?" Blake asks, causing my eyes to look up at him as I swirl my tongue along the tip of his cock. "Is sucking me off making you wet?"

I look at him through hooded eyes and give him a nod before sliding him back into my mouth.

"Let me have a taste." It's not a question, but a command.

I give his cock on more lick and sit up so that I'm straddling him again, bringing the hand that was just in my pussy up to his lips.

Blake's eyes stay on mine as he takes each of my fingers in his mouth and sucks them clean.

For a second, he closes his eyes as if to savor my taste.

"Just as sweet as I fucking remember," he says, taking my face in his hands and kissing me like there is no tomorrow.

His tongue dances with mine, and for a few minutes I get lost in everything that is Blake Jacobi.

As our mouths explore each other, I feel one of his hands land on my waist, while the other makes its way between my thighs.

He lets out a hum when he finds my panties already pushed to the side and me wet from having him in my mouth.

"You're bare," he says, sliding two fingers along my folds.

I nod. "I like it better that way." I say against his mouth. Thank God for Brazilian waxes.

"I think I do, too," he says, right before his thumb makes contact with my clit, and he draws lazy circles against the bundle of nerves.

His fingers continue to slide through my folds until they are at my entrance teasing me ever so slightly.

I grind against him, needing more of him, and thankfully he listens, quickening the pace of his hand.

His mouth makes it down to my neck and he kisses me there as his fingers work me in the most spectacular way.

When he slides a finger in me, and then two, I'm a panting mess and feel the need to come right there and then.

"Blake," I say, moving my hips in motion with his fingers.

"You want to come, Sophia? You want to coat my fingers with all that you got?" He licks his way up my neck until he makes it to my ear. "Come on my fingers, baby. Come all over them, and after you can ride my cock, and I can make you come again. Do it, Sophia." He orders, and I can no longer hold my release in.

I come all over his hand just like he told me to, loving every single second of the orgasm-induced high that he has put me in.

"Good girl," he says in my ear, his fingers still on my pussy spreading my release all over. "I can't wait to see you bouncing up and down my cock and screaming out my name."

He finally takes his hand out of me and brings it up to his mouth to lick it clean just like he did with my fingers.

There is something sexy about watching him licking my taste off his hands. Seeing it already has my body ready for more.

Blake leans in to give me a quick kiss before grabbing me by the waist and removing me from his body so that he can get out of bed, getting rid of his shorts and briefs in the process, and walk over to his bag. He pulls something out, and within seconds, he's back in bed, pulling me back on to his body.

I sit on his lap, as he takes the condom that he grabbed from his bag and starts sliding it on.

As soon as he is covered, he wastes no time in placing his mouth on mine again, this time with a lot more hunger than ever before.

My hands find their way into his hair, and I pull on the strands tightly, bringing me as close to him as I possibly can.

We detach for a few seconds so that he can slide my T-shirt off my body, but as soon as it's gone, we go back to devouring each other's mouths as if this is the last time we will ever be together like this. And in a way, it might be because I don't know how many more hookups with Blake I can take without confessing to him how I really feel. This might be the last time.

Might as well make it worthwhile.

I start grinding against him, moving my hips up so that my pussy is sliding against his cock.

The need to have him inside me grows with every passing moment.

Blake must be reading my mind, because he wraps an arm around my waist and lifts me up so that he can angle his cock right at my entrance.

I let out a moan as I slide down on him, and the second that I'm seated with him fully inside of me, my mind travels back to the last time his cock swelled in my pussy. It feels like it was so long ago, but it also feels like it was yesterday.

We take a second and just watch each other before we do anything.

We don't move, we don't say a single word, we just stay still, taking not only the moment in, but each other.

Our eyes stay locked until it becomes unbearable. I start to move my hips, taking everything from this that I can.

I ride him with no regret.

My fingers dig into his shoulders, and I take everything that I can.

Because after this, I'm going to try my hardest to move on from Blake. I'm going to try my hardest to put my feelings for him away because I can't take any more of this back and forth.

Today is the last time I will pour my heart out to this man with everything that my body has to offer and pretend that what we did didn't affect me.

Blake digs his fingers into my hips as if he knows this is the last time we will be together like this. He kisses me the same way.

I pant out his name, and he moans out mine.

It doesn't take much for me to reach the edge again, but I still speed up my movements, to get us both where we need to be faster.

Blake's face falls to my neck, and when he plants a kiss just under my ear, I unravel for him, giving him everything I have.

He uses my body to get there with me, and soon, he is grunting into my neck and calling out my name.

This night was everything we both needed, and I won't regret a single thing.

But I have to do what's best for me and put an end to this.

CHAPTER TWENTY-FIVE

BLAKE

A BEEPING SOUNDS OUT, causing my eyes to pop open straight into the sunlight making its way into the room through the gap in the curtains.

You would think that for the amount of money a room at this hotel costs, they would at least put different blinds in their rooms so that the sun doesn't creep in.

As I sit up on the bed, I look over to my right and notice the side of the bed where Sophia slept, is empty, and for a second, I think that she left without saying anything, but then I hear the shower running, and I relax.

Rubbing at my eyes, I grab my phone from where it lays on the bedside table. I don't remember putting it there, but at least it's there and not somewhere else, like down at the restaurant.

Picking up the phone and checking the screen, I see there are over a hundred messages waiting for me to open them and over fifty calls waiting to be returned.

I open a message from Liam first in the group thread with him, Christian, Logan, and myself. The second the message pops up on the screen, I can't help but smile. It's a picture of him with his newborn daughter. In all the time I've known the guy, I haven't seen him this happy.

Who knew a one-night stand could end with happiness and a baby?

I send a quick text saying I will stop by the hospital later today and move on to the other texts.

There's a few from my buddies back home, congratulating me on the win and saying that they are going to be making the trek to Chicago to attend the parade and to celebrate. I respond to a few, starting to get back into the high I was on last night when the game ended.

I answer a few more messages from a few other friends and teammates, until there are only a few left to answer.

One message that makes me want to stop answering all together—one from my dad.

I figured after he told me those lovely four words last night, I wouldn't hear from him until either the season started again, and he wanted tickets to impress his buddies, or Christmas, since that's the one time a year he tries to act somewhat like a decent father.

I sure as hell wasn't expecting him to send me a text this morning, telling me that he wants to grab a meal together to celebrate the win. I'm half tempted to answer the message by telling him to fuck off because I know for a fact this meal together isn't just going to be attended by the two of us. His buddies from work will no doubt be joining us. But I'm also tempted to say yes, mostly so that I can show him I can be a good son, even if there are times he isn't a good dad. I already kind of blew him off last night. I would feel bad if I did it again, even if it's something I'm used to doing.

Part of me thinks it might be time for a change when it comes to my relationship with Roy Jacobi.

After shooting him back a message, letting him know that

we can meet up tomorrow, I quickly move onto the next set of unanswered messages. This time from my sister.

Jainie graduated from high school about a week ago, and as a graduation present, she asked Mom if she could go to Europe for the summer before she started college in September. Mom was hesitant but agreed to let her go. Both Hunter and I paid for it to give our sister the best summer that she could have.

This trip was planned before she even started her senior year, when we didn't even know if the Knights were going to be contenders for the Cup. When we made the Finals, Jainie wanted to move back her trip, but because the dates were so close, nothing could be changed.

Well, it could have if she paid more money, something that both Hunter and I were more than happy to give, but she didn't want to take it. So she missed the last two games we played.

I talked to her yesterday before heading to the arena, and the girl was literally crying about the fact she was going to miss the game. I can only imagine how she's going to be today.

Instead of texting her, I hit the dial button and give her a call.

Jainie answers on the fourth ring, sounding annoyed as hell.

"Finally. I've been texting you for hours, you know?" she says, and if she was in front of me, I know for a fact she would be rolling her eyes at me.

Before I respond, I check the times she texted and the current time. It's ten in the morning, and she only texted at seven.

"You only started texting me three hours ago," I tell her, leaning against the headboard and dragging the sheet over the lower half of my body. Being naked while talking to my sister is weird as hell.

"Hello! I also texted you after the game ended, and you didn't even respond to that," she throws out.

God, she sounds like Mom.

Pulling the phone away from my ear, I check her messages again and see that she did in fact text last night, and I'm just seeing it now.

"Sorry, Jain. Last night was a little crazy, and I didn't really take the time to look at my phone." Last night was more than just a little crazy, especially given who I ended up sleeping with at three in the morning, but I don't say that to my sister.

"Given that your team won the Cup last night, you are forgiven," she says, in a calmer voice, but the calm doesn't last forever, because it quickly fills with excitement. "I'm so damn proud of you, Blakie! I really wish I could have been there to watch it!"

I ignore the use of the nickname Blakie because it reminds me of when Sophia used it last night and give her a response.

"Thanks, sis. Don't worry, you'll be at the next one. I'll get together with Hunt and make sure that we win another Super Bowl and Cup in the same year."

"Oh my god, you better. That would be so much fun. And if Maddox and the Miners win the World Series a few months later, it would be like a trifecta," she says, mentioning one of Hunter and Selena's baseball player friends.

"That would be awesome," I tell her, thinking of all the things that have to get in line for something like that to happen. "Are you having fun at least?"

"Yes. I still wish I was home so I could have seen you win, or even for the parade because who doesn't want to ride on a float, but I am having fun. I'm glad I got the chance to do it. It's only been a week, though, so that could change."

"Well, if it does change, call me, and I will get you on the first plane out," I say, just as the bathroom door opens and Sophia walks out wearing the same clothes she was wearing for the game.

She looks absolutely beautiful, even more so with my name on her back, but from the way she's looking at me, and the way she is dressed, there isn't going to be a repeat of what we did a few hours ago.

"I'll hold you to it." Jainie laughs in my ear, pulling me out of my Sophia-filled thoughts.

"Just let me know," I say, and Sophia raises her eyebrow at me as she goes over to my bag and dumps the shirt she was wearing on top of it. "Hey, Jain. Can I call you back later?" I say into the phone.

As much as I want to talk to her right now, it feels like there are other pressing issues that I have to take care of.

"Yeah, call me back whenever, just check the time first. I don't want to talk to you at two in the morning."

"I will. I promise. Have fun," I say to her, and before she can even respond, I end the call and turn my attention over to the woman who looks like she wants to run out of the room and never say another word to me again.

It would fucking break me if she were to do that.

"How long have you been up?" I ask, feeling a bit awkward about it.

Why does this feel like our night four years ago? Maybe because we're a few weeks shy from the anniversary of when it happened, and all of this feels exactly the same.

But instead of her waking up in bed alone while I take a shower, it's the other way around.

"About an hour," she says, her voice small and low.

"Why do I get the feeling that the conversation we are about to have is going to be a tough one?" I meant to keep that question in my mind, but I somehow let it leave my mouth.

Sophia just continues to look at me as if she wants to run.

"Maybe because it might be," she says, before taking a pause and sitting on the edge of the bed opposite of me, with her gaze down on her hands. "We can't keep doing this, Blake."

When she turns to look at me, her eyes are shining with unshed tears.

Here I was, not telling her how I really feel about her because if I did, and it ultimately didn't work out, I didn't want to lose her or our friendship, or worse, hurt her, and yet, as I look at her, I see that I'm doing just that.

Just tell her. Fucking tell her how you feel.

Fucking tell her.

Grow some balls and let the words come out.

It's not that fucking hard.

"Soph," I start, the words on the tip of my tongue, but she shakes her head at me, ultimately stopping me.

"This isn't healthy. For either of us. Yes, we've only gotten together twice, and once was four years ago, but next time could be in a week or a month, and we can't keep blurring the lines like this. We were able to put it behind us last time, and maybe we'll be able to do the same this time, too, but I don't know if I can handle another." The way a tear escapes from her eyes has me wanting to crawl over to her and wipe every single tear that dares to escape.

Just tell her, and she will stop crying.

Saying fuck it, I wrap my body in the sheet and climb out of bed. I walk over until I'm standing right in front of her. She looks up at me with her doe eyes, as more tears escape.

I kneel down in front of her and take her hands in mine.

Instead of confessing and giving her my whole heart, I let fear take over again and say something different than what I had planned a second ago.

"Tell me what you want, Soph. Tell me, and I will give it to you," I say, because it's easier to give her her wants than give in to mine.

Subconsciously, I'm hoping her wants are on the same level as mine.

Fuck, I hope so. Because this whole interaction is telling me that I'm too much of a pussy to give her the whole damn truth.

Sophie looks down at me for a long minute, her bottom lip between her teeth and her eyes filled with tears.

"I need my friend more than I need nights filled with sex."

And I need to tell you how I really feel and show you that you own my whole damn heart, and that I need you more than I need to breathe, my mind wants to scream out, but I don't let it. Because giving her what she wants is more important to me.

I squeeze her hand tightly in mine.

"You have me. As your friend, as whatever you need, and not a single night we've had will ever interfere with that." I try to push down the ball of fucking emotions forming in my throat. "I don't regret a single night with you, Soph. Not four years ago, not now, and if it ever does happen again, I won't regret it then either. But if you don't want it to happen again, then it won't. You have my word."

Having a night with her here and there may not be enough to satisfy my hunger, my cravings, and my wants for this woman, but for her, it's not the same. I can see it in her eyes.

She wants to protect and save our friendship, and she wants to do everything to keep it that way.

I do, too.

Which is why I can't tell her what my heart is so desperate to say.

"You won't hate me?" she asks, squeezing my hand back.

"Why would I hate you? You're setting a boundary for us. There's no reason to hate you. Now if you start cheering for Florida after they broke my nose, then I would hate you." I have to throw a joke in there so it seems like everything between us is okay. And for the most part, it is. It's just one of us has to get over our feelings and get our head in check about the other.

Me, it's me who has to do that.

Sophia lets out a little laugh. "Never. Unless you get traded to them. Then I will think about cheering for them."

"Take those words back. That is never going to happen." I give her a smile.

We look at each other for a few seconds, small smiles on both of our faces and hands still intertwined on her lap.

"We're going to be okay?" she asks, her voice just as small and low as it was earlier.

"We're going to be okay. Always and always, remember?" I say, holding her hand as tightly as I can.

"Always and always."

If only I could say those three words in a different context, maybe then things between us would be a lot easier.

A lot less regret when it comes to our bodies joining together as one.

CHAPTER TWENTY-SIX

SOPHIA

I NEED *my friend more than I need nights filled with sex.*

Those words circulate in my head even days later.

There were so many different words that came to mind as soon as I stepped out of that bathroom, but as soon as I sat down on that bed, I forgot them.

And instead of telling Blake the words I spent the majority of my shower thinking up, I gave him only half the truth. That I needed my friend more than anything. I should have just admitted everything.

Part of me is glad I did it that way, part of me isn't. Part of me hates myself for it, but the other is happy because even if I broke my heart saying those twelve words, I liberated myself from the hold my feelings for Blake have on me.

At least, that's how it feels.

Because if it didn't feel that way, I wouldn't be here getting ready for a date.

A *date*. With Elijah, the guy who I met at the hospital the day of the Cup Finals.

Since junior year in high school, I've been on my fair share of dates, a large majority of them being first dates.

For every single one of them, I have been nervous. Something about meeting new people and the act of trying to get them to like me always has my leg bouncing up and down, thinking something is going to go wrong.

Things don't usually go wrong. A large percentage of the time the guy and I hit it off and set up a second date, but that doesn't stop me from feeling like I want to puke before every single one.

It's like a cycle. Find date, get nervous for said date, puke, and then go on date and act like everything is fucking peachy.

And since I'm going out for the first time in almost a year, my nerves are at an ultimate high.

Elijah texted me two days after the Cup Finals and asked me on a coffee date. Given who I woke up next to the morning after the game and the conversation we had, I was going to decline his invitation. It didn't feel right to accept a date when I basically stomped on my own heart. But I then remembered what I told myself that night. I have to do what's best for me, and what was best was walking away from my feelings for Blake and trying to be happy.

So without a second thought, I texted Elijah back and accepted his invitation for today.

I thought the second the message said delivered, I was going to feel relaxed, that the nerves weren't going to take over my body as if it was their host. I couldn't have been more wrong.

Since everything was finalized for this date, my stomach has been churning as if it was trying to tell me going out with Elijah is a really bad idea. But it's just my nerves trying to play mind tricks on me.

From what I can see, there's nothing bad or wrong with Elijah. From what I can tell, he's as sweet as they come, so there shouldn't be anything to be nervous about, but apparently my body is not comprehending that just yet. So it's drowning me in nervous energy.

And at the worst time.

I'm supposed to meet Elijah in an hour, and not only have I not picked out what to wear, my hair is not cooperating, and my stomach feels like it's going to jump out of my body.

"It's just pre-date jitters. The second you see him, it will be all gone," I tell myself as I drag on a skirt I bought years ago and have yet to wear.

As soon as it's on, I walk over to the full-length mirror I have behind my door and check to see how I like it.

Looking at myself, I can see why it's been at the back of my closet all of this time. The material does nothing for my body. If anything, it makes me look boxy. I have half a mind to say screw it and pick something else, but when I look at the time again, I see that my hour just got shorter. There's no time to pick something else out and fix my hair.

"Fuck it. I'll wear something cuter on our second date," I say to my reflection and head back to my bathroom.

Hopefully a few more passes of my straightener will be able to control the frizz. I doubt it, though, since the humidity in Chicago is already rising. It's days like this that I miss living in Missoula.

I spend the next twenty minutes fussing with my hair, until I finally get it to look at least a little decent. Once that's done, I slide on my shoes and make sure that I have everything I need and start heading to the door.

There's a slight chance I'm going to be a few minutes late, but that's okay. As long as I get there, that is all that matters.

I'm grabbing my keys from where they are on the kitchen counter, when I hear the front door opening.

Instantly, I stop walking, and my eyes go wide.

No fucking way.

There is no way Blake is here right now.

He wasn't supposed to be home until later.

But sure enough, a few seconds go by, and Blake walks deeper into the apartment with his duffel bag slung over his shoulder.

"Hey," he says, eyeing me right before throwing his bag on the couch.

"Hi," I say, surprised. He wasn't supposed to be home right now. "What are you doing here? I thought you guys weren't going to come back until tomorrow morning."

Blake and some of the other Knights took a trip out to California to visit their version of the Magic Kingdom to celebrate the Cup win. He told me if he wasn't back tomorrow morning, they would for sure be back by the afternoon. That's the reason why I even set up my date for today. One because I had the day off, and two so Blake wouldn't be here when I left.

I knew I should have set up the date for a day he wouldn't be here at all. What the hell was I thinking?

In the days since the Cup win, eight days to be exact, things have been more than awkward between Blake and me. Just like it was the last time. The only difference now is that we live together, and at times it's hard to keep certain thoughts from popping into my head.

The fact he hasn't been home much these last few days has been helpful, but that still doesn't stop my brain from thinking about the way he made me feel while I'm in bed alone or even showering.

Something I definitely need to put a stop to if I start seeing Elijah in a more serious way after today.

Blake looks over at me, and at first he has a smile on his face, but that smile quickly turns into a look of confusion.

"Um," he says, his eyes moving down to my exposed legs for

a second before moving them back up to my face. "We had a change of plans and decided to come home earlier."

His eyes move down to my legs again, and I try my hardest not to be affected by it. Why do thoughts from our first night together start to take center stage in my head? Because this look he is currently giving me is almost the same as the one he gave me that night all those years ago.

"Where are you going?" His voice brings me back to the present.

Lie, Sophia. Lie to him. He doesn't need to know where you're going all the time.

But what if Elijah is a serial killer, and I need rescuing?

I really need to stop watching the true crime videos I find online.

Taking a deep breath, I give Blake a smile and tell him. "I'm going on a date."

"You're going on a date?" he asks, his words coming out slowly like he is trying to comprehend them as he says them, while his eyebrows climb up to his hairline.

"Yeah," I say, giving him a nod. "It's just coffee, but it's still very much a date."

Why do I have the sudden urge to explain myself? I don't owe Blake anything. Sure, he's my best friend, and I don't keep anything from him, just my feelings, but that doesn't mean that I have to explain myself to him or why I'm going on a date.

Sleeping together doesn't give us a say in who we see or when we see them. More so when we treat sleeping together as if it doesn't mean anything afterward.

"Do I know this guy?" he asks, scratching the back of his head, looking awkward.

An awkwardness that's starting to fill the room and make my nerves go up another level from where they were.

I give him a shrug. "I don't think so. I met him at the hospital last week, and he asked me out, so I said yes."

"Why didn't you tell me about it?"

Why indeed.

There are so many reasons why I didn't tell Blake about this date, but there isn't a single one I'm willing to say out loud.

"It must have slipped my mind, I guess. What with all the celebrating going on." I lie through my teeth.

Lying to Blake has started to become a whole lot easier, and I fucking hate it so much.

"Slipped your mind," he repeats, making sense of the words.

I give him a nod. "Yeah."

He gives me a nod back and just looks around the room as if he were inspecting it for the first time. I watch him as he does it, and I can't help but notice that he looks hurt.

In all the years we've been friends, we have always been open about things with each other. We don't tell each other everything, and there are definitely things about the other that we might not know, but things like going on a date or seeing someone new, we definitely share.

I start to feel bad I didn't tell him about Elijah sooner, but if I am going to do what I said I was, I can't continue to live my life as if Blake is everything to me. As if only he owns a part of my heart when I haven't even handed it over.

He is everything to me, but not in the way I want him to be.

Blake doesn't say anything, and at this point I don't think that he will. It might be best for me to just go. I'm already going to be late to meet Elijah. I don't want to add more time to that.

"I should get going. I'll see you later, okay?" I say, making my way to the door, but still keeping my eyes on him.

He turns, and for a second, he looks at me with a face that is void of any expression, but then it quickly transforms into a small smile. My least favorite smile of his.

"Yeah, I'll see you later."

I give him a small smile back and walk the last few steps to the door, opening it.

"Hey, Soph?" Blake calls out, stopping me as one foot steps over the threshold.

Pausing, I turn back to look at him and see that he is playing with his hands, all the while he is looking at me like he wants to tell me something.

Tell me not to go, Blake.

Tell me not to go on this date.

"Have fun, okay? You deserve it."

Six words I have no reason to hate, but I do.

"I will." With one more smile in his direction, I walk out of the apartment and close the door behind me, feeling as if I want to cry.

I push those feelings to the side and take a deep breath before I start making my way out of the building and to the coffee shop where I'm meeting Elijah.

The whole walk there, though, I'm not think about Elijah and what the date might bring. No, instead, I'm thinking about Blake and how I wish I was willing to throw our friendship away and tell him how I really feel about him.

Maybe finally telling him will make things easier.

But what if it doesn't?

That question scares the crap out of me and gives me enough push back to not do what I want.

And because of that, I'm going on this date.

Because I need to move on and let myself be happy with someone who is going to feel the same way about me that I feel about them.

My thoughts finally shift to Elijah when I arrive at the coffee shop and see him standing out front, looking down at his phone, waiting for me.

The butterflies that appeared the first day I met him appear again, and I can't help but to smile a little bit.

This is something that I need. I know it is.

Taking a deep breath, I walk over to Elijah, and when he looks up and gives me a big smile, I can't help but to smile back.

"Hi," he says, his smile growing even more.

The fluttering in my stomach is getting even more pronounced and making me feel like I did back at the apartment. But I think it's more giddiness than nerves this time around.

"Hi," I say back, feeling like the giddiness wants to take over.

That feeling gets even stronger when he closes the distance between us and places a peck against my cheek.

Elijah pulls back and gives me a beaming smile. "Are you ready to get this coffee date started, pretty girl?"

Overdrive, my body is in overdrive.

I give him a nod. "More than ready."

Fuck, I sure hope so.

It's time to put my nervousness aside and have fun like Blake told me to.

CHAPTER TWENTY-SEVEN

BLAKE

A DATE.

Sophia is on a fucking date and not even two weeks after I had her under me, screaming out my name.

I don't know what I hate more, the date part, the fucker who asked her out, her for even agreeing to go out with him, or me because I'm too much of a chickenshit to tell a girl how the fuck I feel.

Given the anger I feel right now, it's a combination of all four, but it's mostly on me. All because it feels like a fucking endless cycle that could be stopped if I finally admit to myself I'm in love with my best friend. But I'm too fucking stubborn.

Maybe if I admit how I feel to Christian or Hunter, one of them will beat the stubbornness out of me, and I will be able to grow some balls and admit my feelings to a girl.

I'm sure they would fucking love that. Beat the crap out of me and ridicule me while they do it. I will never hear the end of it.

Shaking my head, I throw the thought of a beating out the window. Maybe if things don't work out with Sophia and this dude she is meeting for coffee, I'll consider it. For now, I'll continue to live with my stubbornness and watch her be happy with some fucker who doesn't deserve her.

Fuck, what has my life come to?

You would think since the Knights won the Stanley Finals not even two weeks ago, I would still be living off the high, but yet, here I am, back from one of the happiest places on Earth, moping on my couch, grumbling about how my best friend is on a date.

I need to get my shit together.

Instead of continuing with my moping, I decide to text my brother to see if he and Selena are still in the city.

They flew in from San Francisco for game seven and said that they were going to stay in Chicago for a few days. Not only to celebrate with me in case the Knights won, but because the San Francisco Miners were going to have a game against one of the Chicago teams, and they wanted to support Maddox Bauer, one of their friends and a pitcher for the Miners.

The baseball game was yesterday, so there is a slight chance my brother is back in California already.

Thankfully though, a message from him comes in telling me they are still at their short-term rental.

Not even thinking about it, I get up from the couch, grab my keys and wallet, and make my way over there.

Better to be surrounded by actual people than sitting around and googling every single coffee shop within a ten-mile radius so that I can go to every single one of them, find Sophia, and interrupt her date.

Who even chooses to go to a coffee shop on a first date anyway? If it were me, I would have taken her to her favorite Thai place, and even though it's summer, I would have rented out an ice rink and taken her ice skating so everything would come full circle.

But it's not me.

It's some asshole who she met at the hospital God knows when.

I'm fucking glad that fucker doesn't know her well enough just yet because if he did, and took her on my date, I would be charged with strangling him to death, that or figuring out a way to decapitate him with my skates.

Wow, that got dark quick.

I really do need to get my shit together.

At the very least the dark thoughts made the walk over to Hunter and Lennie's rental quick because one second I'm walking out of my own building, and the next I'm standing at their front door.

I guess when you are thinking about murdering someone for dating the woman you are in love with, you lose all sense of your surroundings.

Clearing my head a bit, I knock on the door of the brownstone and wait for someone to open it for me. I would just walk in, but I really don't want to see them doing things that will make me want to burn my eyes out. I did that once a few years ago, when I went to visit them in San Francisco, and it has scarred me for life. There are images in my head of my future sister-in-law that shouldn't be there.

When the door doesn't open after a few seconds, I start to think maybe I am interrupting something, and I'm definitely going to be getting a visual I don't want, when the door opens, and I see my brother standing there with a shirt on.

"What?" he asks, opening the door wider for me.

"What, what?" I ask, walking into the house and taking off my shoes.

"You made a face when I opened the door," he says, crossing his arms after closing the door.

I give him a shrug. "I was just surprised you actually have a shirt on. Seems like every time I visit you, you're in the middle of defiling Lennie."

"We don't fuck like bunnies twenty-four-seven," he answers, guiding me through the house, heading to the kitchen.

"You could have fooled me," I say under my breath, which earns me a middle finger.

Walking into the kitchen, I see that Selena is at the island dropping something into a pot.

Fuck, yes. She's cooking.

With a smile on my face, since I know I'm going to be eating well with whatever Lennie is making, I walk up to my future-sister-in-law and place a kiss on her cheek.

She looks up at me then to the entryway of the kitchen. "Where's Sophia?"

I guess it's weird when two people who basically do everything together aren't together.

I give her a shrug. "She's on a date or something," I say, snagging a piece of tomato from the cutting board in front of her.

The look that Hunter and Selena give each other when I say the word date is definitely not missed, but I choose to ignore it and continue to steal pieces of tomatoes.

"'A date or something,'" Hunter repeats my words, like he can't believe it. Yeah, well that makes two of us.

"Yup," I say to him, mid chew.

"And you're okay with that?" he asks, and I notice Lennie has a worried look on her face as she goes back to making whatever meal she's making.

I look up at my brother. "Why wouldn't I be?"

Hunter just gives me a knowing look but doesn't say anything.

I'm not stupid. I know my brother knows how I feel about Sophia, or at the very least I think he does. He hasn't straight up told me he knows, but I have a strong feeling that he does. This conversation is just proof of that. The guy has been telling me to make Sophia mine since I was fifteen.

Sometimes I wonder if he would rip me a new one if I told him about our two nights together.

Hunter just shakes his head. "No reason," he says and lets out a sigh. "I just figured you would feel a certain way about it."

Is he finally going to call me out?

"And what way is that?" I ask, not sure why I'm getting defensive about it.

My brother looks at me straight on, while his fiancée is trying to cut vegetables in between us with her eyes everywhere but her knife.

"The way that finally has you telling that girl how you feel about her." And there it is. The official callout.

"And how do I feel about her?" I ask, because of course even when I'm being called out, I still can't admit it.

"Dude, I've seen the way you look at Sophia. You're in love with her, and you're too chickenshit to say it. To her and possibly even to yourself."

I let out a sigh because he's right. Of course, my older brother is right, and I fucking hate him for it.

But just because he's right doesn't mean I'm going to leave here and go straight to whatever coffee place Sophia is at right now. One, I don't know where exactly that is, and two, I don't want to be an asshole best friend.

"How I feel about her doesn't matter," I say because it's the truth. "If she wants to date, she can date. If she wants to go to coffee with some douche she met at the hospital a few days ago, then she could go get coffee with some douche. I have no say with what she does or who she sees, and I'm okay with that as long as she is happy."

Hunter looks at me with a stoic face and his arms crossed

over his chest. I know he wants to say something, but he stops himself when Selena looks up at him.

Whatever expression the girl is giving him is enough for him to drop it.

"Fine. As long as you're happy with that choice," he throws out before walking over to the fridge behind me and taking out some water bottles. My season may be over, but his is about to start, and he can't be drinking all the beer in the world.

As for his statement...

I'm not happy with Sophia dating, a part of me never has been. Even when both of us were in relationships. But I stand by what I said. As long as she is happy, then I'm okay with it.

And if she ends up marrying this douchebag, I will be okay with it, too.

Maybe. Who the fuck knows. This is their first date. There's a good chance that it will never lead to that.

Instead of responding to my brother, I wrap an arm around Selena and look down at the pot of food in front of her.

"Please tell me that you are making a Mexican dish of some kind." It looks like soup. Even though it's the middle of June and a million degrees outside, I'll still eat it.

"*Albondigas*," she says, looking up and giving me a smile.

"Fuck yes. I've been dying for some home-cooked Mexican food," I say, trying to forget about where my best friend is.

"Um, you live with a roommate who is half Mexican. She can cook for you whenever you want." Selena walks out from under my arm and gives me a weird look as she grabs the pot and takes it over to the stove.

"Look, I love that girl, I do, but she can't cook for shit. The fire department has been over more times than I can count because she's burned something."

My mind goes back to just last month. I had gotten home from an away game, and there was smoke all over the place because she left some sweet potato fries in the oven for way too long. The whole place stunk for a week. I'm surprised we haven't been kicked out of the building yet with all the fire scares we've had.

Selena just lets out a laugh and goes back to cooking while Hunter and I take a step back to not be in her way.

Eventually everything is in the pot and needs to cook for a while before we are able to eat, so the three of us make our way over to the living room and put on a movie.

Halfway through the movie, Selena turns to me excitedly.

"I forgot to tell you," she says, shifting her body so that she is sitting on her knees with a huge smile on her face.

"You're pregnant?" I ask, taking a sip from my water.

The comment earns me a slap against my arm.

"No, but I did tell your brother we should start thinking about dates for the wedding," she says, her smile growing more if that's even possible.

"Wait, really?" I ask, looking from Selena over to my brother, who gives me a nod. "That's fucking awesome!" I say, wrapping Lennie into a hug.

Hunter and Selena got engaged last year after Hunt won a Super Bowl ring. The dude didn't even wait to get off the field to do it either. In the middle of all the celebration and the confetti falling onto the field, he got on one knee and proposed to Selena. Of course, she said yes, and they have been living in engaged bliss ever since.

When it came down to actually getting married, they said that they were going to wait until Selena finished her master's degree. Last I heard, she was finishing up in December, so that's probably why she decided it was time for them to start planning. Without a doubt, it will be the sports wedding of the year.

"When are you thinking?" I ask once I detangle myself from my brother's fiancée.

"Probably next offseason. Gives you and me a chance to actually attend and not worry about any games or practices."

I give him a nod.

"I also wanted to ask you something with regard to the wedding," Hunter says, taking my head out of the mental calendar I'm creating.

"What's up?" I ask, trying to think of what he could possibly ask me.

"Think you'd want to be my best man?" The question rolls off his tongue, and it fucking shocks me.

As a kid, whenever I thought of Hunter getting married, I figured I would take no part in it. What with our age difference and how we were estranged from each other for a few years. I always thought that the role of best man would go to one of his friends or a teammate, not me.

"Really?" I ask, a little stunned.

"Really. I wouldn't have it any other way, little brother."

Wouldn't have it another way.

Never did I think I would hear those words come out of his mouth.

Why do I feel all emotional right now?

Through all the emotion, I find myself nodding.

"Yeah, I'm down to be your best man." I say, trying to play it down, but the smile on my brother's face is making it hard.

Holy shit, I'm going to be his best man. I don't know why, but that feels more exciting than winning the Cup.

"I guess now that we have a best man, we should pick out a date," Selena says, and right away, her and Hunter start throwing out dates they can use.

While I listen to them talk, I think about the future. About how one day, there is going to be another wedding.

One where the bride is Sophia, and instead of me being the groom, like I thought I would be if I just told her how I feel, I'm the one standing behind her as her best man or maid of honor or whatever the fuck she wants me to be. I'll be standing behind her and not next to her. I'll be standing there and watching as she marries someone, as she professes her love for him.

And it will all be because I was too much of a chickenshit.

I came to see Hunter and Selena so it could serve as a distraction.

But instead of a distraction, all this visit did was paint a picture of an unhappy life, one where I'm unable to love Sophia.

All because of stubbornness.

If things don't work out with this guy, I'll tell her.

Yeah, that's what I will do. If things don't work out, I'll tell her.

CHAPTER TWENTY-EIGHT

SOPHIA

Four months from present day

"THAT SMILE you're wearing is pretty big. Do you want to tell me who put it there?" Chloe asks as we make our way into the Knights arena for the second home game of the season.

Even though it's only the second home game, the place is packed with people. Winning the Stanley Cup really brought in more fans for the Knights, especially with all the press the players have been getting these last few months. Everyone on social media loves them, and now everyone is wanting to get a piece of them in person.

I dodge a few people as Chloe carries Emma to the elevators.

"It's Elijah," I say to her when I finally catch up to her, a smile spreading across my face yet again.

"Oooh, the elusive boyfriend," Chloe says, wiggling her eyebrows at me as she pushes the button to call the elevator. "Is this the day I finally get to meet him?"

My face turns a little red as I follow her and her baby into the steel car. Elijah and I have been officially together for three months now. We really hit off on our coffee date, and we both decided that we wanted to see each other again. I was a little reserved about it at first, but I was able to get over it quickly. From there, we went on date number two, and then two turned into three and four, then a month in, we finally put a label on it.

It's been an awesome three months, filled with a lot of fun and a whole bunch of smiles. But in those three months, I have yet to introduce Elijah to Blake or our hockey family or even my parents. I've introduced him to my friends at the hospital and some of the girls from school, but not the most important people in my life. I've told them about him, and most of them have said how I look happy, but that hasn't been enough for me to bring him around. Don't get me wrong, I want to introduce them. I just find every excuse in the book not to.

Why?

I have one theory, and that theory is Blake.

Every girl should look forward to the day when she introduces her best friend to her boyfriend and sees them become just as close. That's a day she looks forward to, a day she hopes for.

But something deep inside of me tells me that isn't going to happen.

In all the years since we have discovered dating, I've tried to strike up friendships with most of the girls Blake has dated in some capacity. Apart from Gwen, who was just a bitch from hell, most of his girlfriends have liked me. I haven't kept in touch with them since Blake kicked them to the curb, but I was still their friend in some way. Blake, on the other hand, has probably liked maybe one guy out of the five or six I've dated for longer than a month. According to him, there is always something wrong with them.

And the feeling in my gut tells me he is going to find something wrong with Elijah. So I've been holding off on bringing the two together, and because the Knights and their significant others are an extension of him, I've held off on bringing Elijah around them, too.

As for my parents, well, that's normal. I don't bring anyone around my dad unless we've been together for at least a year and are extremely serious. For the record, that has only happened with Theo and look how that turned out.

Stupid, cheating, ass-face.

Emma coos in her mother's arms as the elevator doors close, taking me out of my thoughts enough to answer Chloe's question.

"Maybe," I say as I watch Chloe take care of her daughter. "He's here at the game, but he's sitting down by the ice with his friends."

"Why didn't you invite him up to the suite?" Chloe asks as the elevator arrives at the suite level.

Usually, we sit down in the stands with everyone else, rarely taking advantage of the suite Liam, her baby daddy boyfriend and Knights starting forward and captain, reserves almost every game. We like being around all the commotion, or we did before Emma was born a few months ago. Chloe brought her to a preseason game a few weeks ago, and it was a little loud for her little ears, even with noise-canceling headphones. So we decided it was best to just use the suite and invite a few other of the wives and girlfriends who have little kids.

We also invited Eliana, Christian's girlfriend, up here with us, but since the girl is the team's photographer and is working throughout the game, she can't be up here.

"I don't know," I say, giving Chloe a shrug. "This is basically the WAG's suite, and given that I'm not even a WAG, it would be awkward being up here with my boyfriend while everyone else is cheering on their men."

"I guess," Chloe says, giving me a smile while she shakes her head. "So, if you didn't invite him up here, why aren't you sitting down there with him and his friends?"

I don't have an answer to that.

"Because I'm helping you with Emma," I answer because apparently I can't come up with any other excuse as to why I'm not watching this game with my boyfriend.

Why aren't I watching this game with my boyfriend?

"You mean the four-month-old baby who is about twenty seconds away from falling asleep?" she says, giving me a pointed look as she rocks her baby back and forth.

I look down at the baby in her arms, and sure enough the Crawford-onesie-donning child's eyes are closed, and she is cuddling deeper into her mom's arms.

"I'm also up here to keep you company," I throw out because I really have no reason to be up here.

"There will be plenty of kids and other wives and girl-friends up here who will keep me company. Go down there and watch the game with your man," Chloe urges, nodding back toward the elevators.

There is no reason for me to hesitate with her command, so why am I?

There is nothing in the world that should be stopping me from going down to the stands and watching a hockey game with my boyfriend.

But what if Blake sees us?

And what if he does? I have to pull the Band-Aid off and introduce them eventually. Besides, he's going to be too distracted by playing in the actual game to even look up at the stands.

With a smile in Chloe's direction, I pull out my phone and shoot a quick text to Elijah, asking to see if they still have an extra ticket.

We had talked about attending the game together, he even

bought the seat next to him, but in the end, I decided to come up to the suite.

That extra ticket could have gone to one of his friends, so it's better for me to ask than just go down there and come right back up because someone else is in the seat that was meant for me.

Within seconds, a text message pops up on the screen, and the smile I had on a few seconds ago goes from a small one to a full-blown grin.

Chloe lets out a laugh at my expression and shoos me away as she and Emma continue their way to the suite to catch the start of the game.

Pocketing my phone, I make my way down to the lower level and look for Elijah.

Thankfully I don't have to look a whole lot because he meets me at the door to the section he and his friends are sitting in.

When he turns to look at me, a huge smile spreads across his face, but for some reason, it slowly starts to fade.

"Is everything okay?" I ask, closing the distance between us and placing a kiss against his lips.

Elijah looks me up and down when I pull away from him, his face and eyes are not giving me anything to go off of.

"Do you usually wear a jersey to games?" he asks, his tone unreadable.

I look down at what I'm wearing. This is normal for me when it comes to attending a hockey game—leggings and a jersey. Sure, sometimes I do dress up, but not all the time. But did Elijah expect me to wear a skirt or something?

"Not all the time," I say, giving him a small, nervous smile. "Only when I'm too lazy to pick out an outfit or when I'm coming from the hospital. It's just easier."

He lets out a hum as he gives me a closed-lipped smile, but

he doesn't say anything. He just takes my hand and leads me down to the seats.

As we walk down the stairs of the arena, I can't help but feel some tension rolling from Elijah's body to mine, but I don't read too much into it. Maybe he wanted to see me in something more form-fitting.

Next time we come to a game, I will try to plan better. If I have the time.

That's the game plan, but as the game starts, and Knights are playing like their asses are on fire, the tension coming off Elijah gets a whole lot more intense. And I feel it directed straight at me.

He doesn't say more than two words to me during the first period, and during the second and third, that word count goes down to zero. He doesn't even talk to his friends, which I find even more weird.

I guess whatever his issue is, it has very little to do with what I'm wearing. Because who gets this mad over a damn outfit?

I try to give him space most of the game, occasionally trying to make him smile with a peck on the cheek, but that doesn't help any. He just scoffs.

By the end of the game, which the Knights won three to one, I'm slightly irritated. If I knew he was going to act like this the whole game, I would have stayed up in the suite. At least then, I would have had some baby time with Emma.

As everyone starts making their way out of the arena, I look down at the ice and see Blake looking around. Since he has made it to the NHL, we've made it a habit of sorts, win or lose. I will go down to the ice and give him a few non-encouraging words about his game. Long gone are the days when I would yell how much he sucks from the stands. Well, not long gone. I did it all postseason, but a few of the dirty looks I got, especially when

Blake was doing well, made me stop. Now we have this little tradition that I don't want to put a stop to.

"Do you guys mind if I go down to the ice and say hi to my friend?" I ask Elijah and his friends. I don't need permission to do things, but I rather not be rude and just leave them when they are heading in a different direction.

Elijah makes a face, but he doesn't say anything or even makes sound, but his friends do.

"Would it be okay if we go with you? We would love to meet him," Marcus, Elijah's best friend asks, a smile growing on his face.

I guess introducing them to Blake in a public place is better than anything.

Ignoring Elijah and yet another one of his scoffs, I give Marcus a smile.

"Yeah, I would love to introduce you guys to him," I answer, and all of them, besides Elijah of course, look excited.

Seriously, what is up with him today? The Knights are his favorite team. I would have thought he would be excited not only because they won, but because he's about to meet one of the players. I must have missed something, but I can't think of any reason why he should be acting this way. Maybe something happened at work, and he was reminded of it? I don't know.

I'll ask him when we go back to his place later tonight, but for now I'm going to go make his friends' night.

As I make my way down the stairs to the ice, Elijah tries to grab my hand, and even though I'm not in the right mind to deal with his moodiness, I let him take it. But when he holds it in a death grip that is almost painful, I pull it away, much to his distaste.

"What is up with you?" I whisper in his direction, stopping to let a family pass by.

"Nothing, let's go say hi to your friend," he tells me, his

voice having a coldness to it that I don't like. I really need to get to the bottom of what is going on with him because I don't know how much more I can take.

Trying to ignore his tone as best that I can, I continue to make my way down to the ice. Thankfully, Blake catches sight of me and the guys and stops at one of the openings to wait for us.

He throws a wave in our direction and gives me a small grin when I close the distance between us.

"Your stickhandling skills could use some work. I wonder what Coach Martinez would say if he was here," I tease, both of us knowing that his stick moved perfectly today. He even got an assist.

"Probably not to listen to his loudmouth daughter because she doesn't know what the fuck she's talking about," Blake teases back, the grin on his face growing a bit.

"Shut up. I know more about hockey than you do. Or did you forget who was raised by the hockey player and who wasn't?"

"Yeah, yeah, keep rubbing it in my face," he says, giving me a playful eye roll before nodding to the guys behind me. "Who are your friends?"

I give Blake a smile and introduce him to Elijah's friends first, since they look the most excited to meet him. When that is all said and done, I turn to my boyfriend with a smile, hoping to see that he is excited to meet an important person in my life, but my smile disappears when I see little to no excitement on his face.

This is definitely not going to be a great first impression.

Might as well get this over with.

"Blake, this is Elijah, my boyfriend, and Elijah, this is Blake, my best friend," I say, waving a hand between the two.

"It's nice to meet you, man. Soph has told me a lot about you. I'm glad I can finally put a face to the person."

Blake, being the good friend that he is, puts a smile on his face and extends a hand out to Elijah over the door separating us, because he knows how much Elijah means to me.

My boyfriend, on the other hand, looks like a petulant child being dragged by his parents to say hi to one of their friends.

Seeing the look on his face makes me want to cry.

Here are two individuals, who at the moment, are important to my life beyond belief, meeting for the first time, and I can already tell that they won't be getting along.

"Yeah, nice to meet you, too," Elijah answers, but instead of shaking Blake's hand, he slides his hands into the pockets of his pants.

Cue the heartbreak.

In the months we've been together, he has never acted this way. He has always been happy and cheery whenever I introduced him to someone in my life. Yet, I introduced him to Blake, and he acts like this? Whatever is affecting his mood better be good.

The two men continue to look at each other without saying a word, sizing each other up. Eventually after a few seconds, Blake breaks the stare down and turns to look at me.

"I'll see you at home later?" he asks because that's a normal question between us, but the way Elijah's jaw is ticking, it's as if this is the first time he's finding out I live with Blake.

It isn't. He's known about it since date two.

After giving my boyfriend a quick look, I shake my head at Blake. "I'm going to stay at Elijah's tonight."

Blake gives me a tight smile, one that tells me he is trying hard to like my boyfriend but failing and gives me a nod. "Alright, then I will see you tomorrow. It was nice meeting you guys."

With that, he skates off and heads down the tunnel to the locker room.

The second Blake is gone, Elijah's friends start heading up, talking about how cool it was to meet one of the Knights.

I look over at Elijah, silently asking why he's acting the way he is, but all I'm met with is a distant expression that gives me nothing.

When we get to his place, I'll ask him. I don't feel like having a screaming match in public.

I slide my hand into his when he offers it and let him drag me up the stairs and out of the arena. The whole time my hand is screaming at me to be released from the death grip that it's currently in, but I leave it where it is, not wanting to make Elijah's mood even worse.

Once we are out of the arena, Elijah walks over to his friends and tells them that we are heading home instead of going with them to grab something to eat.

The words to object are on the tip of my tongue, since I've barely had anything to eat since lunch, but I drop it. Maybe he has plans to order something once we get to his apartment.

Instead of taking the train like we usually do, Elijah calls for a ride, and within minutes, we are leaving the Knights arena behind and heading to his apartment.

The car ride is silent.

Not a single word is spoken, not even to the driver. We just sit in the back seat, my hand on his lap, still in the tightest grip known to man, while he looks out the window, and I look at him.

For the whole car ride, I try to figure out what could have affected his mood so badly, and all I can think of is that it started when he saw me and what I was wearing. I see nothing wrong with it. I'm supporting my friend, but he must be seeing something I'm not.

All the questions are on the tip of my tongue, but I don't speak them.

When the car gets to its destination, Elijah is quick to get out of the car without a single word, leaving me and the driver absolutely speechless.

I take a deep breath before giving the driver a smile through the rearview mirror. "Thank you so much," I tell him before getting out of the car and following my boyfriend upstairs.

The second we are in the safety of his apartment, it is as if all the tension coming off him becomes more intense.

"Did you have fun at the game?" he asks, taking off his jacket, like he didn't just spend the last three hours in his own emotions.

It takes everything in me not to blow.

"I was having fun until my boyfriend decided to act like an asshole," I let out, pulling at the sleeves of my jersey.

"An asshole, huh?" he asks, nodding his head in the process.

"Yes, an asshole. You didn't say more than two words to me during the whole game, and when we went down to talk to Blake, you didn't even shake his hand," I say, trying not to let my anger show, but it's becoming hard.

"Yeah, well I had a reason for that," Elijah tells me, his face as stoic as it has all night.

"Oh yeah? And what reason is that?"

The second the words leave my mouth, everything becomes a blur.

One minute there is about fifteen feet between me and Elijah, the next he's right in front of me, his hands wrapped tightly around the tops of my arms, and he has me pushed up against the wall.

A whimper escapes me when Elijah brings his face closer to mine with a snarl on his face instead of a smile.

"I was acting like an asshole because my girlfriend was

fucking embarrassing me. Not only are you wearing another fucking man's name on your back, you were also cheering him on like you wanted to get on your knees and suck his cock." He spits out the words, while his fingers dig not only into the material of my jersey but into my skin. Pain radiates through both my arms as they ask for relief. "Do you know how that fucking felt? To be sitting there with my friends, while my woman was screaming out another man's name. It felt like I was a fucking joke, and they were laughing straight to my face."

He shoves my body back, my head hitting the wall.

"I-I-I was supporting my friend," I stutter out, trying my best to wiggle out of his grip, but he's too strong for me.

"I don't give a fuck. I don't give a fuck you've known the guy since you were a fucking child. You're mine, and the only man's name that has a right to come out of that mouth of yours is mine."

Tears start rolling down my face, and I feel like crumbling down to the floor because it feels like Elijah is seconds away from letting go of my arms and slapping me across the face.

I need him to let me go.

I continue to try to wiggle out of his hold some more, but he just holds me tighter, pushing me further into the wall, leaving no space whatsoever.

"Elijah, you're hurting me," I say, my voice barely a whisper.

"Do you think I care? You embarrassed me. You disrespected me," he says with a snarl.

The tears continue to flow down my face, and even as he sees them, he doesn't budge.

"I'm sorry. I didn't mean to do it. Please let me go. You're really hurting me," I plead for him to let me go with everything I have before the situation becomes worse.

Something comes over his face like he realizes what he's

doing is wrong. It takes him a second, but he finally lets me go, letting me fall to the ground.

Instead of getting up right away and running away from this place as fast as I can, I stay on the floor and try to collect myself.

I'm okay.

I'm okay.

"Sophia, I'm sorry," Elijah says, sounding close but far away at the same time. "I shouldn't have done that. I let my anger get the best of me. I promise you it won't happen again."

His words sound sincere, and when I look up at his face, I see the apology in his eyes, silently telling me he means every word.

And every inch of me is saying to believe him.

I just don't know if I can.

CHAPTER TWENTY-NINE

SOPHIA

IT'S DARK OUTSIDE.

Darker than it was when we left the arena and headed to Elijah's.

It has to be late, but how late, I don't know. I haven't checked my phone since I left Elijah's, and I really don't want to check it now. More so because I don't want to see the messages that might be waiting for me from my boyfriend.

After Elijah let me go and apologized, he acted normal, asking me what I wanted to eat and if I wanted to watch a movie before bed. Like he had forgotten he had his hands digging into my arms and had shoved me against the wall.

As much as I wanted to play along and forget about what had happened, I couldn't. So I got up from the floor and told him I was going to head home. I felt bad doing it. I apologized a hundred times for it.

From the looks of it, he was upset, but nodded and let me go. He apologized again as he walked me to the door and kissed me goodnight.

As I left the building, I knew that I should call a car to take me home, or even wave a cab over, but I decided against it and started to walk. It wasn't that far of a walk anyway.

So, I walked, and I walked, and I walked, until I was standing in front of the building where Blake and I live.

Now I've been standing outside for God knows how long.

I should really go inside. It's getting darker and colder.

But I can't seem to make my feet move. So I stare up at the building some more. Not really seeing any of it.

It's when I hear a dog barking in the distance that I'm finally able to break out of my trance and make my way inside.

It takes me a minute to push the button for the elevator, though, but the second I do and step inside, I let out a sigh of relief. One step closer to being home.

When the elevator arrives at our floor, I don't hesitate getting off and walking down the hall to the apartment. When I reach the door, I take a second to just look at it. I should be opening it and heading straight to my room to put an end to this night once and for all, but I just stand here, looking at the door.

Halloween is in about two weeks, and I thought it would be nice to put some decorations up. I had to make do with solely decorating the front door since we don't have a front yard or a small porch where I can put up those animatronics that scare people or even have pumpkins.

Looking at it now, though, I want to rip everything off. Every single inch of caution tape, every little paper black and white pumpkin I put up, my hands itch to rip off. There's no reason to, it looks nice, and I'm sure the kids who live in the building will like it when they come by to get candy. But everything from the last few hours is just boiling inside of me and ripping off the decorations seems like a logical thing to do.

He apologized. You know he didn't mean to grab you like that or even yell. You have no reason to be angry at Elijah.

Right. No reason.

It was just a one-time thing, a heat of the moment. It won't happen again.

I think it's the fact it even happened once is what has me feeling all types of emotion.

I don't know if my blood is boiling because I'm angry about it or sad.

Whatever it is, I try to push it down, at least until I get into my room.

Blake shouldn't be home. The Knights won. He's probably out celebrating with the guys. So I can go in and head straight to my room and just forget about tonight.

Taking a deep breath, for no other reason other than to compose myself, I slide my key into the lock and open the door.

The apartment is dark, and for once I'm thankful for it.

I take off my shoes, and basically throw my keys and my bag onto the entryway table and start walking deeper into the place.

"Hey," Blake's voice sounds out as I pass by the kitchen, and I jump slightly.

How did I miss the glow of the kitchen lights? And why the hell is the rest of the apartment dark? Blake is a turn-on-every-single-light-in-the-whole-place kind of guy.

"What are you doing home?" I ask, my voice shaking as I try to keep all the emotions flowing through my body controlled.

I'm partially glad the lights are turned off everywhere but the kitchen because if he fully sees my face right now, there is no doubt he will know that something is wrong and will see how close I am to bursting into tears.

"It's after midnight," he answers, giving me a weird look.

"What?" I ask because no way he's right. The game finished around nine. No way it's already the next day.

"It's twelve fifteen or something. I grabbed a drink with the guys and then came home. What are you doing home? You said that you were staying at Elijah's tonight."

I take out my phone, and sure enough, Blake is right. It is after midnight. Was I seriously wandering around the city for a whole two hours?

"Soph, you okay?" Blake asks, his voice sounding closer.

I look up and see that he is walking out of the kitchen and toward me. I take a step back.

If he comes anywhere near me, I'm going to burst, and if I do, he's automatically going to assume that Elijah did something and go hunt him down.

As much as I'm mad at Elijah for the way he put his hands on me, I don't want Blake to go and fight him.

So I answer him.

"Yeah, I'm fine," I say, closing my eyes for a second before opening them back up again and giving Blake a smile. "I was going to stay over at Elijah's, but I started feeling funny, so I thought it was best for me to come home."

I should tell him what happened. I should tell him how my arms ache and how there were more than a few minutes where I was scared of my boyfriend. But I can't find the words.

It was just a one-time thing. It won't happen again. There is no reason to worry Blake.

"Want me to make you soup or something? I think we still have that sopa de fideo your mom froze when she was here a few weeks ago. I can heat that up for you," he says, coming closer to me and placing the back of his hand on my forehead to check if I have a fever.

I love that he is being this sweet and caring, but I can't take it right now.

"It's okay. I'm just going to go to bed," I say to him, and I see his face fall a bit as I say the words. "But I will definitely take you up on the fideo tomorrow, if the offer still stands." I try to give him a smile, but I don't know if he can even see it in the limited light.

"Always."

"Thank you," I say, going on my tiptoes and placing a kiss against his cheek. "I'll see you in the morning, okay?"

"Okay," he says, giving me a nod and a smile that doesn't quite reach his eyes.

With another smile, I turn away from my best friend and make my way down the hallway and into my room.

The second my door is closed and locked, I turn on the lights and quickly turn to face the mirror.

I hurriedly take off my jacket, my Jacobi jersey, and my long-sleeve shirt before looking down at my arms.

I had hoped I had just imagined it, that Elijah hadn't grabbed me as hard as he did, and there was no way that there were going to be any marks on my skin.

But I was wrong.

Even through the fabric of the jersey that I was wearing and my long-sleeve shirt, his grip made it through to my skin, and now I have two distinct bands on both of my upper arms that will no doubt be bruises in a few hours.

Tears start to run down my face the longer I look at myself in the mirror.

It won't happen again.

This won't happen again.

I'll do everything I can to make sure it doesn't, and if that means not cheering on my best friend, then so be it.

Elijah apologized.

And it won't happen again.

CHAPTER THIRTY

BLAKE

Two months from present day

CHRISTMAS BREAK.

The time during the hockey season players look forward to. Three days of no hockey. No thinking about the next practice, the next game, absolutely nothing about the sport. Three glorious days where the only thing that matters is taking a small break and spending time with friends and family.

I've been looking forward to this break. This season has been kicking my ass physically, mentally, and everything in between. Winning a championship the previous season pushes you to a limit you aren't sure you are able to recover from. So when the three-day break came around, I was hoping I would get at least one full day on the couch just vegetating, before jumping back into the grind of hockey season. Doing absolutely nothing for a full twenty-four hours sounds amazing, but of course, that isn't going to happen.

Because not only is it Christmas, but there is also a damn football game in San Francisco I have to attend. So my day of doing absolutely nothing is now filled with travel and spending time with family.

The second I got the Gold's schedule for the season, I should have thought of an excuse to get out of this game, but of course I didn't.

Now I'm having another California Christmas.

I can't really complain, though. Not only do I get to see my brother play, live and in person, something I don't really get to do all that often, but I also get to see my mom and sister and eat good food. All of that makes up for me not having one day on the couch.

Well, almost makes up for it.

If Sophia was here, I wouldn't even be thinking about vegetating on my couch.

For the first time since we were teenagers, Sophia and I are spending Christmas apart. Ever since that Christmas when we were fifteen, we have done everything to not spend the holiday in different parts of the country. Football games, family dinners, whatever it may be, we have always been together. For the last few years in high school, college, and when we moved to Chicago. It didn't matter what we had going on in our lives, we continued the tradition from when we were kids into adulthood.

But this year, she's back in Illinois, and I'm in California. She's spending the holiday with Elijah and his family, with her parents flying in, and I'm spending it with my family. What kind of fucked-up shit is that?

Her spending a Christmas with her boyfriend shouldn't bother me. I should be happy she is happy and in a serious relationship, where she is introducing her parents to her boyfriend. I should be fucking ecstatic their families are going to come together and probably have a great time. But I am bothered, and I'm not happy about it one bit.

And it has everything to do with her fucking douchebag of a boyfriend.

He seems nice and whatever, but there is something about the guy that rubs me the wrong way. Ever since I met the dude, and he didn't bother to shake my hand, I haven't liked him. I thought maybe that was going to change in the two months since, but my dislike has only gotten stronger.

Granted, I haven't spent a whole lot of time with him, just a few quick meetups at the apartment whenever he is picking up Sophia, but even spending a few minutes with him isn't all that pleasant.

Add on I've barely seen or talked to Sophia these last few weeks, what with her spending almost every single night over at his place, barely coming home, and it makes me dislike him even more. She hasn't even gone to one of my games since October. I was looking forward to spending at least one full day with her, and now I'm not getting that.

Or a chance to give her a Christmas gift. Something I've been planning for weeks.

Just thinking about it is pissing me off.

And apparently it's enough for people to notice because Jainie comes over to me and pinches my cheeks.

"Ah, why do you look all sad, Blakie?" she asks, giving me a cutesy voice that you would give a puppy.

"I'm not sad," I say, swatting her hand away.

"Sure, you aren't." Jainie lets out a snort and gives me an eye roll, before taking a look around the suite we are currently in at the Gold's stadium.

We're currently about twenty minutes away from kickoff. It may be a Christmas Day game, but not only is the suite packed with my brother's friends and family, the whole stadium is packed, not a single empty seat anywhere.

I guess I'm not the only one here today hoping the Gold beat Baltimore today.

"Lennie," Jainie calls out, waving her over from where she is talking to her best friend, Jennifer. Both women look over at us and walk over. "Does he not look sad to you?"

Both Selena and Jennifer look from my sister to me, and within a second, they both look at me like they want to give me their condolences for my puppy dying or something.

Selena cringes a little before she says anything. "He does."

"Yeah, why are you all mopey, little Jacobi? It's Christmas. Why aren't you all happy and cheery like a little elf?" Jen says, using almost the same voice my sister did.

I roll my eyes at all three of them.

"I'm not sad," I say to them, trying to drill it through their heads.

All three women look at me like they don't believe me, and it takes just a few seconds of getting that look from the three of them for me to let out a sigh.

"I'm not sad," I say, telling the truth. "I'm pissed off more than anything else, but not sad."

"Let me guess, girl problems?" Jen asks, a slight smirk on her face, while my sister and Selena look at each other, both of their facial expressions going from teasing to sad.

I guess I'm not the one looking sad now.

Yesterday, I had more than a few drinks flowing through my body as we celebrated Christmas Eve with Selena's family, and the alcohol may have caused my mouth to start talking. I may not have told the two of them and my brother about my feelings toward Sophia, but I did tell them how I hated that it felt like I was losing my best friend. How I hated that I wasn't seeing her as much and that we are solely communicating through text.

They let me talk until I couldn't anymore.

So by me telling them my anger from yesterday is carrying over into today, they understand and are going to be careful with what they say. Jen wasn't there, so she isn't going to be, which I appreciate, but I don't know if I can take it right now.

That doesn't stop me from giving her a small smile. "Something like that."

"She'll come around eventually. Have faith," Jen says, patting me on the shoulder.

Have faith.

I've been having faith since I was fifteen and look where it has gotten me.

"Yeah, I'm not sure that faith is going to help," I say, still with a smile on my face. I'm about to make a joke when my phone goes off.

Without thinking, I pull it out and check the caller ID.

I was expecting a call from Logan, or maybe even Christian to ask me what time I'm flying back to Chicago since he is also in California, but it isn't.

It's Sophia.

For a quick second, I think about ignoring her call, to let her feel a bit of what I'm feeling, but I decide against it.

No matter what, I really want to hear her voice right now.

"Excuse me, ladies," I say to the three women and walk out of the suite.

I have never needed privacy to talk to my best friend. I don't know why I'm seeking it out now.

I watch the phone ring for a few more seconds before I slide the icon over to answer.

"Hey," I say, blocking out all the noise and focusing on Sophia and what she is about to say.

"Hi. Feliz Navidad, Blake." Sophia's voice sounds out, and I can't help but smile.

"Merry Christmas, Soph," I say, hoping that she can hear me smile through the other side.

"Sorry, I didn't call you yesterday. I lost track of time trying to help Elijah's mom with everything for this morning."

"It's okay," I say to her, before something clicks in my brain. "Wait, you didn't celebrate last night? I figured you and your mom would be pulling out all the stops to show Elijah's parents a real Noche Buena."

"Oh, yeah. That was our plan," she says, almost sounding nervous. "But we decided not to do that and just celebrate today. It was just easier that way."

"You guys didn't do anything last night?" I ask, getting curious.

"Not really. My parents stayed at our place, and I had dinner with Elijah and his parents and just watched a movie afterward."

Never in my life have I heard of Sophia and her parents not celebrating Christmas on Christmas Eve. No matter the circumstances. So hearing they didn't celebrate last night isn't sitting right with me.

"That doesn't sound all that fun," I say to her, and it doesn't.

I think back to all the Christmas Eves we have spent together, and I think we've only watched a movie once, and that was because Sophia was sick and wasn't up to doing all the fun things we usually do.

"It wasn't, but it was what was easier for everyone," she says.

"What the fuck does that even mean?" I ask, the question slipping out from my mouth. I didn't mean to say it out loud, but I guess just like yesterday, I can't control what I say.

"Nothing, forget I even said anything. How was your night? And this morning? Did your mom like the coat you got her?"

As much as I want to tell her I don't want to forget about her not celebrating Christmas the way that she has done all of her life, I answer her questions.

"Last night was good," I start, letting out a sigh, trying to control my anger as best that I can. "Selena's parents and sisters came up, and we all celebrated at their house and opened gifts. And yeah, my mom loved the coat. She is wearing it now."

"That's good. And are you guys at the stadium already?" she asks, and I can hear longing in her voice, like she wants to be here, too, but for now her questions will do.

"Yeah, we got here a little bit ago," I say, trying to match her energy, but I know I'm not succeeding.

"Tell Hunter I cheered him on from here. Elijah and his dad aren't big football fans, so I won't get a chance to watch it."

She is changing everything about herself for this asshole and his family, isn't she?

"Go back to the apartment and watch it with your dad," I suggest because just like she never misses watching one of my games, she never misses one of my brother's either. At least she never used to. Now that she's with Elijah, things are changing.

"Oh, my parents are going back home in a little bit," she throws out.

Why the fuck would they do that? That sure as hell doesn't sound like them.

The question is on the tip of my tongue, but I don't speak it.

This conversation is drawing up so many red flags, it's pissing me off more than what I already was.

"Right," I say, trying to make sense of everything.

"I have to go. I just wanted to give you a quick call to say merry Christmas before the game started. Have fun, yeah? And cheer on Hunter for me?" she says, her voice shaking just a tiny bit.

If it was any other time, and I was at a game, and she wasn't, she would have demanded that I switch her over to FaceTime so that she could experience every single second of the game, too. Even if it was through a screen. I guess times change.

"Yeah, I will," I say, sounding defeated and feeling like not only did I let the girl of my dreams slip through my fingers, but feeling as if I'm losing my best friend. "Thanks for calling, Soph."

"Of course. It wouldn't be Christmas without at least talking to you," she says after a few seconds of silence. Is it just me, or does she sound sad?

"Right," I say, because I can't come up with anything else.

"I have to go," she says again, this time in a lot more of a hurry. "Merry Christmas, Blakie."

"Merry Christmas, Soph," I say into the phone, and not even a second later, the call ends and I'm left feeling all types of emotions.

The call and hearing her voice were supposed to help me get over my mood and let me start enjoying myself, but instead, my mood just got worse.

As I pocket my phone, my knuckles grace the small cardboard box that I've been carrying around since yesterday in hopes that my best friend would show up out of nowhere, and I'd be able to give it to her.

Taking the box out, I look down at it for a second before opening it.

Inside, are two small pictures of the two of us, cut up into little circles so they would fit perfectly into the locket I gave her all those years ago.

The pictures have never been changed, so I thought this would be the year she could do that.

I look down at the two little pictures, seeing us wearing smiles and embracing each other like we never wanted to let go and feel a sharp pang in my chest.

This is it. My worst nightmares are finally coming true.

For years, I was afraid of telling Sophia of how I felt about her because I didn't want to lose her. Yet, here I am, not having said a single word to her about my feelings, and it feels like I've lost her anyway.

I'm losing my best friend.

And I fucking hate it.

CHAPTER THIRTY-ONE

SOPHIA

A TEAR ROLLS down my face as I look at the screen of my phone go black after ending the call with Blake a lot faster than I wanted to.

For a while now, I've been feeling like a part of me has been missing. Like a giant hole has opened up in the ground and sucked me in, and I lost everything that made me *me,* and I've been trying to find myself ever since. That feeling intensified yesterday morning, and it went from something being missing to something being ripped away from me.

And that feeling intensified as I talked to Blake.

Especially with all the lies I told him.

A few weeks ago, Elijah told me what we were doing for Christmas. Told, not asked.

It didn't matter that I already had plans to fly to San Francisco with Blake and his family, to spend Christmas with them and attend Hunter's game. It didn't matter that my parents already had plans to go visit my grandparents in Boston and had asked me to go with them before flying to California. He didn't care. Elijah just made plans for the both of us and expected me to go along with them.

I wasn't going to at first, but then I thought about it.

I thought about what would happen if I made him angry again. For the last two months, I've been doing everything he has wanted, everything that he has asked of me, all so he won't get mad and do to me what he did back in October.

So far, it has worked. He hasn't put his hands on me again. Not like he did that night.

Part of me thinks it's because he really meant his apology and meant it when he said it was never going to happen again. The other part of me is saying it's because of how I've been acting around him, and for all I know, one wrong move and his apology and his promise goes in the trash.

Everything in me wants it to be the former, but deep down, I know what the truth is, even if I can't admit it to myself.

So I said yes to spending the holidays with his parents, while Blake went to California with his family, and my parents went to Boston. I lied to Blake about my parents being here, and I told my parents I was having the time of my life. When in reality, this is probably one of the worst Christmases I have ever had.

Elijah's parents are amazing and are really trying to include me in things as best as they can. Trying to have conversations with me. Trying to get to know me, asking me questions about my life and the type of Christmases I had growing up. I try to answer each and every one of their questions with a smile and as enthusiastically as I can, but it's their son who is making me overthink what I say and making me wish I hadn't come.

He's fine when I just talk about myself or my parents, but every time I mention Blake and his family, hockey or blood, something shifts in Elijah. Whether it be in his eyes or his body posture or how his jaw is set, something changes, and I take notice right away.

It makes me think he is going to blow up and shove me

against the wall again for even mentioning my best friend, but he hasn't done anything. He just stays quiet for a while, and then an hour or so later, he goes back to being his normal self. That is until the topic comes up again.

This has been going on for three days, and I've been on high alert since. I don't know how much more of this I can take.

Of this holiday, and of how uneasy I feel in this relationship. I want to feel like me again, and I don't think continuing in this relationship with Elijah will let that happen anytime soon. The call with Blake is proof of that. I have never lied to him like that, and I don't want to do it ever again.

Footsteps sound out in the hallway, and I quickly pocket my phone, wiping at my face to hide any evidence I've been crying.

I snuck away while Elijah and his dad were watching the basketball game to call Blake. No doubt in my mind, Elijah has finally noticed and has come looking for me.

I did nothing wrong by calling someone who has been in my life since I was five years old, but he probably won't see it that way.

A part of me hopes the footsteps belong to his mom or even his dad, but when the bedroom door opens, and Elijah appears, that hope disappears.

"Hey, what are you doing up here?" he asks, coming into the room and closing the door behind him.

I give him a smile, trying to hide all the turmoil I'm feeling. "I was just talking to my mom," I lie.

"Didn't you talk to your mom earlier?" he asks, crossing his arms, looking at me like he doesn't believe me.

"I can talk to my mom more than once in a day," I say, my defenses going up.

Elijah nods, closing the distance between us. "You could have talked to your mom downstairs. You didn't have to come up here and talk to her in secret."

"I didn't want to disrupt you and your dad watching the game. Besides, it shouldn't matter where I talk to her. If I wanted to talk to her up here, then I'm allowed to do that."

"It does matter. Especially if you weren't really talking to her and instead were talking to someone else," he spits out, coming even closer to me. The way he is approaching has me taking a step back.

Like Blake. I shouldn't have lied to Elijah.

"Who else would I be talking to?" I ask, my voice shaking in the process.

"Maybe Blake?" He snarls as if even the mention of Blake disgusts him.

Why does he hate him so much? What is it about my relationship with Blake he can't stand?

I don't know, but I can't take it anymore.

Letting out a sigh, I tell Elijah what he already suspects. "I was talking to him," I admit. "I'm sorry I lied. I know how you feel about him, so I just thought it was best I didn't tell you. I just wanted to wish him a merry Christmas. That's all."

I stand there wringing my fingers together, watching Elijah's face. It's completely unreadable, and it scares me more than it should.

Elijah just stands there, looking at me, his stance rigid. For a second, I think he is just going to stand there and not say anything or even walk out of the room.

But of course, I'm wrong.

My mouth opens to say his name, to ask him what is going through his mind, when his hand comes up, and he wraps it around my neck, while he slams me against the dresser.

"Is this what it has come to? You lying to me? All because you can't go two fucking days without talking to that fucking bastard? What the fuck will my parents think when they see my girlfriend is a two-timing bitch who had to talk to another man while in their house?" he snarls in my face, the grip on my neck growing tighter, almost closing off my air supply completely.

"I'm not," I gasp for air to get the words out. "I'm not cheating on you. I was just talking to my friend." I say, defending myself, tears burning my eyes.

"The fuck you were. I see the way he looks at you and the way you look at him. You want him, just as much as he wants you, but guess what? He can't fucking have you because you're mine, and he would have to kill me before he can get his hands on you."

"Elijah, I can't—" I start to say, as I claw at his hand to let me go, but he tightens his hold on me even more, taking away my ability to breathe.

"You can't what? You can't breathe? Good, maybe now you are able to feel the pain that I go through when you mention another man's name. I already told you once, Sophia. The only man's name that should be coming out of your mouth is mine. Not only that, but I'm also the only one you should be thinking about. Not fucking Blake Jacobi."

His face is mere inches from mine, but I can't even concentrate on the closeness. All I can see is the black spots that are infiltrating my vision from the lack of oxygen.

Needing air, I dig my nails into his skin and try my hardest to pull him off me.

He gets the picture, because he loosens his grip just a bit, just enough to let some air into my lungs.

"Lie to me again, Sophia, and see what happens," he threatens, his hand falling completely from my neck as he steps back.

I suck in as much air as I can, as I crumple to my knees while I try to keep my sobs from sounding out and alerting his parents to something being wrong.

"Compose yourself and come back downstairs. Change your shirt while you're at it. I don't need my parents asking questions as to where you were or why your neck is red," he says, as he walks over to the bedroom door.

I watch him the whole time. My eyes may be filled with tears, but I watch him as he wraps the hand that was just around my neck, around the knob.

"Oh, and start thinking about ending your friendship with Jacobi. I don't know how much more of this shit I can take," he says, right before he rips the door open and walks out like we just had a normal conversation, and I'm not left on the floor gasping for air.

He broke his promise.

He said that he was never going to let it happen again, and yet, it did. And this time, he didn't apologize for it. He just walked away like it was nothing.

Elijah hurt me again.

I need to walk away. I need to leave him because next time could be worse.

I need to break this off before there is a next time. I need a plan because no way is he going to let me go easily.

CHAPTER THIRTY-TWO

BLAKE

A week before present day

"YOU KNOW, at first I was a little peeved Liam was the only one of us who was going to go to the all-star game, but seeing all the things that he has to do while he's there, it makes me glad I wasn't picked," I say to guys as I scroll through the schedule that was sent to Liam for all-star weekend.

Christian, Logan, and I are all sitting around Liam's kitchen counter after eating a meal he had promised us. Well, not really promised, more like he was forced to cook for us.

A few weeks ago, he and Christian made a bet on a Gold's game, and the loser was set to cook the winner a three-course meal. And because Logan and I are always down for a home-cooked meal, especially one that isn't coming from our own kitchens, we added ourselves to the wager.

I'm not usually one to place bets when it comes to my brother and his team, but I'm all for others doing it and it bene-fiting me.

I'm not going to lie, the chicken he cooked was fucking amazing, and it had three grown men fighting for more. I'm a little bit disappointed he didn't poison us. Maybe he would have if Chloe and Eliana weren't at the table.

"Sounds like a fucking nightmare," Logan grumbles next to me as he takes the tablet from me and looks over the schedule himself. "Cameras everywhere, everything you do for people to see."

"I'd be all for it if the dodgeball game included players and coaches and not just mascots. There are a few people I wouldn't mind nailing with a rubber ball," Christian says, from where he sits at the counter.

"Bradford being at the top of that list," I respond, which earns me a nod from my teammate.

"Oh, how I want to punch that fucker in the face every time he walks into to the locker room," he says, his face scrunching up in disgust.

"We can't afford you being suspended again." Liam throws out, which causes Christian to shake his head.

Kalen Bradford is a player the Knights acquired back in September. He's an okay player, but the dude is a douchebag and a half who thinks the world revolves around him. He was causing trouble for the team before he was even signed, what with him blackmailing Eliana and all that. Things got heated with Christian and Bradford at the start of the season, which ended in a fight between the two of them and Logan. All three of them got suspended for two games and were fined. Because Eliana is not only Christian's girlfriend, but also Coach's daughter, nobody really likes the guy. Even more so when he refuses to get traded to another team.

Now, we just tolerate him on the ice, but off it, we can give two shits about him.

"Or thrown in jail," Eliana says, as she comes up behind her boyfriend and wraps her arms around him.

"If I get to beat the shit out of Bradford one more time, I will gladly take the suspension and one night in a jail cell." Christian leans over and places a kiss against her temple.

"Of course, you would." Eliana answers, rolling her eyes at him.

The conversation moves back to the all-star game, and when Chloe comes out with a fussy Emma in her arms, the conversation turns to us each taking a shot at soothing her when she starts crying and screaming at the top of her lungs.

It turns out that Logan is a damn baby whisperer because the second the little girl is in his arms, she calms down, and the tears stop completely. Emma even smiles up at the broody asshole who looks like he's never handled a kid in his life and is about to burst into tears himself.

"Damn, you want to move in?" Liam throws out as he looks at our teammate with his little girl.

"No," Logan says, his eyes going wide as if he thinks that Liam is actually being serious.

For the next few minutes, Christian, Liam, and I all throw jabs at Logan about how he can be scary as shit on the ice, but the second he has a baby in his arms, he becomes a huge-ass teddy bear. Well, at least with Emma. Chloe even takes a picture of the two of them and sends it to him.

No doubt in my mind, that little girl is going to have him wrapped around her little finger in no time. She might even make him smile every once in a while.

After being in Logan's arms for about fifteen minutes, Emma ends up falling asleep. Which we all take as a cue to head out, not only to let the baby sleep but also to let her parents rest a little bit.

We all say goodbye and head out.

As we make our way down to street level, Christian suggests we go grab a drink before heading to our respective places, but as I'm about to accept his offer, my phone goes off with a text message notification, distracting me.

As Logan, Christian, and Eliana talk about where to go, I pull out my phone and check my messages.

SOPHIA

What time are you going to be home?

I LOOK at her message for a quick second before I type out a reply.

BLAKE

I'm just leaving Liam's and was thinking about going to get a drink with Chris and Logan. So later?

SOPHIA

Oh, okay.

WHAT DOES SHE MEAN BY, "oh, okay?" And why is she asking me what time I'm going to be home?

If I thought I barely saw Sophia before Christmas, that was nothing compared to how things are now. Since Christmas Day, she hasn't spent more than two hours at our place, at least not with me there. It's as if she is avoiding me. She's not there when I leave, and she's not there when I come back. And don't even get me started on my text messages and phone calls to her. I don't hear from her for days.

So her asking me when I'm going to be home is raising all types of flags I'm not sure that I want to ignore.

ME

I'll be home in twenty minutes.

I RESPOND, and she quickly sends a heart emoji that just confuses me even more.

"I'll take a raincheck on the drink," I say to my friends, pocketing my phone.

"Why? What's up?" Christian asks, his eyebrows bunching up in the process.

"I don't know. Soph just texted asking what time I was going to be home. So I want to check out what it's about," I tell him.

Out of all of my friends, family, and teammates, Christian is probably the only one who knows a bit more than others. Not because I've told him anything, but because he has put the context clues together. I might have also told him a time or two how much I hate Sophia's boyfriend.

"Alright. We'll text you where we end up, just in case you feel like joining us later," he tells me, and the others nod in agreement.

With a quick goodbye, I head to the nearest train station and make my way over to my apartment.

The whole way home, I can't stop thinking about what could be going on with Sophia. Did she and the douchebag have a fight? Did they break up? So many scenarios move through my head, but not a single one is what I expect when I walk into the apartment.

All the lights are turned off, expect the lamps on the end tables next to the couch. Apart from the lamps, the living room is being lit up by the TV above our mantel. I look over at the kitchen counter and see it overflowing with pizza, candy, popcorn, and beer. And as I walk deeper into the living room, I see the mountains of pillows and blankets in between the couches.

What did I just walk into?

This better not be a romantic night between Elijah and Sophia because if it is, I might actually strangle the bastard.

Sophia is nowhere in sight, so I call out for her.

"Sophie!" I yell out, in the direction of her bedroom. One she hasn't slept in in weeks.

Right away, she comes running out. "Hi," she says, giving me a bright smile. One that I have missed seeing so damn much. "I didn't hear you come in."

"Hi," I say back, returning her smile. "What's going on?" I ask, nodding toward the makeshift fort that is missing a roof and walls.

"I thought it would be fun to have a movie night. You know just the two of us. It feels like we haven't done that in a while," she says, her voice shaking a bit, like she is scared I'm going to turn her down.

I'm not because she's right. We haven't done it in a while. Maybe not since the summer. Time got away from us, what with hockey and her finishing up her nursing degree. Then Elijah came into the picture, and that put a bigger dent into our hanging out.

"It's definitely been a while," I say, feeling excited for the first time in weeks.

"So, what do you say? You, me, a bunch of junk food, a pillow fort, and a *Fast and The Furious* marathon?" she asks, and for the first time in what feels like forever, I see a brightness in her eyes I haven't seen in a long time. One that squeezes at my heart every single time it's directed at me.

Sophia looks absolutely breathtaking, and she doesn't even know it.

Instead of telling her what is going through my brain, I give her a bright smile and an enthusiastic nod.

"Let's do it."

"I MAY BE the only one who likes the third movie," Soph lets out about ten minutes into the third movie of the night.

We've been at it for hours, with no end in sight, and I fucking love it.

Not only am I spending time with my best friend, but I'm getting to listen to her laugh and talk absolute nonsense all while feeling her close by. I knew I missed her, missed us, but I didn't know just how much until I was rewarded with this little gift.

"I think you might be the only one who likes any of these movies. They are fucking horrible," I say to her, placing a hand behind my head.

My eyes are on the screen, so I completely miss Sophia grabbing a pillow and slamming it against my face for my comment.

"Take that back," she tells me, slamming the pillow against my face again. "These movies are a masterpiece."

I start to laugh as I grab a pillow of my own and swing it her way. "*Inception* is a masterpiece. These are wannabe car movies with explosions and people dying."

She lets out a gasp as if I insulted her. "I cannot believe you said that. Now you really need to take it back."

"Not a chance," I say, a smirk starting to spread across my face.

Sophia sits up, almost towering over me. "Take. It. Back," she says, a smirk of her own starting to form.

I sit up, bringing my face mere inches from hers. "Never."

We have a stare down for about ten seconds before a pillow hits the side of my head, and there is not a second of hesitation on my part before I swing my pillow and get her back.

Sophia's sweet laughter, mixed together with mine, fills the room, and it's not only music to my ears, but also to my heart. I've been needing this. I've been needing a night with her, where it's just the two of us, laughing our asses off, acting like we did when we were kids.

We have had countless pillow fights throughout the years, but this one will definitely go to the very top as one of my favorites.

We continue to pound at each other with the pillows, not getting the least bit tired. Soon the pounding goes to trying to escape and each of us pulling the other back.

Somehow, someway, I end up on top of her, while she lays under me looking like an angel sent down for me and only me.

The pillow fight is completely forgotten, and all there is me and Sophia, staring at each other's faces, and our smiles not going anywhere.

"I've missed you," I say to her, the words escaping me with no regard for what my brain wants.

Sophia's smile dwindles a bit, becoming faint, as she reaches up and takes one of my curls between her fingers.

"I've missed you, too," she says, almost in a whisper.

"Then come back to me, Soph. Come back to me. I want you back. I want my best friend back," I say, the words almost escaping me like a plea.

I feel Sophia shift under me a bit, and then her hand is

sliding into my hair, grabbing onto me like I'm her saving grace, but that isn't what has my attention.

What has my attention is how her other hand comes up and cradles my cheek while her eyes fill with tears.

"I want to," she starts, her voice shaking in the process. "I want to come back."

A tear escapes from the corner of her eye, and I'm quick to wipe it away with my thumb.

"Then do it. Come back to me, and our nights will be just like this one. Filled with laughter and memories we will remember forever. You just need to come back."

"It's not that easy," she says, more tears making their way out.

"Why not?" I ask, caressing her cheek just like she is caressing mine.

"I have to do something first, but after I do that, I will come back to you. I will come back to you and give you everything I am. I promise you. I just need time."

I take a second to look into her eyes and to comprehend her words. I go through everything she just said at least three times, but I still don't understand it.

As much as I don't want to, I pull away from her and sit with my back to the couch and watch her as her eyes follow each one of my movements.

"What do you have to do?" I ask, hoping it's easy, and it's something that I can help her with. Because I meant everything I told her. I want my best friend back. But not just my best friend, I want her.

I want her laughing beside me as we create memories, and maybe then I will have the courage to tell her she owns every inch and ounce of my heart. Maybe then, even if it takes time, I will be able to make her mine for good. If she will let me.

She crawls over to me, taking my face in her hands so I'm

able to look straight into her eyes and see the conviction and the strength that is radiating off her.

"I'm going to break up with Elijah."

It takes me a second to fully understand what she is saying.

"You are?" I ask, just to make sure.

She gives me a nod. "Yes. I need to."

"What do you mean by that? Why do you 'need to?'" I ask, my hands itching to reach for her and bring her closer to me. Bring her closer to me and kiss her like I've been dying to do since last June when I last got a taste of her.

More tears form in her eyes, but they don't escape. "I just do."

As she says the words, I can't help but think that she is doing it just because I'm telling her I want her back. That she feels like she has to do it because I want her to. I want her to be happy, and if he makes her happy then we will be able to move past whatever is going on between us and get her that happiness.

"Soph," I say, bringing my hands up and placing them over hers. "Don't do it for me. Don't break up with him because I told you to come back to me. Don't let me sway your decision."

"I'm not." She pauses, taking a deep breath before continuing again. "I'm doing it for me. I'm breaking up with Elijah for me because I want to do it and because I want to live a life where he's not in it. I don't love him. I never did, and I never will."

CHAPTER THIRTY-THREE

SOPHIA

3 days before present day

IT SHOULD HAVE NEVER GOTTEN this bad.

At the very first sign, I should have walked away and never looked back. But I lived with the thought that it was going to be a one-time thing. That he had apologized and that he meant it, and it was never going to happen again.

But it did happen again, and again, and again, even when I promised myself that I was going to leave before it got worse. Even if I promised myself that I was going to break it off before there was a next time.

I broke the promises I made to myself. I didn't follow through with my word. I stayed because I kept telling myself it was going to get better, that things were going to change. But things didn't get better, and things didn't change. If anything, everything got worse.

Ever since Christmas, it's as if my life has revolved around two things, and those are being a nursing student and Elijah. Nothing else. I go from the hospital to classes to Elijah's apartment, and that's it. A few visits to my own home have been sprinkled in here and there, but only when Blake is at practice or at an away game, and even then, Elijah is always with me.

No matter what I do outside of work, Elijah is always with me, dictating the things that I do, the things that I wear, the things that I say to people. No matter who I talk to, whether it be my parents or even Chloe and Eliana, I have to be careful with what I say. If I even mention Blake in some way, or even one of his siblings or Selena, he gets angry with me, and I can never calm him down.

Since we got back from his parents, he has hurt me three more times. Three more times that shouldn't have happened if I had left at the very beginning.

Two were shoves, against the refrigerator and the bathroom door. The last one though, the last one was the turning point, and when I finally told myself it was time to walk away. The last one was a slap across the face. He had shoved me against things and wrapped his hand around my neck, but never actually hit me in any way. The second he did, all because I had been talking to my dad about us going to a game together, I made up my mind.

I wasn't going to take it anymore.

I wasn't going to lose myself any more than I already have because my boyfriend has an issue with who I'm friends with. I've explained to him more times than I can count that nothing is going on with me and Blake. I've told him I'm fully in this with him and that Blake wouldn't get in the middle of it, no matter how I might feel about him now or felt about him in the past. But no matter what I said, what I did, Elijah wouldn't listen, or even believe me.

He would just get angry and take it out on me, and I can't take it anymore.

So, I started to put a plan in place to walk away. I thought about just telling Elijah, of telling him that we were done and to never come near me again, but the fear of what he would do kept me from doing that. If he got angry with a simple phone call, what would he do if I ended it between us?

I didn't want to find out.

So, I decided that no matter what I did, I was going to do it with caution. Caution also meant I had to take my time.

I didn't want to, but it was necessary.

For weeks, since the hospital and school were the only places that Elijah wouldn't go with me, I would take some of the stuff I had taken to his place with me. Clothes, toiletries, anything that could possibly fit in my bag, I would take it and sneak it home whenever I got the chance.

Sneaking away to go home shouldn't be necessary. I should be free to go there whenever I want without any fear, but unfortunately, that isn't the case.

I didn't realize just how much stuff I had over at Elijah's until I was trying to get everything out.

For a solid week, I stressed about how I was going to get everything out.

Thankfully, it seemed like a higher power was looking after me because a few days later, Elijah had to go to Springfield for two days for a work conference. One I couldn't go to. When he told me that, every single cell in my body jumped up in excitement.

The second he left for the conference, I started packing up all the things that didn't fit in my work bag and started moving them home. Thankfully, Blake was gone on a stretch of away games, so he wasn't home to ask any questions.

But I knew I owed him an explanation. A big one.

From the second I told myself that I wasn't going to do anything to anger Elijah, my relationship with Blake started to suffer.

I was miserable without my best friend and not seeing him,

or even talking to him in the way that I wanted to, killed me so much.

So when Elijah left, I thought it would be the perfect time to start repairing the relationship I had started to destroy.

Seeing the smile on Blake's face when he walked into the apartment and saw what I had planned was everything I needed at that moment. It broke my heart that I couldn't even remember when the last time he had looked at me like that was. My heart broke even more when he told me to come back to him.

When I heard those words coming out of his lips, I wanted to scream out how much I loved him. I wanted to tell him I will always come back to him because I was his, and he owned every single part of me. He always has, and he always will, no matter if he didn't feel the same way.

But in that moment, as I looked into his eyes, and I held his face close to mine, I realized something. Elijah was right about something. Blake does look at me a certain way.

Blake looks at me like he loves me in the same way that I love him. I don't know when he started looking at me like that, but I hope it never goes away.

The second I saw that look, I vowed to myself that I would follow through with my plan and end things with Elijah once and for all so I can come back to Blake. Maybe then we can give this love between us a real shot.

I may have broken the promise to myself, but I won't break any promise I made to him. I will come back to him. No matter what.

Almost everything I had at Elijah's is back home. There's nothing left for me to take back, and if there is, he can fucking keep it. I don't want it.

I'm close to the end. I can almost see the light.

As soon as Elijah came home, I was going to do it. I was going to leave and never look back.

But when he walked through the door, all of that went out the window.

I'm sitting on the couch as he walks into his apartment, his weekend bag in his hand and a smile on his face.

Lately, he has been wearing a stoic expression, not a single smile in sight. Seeing him sporting one now has all the hairs on the back of my neck standing up.

"How was your trip?" I ask, trying to act as calm and collected as I can.

"It was fine," he says, putting his duffel down and coming over to me and placing a kiss against my lips.

I want to pull away as his lips meet mine, but I don't.

"That's good," I say, when I pull away from him, giving him the best smile I can. "I was wonder—" I start to say but he cuts me off.

"Let's take a trip," he says out of nowhere.

"What?" I ask, looking over at him with what I'm sure is a confused expression.

He wants to take a trip? I'm here trying to break up with him, and he announces that he wants to take a trip?

"Let's take a trip," he says again, as if his words make perfect sense. "Let's go somewhere, you and me. Let's take the next few days off and go somewhere." Elijah gives me the smile I first fell for and starts leaning in, his mouth barely brushing against the skin on my neck.

A shiver runs through my body, but it's not a good shiver like he thinks it is.

"I-I don't think that would be a good idea," I stutter out, trying my hardest to keep my composure and do what has to be done because if I don't, he is going to get his way, and I will forever be stuck in this endless cycle.

"It's a great idea," he says, his lips finally meeting my skin, and all I want to do is jerk away from him, but it feels as if I'm paralyzed.

My head is swimming with thoughts of what he could do if I tell him no.

"Wh-where would we g-go?" I ask, trying to keep the shakiness in my voice at bay but failing, and Elijah is taking notice. I can see it in his face when he pulls away from me, but he doesn't call me out on it.

"Anywhere you want to go," he says, his voice not matching the hardness of his face again.

"Anywhere I want to go," I repeat with so much fear running through me.

He's giving me the option, but the only place I want to go is anywhere he isn't.

"Yeah, anywhere," he says, taking my hand in his and holding it in a tight grip. "We haven't done a trip just the two of us. Let's go somewhere for a few days and clear our heads and come back better than ever."

His grip tightens even more, all the while he gives me a knowing look. One that tells me he knows what I was about to say, and there is no way in hell he is letting me go that easily.

He must have noticed. He must have noticed that most of my stuff isn't here anymore and put it together that I want to leave. He must think going on a trip is going to help things, but that thought couldn't be further from the truth.

"I have work," I say, trying to find any excuse to get out of this other than telling him I don't want to go anywhere with him.

Even when he has hurt me, I can't find it in me to hurt him back.

"Screw work," he says, almost forcefully. Like the decision has already been made, and I have no say in it. "Let's just go,

Sophia. You and me. I'll make it the best trip ever. Just pick the place."

Pick the place.

Anywhere I want to go, he will take me.

If I do this, if I go on this trip with him, that will be it. One trip, and as soon as we are back home, it's done between. I can give him this.

I can.

But not without a few caveats. If I go, it will have to be to a place where I can run if things get bad. It has to be to a place where I know I will have people there to take care of me if anything happens. People who I can run to and will do everything in their power to keep me safe.

There are few places that have that, but one of them he won't think about too much if I pick it.

I give Elijah a nod. "Okay, let's go somewhere then."

He gives me a smile that says that he has won. Little does he know it's actually the opposite.

"Where would you like to go?" The question rolls off his tongue.

"Let's go to San Francisco. It's quick, and close to the coast."

He nods like he thinks my idea is perfect. "San Francisco it is."

WITHIN MINUTES of me saying San Francisco, Elijah booked us a flight for that same night and a hotel.

I couldn't believe I was doing this. I was supposed to break up with the guy, but instead I'm heading across the country with him on a pointless trip.

As he packed a bag, I thought about why he suggested a trip so out of the blue. Apart from him realizing what I was doing and trying to see if he can fix it, he had to have another reason.

It's not until I get a text notification from Chloe asking if I can stop by the apartment while they are in Arizona for the all-star break to check on her one plant does it click.

It's the NHL bye-week. The Knights don't have any practices or games to keep them from living normal lives for a few days.

Being an avid hockey fan, Elijah knows this and probably thinks since Blake is essentially off this week, I will seek him out.

Elijah is taking me on this trip to keep me away from Blake. At least that's what I think. And I sure as hell wouldn't put it past him to do just that.

"Where's your bag?" Elijah asks as he steps back into the living room, his duffel repacked and ready to go.

"What?" I ask, my head spinning in all different directions.

"Your bag. Where is it?" he asks, a bite to his voice.

"Oh, um." Think, Sophia. Think of a reason as to why none of your clothes are here. "I didn't like anything I have here, and I was wondering if we could stop by my place on the way to the airport. It would only take a second."

"Sophia." Elijah's jaw starts to tic and right away, I think he is going to get angry and throw something.

"In and out, I promise. I want to look pretty for you in San Francisco," I tell him, the words making me want to vomit. "Please."

"Fine, let's go," he says, sounding a little annoyed.

I don't care if he's annoyed. I'm just glad I at least get to go home for a few minutes.

Hopefully Blake is there, and I can tell him where I will be. I can text him, but I know the second that we get in the car,

Elijah is going to be looking over my shoulder the whole time, checking to see who I'm texting or getting mad if I don't give him my full attention.

Going to the apartment is what is going to work best.

After grabbing our essentials that are needed to fly and Elijah's duffel, we start making our way out of the apartment and get into the rideshare waiting for us outside.

The whole ride to the apartment is tense, and it gets even more tense when we get there, and I tell Elijah to wait for me in the car.

"You can't be serious," he throws out, catching the door before it slams shut behind me.

"It will only take a minute, I swear," I say, not looking back as I run into the building.

The whole elevator ride up to our floor, I'm a ball of nerves, hoping that Blake is home and not with the guys or worse yet, somewhere else, like Montana or something.

The dark apartment doesn't give me anything. It's late, almost ten at night, and even knowing that, it doesn't stop me from being loud as I open the door and running straight to Blake's room.

"Blake! Please tell me you're home," I yell out once in the hallway.

Not even a second later, I hear his feet hit the floor, and it's not long after that his bedroom door opens up.

There he is standing in the doorway, only wearing basketball shorts and no shirt.

I see a questioning look on his face, but I ignore it.

Without any hesitation, I walk straight into his arms, trying my hardest not to lose it as I press myself onto his bare chest.

"What's going on?" he asks, holding me tighter to his body.

If it were up to me, I would tell him to hold me and never let me go, but I have something to do before I'm able to do that.

I have to leave Elijah before I can give anything with Blake a real shot. Because that's what I want. I want Blake, and I don't care if I lose him in the long run, or he doesn't return my feelings. Once this is all done and over with, I'm going to tell him how I really feel. I owe myself that much.

"Soph, you're scaring me here. What's going on?" Blake says, pressing his face into my hair.

God, I had no idea how much I've missed him until this very moment.

Unwillingly, I pull myself away from him, and I try to compose myself as best as I can and try not to break down.

"Nothing," I say, trying to give him a smile. "Well, not nothing," I say, turning toward my room. Thankfully, Blake follows. "I came to pack a bag and to tell you that I'm going to go to San Francisco with Elijah for a few days."

"Okay?" he says as I grab the luggage I stowed in my closet a few days ago.

I hurriedly pack clothes into the luggage, not even looking at what I'm grabbing. "It will only be for a few days, but I wanted to tell you just in case anything happened."

"In case anything happened? What the fuck does that even mean?" he asks, standing by the door, watching as I move through the room erratically.

"Nothing," I say, fishing out a pair of shoes from under my bed and stuffing it into the luggage before zipping it up.

"Sophia," Blake says with desperation sounding in his voice. It hurts me to hear him like this. It hurts me enough to slow down and look over at the man I've known my whole life. The man who has been my everything since I was five years old. My protector, my friend, the love of my life.

I forget about packing and go over to him. When I reach him, I let my right hand reach up and slowly caress his cheek.

"I promised you that I was going to come back to you. That's what I'm doing. I'm coming back. I just need to go to San Francisco first before I can do that, and as soon as I get back, I will explain everything to you. I promise. I'll make everything better between us. I promise that, too." The whole time I speak the words, all I can do is hope I don't break a single one of these promises, because Blake deserves so much better than that.

"Soph," Blake starts, worry coating every single inch of his expression, and all I want to do is take it away.

So, I do.

Getting onto my tiptoes, I give myself as much height as I can to reach up and place my lips against his.

For months, I've thought about his lips against mine. Of how they felt on mine the last time, and how I wanted to drown in that feeling a million times over. For a few short seconds, I do. For a few seconds, I drown in everything that Blake is and everything we could be when all of this is over.

I have to be strong and walk away from Elijah. For me. For him. For the future we could possibly have together.

His hands land against my body and pull me closer to him, taking all the worries flowing through me away.

As much as I don't want to break this moment, I have to. I have a job to do, and as soon as it's done, I'm coming back to him.

"I have to go," I say, pulling away from him, but just enough to lean my forehead against his.

"Don't."

"I don't want to, trust me, but I have to. We'll talk when I get back, okay? The second I step off that plane, I'm yours." I mean that in every single way, but I don't tell him that.

"Promise?"

"I promise," I say, placing another kiss against his lips but just a chaste one.

When I pull back, I give him a smile before turning and grabbing my luggage.

Blake follows me as I walk to the door, neither one of us saying anything besides bye and see you later as I walk out.

A few days.

That's all I need.

A few days, and I will be in Blake's arms where I hope to stay forever.

A few days, and I will be out of this nightmare and moving on with the man that I should have told I loved a long time ago.

Just a few more days. I can do this.

CHAPTER THIRTY-FOUR

BLAKE

IT TAKES ME THIRTY SECONDS.

From the second Sophia leaves our apartment, it took me thirty seconds to make sense of everything that she said and make a spur of the moment decision. Something that I hope I don't regret in the long run or have it be something that Sophia hates me over.

If she's going to fucking San Francisco, so am I.

There is no hesitation running through my body as I head back into my room and start packing a bag so that I can head to the airport and catch the first flight out to California I can. I'll fly to Sacramento and drive to San Francisco if that's what I need to do. I just need to be in the same state as her.

In case anything happened.

Those four words don't sit right with me. I fucking hate them.

What could happen?

All I could picture in my head is fucking Elijah putting his hands on Sophia, and I see red. So much fucking red.

Fuck.

He doesn't hurt her, does he?

I try to think of the few times I've been around them and the times that she has come home after spending time with him. Nothing stands out. Nothing is yelling out red flag to me.

If that was something she is going through, she would tell me. Right? Sophia would come to me if she didn't feel safe in a relationship, right?

Everything in me is saying that she would, that she would come to me right away if that were the case, but things have changed these last few months. We don't see each other all that often. Up until three days ago, we hadn't had a deep conversation in weeks. A lot of shit could have gone down in her life she hasn't told me. There have definitely been things that have happened to me that she doesn't know about. She could be keeping so many things from me, and this could be one of them.

You can't go there. You don't know if that is something she is going through.

Right. I don't really know and coming up with scenarios in my head isn't going to help anything.

Trying to put that thought out of my mind, I pack a bag as if I am going to an away game and only need the essentials. But in this case, the essentials don't even matter. I just need to go and make sure that if anything does happen, I'm there for Sophia in whatever way she needs me.

The second my bag is squared away, I start looking for a flight.

Which just becomes a frustrating task when the only flight I'm able to find a seat on is first thing in the morning, but I don't hesitate in buying it.

As soon as I buy the plane ticket, I do the only thing I can think of. Call my brother.

Three rings, and he answers.

Before he can even say anything, I speak.

"I need a place to stay. Think I can use your guest room for a few days?"

Going to San Francisco may be a futile thing, but if Sophia ends up needing me there, then so fucking be it.

For her, I will do anything.

Including flying across the country because my gut tells me to.

CHAPTER THIRTY-FIVE

SOPHIA

Twelve hours from present day

I SHOULDN'T HAVE AGREED to this.

When he suggested a trip, I should have put my foot down and said no. I should have left that night, but instead, I decided to be complicit and go through with going on a trip with someone I don't even want to touch me, then break up with him when I get home.

From the second I got back in the car after stopping at my apartment, tensions have been high. Elijah barely spoke to me on the way to the airport, and once we made it past security, it was curt, no more than two-word responses.

Thank God we were on a redeye flight and had the chance to sleep. I have no idea if I would have been able to handle almost four hours of sitting next to Elijah and being on pins and needles the whole time, hoping I didn't say the wrong thing and make him angry. It has been three weeks since the last time he took out his anger on me and I'm going to do everything in my power to keep him as calm as I possibly can. Especially with what I need to do at the end of this trip.

When we landed in San Francisco, things got somewhat better. And by better, I mean that Elijah transformed into a whole different person. He was smiling, laughing, and holding my hand, as if everything was normal. As if I hadn't been afraid of him for weeks, and we'd been living a happy life. As if our relationship has been an absolute dream, and he has always been the caring and loving boyfriend he was at the beginning.

I've seen glimpses of this Elijah here and there these last few months and seeing those glimpses has definitely been part of the reason I continued to stay.

Because there have been times throughout our relationship where he was caring and kind and showed me he could really be a great boyfriend. A great man. A part of me hoped the loving and caring side of him would overpower the other, but I was wrong. There is nothing that could overpower that side of him. There isn't enough hope in the world that could make me stay any longer. I've seen who Elijah really is, and I want no part of it. I no longer want to get my hopes up, that the kind version of him would stay. That he really is putting in the effort to keep his promise to never hurt me again, or to never raise his voice at me again. Because no matter what, every single time, those hopes always came crashing down.

This time, though, I'm not getting my hopes up. This time, I'm not falling for this facade he is giving me. I'm not falling for the loving boyfriend act. This time, I know even if he acts as if he will keep the promises he made me all those months ago, he will never hold himself to his word. He might change at some point in the future, but I don't want to suffer through it, just waiting for that change to happen. Just hoping there will never be a next time. I can't live like that. I don't think anyone can or should.

As much as I want to hate Elijah, though, I can't. Not fully, anyway. I want him to be happy to a certain degree, even if it kills me. Which is why during our first two days here in San Francisco, I've been trying to act as if everything is fine and dandy. Because a happy Elijah keeps the angry one away.

But as the hours pass by, it's becoming harder and harder to keep up the pretense that I'm happy and want to be here. Especially when I have no idea when we are going to head home.

There's only so much two people can do in San Francisco in February. Every time someone asks us how long we are in the city for, I look at Elijah for the answer, and every time he just smiles and says a few days. My guess is that we're here until the end of the bye-week, but who knows.

Since we've been going since the second that we landed two mornings ago, I asked Elijah if we could spend a few hours in our hotel room this morning, instead of exploring the city like we have been since we got here.

Surprisingly, he said yes. I thought that he was going to fight me on it, but he didn't.

Since we are staying in, I'm thinking that this might be the perfect opportunity to talk to Elijah and share everything I've been feeling and finally pull the plug on this.

He has to see that I'm not happy, that I'm scared of him. He has to know a few days away, exploring a new city, isn't going to change anything. No matter how different he has been acting.

Maybe he does see it, and this will be the one thing that doesn't bring out the anger.

There's only one way to find out, and that is to finally rip the Band-Aid off and leave the bedroom and go talk to him.

Taking a deep breath, I center myself as much as possible and walk out of the bedroom and into the small living room the suite that Elijah booked for this trip has to offer.

"Elijah," I say, seeing he's currently watching a rerun of last night's basketball game. I've noticed that this has been his go-to sport to watch. Not a single hockey game has played on his TV back home since I introduced him to Blake.

"Yeah?" he answers, not looking away from the screen.

As much as I feel like his attention should be on me during this conversation, it might be better if he's distracted.

"I was wondering if we could talk about something," I say, taking a seat on the small couch with him, leaving a few cushions between us.

As soon as I sit, Elijah surprises me.

Instead of keeping his attention on the game like I expected him to, he turns to look at me, concern crossing his face.

Now he's concerned. Not when he had me pushed up against the fridge or when he had his hand wrapped around my neck, not letting me breathe.

Don't think about that. If you do, you won't be able to get through this. You need to stay calm.

Right. Calm. I can do calm.

"Is everything okay?" he asks, muting the TV, giving me his full attention.

I swallow down the ball of emotion that is forming in my throat and take a good look at the man in front of me.

No more butterflies flutter in my belly when I see him. I no longer blush when he touches me. I no longer have any love for him in my heart. At the beginning, I was so excited to be with him and to see what we could be together, but now, none of that excitement exists, and I can't help but to be angry at myself for letting it go on for this long.

"I-I," I start, trying to find all the right words to say but having a hard time. "I think once we get home, it might be a good idea for me and you to take a step back from this."

As soon as the words leave my mouth, I can't help but to feel proud.

I'm doing it. I'm really ending things between us.

Not a second goes by before all the concern disappears from Elijah's face, and he goes absolutely cold.

"What do you mean by that?" His jaw is set, and the words come out through clenched teeth.

"I don't think we should be together anymore. Things between us aren't working out, and I think both of us will be better off if we went our separate ways." I say, feeling like a huge weight has lifted off my chest and like I can finally breathe.

I sit there, waiting for Elijah to say something. I can see the anger flowing in his eyes, and all I can hope is that it isn't the type of anger that I hate.

"Our separate ways," Elijah eventually repeats, getting up from the couch and starting to pace the length of the small living room.

I stay seated on the couch, just watching him, holding on to all of my strength. If I don't, I might cave and tell him that I was just joking around, that I don't want to end things, solely to keep his anger at bay.

"Yes. It's for the best," I say, proud of myself that my voice isn't wavering. "Things between us aren't working anymore, Elijah. We can't keep going like we are. We both deserve better than that."

I wanted to say I deserve better than that, that I deserve better than him, but I couldn't find the words. I have to make this about both of us because maybe then there won't be a fight. Maybe then, I won't have another bruise to add to the memories I have of him.

Elijah lets out a snort, stopping mid pace to look over at me. "This is fucking rich. I take you on a trip, and you repay me by breaking up with me? That's a bitch move."

His words have a sting to them, so instead of looking at him as I answer, I look down at my hands. "I've been wanting to do this for a while. I just hadn't been able to find the courage to do it until now."

I close my eyes, hoping that he takes my honesty for what it is and that he doesn't let his anger take over.

But of course, that hopefulness is futile when I hear him step closer to me, and I feel his hand slide into my hair. He pulls so tightly and painfully that tears spring into my eyes when he makes me look up at him.

"You want to know why things between us aren't working anymore?" He spits out, anger enveloping every inch of him. His fingers dig into my scalp, and I can't help but to let out a whimper filled with fear. "Because of you. Because you are a whore of a bitch who would rather spend time with that joke of a hockey player instead of her boyfriend."

"That's n-not true," I let out, tears starting to stream down my face.

"Shut the fuck up," he says, right before his hand slips out from my hair and slaps me across the face.

The slap rings out, and my whole face goes numb from the impact. I try to reach up to soothe the pain, but Elijah stops me, reaching down for my hands and pinning them in place.

"Elijah, please," I say to him, begging.

"Please what? Let you go? Not a fucking chance in hell. I'm not letting you go or letting you walk away from me. Do you understand me? Nobody fucking leaves me," he spits out, almost in a growl.

That's when everything shifts. That's when everything gets worse.

One second, I'm on the couch looking up at him. The next, another slap lands against my face, and I'm falling to the floor where I start crying hysterically as Elijah drags me up his body so that I can look him in the eyes. All the while I beg him to stop.

Everything happens so fast, but somehow when he swings his hand back to slap me again, I'm able to escape him just for a few seconds. Enough to run to the bedroom and get away from him.

Enough for me to reach for my phone and call the first person that I can think of. Blake.

He may be in Chicago, but maybe he can still help in some way. Maybe he can call his brother, who can call the police here in San Francisco. Maybe he will be able to come up with something that I can't, to get me out of here.

As Elijah starts to kick at the bathroom door, I drop the phone and make myself as small as possible, my right hand instantly wrapping itself around my locket, while I wrap myself into a ball and let out a sob.

I should have walked away sooner. I should have left him a long time ago.

I only have one person to blame for being in this situation, and that person is me.

CHAPTER THIRTY-SIX

BLAKE

I'M jerked awake by a sound. It takes me a second to figure out it's my phone vibrating on the nightstand next to the bed.

I look over at the alarm clock that is also sitting on the table and see that it's just after eight in the morning. I was watching a movie last night, and I must have fallen asleep.

Grabbing my phone, I look at the caller ID and sit up right away when I see Sophia's picture looking back at me.

Not another second is wasted as I slide the icon to answer the call, getting up from the bed in the process.

"Hey, Soph," I say into the phone, trying to keep my voice calm and not freak out she is calling me.

I wait for a response from Sophia, but she doesn't say anything. The only thing that I'm able to hear is muffled crying and what sounds like banging in the background.

"Sophia." I say, a little more sternly, a little louder, hoping that she will hear me, because it sounds like the phone isn't anywhere near her.

But she doesn't say anything. The bangs just continue to get louder and so do her cries.

"Sophia!" I yell out, but still, she doesn't respond. I don't think she can hear me.

"Fuck this," I say to myself, putting the phone on speaker, throwing it on the nightstand, and quickly moving through my brother's guest room and throwing on the first shirt I grab from my bag and sliding on the first pair of shoes I can find. Thank fuck I slept in fucking shorts.

I couldn't give two shits what I'm wearing right now. The quicker I get to wherever Sophia is, the better.

I quickly grab my phone again and run out of the room, straight to Hunter's garage. He and Lennie are in Montana this week, since his team didn't make it to the Super Bowl. I was supposed to join them, but when this whole thing with Sophia came up, I bailed on those plans and came here.

My brother doesn't know the whole reason why I had to come to San Francisco or why I asked to stay at his house. He just told me to make myself at home and gave me the liberty to use any of his cars if I needed.

I grab the first set of keys I'm able to find and walk over to the corresponding car, the whole time I'm listening to Sophia cry as the bangs get louder and more frequent.

"Soph, I need you to tell me you're okay." No response. "Sophia! Please tell me that you can hear me, and you're okay," I say into the phone as I get into my brother's SUV.

Still no response from Sophia but the bangs and her cries continue to sound out and eventually are accompanied by muffled yelling.

"Stop being a bitch, Sophia, and open the fucking door. I'm done playing games. Get the fuck out there. Now!" I hear Elijah yell out right before a loud bang comes through.

Motherfucker.

I hear his voice and Sophia's cries, and all I see is red. So much fucking red. This bastard is going to pay for what he is putting her through, and he won't even see it coming.

Keeping myself on the call, I open up the location app on my phone. From the second we got phones when we were kids, Soph and I have shared our locations with one another. Sort of a piece of mind that is used occasionally, and it's coming in handy today.

Tapping on her name, I see exactly where she is and that the hotel she and the sorry-excuse-for-a-man are staying at is about twenty-five minutes away from Hunter and Selena's house. Given the time of day, though, there will be traffic, so there is no doubt in my mind it will take longer.

I click on the location and speed out of the garage and out of the semi-quiet neighborhood.

The whole drive, I'm not only going way over the speed limit, dodging cars left and right, I'm also yelling into the phone, hoping Sophia will hear me through everything and tell me that she's okay. But no matter how much I yell and beg for her to pick up the phone, she doesn't say anything back.

Adrenaline is running through me the whole drive. I speed down the highway trying to get to the city as fast as I possibly can. At times, the traffic makes it seem almost impossible.

My blood boils every time I hear Elijah's voice coming through the line. Every time he calls her a name, I want to pummel my fist into his mouth and never hear another word from him.

In case anything happened.

This is what Sophia meant.

This is why Sophia looked fucking terrified when she stopped by the apartment a few days ago. I don't know how long this has been going on, but I'm going to do everything in my power to put a stop to it and make sure it never fucking happens again.

I push down on the gas as I start to see the cityscape in the distance, and I push down on it even more when the call drops as I get off the highway and onto the city streets.

"Fuck!" I yell out, hitting the steering wheel in the process.

I try calling her back, but her phone just rings before it goes to voicemail.

And that's what continues to happen as I call her thirty more times as I make my way to the hotel.

Not a single call is answered, and by the time I reach fifty calls, I'm pulling up to the valet station at the hotel, ready to jump out without putting the car in park.

"Sir!" The valet attending yells outs as I jump out of the SUV and run into the lobby of the hotel and head straight to the front desk.

If the location app gave me specific locations, I wouldn't be having to waste my time trying to find the room she is in.

"Sir, is there something that we can help you with?" The girl behind the desks asks, looking at me with concern in her eyes, as if she is trying to figure out if I'm a crazy person or not.

"I need you to tell me what room Elijah Swanson is in," I order, my tone a lot harsher than it needs to be, but I don't care. I need to not only find Sophia, but also see with my own eyes that she is safe.

The girl starts shaking her head. "Sir, I'm not at liberty to give out any guest information," she tells me, looking over my shoulder, no doubt alerting a security guard or something.

"I don't give a shit. My friend is here with him, and she just called me. From the sound of it, things are getting nasty. So, tell me what room he is in, so I can make sure that she is fucking safe," I let out, my whole body shaking in the process.

The girl's eyes go wide again, but this time with concern.

I need to see Sophia. I need to fucking see her.

"Sir," she says, and again with a shake of her head, fighting with herself over doing the right thing.

"Security can go up with me. Just tell me what room Elijah Swanson is fucking in. If nothing is wrong, you have my permission to kick me out of this hotel. Please." I'm willing to beg. I'm also willing to go to every single room this hotel has just to find Sophia. I will kick through every single door until I have her in my arms.

The receptionist must see something in my eyes, or hear the desperation in my voice, because she gives me a look of pity before she lets out a sigh and throws a nod at me. I watch as she goes to her computer and reaches for a key card.

"Room 1464," she says after a minute, handing me the key card. "He's in room 1464."

I let out the biggest sigh of relief imaginable. "Thank you."

She gives me a nod and points me in the direction of the elevator.

I give her thanks once again, and head to the elevator. Before the doors close, I yell out for her to call the police, and right away she gives me a nod.

It takes the elevator twenty seconds to climb up to the fourteenth floor, and the whole time, I will the steel box to travel faster.

A lot of shit could have happened since the call dropped, and I don't know what I'm going to walk into once I reach the room.

The second the elevator stops, I'm standing there waiting for the doors to open. When they are open just enough, I wiggle through and follow the room number signs in the right direction.

It takes two whole damn minutes to find the room, and the second that I do, everything goes absolutely silent for me. I can't hear a single bit of noise as I look at the door. The door that is separating me and Sophia. Nothing makes it into my ears. Absolutely nothing.

Not until I hear Sophia's voice.

Not until I hear Sophia's cries and her asking Elijah to calm down.

The second I hear her, it's as if everything is enhanced, and nothing in the world matters but her. And right now, it doesn't.

The only thing that matters right now is Sophia and making sure she is okay before I take her in my arms and get her out of here.

I hear Elijah yell at her to shut up, and that's when I lose it and let the adrenaline in me roam free.

Using the key card that the receptionist gave me, I push the door wide open, slamming it into the wall behind it.

My eyes start to search the second the door is wide open, and when I see the image before me, I know I will be seeing it as long as I live.

Sophia is looking at me with eyes wide and fear in every single millimeter of her brown irises and her beautiful face, as she is curled into herself by what looks like the door leading to the bedroom. All the while, Elijah looks like a rabid animal as he hovers over her.

When his eyes land on me, his hands form into fist, and he starts charging at me, but I don't give a shit.

I charge back as red clouds my vision.

And I don't stop.

I don't stop when I hear a crack.

I don't stop when I feel Sophia yelling at me to stop hitting Elijah.

I don't stop when she tries to pull me away from him.

I continue to see red until someone slaps handcuffs on me and starts reading me my rights.

I see red until I realize Sophia is looking at me the same way she was looking at Elijah. Like she was scared of me.

That's when I realized I messed up.

Not only am I going to jail, but I just possibly lost the woman who owns my heart because of it.

Part 3

CHAPTER THIRTY-SEVEN

SOPHIA

Present day

SO MANY MEMORIES of me and Blake run through my head, including the ones from last night.

There have been so many damn turning points in our friendship. There have been so many chances where I could have told my stubbornness to fuck off and told him how I felt. There were so many times where I could have gotten over my fear of losing him and spoken my heart out.

My quinceañera, that party after high school graduation, our first time together, during college, when we moved in together, when he won the Cup, our second night together.

So many damn times, and yet I didn't do anything and look where it got us. At a police station in San Francisco of all places, with Blake facing battery charges and me about to press those same charges against my boyfriend.

Or should I say ex-boyfriend? Because no way in hell am I going to be in the same room as Elijah willingly ever again. Not after what he did last night. I'm officially walking away from him, and I hate it that it had to go this far for me to finally do it.

I let out a sigh as I lean back in the metal chair I'm currently occupying. I saw a lot of things on my bingo card of life, but this was definitely not one of them.

So many "if onlys" pop into my head, and I don't know how to feel about them. If only I had ended things with Elijah when he first shoved me against the wall in his apartment. If only I had walked away from him at Christmas when he choked me and basically had me isolated from everyone I love. If only I had been truthful to myself and to Blake. If only I could go back in time and make sure none of this ever happened.

If only, if only, if only.

I can't change the past now, no matter how much I absolutely want to, but I can change my future, and I'm going to start doing that by talking to the police and getting Blake out of jail.

It's been an hour or so since I got here, and in that hour, the only thing someone has done is come get my name and get a copy of my driver's license. They looked at me weird when they saw the Illinois license, but they didn't question it. They just walked away. That was about thirty minutes ago, and now I just continue to wait.

It's already been a long day, what with me spending time talking to police at the hotel and then a few hours at the hospital getting checked out, so waiting here just adds to it. In a way, it's making me desperate.

As I sit here, my phone rings in my hand, and I don't hesitate to see who's calling me. For a second, I panic thinking that it's Elijah again, but I relax when I see that it's Eliana.

Why she's calling me, I don't know. As much as I want to talk to her and tell her everything that is going on, I just let the phone vibrate away. If I talk to her, there's a chance that I will have an emotional meltdown, and I can't have that. At least not yet. I haven't broken down since the cops took Blake away hours ago, while I yelled at them that he was acting in self-defense, and I don't plan on doing so now. I need to save my strength for the police officer who's going to take my statement.

I should call my parents, though, and Patty. There's a slight chance this might leak out to the press in the next few hours, if it hasn't started to already, and they need to know before it does. They shouldn't be finding out that way. At the very least, I should warn them.

Ignoring Eliana's call, I go into my messages and start a thread that has my parents, Patty, Hunter, Selena, and Jainie and type out a message.

HI. **I wanted to let you all know that Blake and I are in San Francisco and something happened where Blake was arrested for battery. We're both okay, and I'm trying to get him out. As soon as he's out, I will let you know. I wanted to say something before it hit the news.**

THE MESSAGE DOESN'T EVEN SAY DELIVERED for a whole minute before my phone starts to ring again. This time with my mom calling. I contemplate ignoring her, but I already worried her with my text, so if I don't answer, I will worry her even more.

So, I answer.

"Hi, Mami," I say into the phone, feeling tears starting to form in my eyes.

"Sophia, what's going on?" Her voice comes through, sounding a bit scared and full of worry.

That worry is going to get a lot stronger once I answer her question. "Everything is fine," I say to buy myself some time.

"Sophia, tell me what's going on right now. Why are you two even in California?" she asks.

I have the same question for Blake.

I know why I'm here, but why is he? Last time I checked, he was going to Montana for a few days to spend time with his mom and Hunter. When did those plans change?

As for me, I had told both my parents last week I would be staying in Chicago instead of going to Montana with Blake this week because I had to work some hours at the hospital. Which was the truth before Elijah decided to spring this trip on me. My stomach churns as I remember the number of times I have lied to my parents since Elijah and I got together. It's a lot, and I hate it so much.

"Sophia Martinez?" a male voice announces into the waiting room of the police station.

I raise my hand to show him that I'm here.

"Mom, I'll tell you everything, I swear, but it will have to be later. I have to go talk to a police officer," I tell her, getting up from my chair.

"Police officer?" she asks, sounding like she is about to go into a panic attack.

"I'll call you later," I say, quickly hanging up and walking over to where the officer is.

The guy gives me a small smile. "Miss Martinez, I'm Officer King. I'm sorry we have to meet under these circumstances," he says, holding out a hand.

"Me, too," I say, shaking his hand, nerves running through me like crazy.

"Follow me, there's a free room where we can talk." He waves for me to follow him.

Officer King leads me down a long hallway and into an interrogation room at the end. I guess they treat everyone like criminals, no matter what.

A chair gets pulled out for me, so I take a seat, while Officer King sits across from me.

"Miss Martinez—" Officer King starts, but I interrupt him.

"Call me Sophia. Please," I say, because being called Miss Martinez makes me feel like I'm talking to the principal or something.

Officer King gives me a smile. "Sophia," he says with a nod. "My colleague has informed me you are looking to press charges in regard to a domestic violence dispute that happened earlier today?"

I swallow the lump forming in my throat. "Yes, that's right."

He nods and looks down at his notes. "Against Blake Jacobi? That's who was arrested by us."

I shake my head and when he looks up say, "No, the charges would be against Elijah Swanson. The individual who was taken to the hospital with a broken jaw."

I watch as King moves his eyes from mine to my cheek where an open hand made contact more than a few times.

The slaps weren't hard enough to break anything, but they were hard enough to leave a bruise. At least that's what the EMTs that checked me out said. Same thing with the nurses who checked me out at the hospital.

"Has Mr. Swanson been violent with you before?" Officer King asks, concern filling his eyes.

"Yes," I admit for the first time since I've gotten together with Elijah.

"When did it start?" he asks, taking out a voice recorder and turning it on, followed by opening up his notebook.

One single question, and my mind goes back to when Elijah and I started and how I went from having butterflies fluttering in my stomach from being around him to being absolutely terrified of him. Every single detail comes back, but the memories from this morning take center stage.

SOMEHOW, *Elijah was able to open the bathroom door. I don't know how, but somehow he was able to do it without breaking it down. Maybe he found a secret key somewhere, maybe he's a master at picking locks, I don't know, but what I do know is that now I have nowhere to run.*

Nowhere to hide.

"You're such a whore, Sophia. You couldn't just let me take care of you, could you? You had to go and piss me off every step of the way and look at you. Running away from me, like you actually think you have a choice."

"Elijah, please," I plead, looking up at him, trying to see if the kind side of him is still there somewhere and hope he will come out and realize what he is doing.

But the more I look at him, the more I wonder if that side of him was just a facade. Just a face he would put on so that people fall for him and see him as nothing but a great guy. I also can't help but wonder if I'm the first person he has done this to. Are there others out there who fear Elijah just as much as I do right now?

"Shut up," Elijah says through clenched teeth, his hands forming fists as he comes closer to me.

I move my body back until it hits the shower door, and I have no more room to move.

"Don't do this, please." I say to him, tears streaming down my face, and I make no effort to stop them. "I'll take my words back. I won't walk away from you, just please stop."

As much as I don't want to say those words, right now I will do anything to make him stop acting like this. And if that means I have to lie to him, then so be it.

Elijah's face contorts a bit as he comes closer to me, until he is eventually crouched down in front of me. His body inches from mine.

"Want to know something, my beautiful Sophia?" he asks, reaching his hand out so that his knuckles can glide against my cheek, his voice as sweet as honey. "I can tell when you're lying to me. This pretty face of yours isn't able to hide anything from me."

He glides his knuckles down my cheek and down my neck, where he keeps it, moving them up and down as slowly as possible. I watch him as he does it, his own eyes staying on his hand as it moves.

I try not to react to his words. I try to keep as calm as I possibly can, but I know that I'm failing. Part of me knew he could see right through every single lie I told him. Part of me knew he could see through my words of love and adoration. But the one thing I can't wrap my head around is if he could see right through me, if he knew that my feelings and love for him were disappearing, why didn't he let me go? Why did he continue the ruse that things were working between us?

Because he wanted me to be his, and he never cared about how I was feeling. All he wanted was to be in control, and he was able to get that.

I open my mouth to say something, but Elijah stops me by stopping his caresses and wrapping his hand around my neck, almost blocking my airway.

"You're mine, Sophia. And you will be mine until I say so," he says, a smirk spreading across his face, causing my stomach to churn even more.

With his hand wrapped around my neck, he lifts me as best he can and drags me out of the bathroom. I fight him the whole time.

At one point, I'm able to dig my hands into his face, which hurts him because he jerks away and lets out a curse, loosening his hold on me. Which is enough to let me fall to the ground.

I take the deepest breath I can as I try to crawl away from him, but I'm brought to an abrupt stop when Elijah shoves me against the floor with his foot, before pressing it against my side and holding me down.

I let out a gasp when I feel the weight on me, and then a scream when he presses down even harder. It feels like he's going to break my ribs if he presses down on me even just a little more.

"Elijah, you're hurting me," I whimper out, trying to wiggle out from under him, but I can't. It's as if all the strength in my body has evaporated.

"That's what you fucking get for wanting to leave me." He presses down harder, and I can't help but let out another cry.

A noise for the other side of the door distracts Elijah just a bit, not a whole lot but enough for him to shift and give me enough time to get out from under him and move toward the bedroom.

After a second or so, Elijah forgets about whatever could be going on outside and turns his attention back to me looking as if he wants to back hand me and leave his mark.

I can feel so many tears streaming down my face as I look up at him, and I feel so much damn fear running through my body.

I just want this to stop.

Please, I scream out in my mind. Please make this all stop because from what it looks like in Elijah's eyes, there is no end in sight.

For a second, I think I'm never going to make it out of this room.

And that's my thought when the door slams open, hitting the wall behind it.

As soon as I see who is standing in the doorway, I let out the first sigh of relief I've felt all morning.

Out of all the people I thought would burst into the room, Blake wasn't one of them. He was supposed to be in Montana. He has no reason to even be in California, so why is he?

The answer to that question doesn't matter because he's here, and I might have the chance to make it out of this room.

His name is at the edge of my mouth, about to come out as a plea, as a saving grace, but it gets stuck in my throat when Elijah charges at him and starts to swing.

I sit there in absolute silence and fear as I watch Blake and Elijah start throwing punches at each other. I will myself to move to stop them, but I can't seem to do anything but to watch.

It's not until I see blood when I am finally able to pull myself out of whatever stupor I was in and get up and try my hardest to pull them apart.

Nothing I do works, though.

No amount of screaming or begging or using all the strength I have can pull them apart is enough to stop them.

"Blake, stop. Please," I beg, grabbing at his arm as he swings it back and hits Elijah right in the jaw.

They go at it and continue even as both of them become a bloody mess.

Tears continue to stream down my face, as I start to fear for Blake and everything that he is sacrificing with what he is doing.

The tears are ever-present even as police officers storm into the room and break the two men apart.

But they quickly evaporate when the paramedics arrive and take Elijah to the nearest hospital because of a broken jaw. And they are almost nonexistent when they cuff Blake and take him away. By then, I felt absolutely numb.

Soon, the room starts to clear out, and I'm getting taken to the hospital to get checked out. It's when I'm left alone that I'm finally able to process everything.

It's in the silence I conclude that all of this could have been *avoided if I didn't let fear dictate me. But I did, and now Blake is in jail and will possibly lose his place on the Knights because of it.*

And if he does, it will be all my fault.

I have to fix things. How I will do it, I have no idea, but I have to try. Because if I lose Blake, I don't know if I will survive.

OFFICER KING LISTENS to every word I say. From the first time Elijah got violent with me to everything I said as I got lost in the memories of a few hours ago. Every single word he listens to, not once interrupting me, solely writing down the occasional note.

The majority of the time I was talking, I got lost in the memories, but there was a time or two during it all, I would step away from the memories and look at Officer King and the facial expression he was giving me.

Most of the time he was unreadable, but there was a moment where he looked at me with all the pity in the world, and I hated it.

He was probably thinking I was stupid for staying with Elijah for as long as I did. And if he was, I wouldn't blame him. I was stupid.

"My colleague told me that you had evidence," Officer King says, a few seconds after I finished telling him everything I've been going through.

I nod. "I do."

"Do you have it on you?" he asks as he looks up from his notes.

Again, I give him a nod.

Without saying anything else, I pull out my phone and go straight to my pictures and scroll through until I find my hidden folder. After I unlock the folder, I place my phone on the table and slide it over to Officer King.

When Elijah and I got together, taking pictures so they could possibly serve as evidence one day was the furthest thing from my mind. I didn't even take them when he left marks on my arms the first time that he shoved me.

I didn't think about taking pictures until Christmas. When I saw the way my neck bruised after he choked me, I decided it was best to take a picture. Even though I told myself countless times that it was never going to happen again, another part of me told me that I had to have a record of it just in case it did. Because the authorities are more willing to believe someone with evidence, right?

So, I took pictures of that bruise and every bruise that came after it, including the ones from this morning. There might not be many, but it's enough.

Officer King looks at all the pictures I have saved, nodding at each one and taking notes as he goes along.

After a minute or two, he hands me back my phone.

"Would you be able to send me those pictures?" he asks, nodding toward the device in my hand.

"Yes," I say.

Within seconds, the friendly officer rips a piece of paper from his notepad and quickly writes down an email before handing it to me. I send the photos over to him right away.

"In reference to this morning, do you think Blake Jacobi acted in self-defense? That he went after Mr. Swanson in order to defend you and himself?" King asks.

I answered those questions earlier after Blake got arrested and the arresting officers came by the hospital to question me, but even if I did, I don't hesitate in answering them again. "One hundred percent. I've known him all of my life, and Blake isn't one to look for a fight, no matter what he does for a living. He will only go after someone if that person is threatening him or someone he loves."

Officer King nods as he looks down and takes a few more notes.

"For right now, I think that I have all the information I need. If there is anything else you might remember, feel free to give me a call at the number on this card," he says, as he pulls a card out of his pocket and hands it over to me. "If I have any questions for you, I will call the number you gave my colleague. Do you have any questions for me?"

"Blake, will he be able to go home tonight?" I ask, wanting to see Blake more than anything.

Officer King gives me a closed lip smile. "I will try, but given the charges, he might have to stand before a judge before he is able to go home." My whole body deflates. "But given what you just told me, I think there's a chance we can get the charges dropped. It might take a few hours, and it may not work, but we can try."

"That's all that I ask." I say, giving him a small but appreciative smile.

We don't spend much longer in the interrogation room. After he tells me a bit more information about what to expect about this whole process and how I can go home to Chicago whenever I'd like, we go our separate ways.

Walking out the police station takes a lot more effort than I was expecting. I feel drained but also defeated because Blake isn't walking out with me.

I think about going somewhere to wait just in case Blake does get released today, but I have nowhere to go.

I'm in a strange city where the only people I know are either in jail, in a hospital, or out of state.

So instead of calling a car or jumping on a bus to take me somewhere, I decide to head over to the coffee shop across the street that looks to be open. I can wait things out there, and once they close, I can go find a hotel for the night and wait it out there, before coming back in the morning and repeating the process.

Because no matter what, I'm not leaving San Francisco until Blake is with me. Whether he hates me or not.

I'm going to wait for him until the end of time. I'm declaring that right now.

And I don't care if it scares me.

CHAPTER THIRTY-EIGHT

BLAKE

EVERY SINGLE PART of me is fucking stiff.

The last time my body screamed at me like this, I was slammed into the boards by a defenseman from Toronto. My whole right side of my body was bruised. and I couldn't skate properly for a whole two days.

I have a feeling that this stiffness is going to last longer than two days, especially after spending the last ten hours sitting on a damn bench made out of cement. Whoever designed jail cells really wanted the individuals occupying them to suffer because fuck. No matter what way you adjust, everything is always hard.

And smells like piss.

You would think that getting arrested in a city like San Francisco would have some benefits, like at the very least, nice smelling facilities, but that's not the case whatsoever. The whole damn place smells as if a sewer and a dump came together in a damn port-a-potty.

I could go the rest of my life never smelling this stench ever again, and even then it won't be long enough.

I look over at the clock that is just outside of the jail cell I currently occupy, the one that has been taunting me since I got here, and let out a sigh.

Ten hours and seventeen minutes. I've been in here for ten hours and seventeen minutes, and I don't see myself leaving anytime soon.

I was able to call someone around hour six, after I was processed, and the first person I thought to call was Sophia. Given the circumstances, though, I didn't think that was a good idea, so I ended up calling Christian. I knew he and Eliana were going to be in California for bye-week, and even though he gives me shit every single day, I knew no matter what, he would come and try to bail me out. We may not be bonded by blood, but we are definitely bonded through something else.

My second call was to my lawyer, who told me they would try to take care of this from Chicago. According to him, if he had to get on a plane to San Francisco, he would.

But that was four hours ago, and if Christian or my lawyer can't bail me out, I doubt anyone can. I'll probably have to stand in front of a judge or something before I can even go home.

Which means I'm probably getting charged. Which also means that if the Knights get wind of this, I'm probably going to be kissing my position on the team goodbye. That is if they don't already know. I'm sure someone already leaked my arrest to all the news outlets that would listen.

Everyone I know is probably looking at my mug shot right about now, talking shit about how I beat up Elijah Swanson, a fucking golden boy. I wouldn't pass it by the bastard himself to send a tip into a gossip site to spin the story and make him look like the innocent party.

If anyone is innocent here, it's Sophia.

I knew I didn't like the fucker, and now I know why.

He never fucking deserved her, and I hope he rots in a hole full of fucking mice for the shit that he put her through.

I may not know the whole extent of it, but I know what I saw in that room, and nobody should ever be that afraid of someone. Especially not someone who should be protecting them.

I never want to see that asshole ever again, but if I do, I'm going to finish the job. Consequences be fucking damned.

I look over at the clock again and see that the hands have barely moved.

Ten hours and twenty minutes.

Who would have thought that sitting in a cell would make time crawl at the pace of a snail.

Trying to distract myself, I lean back against the concrete wall and close my eyes, clearing my head of everything, to see if the time passes just a bit faster.

It works for all of thirty seconds before my mind starts replaying the morning all over again. As much as I tried to put what happened this morning at the back of my mind, everything and anything brings it to the forefront.

I replay every single moment. From the second I answered Sophia's call to when I was taken away by the police and landed myself in this damn concrete box. Every single moment continues to run through my mind as if it were live, and I can't escape it.

The thing that I see the most is Sophia and the way those brown eyes of hers looked at me as paramedics were taking care of Elijah. How they looked at me as the police slapped cuffs on my wrists and started to whisk me away.

I couldn't get a good read of her, but I definitely felt a coldness coming from her. That's never something I've felt coming from her, especially not direct at me. I fucking hated it.

But what I hated the most was when the cops whisked me away, she didn't fight them on it. She didn't say a single word. She just stood there not doing anything.

I've asked myself a lot of questions during these last ten

hours, one of them being if this whole situation changes things between me and Sophia, and the only answer that I can come up with is yes. This changes a lot of things.

Because of my actions, because I put someone she cares about in the hospital, I probably lost Sophia. As a friend, a roommate, as everything. This is something that is going to be hard to come back from.

If only I had thought about things for a little longer before entering that room, then maybe we wouldn't be in this situation.

But the only thing I could think about was her, making sure that she was safe, and the way her lips felt against mine after she told me that she would come back to me. I wanted to do everything in my power to make sure she kept that promise, but now, after everything, that is probably gone.

I look at the clock again. Ten hours and twenty-five minutes.

A sigh escapes me. Looks like I'm sleeping here.

"Jacobi!" My name sounds out through the holding cells.

Not even bothering to get up from where I'm sitting, I look over at the police officer who called out my name. I watch as he walks over to the cell I'm in and starts unlocking the door.

"What's going on?" I ask, not even trying to get up.

"It looks like you'll be sleeping in a bed tonight. We're letting you go," the officer says, holding the cell door open and nodding for me to get up.

"What?" No way did he just say that they are letting me go. The last I've heard, I have battery charges up against me. No way in hell they would just let me walk out of here without talking to a judge first.

"We're letting you go," he says again, nodding at me to get up.

I finally do and walk out of the cell with so much confusion running through my head.

"Why?" I ask the guy, trying to make sense of it all.

The guy legit shrugs. "Don't know. I was just told to release you. But a fellow officer is out in the front, waiting to talk to you. If anything, I would get in contact with your lawyer and make sure everything is squared away."

I can't help but wonder if Christian and Tyler, my lawyer, put their heads together to get me out of this mess. As long as they didn't involve the team, I should be fine.

I give the police officer letting me out, a nod, and follow him as he guides me away from the holding cells. Before walking through the door I guess leads to the front of the station, the officer hands me a bag with all the belongings I had on me this morning.

Phone, wallet, keys.

Crap.

Hunter's SUV. It's still at the hotel. After everything that happened there this morning, I'm sure not a single employee wants to see my face ever again. Maybe I can convince Christian and Eliana to go pick it for me and take it to my brother's house.

I'll figure it out later. Right now, the only thing I can think of is getting out of here and seeing if Sophia will answer one of my calls.

I need to make sure that she's okay, and I couldn't care less if she hates me. I need to see her, talk to her, and once I do, I'll be able to handle anything that comes my way.

The cop leads me out to the front of the station, quickly telling me where to wait so I can talk to his colleague, before giving me a nod and walking away.

I turn the corner to head where I was told to go, but I stop when I see Christian and Eliana sitting in the waiting area, a few feet away.

The second I see them, I let out the biggest sigh of relief.

I knew Christian would bail me out.

Both of them look up as I approach them, and I notice they both look to be as relieved to see me as I am to see them.

"Oh my god, your face," Eliana says, getting up from the chair she is sitting on and walking over to me, eyeing what I'm going to guess are cuts and bruises all over my face. I wouldn't know. I haven't had a chance to look at myself in the mirror, but I'm sure that even for a hockey player, it looks bad. There are parts of my face that sting like a fucking bitch.

"It's nothing that I can't handle," I say to her, giving her a reassuring smile.

"If you look like this, I'm afraid to ask what Sophia's boyfriend looks like," she says, grabbing my chin and moving my face from side to side to inspect the damage.

"I don't give a fuck what he looks like," I say, feeling the same anger I was feeling this morning start coming up again.

Before I was brought to the police station, I heard one of the paramedics say that Elijah might have a broken jaw.

That fucker should have a lot more broken bones for the shit that he did. If I can go back and break the rest of his face, I would.

"At least you're out," Christian says, clapping me on the shoulder.

A pain radiates down my whole arm when he does that, and I can't help but to wince.

Great. A beat-up face and a hurt shoulder. If I don't get kicked off the Knights for this, I'm probably not going to be seeing the ice anytime soon anyway.

"Thank fuck for that," I say, massaging my arm before extending it to him. "Thank you for bailing me out, man. I owe you one, times a fucking million."

Both Christian and Eliana look at each other before looking back at me with a confused look on each of their faces.

"We didn't bail you out." Chris says, sounding as confused as he looks.

"Then how are they letting me go?" I ask, but they both just shake their heads, not knowing what to say.

"Blake Jacobi?" A male voice asks from somewhere behind me.

Turning, I see a guy in a suit standing at the edge of the waiting area looking right at me. I guess this is the other cop I was supposed to talk to.

"Yeah, that's me," I say, approaching him.

The man holds out a hand for me to shake. "Nice to meet you. I'm Officer King. I'm the lead on your case."

"Nice to meet you, too," I say, before shaking his hand. "Can you tell me why I was released? Did my lawyer post my bail?" I ask because that seems like the logical explanation.

"No, actually the charges against you were dropped," he states, giving me a curt nod.

What the hell? I beat the shit out of that bastard. How the hell were my charges dropped?

"Dropped? How? Why?" So many questions dance around my brain. Why would he drop the charges? I for sure thought the asshole would use everything in his arsenal to take everything he can from me. He already took my girl. I wouldn't have put it past him to take away my hockey career, too.

"We were able to talk to someone, and they were able to show us that what happened today was self-defense. You were protecting them from harm. And given the evidence they handed over, the district attorney's office thought it would be best to drop the charges against you now instead of waiting for you to stand before a judge."

My head spins from all the information getting thrown my

way, but the one thing that is at the center of it all is just one small important piece.

They were able to talk to someone.

I don't have to guess who it was.

It was Sophia.

She talked to the cop to protect me, not her bastard of a boyfriend.

I thought after this morning, she would be cursing me out and hating me for what I did, but instead, she is showing me that she is on my side.

I should have never doubted that she wouldn't be, yet I did.

Fuck.

Her standing beside me isn't the only thing that has me reeling. She handed the police evidence, which means that whatever Elijah put her through this morning has happened before and wasn't a one-time thing.

I didn't want to believe it. I didn't want to think those scenarios that I had thought up after she left our apartment were true, but they are. The fucker was being abusive toward her, and I didn't know.

She didn't tell me, which I can't fault her for because she was probably terrified.

Either way, I wasn't there for her when she probably needed me the most.

When we were five, I promised her I would protect her, but in these last few months, I broke that promise.

Now my need to see and talk to Sophia is all that more urgent.

"She pressed charges against him, didn't she?" I ask Officer King.

He gives me a curt nod, already knowing who I'm talking about. "She did, but pressing charges is just the start of it. If he fights her on it, this can take a while to resolve. She's going to need someone in her corner every step of the way."

Officer King says the words as if I don't already know that.

I want to tell him that after today, I'm always going to be by Sophia's side, even if she tries to push me away. As her friend, her protector, as whatever the fuck she needs me to be. I will be there for her no matter what because no way am I going to let the woman I love, who owns every single part of me, down again. I've already failed her, and I'm never going down that road ever again.

"She will," I say affirmatively. Not only will she have me, but there are a lot of people in our lives who will stand by her side no matter what.

With that, Officer King offers me his hand again and his card before going on his merry way.

"What happens now?" Eliana asks, giving me a look of concern.

I look down at her and give her a small smile. "Now, I have to go find Sophia. I need to know she is doing okay."

Both Eliana and Christian nod in agreement. I don't know when it happened but these two seem to be so damn in sync that I don't know whether to find it cute or annoying. I'm going with the second one.

"Maybe you will have better luck getting ahold of her. I've been calling and texting her since you called Christian, but she hasn't answered," Eliana says, looking a little hurt by it.

"She was probably freaking out," Christian offers her, and I nod in agreement.

Sophia may have just met Eliana at the end of last summer, but she loves and cares about her so she wouldn't be ignoring her just because.

Pulling out my phone out of the plastic bag it was placed in,

I power it on, surprised it's not dead, and go into my location app, ignoring all the notifications that are coming through.

If she didn't answer Eliana, there is a slight chance she's not going to answer me. Might as well show up wherever she is to talk to her.

Her location takes a second to load, and as soon as it does, I can't help but let out a sigh of relief when I see that she's close.

"Apparently, she's across the street," I say to my friends.

"She probably didn't want to be too far away, just in case you were released." Christian lets out.

"Sounds like Soph," I say, giving him a nod.

It doesn't take long for us to decide it's time to leave the police station. When we walk out, I feel like I'm leaving a huge chunk of stress behind. When I decided to follow Sophia to San Francisco a few days ago, I didn't think this short trip would end like this. If I did, I would have tried to prepare mentally for it.

When we reach the fork between the parking lot and the crosswalk that will lead me to Sophia, I turn to look at Christian instead of just saying goodbye.

"Thanks for coming. I know you didn't bail me out or anything, but the fact that you came and didn't leave me to rot in there means a lot."

Christian claps me on the shoulder, a smirk forming on his face, too, like he knows I'm in fucking pain but doesn't give two shits.

"Just because I find you annoying sometimes, Jacobi, doesn't mean I don't see you as another annoying little brother I didn't ask for." He throws me a wink, but then he changes his facial expression from a joking one to a more serious one. "We're family, Blake. Whether we play for the same team or not, we're family. We've connected, and we are going to be there for each other. And if that includes bailing each other out from jail, then we will do it. I always thought that we were going to bail out Logan and not you, but hey, we can't be picky."

"We're family," I say because I might have thought of him the same way, but I didn't think he felt the same.

"We're family. But if I ever walk into my house, and I find you on my couch bare-assed, fucking some girl, I'm kicking you out of the family. I couldn't do it to my actual brother, but I will do it to you."

What the actual fuck?

Eliana lets out a laugh as she takes in my face.

"We might have walked in on his brother once over the summer. Apparently the beach house is popular among the Rodriguez men, and we might have seen things we didn't want to see," Eliana explains, while her boyfriend makes a face.

"I'd rather not know any details," I say, shaking my head at her.

"And I don't want to speak them," Christian says, clapping me on the shoulder again. It's like he wants me to hit him with my stick the next time we hit the ice. That is if I'm still a Knight after all of this.

"Go talk to Sophia," Eliana says, nodding to the building across the street.

Looking over my shoulder, I see a coffee shop on the corner, where she no doubt is.

"We're going to head back to the beach house. Call us if you need anything," Christian tells me, throwing a nod my way.

We say our goodbyes, and they head to the parking lot, and I head across the street.

Before walking into the coffee shop, I check Sophia's location one more time, just to make sure it's the right place. Once I have confirmation it is, I don't hesitate to pull the door open and walk in.

I see her right away, and as soon as my eyes are on her, a wave of emotions crash into me.

She here. She's safe.

And all I want to do is go to her, and wrap her in my arms, and never let her go.

I want to put all the shit we've been through, all the fear of losing, her behind me and finally make her mine.

She promised me that she would come back to me.

She said the words as her lips pressed against mine.

Maybe now, all that can finally happen.

There's only one way to find out.

CHAPTER THIRTY-NINE

SOPHIA

I'M on my second cup of water, sixth cup of liquid.

Since I was going to wait at the coffee shop until it closed, I had to buy something so the employees wouldn't kick me out for taking up space. So, I bought a coffee, and after my third cup, I started to feel all jittery, so I moved to tea, and well, since that had caffeine in it, too, I thought it was better to just switch to water.

There's no need for me to be overly hyper in a small coffee shop while I wait to see if Blake is going to be released tonight or not.

But I've been sitting at this corner table for a few hours now, and the sky is getting darker, so the chance of Blake getting released today are getting slimmer and slimmer.

It's been a long day, and I just want it to be over.

The only saving grace I've had has been the caffeine and the fact that this coffee shop has phone chargers at every table because if I didn't have either of those things, I would be beside myself.

Not that I've used my phone a lot.

For the majority of the time I've been here, my phone has

been off. I've been getting so many messages and phone calls, I don't know what to do with them.

I should answer everyone, especially my parents, Patty, and Hunter, and I would, if I had more information, but I don't. So, I just let the notifications grow.

I started powering off my phone when Elijah's name started to appear on my screen. In the span of about ten minutes, he called fifty times and sent over one hundred messages. I don't know what he said on the calls, but if they were anything like the messages I received, I might have an idea.

Everything from calling me a bitch and a whore to him apologizing for crossing the line, then back to calling me a bitch after the police paid him a visit right before his surgery to fix his jaw. I've read every single message he sent, and after seeing all the names that he was calling me, I decided that it was best to just turn off my phone and not let his words affect me. Especially his apologies.

Elijah is used to me accepting the very few apologies he has given me and us moving on with our lives like everything has gone back to normal.

But not this time.

This time, I'm not going to crumble at his "I'm sorries." I'm not going to accept a single apology and go back to being with him.

I'm done. I no longer want anything to do with him. He could suffer in hell for all I care.

After all the shit he put me through, all the fear and the pain he made me feel, he's not worth a single thought.

I just wish I was strong enough to leave him sooner, but what's done is done. I can't go back and change the past no matter how much I want to. I have to continue on so I can make my future as bright and filled with love as much as I possibly can.

And I'm going to start doing that as soon as Blake is out of jail.

I look out the window and see that the sun is almost fully set, which means I can't stay here much longer.

Letting out a sigh, I turn my phone back on so I can book a hotel because no way am I going back to the one I shared with Elijah.

Ignoring all the notifications for missed calls and text messages, I go straight to my web browser and start looking for a hotel that isn't going to cost me an arm and a leg.

But it's San Francisco, so even the cheapest hotel is going to cost me a few hundred dollars.

Maybe I can message Hunter and Selena and ask if I can stay at their house for the night. That is, if they don't hate me already for putting their brother in jail.

There's a chance I'm going to lose everyone that I love, isn't there? If I lose Blake over this, I will no doubt lose everyone I connected with through him. His family, his friends, everyone.

I've already isolated myself from everyone, thanks to being with Elijah. I won't take much to disappear from their lives completely.

But they're as much my family and friends as they are his, so maybe I won't lose everyone.

I let out a sigh. Thinking about all of this makes me hate Elijah even more.

Giving up on looking for a place to sleep, at least for a few minutes, I slide my phone away and close my eyes, leaning down to rest my head against my forearm.

I close my eyes for a second and try to get lost in the sounds of the coffee shop. Anything to clear my head.

For a few minutes, I drown in the noise and become aware of every little thing. Like someone opening the front door of the place.

I guess there are people in the world who drink coffee at all times of the day.

I keep my head down as I listen to whoever walked in, my breathing keeping in time with their footsteps. I don't know why, but it's a distraction I will gladly take.

But then the footsteps stop, and I have nothing left to drown out the thoughts. I almost let out a groan, but then something knocks against my table.

Maybe a new customer didn't walk in, and it was an employee, and now they've come to tell me that I have to leave.

I guess my time here is done. I really should have continued looking for a place to sleep.

Sighing, I lift up my head to look up at the employee I'm sure is here to kick me out. The words 'I'm sorry' are on the tip of my tongue, but they get stuck in my throat when I see who is standing in front of me.

Tears start from in my eyes for no reason whatsoever, besides the fact he's here. Blake is standing right in front of me.

"Oh my god," I say, not hesitating whatsoever to jump up from my chair and wrap my arms around him.

It feels like forever since I've hugged him, since I felt his arms wrapped tightly around me.

"They let you out," I say, tightening my hold on him.

He does the same, as his hands find their place around my waist and his face presses against my hair, like it's been a long time for him, too.

"They let me out," he repeats, letting out a huge sigh I feel move throughout his whole body.

Even though I don't want to, I pull away from Blake but just enough to still keep our bodies touching.

I look up at his face, and I start feeling sick to my stomach when I see all the bruising that has formed and the few cuts that he has. I can't help but to be happy that Elijah didn't re-break his nose.

But Blake's face still banged up because of me.

"Are you okay?" I ask him, reaching up and gently gliding my finger along each of his cuts and mapping out the bruises.

"I should be asking you that," Blake says, his icy-blue eyes darkening and his hands tightening as he lets them rest against my hips.

It doesn't go unnoticed he is still holding me, that he's keeping his hands on me as if he doesn't want to let go.

I think about his question and give him a small smile. "I will be."

Blake lets out a sigh before finally moving one of his hands off my body and bringing it up to my face. "Soph, you should have told me what was going on."

His voice is filled with pain and just hearing it breaks me in half.

A tear escapes from the corner of my eye, and Blake wipes it away. "I wanted to. More times than I can count, but then I thought that if I left him, I could put it behind me, and I could just put what he put me through behind me and never mention it again."

Blake cringes at my words, his eyes are filled with pain.

He opens his mouth to say something, but then one of the baristas starts up the coffee machine and stops him. He looks around and lets out a sigh.

"We should get out of here and go somewhere we can talk," he suggests, finally letting go of me but only to interlace one of his hands with mine.

He starts to pull me away, but I stay rooted in place. Blake quickly turns to look at me.

"What's wrong?" he asks, bunching up his eyebrows in the process.

"You don't hate me?" I ask, the question that has been on my mind since this morning finally making its way out.

He gives me a look of confusion. "Why would I hate you?"

"Blake, you were just in jail because of me. You were facing battery charges. That's reason enough to take me out of your life and hate me forever," I whisper-yell at him since we are in a public place.

Who knows if the baristas recognized him when he walked in and are secretly taking videos of us.

My best friend looks at me for a solid minute, his eyebrows close to his hairline as if he's surprised by something.

After another thirty seconds, he finally lets out a snort, and now I'm the one that is surprised and confused.

"Why are you snorting?"

"Because I thought you were going to hate me," he says, a small chuckle leaving his lips.

"Why would I hate you?"

Blake lets out a sigh, composing himself in the process. "I beat up your boyfriend, Soph. I heard the paramedics say I broke his jaw," he tells me, cringing a little bit as he does.

"You were protecting me," I tell him, reaching up to soothe his cuts again, even if they don't need soothing.

"I know, but that doesn't negate the fact he was still someone you cared about, and if the police hadn't pulled me off him, I could have done a lot more damage than I did."

The words 'he would have deserved it' are on the tip of my tongue, but no matter how much I want to say them or how true they are, I can't voice them.

Elijah hurt me, physically, mentally, and emotionally, yet I would never want to do the same to him. Even by voicing words.

"But you didn't," I say to Blake, giving him a small smile. "And even if you did, I still wouldn't hate you. I never will."

I look into his eyes for a second as he looks down at me.

They are my favorite shade of blue the world has to offer. I can't count all the times I've gotten lost in them or wished it was his eyes I was staring into when on a date. Whenever those blue eyes look at me, they make me feel safe, protected, special. Most importantly, though, they have made me feel loved, in every sense of the word.

That's what I feel when I look into them now.

And I want to tell him that, but given the circumstances of today and where we are, it might not be a good idea.

But I will tell him because I'm not going to let fear dictate me anymore. It's controlled everything so far, and I'm done cowering from it.

"I will never hate you either," Blake says, his eyes softening up, and his hand tightening around mine. "Let's get out of here."

CHAPTER FORTY

BLAKE

AS WE LEAVE the coffee shop, I call for a car to take us to Hunter and Lennie's.

Sophia and I need to talk, and I don't think having that type of conversation in a public place would be any good. So going back to my brother's house is better. If I could get us out of San Francisco and head back to Chicago tonight, I would, but given everything that we've been through today, I think it's better to stay in California for the night and possibly head home tomorrow.

"Where are we going?" Soph asks, standing at my side as we wait for our car to arrive.

Her whole body shivers as a gust of wind passes. This is the one thing about this part of California I hate. You always have to dress in damn layers. It can go from nice and sunny to cold as a fucking freezer.

Not having a sweater of my own to wrap around her shoulders, I wrap my arms around her instead and bring her body closer to mine.

She has always fit so perfectly next to me. And having her this close to my body, holding her like this, makes me realize just how much I've fucking missed her. I've missed everything about her these last few months. I want to take everything she's offering me and hold it as tightly as I possibly can.

"Hunter and Lennie's," I answer her, checking my phone to see if the car is close by. Two minutes away.

There's a possible chance I'm going to freeze my balls off in two minutes. We could go back into the coffee shop, but it looks like they're closing already.

"Did you call them when you got released?" she asks, leaning her head against my chest and wrapping her arms around me for more warmth.

We're from fucking Montana and live in Chicago. This coldness shouldn't be affecting us so damn much. We should be thinking it's nothing. Yet, it feels like fucking icicles are piercing our bodies. This weather is no fucking joke.

"No, I've been staying there for a few days," I answer her.

"A few days?" she asks, pulling away from me to look at my face. "How long have you been in California?"

Her eyebrows bunch up, and she looks up at me a bit confused. More so with her eyebrows bunched up and her arms crossed along her chest.

I give her a shrug. "The same amount of time you have, give or take a few hours."

"What?"

I check my phone one more time, before turning my body to face hers. "Soph, you came into our apartment all freaked out, telling me where you were going, just in case something happened. I wasn't going to stay in Chicago and not be there for you 'just in case something happened.' So I booked the earliest flight I could. That way I would be close by just in case. Just in case you needed me," I say to her, not giving a shit if it makes me sound crazy. Because who jumps on a plane to follow their best friend and their asshole boyfriend on a gut feeling? Apparently me.

Sophia opens her mouth to say something, but quickly closes it, as if she can't find the words to say.

After a few more seconds, she finds her voice. "You followed me to San Francisco?" she asks, bewildered by what I did.

"Soph," I say her name, closing the small distance between us. "I will follow you anywhere in fucking world. Whether you need me or not. If my gut tells me to go to you, I'm going. No matter what. There will never be a question about it."

She looks up at me in a way I can't really explain. There's astonishment, but there is also confusion. Like she is happy to hear I would follow her anywhere in the world but also confused about why I would even think of it.

The car I requested finally pulls up to the curb, and I let out a sigh of relief that we don't have to stand in the stupid San Francisco cold much longer.

I walk over to the door and open it so that Sophia can get in, but when I turn to look at her, I find her in the same spot she was in a few seconds ago, not having moved an inch.

"Soph?" I say, extending my hand to her.

She looks up at me, that confusion still in her eyes and she says one single word.

"Why?"

"Why what?" I ask, even though I know exactly what she is asking.

"Why would you follow me?" she asks, her voice breaking a bit.

So many fucking reasons, I think to myself.

There are so many fucking reasons why I would follow her, and I want to tell her, I'm finally done with holding back and not telling this woman how I've been feeling for years, but doing it in front of a police station with a complete stranger waiting for us isn't ideal.

If I'm finally going to tell Sophia she is my fucking heart and world, I'm going to do it somewhere private at least.

"There are a lot of reasons, Soph, and I will tell you every single one of them when we get to the house. I promise." I continue to hold out my hand to her, even though I want to go back to her and whisper every single one of my reasons in her ear.

She needs to hear them, no matter how she may feel in return. Though, I may have an idea how she may feel, more so after she left our apartment a few days ago.

After a second, Sophia gives me a nod and slides her hand into mine.

The second we are in the car, we get enveloped in the music the driver has on.

As much as I want to appreciate him for having good rock music on, the day has finally caught up to me. And by the way Sophia leans her head against my shoulder, not letting go of my hand, I'm sure it has finally caught up to her, too.

The car ride is silent. Both Sophia and I doze off the whole drive. It's not until the driver is pulling the car up to the gated house, thirty minutes later, that we both wake up fully.

We are slow to get out of the car, but as soon as we make it past the gate, up the short driveway, and into the house, all signs of tiredness are out the door.

Both of our stomachs growl at the same time, and I can't help but look over at Sophia and give her a small smile.

With everything that has been going on, I didn't even remember I haven't eaten a single thing all day. I woke up this morning with my first thought being Sophia. I didn't even think about food.

"Let's eat something and freshen up, and then we can talk," I tell Soph, nodding toward where the kitchen is.

She doesn't say anything. She just gives me a small smile and a nod of agreement and starts walking over to the kitchen.

We've both been here plenty of times to know our way around.

The second we step foot in the kitchen, we start raiding the pantry and the fridge for anything we can eat. In the days I've been here, I've mostly eaten through all the pasta and chicken my brother and Lennie had. But as much as I want to keep up with my diet, pasta sounds like a shit meal right about now.

"Tomato soup and grilled cheese?" I ask Sophia, holding up a can of soup I found in the pantry.

You would think that a football player who is worth more than a few million and has a personal chef come in to cook him meals twice a week, would eat fresh tomato soup, not from a can. But it works in our favor today.

Sophia gives me a nod, and we move through the kitchen as if it were our own and start making our food.

It doesn't take long, and before we know it, we are sitting at the small dining table that overlooks the hill the house sits on.

We eat in comfortable silence, something we've been used to since we were kids, and when we're done, we head upstairs to wash the day away.

I lead her to the guest room I took over, but the second that we cross the threshold, the comfortable silence we were in downstairs starts to feel a bit awkward.

Where do we go from here?

"Think Selena would be okay if I raid her closet, so that I can shower?" Sophia asks, fidgeting with her fingers and biting down on her bottom lip. Both signs she is nervous.

She's freaking out about the answers I still owe her.

I give her a nod. "I'm sure she would be fine with it." I send a smile in her direction to calm her down a bit. "I saw some clothes in one of the other rooms. Let's go find you something."

As she looks for something to wear, I send out a quick message over to Christian and ask if he can help with picking up Hunter's SUV and Sophia's stuff from the hotel tomorrow. Thankfully, he says yes, so that is taken care of.

The SUV is quickly forgotten, though, when I decided to go through all the missed calls and text messages I've been avoiding since I turned my phone back on. So many names stare back at me on the screen, from everyone from my brother, Isaac, and my father to my publicist and my agent, which tells me the news of my arrest has made it out. There is one name that stands out, though, one name that has me letting out a frustrated sigh, and that is the name Grayson Lane.

If the owner of the team is calling me, that means that shit isn't going to be pretty when I get back to Chicago. I hate to think this, but my time in Chicago may be done and over.

I should call him back. I should call everyone back, but I honestly don't have the energy for it.

The most that I'm able to do is send out a message to my mom, my siblings, and Isaac, letting them know the situation and that Sophia and I are at Hunter's house. I also tell them I'm turning off my phone to de-stress.

For the time being, I ignore my team, Grayson, and my dad. I'll deal with them tomorrow. Though I'd rather not deal with Roy Jacobi, since even though I told myself that it might have been time to repair our relationship last summer, that hasn't been the case, but I'm going to have to do it eventually. I can already hear him calling me a disgrace to his family name for getting arrested.

Shaking my head, I turn off my phone and put it down on the nightstand just as Sophia comes back into the room with some articles of clothing in her hand.

"You can use the bathroom down the hall to freshen up," I say to her, my mind still very much on the possibility of getting released by the Knights.

Sophia doesn't move or say anything. She just stands there, looking over at me like she wants to say something.

"Everything okay?" I ask, getting up from where I'm sitting and walking over to her, keeping some distance between us.

Sophia lets out a sigh. "Yeah, I was just wondering if you were going to tell me your reasons. You said you would do it when we got here."

A small smile forms on my face. "I was. I am. I just figured we needed some time to decompress."

"I've decompressed enough," she tells me, inching closer to me, the small amount of space I left between us decreasing. "Why did you do it, Blake? Why did you follow me here?"

The moment I've been talking myself out of since I was fifteen is finally standing here in front of me, and for the first time, I'm not afraid of it. I'm actually welcoming it with open arms.

It's now or never.

I close the last bit of distance between us and take her face between my hands so I can look into her eyes and do something I should have done at fifteen years old when we were at her quinceañera, and I was about to hand her locket.

Pour my heart out to her.

"Because I fucking love you, Sophia. I've been in love with you for as long as I can remember," I say to her, finally admitting it. A small gasp leaves her lips, and for a second she looks like she is about to say something, but I continue before she can. "I followed you here because I wouldn't have been able to handle something happening to you while you were here and I was in a different state. I wanted to be here for you whether you needed it or not. I would have done the same if you would have gone to

Guam or to Russia because I fucking love you, and if my gut tells me that you need me in whatever way, I'm going to fucking be there for you. Even if nothing is wrong, I would still follow you because no matter what, I want to be where you are."

A few tears run down Sophia's face, and instead of wiping them away with my thumb, I lean down and kiss them away, every single one.

"You love me?" she asks, her voice barely a whisper as my lips touch the corner of hers.

I don't pull away to answer her question. "I've always loved you. Even when I was five, and I didn't understand what the word meant." I move my mouth down a bit and place kisses along her jawline, before pulling back just enough to look into her eyes. "But I've been in love with you for a few years now. I might have been in love with you since I was fifteen. I just never found the courage to tell you. In my mind if I told you, and I lost you, that would have hurt me more than me not telling you at all. Because I can't live a life you are not a part of. I would have taken seeing you marry another man rather than risk losing you. But I'm done holding it in, Soph. I'm done not telling you how l feel about you. Sure, right now isn't the ideal time, what with the shit that has gone down today, but there never might be a right time to say the words, so right now works as good as any." I let out a small chuckle, as I rub my thumb along her face as if it were my lips back on her, kissing every single inch of her.

Sophia looks up at me, so much wonder in her eyes, the tears still pooling at the corners, and her bottom lip trembling.

"You love me." She repeats, but this time, it's more of a statement than a question.

"Always and always," I say, giving her the same words that we started to say when we were ten and have continued to say as the years have gone on.

"Always and always," she repeats my words, as if she is in trance and still digesting everything I just said to her.

Taking her time to take in what I told her isn't something I would blame her for. Today has been like a never-ending day of so many emotional rollercoasters for everyone involved but especially her.

I don't know the whole story yet. I don't know fully what was going on in that hotel room before I got there. Or what would have happened if I hadn't gotten there in time or at all. Seeing your best friend and the woman you love sobbing on the floor and looking up at you like you are her saving grace, then getting arrested because you were protecting her, is traumatic, sure, but not an ounce as traumatic as what she went through, what she had been going through.

Adding me telling her how I feel about her on top of that is more than a lot, and she may not be able to digest everything, not yet.

She may need time with it, and I'm willing to give her all the time she needs. Sophia Martinez is the one woman I would wait forever for. Always and always.

"Today has been a lot," I say, running my thumb along her bottom lip, releasing it from the hold her teeth have on it. "I know we agreed to talk when we got here, but we can just leave it for tomorrow. Go shower and wash the day away so that you can relax." I press a kiss against her forehead, before dropping my hands and nodding toward the door.

I back away from her, even if I really don't want to, and give her a smile.

Sophia continues to stand there, not making a move to leave the room with her eyes never leaving me.

Eventually, after a few seconds, she finally breaks the silence.

"Join me," she says, her words still a whisper, but having strength behind them.

"What?" I ask because no way did she just tell me to join her.

Sophia walks toward me, taking my hand in hers.

"Join me in the shower," she says, interlacing our fingers together and squeezing tightly.

"Why?" I ask her because that seems to be the only question I can seem to form.

This beautiful woman smiles up at me, before closing all remaining distance between us, and leans up to press her lips against mine. Just like she did a few days ago.

"Because I love you, too, and I really don't want to be away from you right now, not even to shower," she admits, giving me another chaste kiss.

"You love me, too?" I ask after a few seconds, bewildered at the fact those four words just came out of her mouth.

A part of me knew Sophia loved me, but it's one thing to think it, and it's another thing to know it.

"More than I can ever express," she says, the tears that were pooling at the corners of her eyes making their way out again. This time, I reach out and let my thumbs wipe them away instead of my lips. "More than you will ever know. You're not the only one who was scared of saying it and losing you. You weren't the only one who let fear make decisions for you when it came to admitting how you felt. But if you are letting the words flow out, then so am I. I love you, Blake Jacobi. Always and always. Hockey or no hockey. I love you, and I hoped for so long that you'd love me the same way."

There's no hesitation. This time, instead of her leaning up and placing a kiss against my lips, I'm the one doing it. I'm the one leaning down and claiming her lips as mine.

Just how I wanted to do it at her fifteenth birthday, just how

I wanted to do it during our first night together, during our second, and so many times in between and after.

For so long, I wanted to claim this woman as mine, and now I'm officially able to.

As our lips move together, I let my hands slide down her body, memorizing every single inch of her that I can.

I have our two nights engraved in my mind, but they aren't enough. I have always needed more. More time with her. More of her. More everything, and I'm finally getting it.

We are both hungry for each other, and I want to mark her mine as fast as I can, but right now, I need to take my time with her.

Unwillingly, I pull away from her, pressing my forehead against hers. "Always and always?" I ask her, her breathing mixing with mine.

"Always and always," she responds, a smile spreading across her face.

"I'll join you in that shower then."

CHAPTER FORTY-ONE

BLAKE

WHEN WE WALK into the bathroom, I let go of Sophia's hand and go start the shower.

Compared to the rest of the house, this bathroom is small, but we will make it work.

As soon as I have the water at a temperature I want— an overly hot shower, which is Sophia's preference—I pull my shirt off my body before turning back to look at Sophia.

She has situated herself on the bathroom counter, her face looking pensive as ever, so I don't hesitate to walk over to her and settle myself between her thighs.

"What are you thinking about?" I ask, placing my hands against her legs and rubbing them up and down against the fabric of her pants.

Sophia lets out a sigh. "A lot of things," she answers, her shoulders sagging a bit.

"What things?" I ask, not stopping the motion of my hands.

"How Elijah saw right through me," she finally answers, looking up at me with sad eyes.

"Saw right through you?" I ask, trying hard to not let hearing the fucker's name affect me. I still want to go back and rip him apart inch by inch.

Maybe when we get back to Chicago, I can have Logan go after him. Dude is Russian, or at least I think he is. He doesn't talk a whole lot about his life besides the fact that he has a brother, but I'm sure he would love to beat the shit of an asshole like Elijah Swanson.

"An ongoing argument we had was that he would notice how you looked at me, or how I would look at you. He would yell about how I was looking at you in the way I should be looking at him. I always told him that I wasn't. That I didn't have feelings for you, and I never would. But that was a lie. It was always a lie, a lie I said to not only convince him but myself, too. I never told him that, though, because if I did, he was going to react in a way I wouldn't like. So I just continued to lie. To the both of us. I even did it this morning." Her voice breaks as she speaks.

"Why did you have to convince yourself?" I ask her, not wanting to hear the answer but knowing that I should.

Sophia looks up at me with big doe eyes, so much uncertainty flowing through them.

"I've been in love with you for a long time, Blake." She starts, taking a deep breath before saying anything else. "Like you said, you would watch me marry someone else just as long as you didn't lose me. I felt the same way. I would have rather watched you have a family and grow old with someone else than lose my friend, lose the little boy I met when I was five, forever. I was in love with you, but after our second night together, I told myself that it would be best for me to shove my feelings for you away. That I should move on and just be grateful I had you as my friend. That's why I started seeing Elijah. Because I was trying to move away from my love for you. But no matter how hard I tried to shove my feelings away, they were still ever so present. I should have realized that what I was doing wasn't working when I had wished you would have told me not to go on my first date with Elijah. I kept telling myself that with time, my feelings for you would settle, and I wouldn't have to continue lying to myself anymore. But that never happened. My love for you has always been there, and it will always be, and Elijah knew that. He knew, or should I say knows, that I love you, and no matter what, that was, *is*, never going to change."

As I hear Sophia speak, I can't help but to hate myself.

If I had grown some balls years ago, she wouldn't have had to do that. She wouldn't have had to shield what she was feeling and lie to herself or to anyone about it.

Anger rolls through my body, but I try to push it down. It doesn't stop me from practically digging my hand into her thighs.

"Had it been going on for a while? The convincing Elijah?" I ask, wanting to know about the situation.

How had it started?

When?

So many questions are circling in my mind, and I'm trying not to ask every single one at once.

Sophia gives me a slight nod, biting down on her bottom lip in the process. "Since the night I introduced the two of you," she answers.

I try to think back to that night, trying to remember when that was. If I remember correctly, she introduced us after a game against San Jose at the start of the season. I also remember her being there for the first few games, but after that game, she hasn't gone to a single one. For four months, I've been playing without Sophia in the stands.

"In October? It started in October?" I ask, my eyes moving down to her cheek. It's discolored, a hint of a bruise marking her face. If she's been trying to convince him that she didn't have feelings for me since October, how many other bruises have landed on her body? Have they only been on her face? The rest of her body? How fucking rough with her did he get?

"Yes," she answers, her chin lowering.

Something pulls at my chest seeing and hearing her like this.

I close my eyes for a second, trying to find the courage to ask my next question.

"How—" I start but quickly pause because I don't know if I can say the question out loud. After a few seconds and Sophia looking back up at me, I'm able to get the words to come out. "How rough would he get?" I finally ask, my eyes not moving away from her bruised cheek, hating the fact that it's even there in the first place. I should be the one with the bruises, not her.

I raise one of my hands and caress the skin with my thumb. She doesn't move, doesn't even flinch.

My eyes stay on the movement of my thumb as Sophia answers.

"This morning was the roughest," she admits. "Before this morning, he hadn't hit me until a few weeks ago, when slapped me across my cheek. He has shoved me a few times and choked me once, but had never hit me."

I'm going to kill him. The next time I see the fucker, he's fucking dead. Screw my hockey career.

A lump forms in my throat, but I'm able to push it down before speaking again. "What did he do to you this morning?"

I don't have to know every single detail, but I want to. I want to know everything she has gone through.

Sophia's bottom lip trembles from between her teeth. She looks like she isn't going to tell me, but that isn't the case.

It takes her a few tries, but Soph finally is able to tell me everything. Not just what happened this morning, but everything she has gone through while being in a relationship with Elijah. She tells me how he grabbed her that first time and shoved her against the wall. How she came home that night because she didn't want to be anywhere near him after that. She mentions the promises that he gave her that night and how she so desperately wanted to believe them. From there, she tells me about how after the first incident, she felt isolated from me and our hockey friends. She tells me about Christmas and how she not only lied to me, but to her parents about how she spent it.

She tells me about every thought, every feeling she had these last few months. Every bruise, small or big that the fucker left on her body. Hearing everything breaks my fucking heart, but when she goes into detail of what happened this morning, it shatters into a million pieces.

Silent tears roll down her face as she tells me every last detail. The hair pulling, the dragging, the stomping on her ribs, the feeling of possibly not making it out of that room. Everything.

I don't know how she does it, but she is able to make it through telling me, without yelling, without breaking into a sob. She may have tears rolling down her face, sliding along her cheeks, but she is as controlled and poised as ever, and I couldn't be prouder.

"I wish you would have told me what was going on sooner," I say as gently as I possibly can.

Soph grabs a tissue from the box that is sitting next to her and blows her nose before she responds. "Me, too. I wish I would have, too. Maybe if I would have, we wouldn't be in this mess. Maybe if I had told you, you wouldn't have gotten arrested and put your hockey career at risk because who even knows if you are still a Knight when we get back to Chicago. Maybe if I had told someone, I would have gotten away from under Elijah's thumb sooner, and I wouldn't have to press charges against or see him again in court. If I had told anyone, a lot of things could have been different. I shouldn't have believed him when he told me it wasn't going to happen again. I should have been braver, stronger. I should have done so many things to not be in this situation."

She bows her head down, but I grab onto her chin and make her look up at me, but she just closes her eyes and shakes her head.

"Look at me, Sophia," I urge her, pleading. After a few seconds, she finally opens her eyes. "You are strong. You are brave. You're so many damn things. And I love every one of them," I place a chaste kiss against her lips, to calm her down as much as possible. "Hockey or no hockey, remember?" I say when I pull back from her. "I couldn't care less if the Knights release me. No contract, no team, matters more than you do. I'd get arrested ten times over if it meant I was there to protect you each and every time. If keeping you safe means giving up hockey, my career, then I'm okay with that because you'd be here with me."

"You shouldn't have to do that."

"No, but I would. For you, I would. Always and always."

A small smile spreads on her face. If only I could see her in full-blown smile that reaches her eyes and hear her laugh in the most uncontrollable way. I last experienced those things during our movie night two weeks ago, and it feels like it has been forever.

"I love you," she says, her hands landing against mine, holding me to her.

"I love you, too," I say, leaning forward and placing my mouth against hers.

For the first time, I kiss this woman like I want to. I kiss her like she is mine, and she will always be. I kiss her with no reservations or because this may be the one and only time I will be able to kiss her like this. I kiss her like I wanted to during our nights together. Like I love her, and she loves me.

Our tongues slide together, and she lets out a moan that makes my whole damn body relax just hearing the sound.

My hands slide down her face, caressing her upper body through her clothes until I reach the hem of her shirt.

I pull away just slightly, both of us already panting, and drag her T-shirt off, leaving her in a bralette that barely covers anything.

The second I see it, I start getting angry. She put this on this morning for him, not for me.

As if she knows what I'm thinking about, Soph grabs my chin and makes me look at her. Giving me a smile that almost reaches her eyes.

"I didn't wear this for him," she tells me, comforting me. "I haven't worn anything for him in a long time."

"I shouldn't be getting mad. He was your boyfriend. A fuck-tard, but still your boyfriend. I know he touched you, but I still see fucking red thinking about it," I admit, because if I can admit something like this to anyone, it's to her, my best friend.

Now it's Sophia taking my face between her hands. "He hasn't touched me in a while. Not since he slapped me the first time. That's when I decided that I needed to walk away, and I no longer wanted anything to do with him. These last few weeks I've just been putting things in motion to end things with him. But not once did I let him touch me."

I look into her brown eyes, getting lost in them. "Are you sure you want to do this now, though? I don't want you to rush into anything. Especially not after today."

Sophia gives me another smile and wraps her arms around my neck, bringing our bodies together and putting us chest to chest.

"Things between Elijah never felt right. I spent four months convincing myself that things would change, that it was just new, and I needed to give it a shot, and then the next four months scared of him and what he might do. Things with Elijah were over for me a long time ago. I just finally got the courage to tell him." Her hands make it up and into my hair. and she starts massaging my scalp through the curls. "I want to do this. I've wanted to do this for a long time, and maybe we should take things between us as slowly as possible, whatever those things may be, but right now, I want to feel close to you. Right now, I want you to take away every bad memory that has invaded my mind in these last four months. Right now, I want you to show me comfort and love and everything in between. I want you to show me how safe I am. I want you and everything you have to offer, Blake."

And I will give her everything that she wants.

Without taking my eyes off hers, I place my hands on her waist and take a step back to give me enough room to slide her pants off.

The second that is done, I take a good look at the beauty who is sitting in front of me. She is absolutely beautiful, but my eyes can't help but zone in on the bruise she has on her ribs, where the asshole pressed his foot against her. I'm surprised the fucker didn't break anything.

Sophia sees that her side has caught my attention and looks down.

"It doesn't hurt," she reassures me, holding out a hand for me to take.

I do, and walk back between her legs, continuing to take off the rest of her clothing. Well, her bra and panties. Once every article of clothing that was touching her body is discarded, I follow suit.

Within seconds, Sophia is naked and in my arms as I walk us over to the shower.

"We're going to owe your brother for a portion of the water

bill since the shower has been running for a while," Sophia states when I put her down.

"I'll take care of it," I say to her, making sure that she is getting the majority of the hot water.

As soon as her shoulders meet the scalding droplets, her whole body seems to relax. She stands under the cascading water for a few minutes, taking a few breaths, as if she is trying to center herself.

I let her be, only stepping up behind her, pressing my front to her back and wrapping my arms around her, happy to have her in my arms once and for all. As she centers herself, I reach for the washcloth and the body wash that are in front of us and start washing the day away.

Sophia is first. I gently slide the washcloth against every single inch of her I can. I fall to my knees, turning her in the process, so that I can clean her lower half, and she lets out a small moan when I slowly glide my fingers along her sex.

"I'm going to make one thing clear to you right now," I say as I run the washcloth down her leg but keep one hand at her core, caressing her.

"What is it?" she asks, her voice sounding breathy.

I lean forward and press a kiss against her mound. "From this moment forward, you're mine, and I'm yours. I love you, and you love me, and unless one of us says otherwise, it's going to stay that way. There isn't a single question as to what we are doing. From this moment until forever, we are together." I place a kiss against her thigh. "That's where things between us are," I say, as I drop the washcloth and let my hand glide up her leg until it lands on her ass and push her body closer to my mouth. "We're together. We will take it slow, as slow as you need, but we are together. Officially. Understood?" I let my nose run along her sex, taking in her scent as it mixes in with the bodywash.

"Yes." Sophia pants outs as my tongue meets her pussy. "I understand."

"Good," I say, lapping at her once, then twice and then a third time before I stand back up, hovering over her.

She looks up at me with a pout because I didn't continue my exploration of her with my tongue.

I can't help but to give her a smirk as I cage her against one of the shower walls, the water now hitting my back instead of both of us.

We stare into each other's eyes, taking in the moment. This day has been a whirlwind roller coaster. So many up and downs, it was fucking exhausting.

Never in a million years did I think that today would be ending like it is.

With Sophia's body pressed up against mine, all slick and warm. I thought I was going to stay in the jail cell and never see her again because of what I did to Elijah, but I was wrong. Thank God I was.

Leaning down, I place my lips against hers, and slowly show her what I've wanted for a very long time. I take my time showing her everything she means to me. I take my time worshipping her body and showing her how much I love her. Everything that we do is nice and slow, each of us taking our time to get to know each other's body in this new light. A light that neither one of us thought was actually going to come to the forefront, but here we are.

At one point, as I kiss my way down her body, taking my time to kiss every single inch of bruising on her ribs, Sophia lets out a sound. A sound that takes me a few seconds to realize is a sob.

I look up at her eyes, and she gives me a smile. Reassuring me that she's okay.

It's a lot of emotion for one day, she tells me, the water from the shower mixing with her tears. The visual breaks my heart, so I try to do what I can to relax her.

Kisses, touches, words.

As we stand under the water, I tell her what she means to me, how beautiful she looks, how much I love her.

I do all of this even as I slide into her hot core and make love to her. The shower isn't the best place for me to show her everything that I want to, but I make do, and when she explodes around me, it's the most glorious image. One that goes right along with the images from our two previous nights together.

The tears continue to roll down Sophia's faces long after the two of us have released all the energy we have into each other.

They continue to come even as we dry ourselves and get ready for bed. And they are still present when our heads meet our individual pillows, and I wrap my arms around her body, bringing her closer to mine.

In those moments before sleep takes over, I do what I have always done, vow to always be there for her whenever she may need me and to protect her if and when the time comes.

This is going to be the last night Sophia cries herself to sleep like this. She will never feel unsafe. Just thinking about the fact she ever felt that way has a lump forming in my throat and tears prickling at my eyes.

It might take some work, but I'm willing to do everything that I can to make her happy.

One step at time, though.

Because today might have been a hard one, but I have a feeling that tomorrow is going to take the cake.

More so when I finally return all the calls and messages waiting for me.

I just have to keep my fingers crossed that when I do return those calls, I still have my hockey career.

CHAPTER FORTY-TWO

BLAKE

SOMEWHERE AROUND SIX in the morning, my eyes pop open. I guess even when I have a few days off and had a day from hell yesterday, my body still wants to wake up as early as possible.

Last time I checked the time, it was around three in the morning. I don't know what time Sophia and I came to bed, but the periodic wake up times made for a long night.

I look over at Sophia and see that she is still fast asleep.

Her hair is all over the place and wild from going to sleep right away instead of waiting for it to dry like she usually does. Even as she sleeps, she is the most beautiful woman in the whole fucking world, and she is all mine. Finally.

Her lips are slightly parted with her pout making me want to lean over and give her a kiss. But I let her be. She had a long day yesterday, and as much as I want to get lost in her and her body, it's better to let her sleep and let her body rest after everything that it has been through.

Without waking her, I untangle myself from her as best I can and get out of bed without so much as a groan from her.

I watch her for a few seconds, a small smile on my lips as I do it.

Never did I think the day would come where she would wake up in my bed and neither one of us had plans to leave, yet here we are, and I couldn't be more ecstatic about it. Because the mornings after our nights together have always had regret, no matter how small, the next morning. Today, there is none, and just the thought has my smile getting bigger.

The smile starts to disappear, though, when my thoughts start shifting toward everything that is still waiting for us. Phone calls, text messages, and I'm sure a press release or two.

There is so much to take care of, so might well start getting it done.

Letting out a sigh, I throw on some clothes and grab my phone before walking out of the bedroom and heading down to the kitchen.

I start the coffee machine before I even turn on my phone. Caffeine is definitely going to be needed for the amount of calls I'm going to have to make.

For a solid minute as the phone powers on, I watch as notifications from last night start rolling in. Surprisingly, it's not as many as I thought, but given the ones that are still waiting for me, it's a lot.

Guess I should get to it.

The coffee machine starts to beep, so I go over and pour myself a cup as I go through the list of people I need to talk to.

Mom. Hunter. Isaac and Maya. My agent. My publicist. Grayson Lane. My dad.

Do I really want to call the man back?

I haven't talked to him since we went to lunch after the Cup win. The lunch that should have been just my dad and me, but ended up being my dad, me, and about five of his buddies from work.

Since then, neither of us has put in any effort to communicate with each other, besides the routine Christmas text, so him calling me now is just as frustrating as him calling me the night before the NHL draft. I know he talks to Hunter and Jainie sometimes but even those calls are rare and far in between. At least that's what I think—my siblings don't really talk to me about the guy who was there for one kid but not the other two.

He's still my father, no matter how much shit he has put me through or what he might say to me when I call him back. He deserves a call back. My mom would yell at me if I didn't.

Letting out a sigh, I plan to call him later today.

For now, I run through the things I'm going to say to my mom, but as I take my first sip of coffee, I hear a door unlock followed by the alarm announcing the front door is being opened.

With my coffee mug in hand, I walk out of the kitchen to the front room.

I guess I can take my brother off the list of people to call.

As I step over the threshold separating the kitchen and front room, though, I see that my brother isn't the only one I will be taking off my list of phone calls.

Hunter throws me a nod when he sees me and quickly moves out of the way so that Selena, my mom, Isaac, and Maya can come in.

I guess it takes an arrest to have a family reunion.

"What are you all doing here?" I ask, grabbing everyone's attention.

Everyone turns and throws small smiles in my direction, but my mom is the first to break the distance between us.

The woman wastes no time to gauge the cuts and bruises on my face. "Next time you get arrested, your first call had better be to me, or I'm going to disown you," she scolds me, her face telling me that she means it, too.

I sigh. "Noted," I say, giving the woman a nod. "Sorry, Ma. I didn't think."

I'm going to have to thank Sophia a million times over for letting my family know what was going on.

"No, you didn't," she says right before she wraps her arms around me, bringing me in for a hug. "What the hell is going on, Blake?" my mom asks when she pulls away from me. "We get a text message from Sophia that you've been arrested and charged with battery, but then neither of you answer your phone after that. Are you going to tell us what is happening, or do I have to kick your ass to get it out of you?"

I may be twenty-two years old, almost twenty-three, and a professional athlete, but my mom still terrifies me. If the woman says she can kick my ass, she will.

I look at her before turning to everyone else who is also waiting for an explanation.

This is going to be a lot harder than calling everyone back because now I have to see their faces.

"Let me go get Sophia, and we will explain everything."

I DIDN'T THINK that repeating the previous day's events would be so damn draining, but it was. Now it's almost two hours later, and my head still hurts just thinking about it.

It actually started to hurt as soon as I started to walk upstairs to get Sophia.

When I walked into the room, I thought I was going to have to wrestle a bear or something because Soph had been dead asleep when I went downstairs. That thought went out the window when I walked into the room, and I found her wide awake. She must have heard my mom's voice because she didn't even ask who was downstairs.

She just gave me a sad smile and got out of bed. I stayed in the room with her as she changed into the clothes she borrowed from Lennie and tried to figure out a way to cover up her bruised cheek.

For a good minute or so, she looked through her purse for something that would cover it up, but she came up empty.

Panic started to flow through her when she realized she didn't have anything with her, everything she brought with her to San Francisco was still back at the hotel. I tried everything that I could to calm her down, and eventually she was able to take a few normal-sized breaths.

I held her in my arms for a few minutes, letting her calm down enough to be able to handle going downstairs and answering every single question that was no doubt going to come her way.

Once she was settled, I placed a kiss against her forehead, and we walked downstairs, hand in hand, something that not a single person in our family raised an eyebrow at.

As soon as she greeted everyone, we went into one of the living areas that this huge-ass house has to offer, and after a few deep breaths, Sophia started telling them everything. I only chimed in when she got to what happened yesterday morning.

The room was tense as fuck. Everyone got angry about the situation. That anger transformed into yelling, not at Sophia or at me, but at everything, and then the yelling turned into tears. I had thought Sophia had cried a lot last night, but those tears were minimal if we compare them to the ones from today.

Every single person in that living room cried with her.

Now hours later, Hunter, Isaac, Christian, and I all are sitting on Hunter's back deck, trying to figure out a game plan for my career.

Christian and Eliana arrived about thirty minutes ago after doing me the favor of picking up the SUV and Sophia's stuff and bringing it all back here. When they saw who was here, they decided to stay—Eliana with the other women upstairs and Christian down here with us.

"How bad is the press?" I ask, a few minutes after someone asked if I had talked to anyone.

Christian ends up answering the question. "Right now, it's not that bad. Your mug shot is out and the fact that you beat up someone. Other than that, not a whole lot of details." Thank fuck. "But just because there aren't any details now, doesn't mean people aren't digging and those details won't make it out soon."

"Great," I mutter out, slouching deeper into my chair.

"I'm surprised the fucker hasn't talked," my brother says from where he sits.

"His time to talk was yesterday. When Sophia hadn't given her statement yet. The second she pressed charges against him, his chance to make Blake the bad guy in all of this was gone. The fucker knows that if he talks now, nobody is going to believe him. It's his word against Sophia's." Hearing the way Isaac's voice breaks has me hating that fucker Elijah even more.

This is the man who practically raised me, who stepped up as a father figure when Roy couldn't. He was even there for me when I needed my brother at times. Seeing him this mad and hearing his voice break as he speaks is something I have never experienced, and I fucking hate it. All I want to do is go to whatever hospital the fucker is as at and finish beating the shit out of him.

If I do that, though, my career would really be in jeopardy. But it would be for Isaac and Sophia, so it would make up for it.

"Where will that go, though? The charges? Do they follow

her to Chicago, or do they stay here?" Christian asks, looking over at me for answers.

I should know the answers to his questions. Before coming to the house, we should have walked back into the police station and asked what the next steps were, but that just slipped our minds.

"I don't know. My mind was all over the place, I didn't even think to ask those questions when I was released. I have the officer's card, though, so I was thinking about calling him since I was already calling the whole damn world," I answer.

I should be reaching for my phone, but instead I just continue to sit here and look out at the scenery in front of me. Anything to keep my mind from exploding.

"Give me the card, I'll call and ask," Isaac says to me, and I give him a firm nod, more than happy to hand over that task.

"Who else is on that call list?" my brother asks, standing up from his seat and going to stand by the small fence that separates the deck from the hill that is his yard.

"Well, you guys were all on there, but since you're here, that takes a good chunk of people off. That only leaves my publicist, my agent, Grayson, and oh yeah, Dad."

"Roy called you?" Hunter asks, almost in disbelief.

I give him a nod. "Yup, and I'm sure he's going to scream my ear off about how I'm a disgrace to the Jacobi name," I say, rolling my eyes.

Hunter just rolls his eyes and lets out a sigh. "I'll talk to him."

I shake my head at him, all the while sitting up in my chair. "No, I'll take care of Dad. As much as I don't want to deal with him, I have to. I put myself in this situation. It's my responsibility, not yours."

As much as I want to delegate this to my brother, I can't. This is my responsibility. It shouldn't have to fall on him.

"Okay, but if you change your mind, I'll take care of it," he offers, giving me a nod.

"Thanks, man."

"Now that just leaves the people who are handling your career," Isaac throws out.

I can't help but let out a sigh and turn to Christian. "What's Anderson saying?"

The fact he is dating our coach's daughter is both a good and bad thing. Good because we can get a feeling for what Coach is thinking, and bad because, well, he's dating Coach's daughter. Holiday dinners sound like they can be awkward as fuck.

My teammate and friend looks at me for a long minute, eventually letting out a sigh. "I talked to him last night, and I told him what I knew and how the charges were dropped, and you were released."

"And?" I push, trying to figure out if I still have a team to go back to when I land in Chicago.

"He sounded relieved but stated that you were still arrested. Some team personnel won't like it and might try to trade or release you. He said if it were up to him, he would keep you as a Knight, but right now it's all dependent on Lane and everyone else."

Of course, it is.

I was hoping for him to tell me the opposite, but hoping for the opposite would be like wishing a damn unicorn would prance across the yard.

"If I were you," Christian starts up again before I can say anything. "I wouldn't put off calling Lane back any longer."

He's right. Of course, he's right. I won't admit that to him, though. I would just go to his head, and it's already so damn big.

Letting out a sigh, I pull out my phone, but instead of calling Grayson back, I call my publicist first to let him know what is going on and to see if he could do some damage control.

Thankfully, he answers on the first ring, and once I tell him that the charges were dropped, he goes into work mode. Within minutes, he comes up with a plan to not only kill my story but to also stop the digging people are going to do into Sophia and what she went through.

I don't care about my story and my image, but I will do anything to protect Sophia and hers.

After my publicist, I call my agent.

According to her, she hasn't heard anything from the Knights about releasing me, but if that call comes, I will be the first to know. I did lose a few endorsement deals, which was fast, I'm not going to lie, but she doesn't see them as a big deal, and frankly, neither do I.

As soon as those two calls are done, I stand up from my chair and mentally prepare myself for the call with Grayson.

The dude is only a few years older than me and hasn't fully grasped how to be a team owner just yet, but he still terrifies me somewhat. Must be the family he comes from.

He must have been expecting my call because he answers after the first ring.

"Blake, I was waiting for you to call me back," he states instead of a greeting.

"Yeah, sorry. I had to get my head straight after yesterday."

"I've been there. Getting arrested is not fun, more so when it's a charge like this," Grayson responds, and I get a feeling that he is speaking from experience.

I don't pry, though, and just ask what I've been dying to know since yesterday.

"Are you releasing me?" I ask, bracing myself against the fence, preparing for whatever news is about to come my way.

Goodbye, hockey. You've been good to me. I have no idea what I will be without you.

"Release you? Why the fuck will I release you?" Grayson asks, sounding almost insulted by my question.

I feel my brows scrunch up in confusion. "Because I was arrested for beating someone up?"

If I was with any other team, they would have said goodbye to me the second they saw my mugshot.

"Do you have a good reason for it?" he asks, and I can't help but to wonder where he's going with this.

"Yeah, I do," I answer without going into too much detail.

"And you were released, I assume, since you are calling me from your cell phone?" he asks.

"Yeah, I was. The charges against me were dropped."

"Then I have no reason to release you," Grayson says, and right away my whole damn body relaxes.

I let my chin fall to my chest, and I let out a sigh of relief.

"Really? I'm still a Knight?" I have to ask because I need all the confirmation I can get.

"You're still a Knight, Blake. And if I have it my way, you will be a Knight for life," he says, and I have never been more relieved in my life.

"And here I was almost puking my guts out thinking I was getting released or traded," I say, a chuckle leaving my mouth. It feels good to laugh a little.

A hand lands on my non-injured shoulder. When I look up, I see that it's my brother, giving me a smile of his own, relaxing me even more.

"Sorry if my calls freaked you out."

"It's alright, man."

"Look, once you get back to Chicago, we'll talk some more. For now, I'll let you go. If you need a few extra days to take care of things, let me know. Your spot on the team will be waiting for you.

"Thank you, Mr. Lane," I say into the phone, so fucking grateful to still have a place on his team.

"Don't call me that. Makes me think I'm my uncle or something. I'll see you in a few days."

The call ends, and I swear the majority of the stress rolling through my body has washed away.

"Damn, and here I thought you were going to be released, and I was finally going to be the fastest one on the team again," Christian jokes.

I turn to look at the fucker and find him shaking his head, but a smirk playing on his ugly face.

"Fuck you," I say, flipping him off in the process.

He starts to laugh, and he is quickly joined by Isaac and Hunter. I shake my head at all three of them for laughing at my expense, but after a few seconds I can't help but laugh with them, too. It's like a high.

The laughing quiets down when the door to the house opens.

"Sorry," Selena says as she stands in the threshold of the open door, her eyes darting from me to my brother. "But, um, your dad is here."

The high that I was just on starts to slowly dissipate.

What is he doing here? Why is he here?

"What? My dad? What the hell is he doing in San Francisco?" Hunter asks the questions that are floating through my head.

Roy Jacobi is supposed to be in Florida last I heard. He only comes west when he's coming to one of Hunter's games or if it's to benefit his work. There's no reason for him to be here now.

Unless he's here for me.

I fucking doubt it, but what do I know? I thought he wasn't going to call me when he found out I got arrested.

Selena looks from my brother over to me. Pity and sadness in her eyes. "He's looking for Blake."

Great.

I guess it's time to have a conversation with my dad, something that I haven't done in months.

This should be fun.

CHAPTER FORTY-THREE

SOPHIA

IN ALL THE years I've been friends with Blake and a part of his life, I can count on two hands how many times I have interacted with his dad. From the ages of five to ten, he was there but not very active in Blake's life like a dad should be. Like he was with Hunter. After the divorce and his move, Roy barely came by to support Blake. I swear, I've seen him around more when Blake officially made it to the NHL than I did when I was a kid.

Roy was never my favorite person, but I've always been respectful whenever he was around.

That's how I'm trying to be right now, especially because my mom and Patty are both in the room, but it's starting to get hard.

Mr. Jacobi knocked on the front door about five minutes ago, and Selena answered. The second she waved him in, he gave her a look of indifference, like he wasn't walking into *her* house.

And here I thought that Hunter was his favorite. You would think because of that, he would show some love to his fiancée, but I guess not. And given the way Selena gives him a tight smile, she noticed the same thing I did.

As he walked in, Selena guided him to the living room where my mom and Patty were with Eliana.

We had been upstairs, mostly just crying all of our eyes out about everything I've been through, when we decided to distract ourselves a bit and have Selena give my mom and Eliana a tour of the house.

We ended up in the living room when the doorbell rang.

I watched as Mr. Jacobi greeted my mom and then his ex-wife. He was cordial but other than that, he was projecting the same indifference he was giving Selena. At least they got some type of greeting, Eliana and I were invisible to the man until I became the bigger person and said hello to him.

He gave me a nod before quickly turning his attention to his ex-wife to tell her he was here to see Blake.

How did he know Blake was even here?

"I'll go get him," Selena said to him, another tight smile on her face, and she scurried away.

Part of me wanted to go with her, just so I didn't have to witness all the awkwardness that was going to float through the room.

But I didn't speak up fast enough, and now, here I am with my eyes playing tetherball between Mr. Jacobi and Patty.

"So, Patty, how have you been?" Mr. Jacobi asks his ex-wife.

With the way that they are interacting, you would never think these two people were married for almost seventeen years.

"I'm fine, Roy. How is Florida?" Patty answers, the sweetest smile imaginable on her face.

"Definitely better than Montana," he says to her, and I'm sure he meant it as a dig.

"I'm glad," Patty answers, actually sounding sincere even if her ex is doing the opposite.

From the corner of my eye, I see that Eliana starts to get up from where she is sitting on the couch next to me, and as much as I want to slap a hand against her thigh to stop her from getting up, I don't. This isn't something she should have to sit through, especially since she doesn't know any of the history that comes with the people in the room.

She gives me a small smile, and she walks out of the room just in time to meet Christian and the other men as they walk into the living room behind Selena.

Christian and Eliana quickly say goodbye to everyone in the room, with Christian telling Blake to call him later, and they excuse themselves.

Once they're gone, the awkwardness shifts into tension, and given the look that I get from my mom, Selena, and Patty, I'm not the only one feeling it.

Something in me is telling me that this day is about to get a hell of a lot more emotional.

I keep my eyes on Blake as he walks in and looks over at his father. His jaw is set tight, and I can see the uneasiness in his eyes. I want to go over to him and wrap my arms around him to comfort him, but I don't. Instead, I study his face.

He's a lot more bruised up than he was last night. If he hadn't spent the majority of yesterday in a jail cell, I would have iced every single bruise and cleaned up the cuts.

Something I should have done to my cheek, too, like I know I should have and was instructed at the hospital to do. Maybe then I wouldn't have had to hold back tears when I saw how my parents reacted when they saw it. My mom had tears of her own, and my dad's eyes burned with so much anger, I thought that he was going to storm out of the house and go find Elijah to finish the job Blake started.

All thoughts of mine and Blake's bruised faces go out the door when Roy stands up from the couch and walks over to his second son.

"Look at you," Roy says with a slight snarl, grabbing Blake by the chin and moving his head in all directions to check the damage to his face. Almost as if Blake is a little boy and fell face first on the ice for the first time, and he's checking him out. Something that I'm sure Roy never did.

Blake swats his dad's hand away and takes a step back.

"Dad, what are you doing here?" Hunter asks, stepping in front of Blake just a smidge. Like he's protecting his little brother from their dad.

"Why do you think? I'm here to check on my son," Roy answers Hunter, but looking over at Blake.

"I'm fine," Blake answers, letting out a sigh and crossing his arms.

"Like hell you are. What the hell were you thinking getting yourself arrested? Do you have any idea what you did by doing that? You can kiss your damn career goodbye. Are you proud of your damn self?" Roy asks, his face getting red as his voice grows louder with each word.

"How did you even know that I was here?" Blake asks.

"You got arrested in San Francisco. It didn't take a whole lot to figure out you were going to go running to your brother to help get you out of this."

"I didn't go running to anyone for help." Blake says, and even if I can see only a fraction of his eyes, I know he threw an eye roll in his dad's direction. "If anything, he came running to me. I was perfectly fine taking care of things on my own."

"Yeah, and look at where that got you. In a damn jail cell with my last name smeared all over the news."

Everyone in the living room watches as Roy steps closer to the two brothers, waiting to see what he's going to do.

"Roy," Patty starts, getting up from her place on the couch and walking over to stand by her sons.

"Can we not do this right now? I don't want to deal with a

lecture from you," Blake says, shaking his head all the while crossing his arms across his chest and meeting his dad's glare straight on.

"We will do this right now. This is fucking serious Blake. What the hell were you thinking?" Roy yells out, stepping close enough that Hunter has to push him back.

"Dad." Hunter interjects, his own face starting to get just as red.

"Don't get in the middle of this," Roy throws at his eldest son, almost shoving him out of the way. "Your brother is throwing his life away. Someone has to knock some sense into him, and you and your mother sure aren't going to do it."

"I'm not throwing my life away," Blake throws out, and this time I'm able to catch an eye roll.

"Like hell you aren't. This stupid stunt is going to follow you forever."

"Then fucking let it!" Blake yells out. "I couldn't give two shits about losing my career. I would do what I did yesterday all over again if I had to."

"And why is that? What the fuck is more important than hockey?" Roy screams, anger filling his voice.

Blake doesn't answer him. Not a single word leaves his mouth. No, Blake doesn't need answers with words because the direction Blake shifts his gaze gives Roy the answer he's looking for.

For a few seconds, Blake looks over at me and silently tells me that I'm more important than hockey will ever be.

Roy scoffs. "Of course. I should have known. Of course, this was about a damn girl."

"Roy!" Patty yells out.

"I would watch your fucking mouth if I was you," my dad says at the same time.

"A damn girl," Blake repeats his father's words. "*A damn girl*," he repeats again, this time shaking his head just as he steps out from behind Hunter and in front of his dad, coming toe to toe, their nose almost touching. Both men stand at over six feet two, but at this moment Blake looks ten times bigger.

Blake pokes a finger into his father's chest, as if he were poking the bear.

"Sophia is more than just a damn girl. If you were more involved in my life, you would fucking know that. You would fucking know that she's been the most important piece of my life since I was five years old. If you were more fucking involved, you would fucking know she's a hell of a lot more important than hockey. That if the choice presented itself, I would choose her a thousand times over. You want to know why? Want to know why I would choose her over a damn sport? Because she's been there through everything. Every tryout, every injury, every win, and every loss, every fucking team, she has been there for me. She was even there for me when you decided to choose Hunter over me and Jainie.

"At ten years old, she was there, hugging me as tight as she could while you and Mom fought about Hunter going to live with you, telling me she will always be by my side, hockey, or no hockey. Sophia has been there through fucking everything! You want to know what I was thinking yesterday? Want to know what was going through my head as I walked into that hotel? I was thinking that the woman I love, the woman I want to spend the rest of my life with, was going through something that nobody should. That she was scared, and I needed to do everything and anything to get her out of there. To fucking protect her. I was thinking that if I didn't do anything, I was going to fucking lose her forever. That that fucker was going to take her away from me. That was what was going through my head. Not hockey, not my career. Her. I was thinking about her because I fucking love her, and if I lose her, I won't know what to do with myself.

"But you wouldn't know that because you never cared enough. You only started to care when I became serious about hockey and started talking about possibly entering the draft. You don't even give a flying fuck about my life because if you did, you would be more worried about Sophia than my fucking career. You just care about the fact that I might lose my contract, and you won't have anything to brag to your damn buddies about. That you will lose those season tickets and that fancy box you love so much."

"That's not fucking true." Roy lets out, his hands forming fists.

"It is because if it wasn't, you wouldn't be here lecturing me for getting fucking arrested. You'd be telling me that I did the right thing, that you'd do the same, but you don't give a shit. You only care about what my career can bring to you, nothing else. If you fucking cared, you would have been there. You would have been there for every game, from when I was five to now, but you weren't." Blake yells out, tears running down his face as he does.

Years of anger, of frustration toward his dad is finally coming out.

I stand up from the couch to go over to him, to comfort him, to be by his side, to do something, anything, but both Patty and Hunter shake their heads in my direction, stopping me.

He needs to do this. He's been holding on to this for years, and this is finally the time to let it out.

"Blake, I've been there—" Roy starts, but he's interrupted by his son.

"No, you haven't. You weren't the one who taught me how to get a better handle on my stick or how to tie my skates properly. You weren't the one who would wake me up at five in the morning, before school, so that I can get more ice time. You weren't the one who took time out of their day while I was in college to do sessions with me so that I could feel ready to sign my first contract. You weren't there for me to talk about girls or give me the damn sex talk. You weren't there to put your hand on my shoulder while I waited to get drafted," Blake says to Roy, and automatically my eyes shift to my dad.

Those were things my dad did. Things my dad has been a part of.

I always joked that Blake was my parents' second child, but in a way, he really was.

"You were never there. Those were all things that Isaac did, and when I got older Hunter was there for me, too, but never you. You were never there for me, so don't say that you were. Financially, sure, but physically or even fucking mentally. Never."

As soon as the last few words leave Blake's mouth, the room gets enveloped in silence. Silence and tension.

I look around, and not only does the majority of the room have tears in their eyes, but it also seems like everyone is holding their breath waiting for something else to happen. Another screaming match. Maybe somebody throwing a punch.

Blake is the one who eventually breaks the silence by letting out a sigh and standing down. He keeps his eyes on his dad as he backs away, but breaks the stare down when he reaches me and turns his gaze to mine.

His icy blue eyes are filled with turmoil and tears, and I just want to take every single bit of it away. I reach up with both of my hands and start wiping his tears away, wishing that I could do more.

At this moment, it's just the two of us. Nobody else is in the room.

And it stays that way for a minute or two, until our little bubble is broken.

"I think maybe you should go, Roy," my dad suggests, most likely so nobody else will have to.

"You don't get to kick me out. This is my son's house, not yours." Roy says, with a bite still in his tone but not as much as there was earlier. This whole thing must have taken a huge toll on him, too.

"Mr. Martinez is right, Dad. You should probably go," Hunter says, letting out a sigh.

"Hunter," Mr. Jacobi says, arguing with him.

"A lot of shit has gone down in the last twenty-four hours, and all of this isn't helping. Take a few days, and then maybe you and Blake can talk about all of this some more, but right now, I think it's best that you go," Hunter responds, putting his foot down.

I can see from his face that he finds this whole thing hard. Hunter has an okay relationship with his dad. From what I hear, it's not perfect, but it's decent. He's trying his hardest to be a respectful son, but right now he is choosing his brother over their dad.

"Is that what you want?" Roy asks, turning to Blake in the process. There's hurt in his facial expression and seeing it has new tears springing into my eyes. I've never seen him like this.

Blake turns fully to face him, and he must see the same thing that I do because he lets out a sigh and hangs his head a bit before he answers.

"I want a lot of things, Dad, especially when it comes to you, but Hunter is right," Blake says, raising his head and looking at his father. "These last twenty-four hours have been a lot. And having a screaming match about how some parts of my child-hood were shitty isn't helping anything. Hunter and Isaac are right, and I think that you should go."

"Blake," Roy starts to argue, but Blake holds up a hand stopping him.

"Asking you to leave isn't me cutting you out of my life, Dad. It's me setting a boundary. I would fucking love to have a decent relationship with you, especially one where I don't have to think that you're only coming around because of my career. I would fucking love it if I didn't cringe every single time I see your name come across my screen. But we aren't going to get there today. You're pissed, I'm pissed, and screaming at each other isn't going to fix things. It will just make things worse." Blake shakes his head and releases a sigh before continuing. "We can meet up whenever you want and hash it out then, but for now, I think you should go."

For the first time since he walked in, or maybe since I've known the man, Roy Jacobi looks defeated and completely saddened at the idea of leaving.

It's like he's just realizing how strained his relationship with his kids really is.

As I watch him, I can't help but realize just how alike he and Blake are, and seeing that expression pass across both of their faces breaks my heart,

Both he and Blake aren't perfect, they both are partly at fault for the type of relationship they have, but hopefully, this opens a door for them.

Hopefully Roy leaves here today and starts thinking about how to make his relationship with his children better. Because if they continue down this path, nobody is going to be happy.

After a long minute or two, Roy lets out a sigh. "Okay, I'll head out," He announces before looking straight at Blake again. "The second you get back to Chicago, you call me to finish this conversation." Roy orders, hurt still very much present on his face, but even with the hurt in his eyes, he still finds it in him to point a finger at Blake as if he were a petulant child.

Blake's face gets hard for a second, but he answers his dad. "I will."

Roy throws him a curt nod before turning to look at the rest of the individuals in the room.

"I'll be on my way," he announces, his head bowing a bit before turning to Hunter. "I'll check in with you later," he says, which just earns him a nod from his son.

As Roy starts making his way out of the living room, Blake lets out a sigh of relief, one that relaxes his shoulders beyond belief, and reaches for my hand.

I interlace our fingers and hold on to his hand as tightly as I can.

My hold on him grows even tighter when I notice Roy stops at the edge of the living room.

"Blake," he calls out, grabbing everyone's attention again. We all watch as he stands there, looking as if he's at a loss for words and doesn't really know what to say. Eventually, he is able to find the words and his voice. "I'm sorry."

Two words full of so much weight, and everyone here can feel it.

Blake looks up at his dad for a good minute, not saying a single word.

It's as he tightens his hand around mine, like he is gathering strength, he speaks. "I'm sorry, too."

With that, Roy gives him a nod and leaves the living room, and a few seconds later the house.

Emotion continues to circulate throughout the room for a few minutes, everyone not saying a single word.

We stay like that for about a minute until Hunter finally breaks the silence.

"I guess one good thing came out of all of this," he says, everyone in the room looking over at him.

"What good thing?" Selena asks, looking a bit confused.

I notice a smirk form on Hunter's face as he makes eye contact with me.

For some reason, I feel a blush creeping up my face as he looks at me like that. Like he knows my dirty secret or something.

"Blake finally got his head out of his ass and told Sophia he's in love with her. Do you know how much money I've lost because of his stubborn ass?"

My mouth drops open.

Hunter knew how Blake felt about me? Blake told his brother but didn't tell me? What the hell?

"I should point out he's not the only one who had to pull their head out of their ass. I could have told him, too," I say, defending Blake. Both of us are at fault here.

While I worry about clearing Blake's name, though, he's worried about something else.

"Hold up, you've been betting on my love life?" Blake asks, sounding annoyed.

Hunter shrugs. "I had to keep myself entertained somehow."

"What the fuck? Who were you betting against?" Blake asks, letting go of my hand and crossing his arms across his chest.

I shouldn't be thinking about this, what with all the emotions we've been going through yesterday and today, but the man looks hot when he stands like that.

All thoughts of Blake being hot get annihilated when Hunter looks over at my dad with a raised eyebrow instead of answering Blake's question.

Out of all the people Hunter could say he was betting against, my dad was nowhere near my list of guesses.

I'm not going to lie, I'm surprised. I thought it would be Christian, possibly Liam, maybe even Selena, but never my dad.

You think you know someone, but then they're betting on you behind your back.

"Dad? What the hell?" I ask after a fake gasp leaves my mouth. I'm not annoyed by this. It's actually a little funny.

"What?" my dad exclaims, holding his hands up, like there's absolutely nothing wrong with betting on his daughter's love life. "I wasn't betting you guys were never going to get together. I just thought you guys would finally admit it to yourselves when you were at least in your thirties."

My mom walks over to the man and slaps him across the head.

"What the hell, old man? No faith in me whatsoever," Blake says, shaking his head.

"I had faith in you," my dad tells him. "My daughter on the other hand, not so much."

A real gasp escapes me this time. "Unbelievable."

Soon everyone starts putting their two cents in on the conversation, with the majority having smiles on their faces as they do. Blake is the only one holding out, but I can see him trying to hold it in but failing.

Eventually he lets the smile go but continues to tease my dad and his brother. And the teasing continues when the betting is forgotten and the conversation moves to Blake and I officially coming together.

And we are officially together, just like Blake told me last night in the shower.

I didn't know how our families were going to react to the news. There may have been a part of me that thought they would be against it, but seeing how they are reacting to the news makes my heart soar.

Seeing both my parents happy at who I'm with is something I've wanted to see for so long, and now it's happening.

For the first time in what feels like forever, I feel happy, content.

But the best thing of all is that I don't feel fear.

I'm no longer scared to say the wrong thing. I'm no longer scared of Elijah's anger.

Fear is something that is no longer going to dictate my life, and I'm going to try and keep it that way.

CHAPTER FORTY-FOUR

BLAKE

I HATED ELIJAH SWANSON, last week, and I fucking hate him even more today.

You would think after he landed himself in the hospital with a broken jaw and because he is facing charges for domestic violence, the fucker would go into hiding and not stir up any more shit.

But of course, that's not what he is doing.

Instead, the asshole is trying to use whatever star power that I have to his advantage. It doesn't matter if I'm at the bottom of the fucking totem pole of famous athletes, he is doing anything he can to not only call Sophia's story bogus but playing the victim. According to the article my publicist sent me this morning, I have anger issues and don't know how to control it.

Like fuck I do.

If I had anger issues, he would have gone to the hospital with a lot more than a broken jaw.

Not only is he trying to damage Sophia's image, he's also been giving me a daily reminder of how much I hate him.

In San Francisco, I knew that if the Knights didn't cut me, then I sure wasn't going to be seeing the ice anytime soon because of how my shoulder felt. I've had enough injuries in my life to know when something is wrong.

And something was definitely wrong with my shoulder.

The day after getting back from California, I reported to the Knights faculty and had the team doctors check me out. According to the team athletic trainer, when I punched the bastard, I hyperextended my shoulder.

I was hoping they were going to tell me that it was just a small strain, and I would be on the ice for the game against New York, but of course that wasn't the case.

The injury was more in the moderate category, which meant I was going on the injured reserve list for at least two weeks. Which meant no home games against Arizona and New York, no away games in Arizona and Anaheim, no hockey whatsoever until I was cleared.

Every day, for those two weeks, I was reminded of that bastard's face, and how if he wasn't such an asshole, I wouldn't be watching my team play without me.

The one thing that makes all of this better, though, is Sophia.

Since we've been back from San Francisco, we've been trying to figure out what normalcy is now that we are together. Which hasn't been hard since we already did so much together and shared an apartment. I think the hardest thing to figure out has been our sleeping situation.

The first night back in our apartment, we stood there for a good five minutes, trying to figure out what to do.

Eventually, I made the decision for us by walking us to her room, where I explored every single inch of her body as if it were my first time.

Sophia and I may be living in bliss, but we still have the cloud of Elijah, the charges against him, and my shoulder injury hanging over our heads.

And hopefully today, one of those things will be an afterthought. What sucks, though, is the fact that it won't be Elijah or the charges he's facing. At the very least, I'll find out if I can hit the ice in two days or not.

I'm keeping my fingers crossed on hitting the ice. I don't know how much more of this damn injury I can take.

And given the look on the team medical doctor's face, I'm going to guess it's not what I might be hoping for.

"What do you think? Am I cleared?" I ask from where I sit on the table in the training room, eager to get out of here and put on my skates. I had already missed enough games. I don't want to miss any more.

"You been resting and doing those exercises I told you to do?" Dr. Watson asks, coming over and moving my shoulder.

I give him a nod. "Yeah. My girlfriend is studying to be a nurse, and she's been keeping me in check," I answer him.

It takes me a second to realize this is the first time that I've called Sophia my girlfriend, and it feels fucking good saying it. For years, I thought about what it would be like for her to have that title, of what it would feel like for her to officially be mine, and now that she is, it's like I won the Cup all over again.

She was meant to be mine, and I'm never letting her go.

"Good," he states, giving me a curt nod.

That doesn't give me the answer I want.

"Please don't tell me you're going to keep me out for another week," I let out, almost sounding annoyed. I'm all for resting and getting better, but my shoulder feels fine, and not even being able to skate is making me crazy. You would think since this is a shoulder injury, I would be able to at least put on my skates and hit the ice, but no. My drill sergeant girlfriend and Watson told me to stay off skates until I'm cleared, because apparently I can fall and hurt myself even more. As if I didn't professionally skate for a living.

Watson moves my shoulder again, not saying anything. After about a minute or so, he drops my arm and gives me a smirk.

Bastard.

"You're cleared. I'll let Shawn and Grayson know they can clear you from the injured list. You might not be able to play against Dallas tomorrow night, but for sure the game against Boston."

"Fucking finally," I say, letting out a sigh.

"I would have cleared you last week, but you wouldn't have been a hundred percent. Everything looks good today, though. Just get back into things slowly and don't go breaking anybody else's jaw."

Only if my girl is in danger.

"I'll try not to," I answer, and a few seconds later, I'm free to go.

No time is wasted going into the locker room, sliding my skates on, and grabbing my stick. The team had practice earlier to prepare for Dallas tomorrow, so there's a possibility that a few guys are still hanging around our practice arena.

As much as I would have liked to get my ass kicked by some drills, just skating on the ice for a few minutes is all I need at the moment.

When I reach the rink, I find it empty of people. Only a few pucks are still left on the ice that the equipment personnel have yet to pick up.

I take a few minutes to skate around the ice to get my feet right. I may have only been off the ice for three weeks, what with bye-week and this injury, but it feels like it has been forever, and I have to get reacquainted with it.

It's crazy because when the season is over, I'm okay with not skating a whole lot, but when it's in season, the only thing I want to do half the time is have my skates attached to my legs.

After a few loops around the ice, I start shooting some pucks into the net. At first, I'm a little stiff—my injury and Watson's words to take it easy are still very much in my head, but after a few slap shots, I'm able to loosen up.

It takes me about a good twenty minutes to feel as good as new, so I just start running random drills by myself.

"You know, when a player is placed on the injured list it means they rest so they can recover from their injury, not go out on the ice and re-injure themselves." A guy's voice sounds out, stopping me mid stride.

I look around the rink and find Grayson Lane standing at the door to the ice, wearing skates of his own and a stick in his hand. I know he's the owner of the Knights and all, but I didn't think the guy even knew how to hold a stick properly, let alone skate.

"Watson cleared me a little bit ago. He said he was going to pass the news on to you and Anderson," I say to him, trying to not sound so damn winded.

Three weeks of no workouts, and I'm like a newbie.

Grayson gives me a nod as he steps on the ice.

"He must have sent that piece of information to my office, and I haven't seen it, since I was driving over here," he says as he reaches for a puck and positions himself to take a shot.

The puck effortlessly glides into the net.

"You play," I conclude because a novice individual would not have been able to make that shot from this distance.

"Yup, played all through high school, was even thinking about joining the draft, but then I fucked up my knee pretty badly, so I quit."

Damn. I didn't know that.

"Is that why you bought the team? To fulfill some sort of dream or something?" I ask, taking a shot of my own. It glides smoothly and lands right next to Grayson's.

"Partly." He shrugs, sliding another puck over and positioning it to shoot it, but instead, he leans against his stick and faces me. "It had more to do with my family. But I did think it would be beneficial for the team to have an owner who actually knew the ins and outs of the sport and not solely be about money. I may not know all of the business side of things, but I'm learning and getting my footing solid."

He shoots his puck, and again, it's smooth as hell.

"Why the Knights, though?" I ask after taking my shot. It hits the edge of the net and doesn't make it in.

"Why not the Knights?" Grayson answers, skating over to the edge of the ice to grab more pucks. "They've been my team since I moved to Chicago when I was five. They were the team I wanted to get drafted to. It was the team my uncle owned at one point. So, when the opportunity came up, I didn't hesitate in taking it."

And here I thought he bought the team because we had a solid chance to win the Cup. Now that I know it was because of a personal connection, it makes me see Grayson in a different light.

I can definitely see him becoming a great owner one day.

Speaking of which...

"Well, I'm glad you bought the Knights. Because if you hadn't, I wouldn't be here right now. Some other owner would have traded me the second he saw my mug shot. Thank you for not doing that." I hold out a hand and right away he shakes it.

"No need to thank me. You're a great player, Blake. I would have been stupid to trade you. Besides, if I was put in that position, I would have done the same thing you did. Especially if it was my sister, then I wouldn't have stopped at a broken jaw," Grayson voices.

"Trust me, I didn't want to," I grumble under my breath, but he caught it.

He lets out a laugh, but quickly controls it. "How's Sophia? I've seen some stuff in the media, and I've been meaning to check in on the two of you, but I keep forgetting."

After we got back from San Francisco, a statement was released by the team's front office, going into some detail about what went down that landed me in a jail cell and my mug shot all over the place. The statement also stated they were going to stand by my side no matter what and weren't going to release me.

But of course, that was all overshadowed by Elijah's damn smear campaign.

That fucking bastard.

"She's doing better," I tell him, my mind going to the smile she gave me this morning before she went to school. A smile that will be engraved in my mind forever, right next to the others. "It's definitely still very much on her mind, more so now that this might go to court."

"Does she need a lawyer? I know a few who would love to help her with her case," Grayson offers.

"She has one, but thank you for offering."

As much as I would like to take him up on that offer, he's already done a lot by keeping me here in Chicago, I don't want to overstep.

"Of course. If that changes, though, let me know, and I will take care of it," he states.

This guy really isn't like other team owners, is he?

"I really appreciate that."

Grayson Lane is actually a cool dude and not just some rich asshole who bought the team just because.

For the next ten minutes or so, we go back to shooting pucks and just talking about absolute nonsense. We don't break until someone else joins us at the edge of the rink.

"Jacobi," Logan calls out, looking like the mean motherfucker he is. Add on that facial expression he's wearing, and not even the President of the United States would want to cross him.

"Yeah?" I call out, taking one last shot before turning to him.

"Crawford and Rodriguez said if I saw you to tell you we're getting together to watch the game," Logan yells out, reminding me of the text conversation the four of us had yesterday.

"Alright, I'll be right there."

Grayson and I clean up the ice while Logan stands on the edge, looking pissed off.

He's always pissed off, but for some reason he looks like he's on an extra level. What's up his ass?

Logan's anger issue gets more intense when Grayson approaches him, and that just confuses me even more.

"I should get going," Grayson announces, shooting Logan a look before turning to me. "That offer, if you need it, let me know, and I will make some calls."

"Sure thing." I say to him, shaking his hand again as a thank you.

"Volkov," Grayson throws in Logan's direction, his eyes even narrowing in the process.

Okay, these two have to have history. What, I don't know if I want to find out.

"Lane," Logan spits out, which causes Grayson to chuckle, which just pisses Logan off even more.

Maybe I should find out because I've never seen Logan so, what's the word? Enraged.

Grayson walks off and leaves me with the big broody bastard who looks like he can melt the ice with his eyes.

"What the fuck is up with you two?" I find myself asking, as I see Logan is watching Grayson leave the rink.

"Nothing," he answers all too quickly. "What did he offer you?" he asks quickly, changing the subject.

"What?"

"He said something about an offer. What did he offer you?" he asks again, no sign of teasing or joking in his tone.

Seriously, what is wrong with him?

"A lawyer for Sophia. If the one she has now didn't work out, he offered to make some calls," I answer, finding this whole interaction weird as hell. "What's going on with you? What the fuck is going on between you and Lane?"

"Nothing," he gives me again. "I just don't like the guy. He and his whole family are a bunch of snakes."

"Snakes?" What the hell?

Living in Chicago these last few years, I've definitely heard my fair share of things about the Lane family, but nothing bad. I can't help but wonder if Logan knows something the rest of us don't.

"Yup. Watch your back when it comes to him."

Okay then.

I guess our team owner isn't as cool as I thought.

CHAPTER FORTY-FIVE

SOPHIA

"JACOBI! What is wrong with you?! You can skate faster than that! Get your shit together!" I yell toward the ice. A few heads turn in my direction, but I don't care. This is my version of cheering on my boyfriend.

Boyfriend.

Blake is my boyfriend. That is definitely going to take some getting used to.

But it feels so good calling him that.

"Oh, I've missed you yelling like that," Chloe says from where she sits next to me in the stands at the Knights arena as we watch them play Boston. Tonight Chloe was able to get a babysitter for Emma and come to the game with me for somewhat of a girl's night. A girl's night while we watch our men work.

"I've missed it, too. It seems like it's been forever since I've heckled him." I say, giving her a smile.

"It has. I've also missed you coming to games. Sitting up in the suite with the other girlfriends and wives is not the same."

Tears start to spring in my eyes at her comment. I missed

coming to games, too, and if it wasn't for Elijah and my fear of what he would do, I would have come every chance I got.

"Chloe, I'm sorry I basically abandoned you this season. I wanted to come, I did. I just didn't want to make things any more complicated than what they were."

My friend reaches over and takes my hand in hers and gives me a good squeeze. "Do not apologize. The situation you were in was definitely a bad one, and you were trying to do everything you could to make sure things didn't escalate." Her own set of tears start to form in her eyes. "Do I wish you would have told me so that I could help you somehow? Sure, but I understand why you didn't. So don't apologize. Please. Even if some of the other WAGS didn't understand me like you did."

I let out a laugh and wipe my tears away. "Aren't you considered like one of the head WAGs, though, since you're the captain's girlfriend?"

I may have only been in the WAG club for about three weeks, but I know a bit about how the elite club works.

"Apparently, but I don't want that title. This time last year, I didn't even know a fraction of the hockey lingo I know now. I'm not qualified." She gives me a smile, as she wipes her own tears away, and I can't help but to laugh again.

"I needed that little laugh," I say to her, squeezing her hand in the process.

"Good, but how are you? I feel like we haven't talked a whole lot about the subject. And we don't have to talk about it if you don't want to. But if you do, the door is open, and I'm here to listen."

I appreciate Chloe.

When we got back from San Francisco, Blake and I looped Liam, Chloe, and Logan in on everything that was going on. Since it was something the media was picking up, especially now with Elijah playing the victim, they had a right to know what was going on.

Since then, the three of them, with Eliana and Christian, have been as supportive as they can.

But as much as I don't want to not think about the whole situation, it's a little hard, now more than ever because the charges I pressed against him just add to the whole situation. One helpful part is the fact the case was moved to Chicago, since most of the situation happened here, but everything else about the case makes me want to have an anxiety attack every time I think about it.

The lawyer I hired to help me with all of this keeps throwing hypotheticals my way and every day, and each and every time a new one pops up, it throws me off course. This type of case can go in so many different directions, so every time I hear of a new one, I start to question if I should continue to pursue it or just drop it. Every time my lawyer tells me that the evidence we have might not be enough to at least put him behind bars for a day, I get discouraged and want to give up on this all together.

It's an internal battle, and I don't know what to do anymore. I just want to be done with it and not have to think about Elijah Swanson ever again. And with every passing day, I wonder more and more if pressing charges was the right call.

Letting out a sigh, I try to center my thoughts and answer Chloe's question.

"I'm okay," I start, trying to find the right words. "But it's starting to feel like a lot," I admit.

Why did I think pressing charges against someone was going to be easy?

"I get that," Chloe says, squeezing my hand again.

I look down at the ice to center myself a little bit by looking for my number ten. Blake was officially cleared to play a few days ago, and this home game against Boston is his first day back. He was able to travel with the team to Dallas, but he wasn't able to play. I know that he's glad to be back on the ice, but a part of me can't help but feel bad because I was the reason he got hurt and wasn't able to play.

Watching Blake for a few minutes as he hits the ice and then moves back to the bench usually calms me in a way not a lot of people would understand. But right now, it's not working.

"I'm thinking about dropping the charges against Elijah," I tell Chloe, the prickle of tears from earlier combing back up again.

"Oh," Chloe says, the roar of the crowd stopping her from saying anything else.

The Knights were able to get the puck away from Boston and are currently making their way to the other end of the ice.

Christian passes the puck over to one of the rookies, who passes it over to Liam, who shoots it into the net, adding another point to the board for the Knights.

Both Chloe and I celebrate quietly in our seats.

"What does Blake say?" she asks a few minutes later.

I shake my head at her, keeping my eyes on the game. "I haven't told him. I should have, especially with everything he has been dealing with like his shoulder, but I don't want to make it seem like all of this happened for nothing."

What if he gets mad? He was arrested and spent hours in a jail cell, on top of not being able to play for two weeks. Some reward has to come from that, but I don't know if I'm mentally capable of going through a whole court proceeding and have it come out in Elijah's favor.

"Soph, it won't be for nothing. You were able to find the courage to walk away from him, and now, you and Blake are together. That's not for nothing. Unless..." she says, pausing for a second before starting back up. "You and Blake are together now, right?"

I take my eyes away from the ice and turn to my friend, giving her a small smile. "Yeah, we are together."

"Then a lot of good has come out of this situation. Pressing charges against someone is a hard thing to do. It can take a mental toll on you. So, if you decide to drop those charges because it's what's best for you mentally, nobody is going to judge you for it. We will all be in your corner, supporting you no matter what." Chloe gives me a reassuring squeeze to drive home her words.

My eyes move back to the ice where I see Blake has made it off the bench again and is trying to take the puck away from the Boston forward.

I keep my eyes on Blake as I ask my next question. One that has been on my mind since that morning at the police station.

"What if he does it again? What if he meets with someone else and gets more violent with her? What if I drop the charges and that happens? People are going to look at me and hate me for not preventing it from happening it again. They could look at it as I had my shot, but I didn't do everything I could to put him behind bars, no matter the length of the sentence."

The crowd sounds out again, but this time in boos as Logan lands himself in the box for roughing.

We really shouldn't be having this conversation at a hockey game, even less so while we sit in the stands, but at this point I really don't care. I need to talk to someone.

I would talk to Blake about all of this, but we've been in a bubble filled with love and happiness since we got back from San Francisco. I don't want to take that way. But I'm going to have to do it. He needs to know what's going on in my mind when it comes to Elijah, and I can't keep up the act that it's not affecting me.

"Your story is out there, Soph." Chloe starts up again once the crowd has gone somewhat quiet. "People will know what kind of person that he is. No blame should fall on you. You told them what kind of person he can turn into. Whether they believe it or not is up to them. If they don't, then their ignorance shouldn't fall on you. It falls on them."

My beautiful friend is right.

The blame shouldn't fall on me. But there are people who are going to try their hardest to make sure that it does, no matter the outcome.

"Thank you, Chloe." I say to her, reaching over and wrapping my arms around her.

"Of course. I'm here whenever you need me."

I give her a smile when I pull back. "I'm sorry I made a hockey game so heavy."

"We should really plan a girl's night on a non-game day. Maybe then Eliana will finally join us, too."

"Whenever you want, I will be there."

The rest of the game ends up turning into a blur. One second we are in the middle of the second period, and the next, the game is over with the Knights barely coming out with the win.

As soon as the game is called, both Chloe and I make our way down to the ice. She heads directly to Liam, and I head to Blake.

This is the first time I'm doing this as something more than his best friend, and for some reason, I'm nervous as I walk down to where he is waiting. Apparently the title shift from best friend to girlfriend was a lot more drastic than I thought it would be.

The nerves go away, though, when he finds me in the crowd and throws a boyish grin in my direction. Now instead of nerves, a swarm of butterflies starts to invade my whole body.

Good butterflies. Butterflies I know will be here to stay, and I won't be letting go of even after I take my last breath.

"'Get your shit together,' huh?" Blake asks, his grin turning into a smirk as I close the distance between us.

"You heard that?" I ask, raising my eyebrows. There's no way he did.

"You're loud as fuck. Even with a crowd of over thirty thousand," he says, leaning down and giving me a chaste kiss on the lips.

I can't even get mad at him for calling me loud anymore.

"Good. Now you can get your shit together."

"I will see what I can do," he tells me just as his eyes move down my body. "Where did you get that jersey?" he asks, his tone shifting a bit.

A blush starts to creep up my face.

Since it was the first game of his I was attending since October, I thought I would pull all the stops out today with my outfit to celebrate his coming off of the injured list. All the stops included faux leather pants, heeled boots, hair and makeup done, and a jersey I took from his closet.

I could have worn any of the other Jacobi jerseys I own, but I thought this jersey would not only make this whole thing special but would go perfectly with my outfit. I was right on both counts.

And because I've been with Blake through his whole NHL career, I know exactly which jersey I'm wearing.

"From your closet," I answer him, giving him a fake confused look.

"That's my first game day jersey," he says, that smirk of his getting more prominent.

"Is it?" I ask, looking down at the jersey as if I had no clue. "I had no idea."

"Cut the crap, Martinez. Yeah, you did. You wore that jersey on purpose," Blake concludes.

And now it's my turn to wear a smirk. "And what purpose would that be?" I ask, folding my arms across my chest.

It doesn't go unnoticed how Blake's eyes go directly there before meeting my eyes.

He closes the distance between us even more and leans all the way down until his lips are at the shell of my ear.

"So I can fuck you while you wear that and only that when we get home," he says right before taking my lobe between his teeth.

Thank God I wore my hair down today. We don't need people seeing what he's doing to me.

Because he's right. That is why I wore it.

"You may be on to something, Jacobi," I say to him, giving him a grin when he pulls away. "Maybe you should hurry up with that shower so that you can go home and find out if that was indeed the purpose of me wearing this jersey." I throw him a wink.

"Fuck," he says, shaking his head. "Meet me by the locker room."

He starts to skate away, but I reach out and take his hand before he can.

"We also have to talk about something," I say, biting the bullet on talking to him about Elijah and how I want to move forward. "So, hurry, yeah?"

"Is everything okay?" he asks, concern covering his face.

I throw him a nod and give his hand a squeeze. "Yeah, everything is fine. I just want to get your thoughts on something."

"Okay, give me a few, and we will go home."

"IS THAT WHAT YOU REALLY WANT?" Blake asks a few hours later.

After the game, instead of coming straight home, we went out to get some drinks with the team to celebrate the Knights win tonight.

If I'm being honest, it felt strange to me. Since Blake signed with the Knights, we have always gone out with the team after a win. Tonight, it felt different, though, since I was there in the capacity of his girlfriend and not just his best friend. It threw me for a loop a bit, but I loved every single minute of it.

Going out for drinks with the team wasn't our first official date, that hasn't happened yet, but hopefully it will soon. I got to spend time with Blake and look into his eyes which are my favorite color of blue. What more can I ask for?

When dinner was done, we came home, and he put on a movie. To de-stress from the game, he said, but I knew what he was doing.

He knew that something was on my mind, and he was doing everything he could to distract me from it. That made me love him more than anything.

Eventually, that distraction had to come to the forefront. I couldn't keep what was on my mind to myself any longer. He had to know what I was thinking.

So, I paused the movie, and I told him.

I told him how my mind was spiraling with thoughts about what to do with the case against Elijah. I told him how I was thinking about dropping charges. How even if we just started this whole process, I was already feeling discouraged about what the outcome might be. I watched him the whole time, more so when I told him that I wanted to drop the charges.

Now moments later, I'm in Blake's arms, getting lost in the heat his body is letting off and how tight his arms are holding me to him.

I nod against his chest. "Yeah, it is."

I go back to the moment where I started thinking about doing this.

Earlier in the week, I had a meeting with my lawyer to talk about the evidence side of things. She said that the more that we have the better.

I showed her and gave her all I have.

She looked at every picture, and one single question started the downward spiral.

Did I have any more?

When I shook my head no, she let out a sigh I can still hear days later.

She told me she would do everything in her power to make sure Elijah is never able to hurt another person again, but with the evidence we have, it would be hard. It won't be enough to put him behind bars. At most he might pay a fine, but even that could be a stretch.

There were no broken bones.

No hospital visits besides the one in San Francisco were documented.

There was nothing that would make this a strong enough case.

My lawyer told me that day they will take this case as long as I will pursue the charges, but that it was going to be a hard one. One that we may lose and may take both a physical and mental toll.

I left that meeting not knowing what to do. Hell I told Chloe, and I still felt the same way.

It wasn't until I was with Blake that I finally made my decision.

As much as I hate the idea, I think it would be better to drop the charges.

"My lawyer is right," I say, pushing myself away from Blake just a tiny bit so I could see his face. "The case isn't strong enough. And if this goes to any kind of court, I don't know if I want to handle reliving that fear again. I would rather walk away than have to deal with that pain again. This doesn't have anything to do with Elijah, in any way, or what he is saying to the press. I have no love for him whatsoever. This is about me and doing what's right for me, and I think dropping the charges is going to be the right thing to do."

Blake looks at me with so much emotion in his facial expression. There's compassion and love and a little of everything else floating around so I can't get a good read on him.

A part of me thinks he doesn't like the idea, and I can see why. We're talking about dropping the charges and letting Elijah walk free with no reprimand. He had me in a corner balling my eyes out, sobbing for him to calm down. If it wasn't for Blake I don't know what that morning would have turned into. Elijah hurt someone who Blake loves, and if places were reversed, I would have wanted to see Elijah pay for everything he did and then some.

After about a minute of looking into my eyes, Blake gives me a nod.

"If that's what you really want to do, then that's what we'll do. I'm going to stand behind you one hundred percent, no matter what the outcome is," he says, reaching out and sliding a strand of hair behind my ear.

"You won't be mad about it?" It's a stupid question to ask,

especially since he just told me he would be by my side no matter what.

His brows bunch up in confusion. "Why would I be mad about it? You're doing what you need and want, Soph. That's not something to be mad about."

"I know, but that morning could have ruined everything for you. Your injury could have been worse. You could have been released or traded. Things could have gone differently. If I were you, I would want me to see this through." I start to ramble, stopping myself from going through a whole monologue that would probably not make any sense.

"You're missing the big picture, Soph." Blake gives me a smile, a sweet one that makes me want to melt right here not the couch. "All of those things could have happened, but they didn't. If they had, I might have been pissed off, but they didn't, and I'm not. I will never be mad about you making a decision that makes things easier on you, that takes a weight off your shoulders."

It feels as if my heart literally skips a beat as I look at the man in front of me. There have been so many times throughout our friendship where I thought his mind would go in one direction, but every time it would go in a different one, and it would surprise me. It shouldn't have, but even after so many years of friendship, there are things about Blake that I don't know.

But I do know one thing. This man will always be on my side. He will always want what is best for me. He will always be there to hold my hand no matter what. Even if he's angry, disappointed, or annoyed with me or at me, he will always be there for me. He was there for me at five years old when I wanted my dad at the rink, and he will be there for me now when I make one of the hardest decisions of my life.

He loves me, and he would do anything to show that love to me, no matter how little that act may be.

A small smile spreads on my face. "Thank you," I say, leaning forward and placing a kiss on his lips. It's small and quick but mighty. "Thank you for being at my side and for loving me."

"Always. I will always be by your side, and I will always love you."

Now it's him who is closing the distance between us and giving me a kiss.

"Have you talked to your lawyer?" he asks when he pulls away.

I shake my head. "No, but I was going to call tomorrow morning to set up a meeting for a few days from now."

"Good." A kiss lands on my forehead. "If my schedule allows it, I'll go with you to the meeting."

"I would really love that."

Not wanting another chaste kiss, I place my mouth against his, hungrily.

Our mouths move in unison and soon it feels like I need a lot more than just a few kisses from my man.

Blake apparently is in the same mind set.

"Let's forget about the fucker Elijah," he says against my lips before moving his mouth down to my jaw. "Let's forget about the charges and talking to the lawyer."

"Okay," I say, almost breathless. I will forget about everything as long as he's the one making me forget.

"Good." I feel like his teeth press against my exposed skin. "Now if I remember correctly, there was a purpose to you wearing this jersey. I think it's time I find out what that is, don't you?"

A giggle escapes me as I pull away from him.

"I think it is."

I pull away from him and stand up from the couch. Blake is

about to stand up with me, thinking we are probably going to the bedroom, but I have other plans.

I push him back down and start taking off the faux leather pants, my panties quickly following, leaving me in just the jersey.

A smirk forms on my face as I see him licking his lips at me.

"Let me show you."

CHAPTER FORTY-SIX

SOPHIA

IT TOOK A LOT.

Both emotionally and mentally to walk into my lawyer's office and tell her I have decided to drop all the charges.

When I was telling her, my mind goes back to the police station and how the female officer who helped me when I walked in looked almost proud when I told her that I was going to be pressing charges. By dropping them, I felt like I was disappointing her and everyone else who had been through something similar. I felt like I was giving up and taking the easy way out.

For a few seconds, I was even second guessing myself and wasn't going to pull the plug. I almost went into a panic attack just thinking about it.

If Blake wasn't there with me, I don't know what I would have done. But he was my saving grace like he has always been. Holding my hand as tightly as possible, whispering words of pride in my ear. Without him, I wouldn't have been able to tell myself I was doing the right thing for me.

For me.

I told myself I wasn't going to let fear of Elijah dictate my life anymore. I need to separate myself from him as much as I possibly can. Right now, he's defining everything I do, and my fear of him is stronger than ever.

I don't want to be scared anymore.

So, I leave that lawyer's office doing what I walked in there to do.

I dropped the charges against Elijah. He might have won this battle, and he may dictate my decisions on occasion, but this is what is best for me, and I'm going to stand by my choice.

No matter what.

This is me growing and hoping my future is bright.

CHAPTER FORTY-SEVEN

SOPHIA

MY FUTURE IS BRIGHT.

For so long it wasn't, but now, it's starting to shine in every direction, and I couldn't be happier for it.

There is so much to look forward to, and tonight is the start of it all.

Tonight, I'm doing something I never thought I would do. Something I had dreamed of but never thought was going to become a reality. Especially with the direction my love life was going just a few short weeks ago. But things changed, and it made this possible.

Tonight, I'm going on a first date with Blake.

We may have been officially together for almost a month, but we have yet to go on a first date, and that changes tonight.

Like every other first date I've had, the nerves are at an all-time high, but not for the same reasons as before.

Before I was nervous because I was putting myself out there and wanted the person who ended up sitting across from me to like me, to think I was worth the effort to plan a second date with.

But this is Blake.

This is the person who has been in my life for years and knows almost every detail about me. The man who has seen me at my worst, at my best, and everything in between. The man I already live with and have in my bed every single day. Not a single nerve that is running through me is about if he will like me or not, or if there will be another date after this. There are no thoughts of puking or sweaty palms.

No, the nerves this time around are different and in the best way.

Tonight, the nerves are there because I want this to be the best first date I ever have. I want to make sure everything is special.

Funny how I want this to be special, but when Blake brought it up, I was so confused by it.

My mind goes to the night he brought it up. It was the day we had gone to the lawyer's office. We had gotten home, and I desperately needed a distraction, and he knew that.

"Go on a date with me." He said, as he walked into the kitchen and started taking things out for dinner.

Pasta and Chicken. It was always pasta and chicken when he was in season, and that was something that I was completely fine with because he made it, and I didn't burn down the apartment trying to cook pasta. I will always happily eat anything Blake makes.

"A date?" I ask, clarifying. Why does going on a date with him sound so foreign?

Blake placed his hands against my cheeks, making me look into his icy blues. I melt every time I see them.

"Yes, a date. One where we get to dress up, and I can show the fucking world the beautiful woman I have on my arm, the one I'm never going to let go of. A date where I can take you to dinner and stare into those beautiful brown eyes all damn night."

That sounds like the best thing in the world. As I take in his words, the activities of the day start to fade from my mind, and the only thing that I could think of is the picture he had just painted for me. A picture that I definitely want to experience.

I smiled up at the man in front of me, and I wrapped my arms around his waist and brought my body closer to his.

"We've never been on a date. You and me," I voiced, my smile growing even more.

"I know—this would be our first." A smile of his own formed on his face, and I loved every single bit of it. "So what do you say? Would you go out on a date with me? I promise to make it worth your while."

The wink he throws at me has a chuckle slipping through my lips.

He will definitely make going on a date with him worth it. He makes everything worth it.

There was no hesitation in my response.

"Yes, I would love to go on a date with you." Best distraction a girl could ask for.

Now here I am getting ready so the two of us can have the most perfect first date ever. Even if I don't know a single thing that is planned. Blake did all the planning. He just told me to be ready by a certain time and not ask questions.

But I have questions. Like what to wear because every single article of clothing I own is currently on my floor, and nothing feels right.

"You need to tell me what to get dressed for!" I yell toward my bedroom door, which is currently closed and shielding me from Blake.

Since this was our first date, I wanted to have all aspects of a date, and since he said I couldn't kick him out of his own house, I locked myself in my room and started getting ready.

"No!" Blake yells back, sounding a lot closer than I expected him to be, which tells me he's right outside the door.

"Jacobi! Tell me," I say, frustrated, pulling out the last name card.

"Just dress like you would for any other date," he answers, his voice a lot lower this time, like he's even closer to the door.

"I would like to remind you this isn't like any other date. This is *our* first date, and it needs to be special. So, tell me what I need to wear so I can leave this room, and we can go on with our night."

A chuckle sounds out from the other side of the door. I'm having a crisis right now about what to wear, and this asshole is laughing. He's lucky my hair and makeup are done, because if it wasn't, I would be taking my sweet-ass time.

"Soph, trust me. It's going to be special no matter what. This is me. I don't give two shits what you wear. Want to know why?" he asks, something landing softly against the door.

"Why?" I ask. No yelling. No frustration. Just emotion threatening to mess up the makeup I spent a good thirty minutes doing.

"Because you will look beautiful in whatever you wear. Whether you wear sweats, or the sexiest fucking dress known to man, I will still look at you the same way and still want to bring you home and lose myself in you until neither one of us knows what day of the week it is," he says, his voice making me want to melt.

He's right.

It doesn't matter what I wear. He will still look at me the same way. Like I'm his whole damn world, when in reality he is mine.

As I stand here taking in his words, I know exactly what I want to wear.

"Okay, give me a few more minutes, and I will be right out," I say to the door, a smile spreading across my face.

"I'll be right here," he says, and I just know he's proudly wearing a smile of his own.

And I know he will be there. Because both Blake and I have done everything in our power to show each other we are in this one hundred and ten percent.

Going through my piles of clothes, I find the articles of clothing I need to get my outfit together.

As soon as everything is in place, I look at myself in the mirror I have behind the door and give myself a smile.

I'm going on a date with Blake. After years of wishing this would happen, it finally is. As I continue to look at myself, I realize all the nerves of making tonight perfect are gone, and in their place are butterflies of excitement.

Excitement for what the night will bring.

Excitement for us.

Excitement for our future.

We're really doing this.

We are really together. We're really showing each other how much we love each other. Holy crap.

With a grin on my face, I take a deep breath and open my door.

The look Blake gives me as I walk out is everything. He looks like he's in awe, and when his eyes drag down my body, it makes me wish we could skip this date and just stay in so we could get lost in each other.

"What do you think?" I ask him, twirling so he can get the whole effect.

When I turn back to him, I watch as his Adam's apple bobs a few times while he tries to find the words.

"I um," he starts but quickly pauses as if I rendered him

speechless. "What if we stay home?" he asks, his hands almost twitching to reach for me as he massages the back of his neck. His eyes not leaving my body one bit.

"Nope," I state, even though every single inch of me is buzzing with electricity to agree with him and have him fuck me right here. "You promised me a date. So, we are going on a date. I don't give a shit if it's to get ice cream and back, we're going."

Blake smiles as his eyes make their way up to mine and closes the distance between us.

"You're going to torture me with this dress," he says, cradling my face between his hands.

That was the plan. Torture him until I landed under him, on top of him or on my knees. I wasn't going to be picky.

But he doesn't know that was the plan, so I act like I don't care.

I roll my eyes at him which just makes his smile grow even more. "It's not like it will be the first time that what I wear tortures you," I say to him, my mind going back to that summer night when we were eighteen, and I wore a skirt that drove him crazy.

If that night had ended differently and not filled with regret, we might not be here right now. We could've been at a different stage in our relationship or not together at all.

Even though it hurt me to act like that night never happened, that's what we needed to do. That night changed a lot of things, but it made Blake and I all that much stronger. As individuals and as friends.

"It's not, but there's a difference between then and now," Blake says, caressing my lips with his thumb.

"And what is that?" I ask, placing my hands over his and holding him to me.

"I will wake up tomorrow and have you in my arms without a single ounce of regret rolling through me. The only thing I will want and get to do is to get lost in you over and over again." His lips meet mine, and I can't help but melt against him and get lost in the feeling of his mouth moving along with mine.

"Okay, okay," I say, pulling away from him, because if I don't, we will never make it out of this apartment. "Let's go. And if you play your cards right, you will definitely get lucky afterward," I say, throwing him a wink, and untangling myself from him.

"Baby, with you being at the goal line, I will always play my cards right."

I really roll my eyes at him this time. "Do you use hockey puns on all the girls, Jacobi? Or am I just special?"

"Oh you're definitely special. There's no doubt about that."

He grabs my waist as I walk to the front door and spins me around until I'm facing him, and our bodies are pressed against each other.

"Hi," he says, his words ghost along my lips.

"Hi," I say back, my arms going around his neck.

"You look really pretty tonight," he says, leaning forward so that his nose touches mine.

"You don't look bad yourself." I smile, my lips moving against his almost feather-like.

"I have a girlfriend to impress, so I had to pull out all the stops." My eyes move down just a bit to see a smirk forming on his face.

"I'm sure she greatly appreciates it," I say, bringing my body even closer to him.

"I hope so, too, want to know why?" he asks, his voice low and deep and everything that makes me wish I could slide his hand down between us and relieve some pressure.

"Why?"

"Because I love her with all that I am, and I hope she feels the same way."

I stop breathing. I stop moving. I stop doing everything and solely concentrate on this man and everything he is. "I do. I do love you with all I am, and that is never going to change."

We stand there, forehead against forehead, for a good minute, just taking each other in. Eventually Blake lets out a sigh and places a kiss against my forehead before pulling away.

"Time to take my girl on a date," he says, taking my hand and interlacing our fingers together.

All I can do is smile as he walks out of the apartment we share.

As we make our way out of the building, I can't help but let the butterflies in my stomach soar.

For so long, this is what I've wanted. I wanted to be brave enough to tell Blake how I felt about him and hoped that if and when I did tell him, it wouldn't ruin our friendship, and I wouldn't lose him forever.

As much as I hate Elijah and everything that he put me through, I'm grateful he gave me this. If it wasn't for what he put me through, I might have never found the courage to leave him and finally tell Blake how much my heart beats for him. If it wasn't for Elijah, Blake and I wouldn't be here right now.

I like to think I would have told him eventually, that I would have confessed to be where we are now, but life changes all the time and maybe eventually might have never happened.

My friendship with Blake has been a roller coaster ride, one I'm sure other people would have gotten off of the first chance they got.

But not me.

Because he is everything I need.

My protector.

My best friend.

My whole damn heart.

Blake Jacobi is my everything, and no matter the twists and

turns that are waiting for us in the future, I will never give him up. I will hold his hand as tightly as possible and hope fear never gets in the way of us being together ever again.

Who knew going to the ice rink without my dad would turn into a whole life with the little boy who tried to tie my skates?

CHAPTER FORTY-EIGHT

BLAKE

I DON'T KNOW how I fucking did it.

I have no clue whatsoever, how I was able to go a whole three hours of looking at Sophia in that fucking dress she has on and not go crazy.

But somehow, I was able to power through, get us through dinner *and* dessert, because of course this girl ordered dessert just to torture me, without dying of blue balls. Thank fuck we are currently heading back home because I have no idea how much more I can take.

The girl is like a damn vixen. Every move, every flutter of her eyelashes, every small movement of her legs, everything she did, even eating, I was attuned to it. It was like she knew I was and just tortured me as much as she could. Like it brought her joy seeing me squirm. I lost count how many times I had to adjust my dick while we were eating, it was that bad.

And Sophia acted as if she had not a single clue.

But she did. I know she did, because if she didn't she wouldn't have taken off her heel and started sliding her foot up my damn leg. Like I said the girl is a damn vixen, and she is lethal when she wants to be.

And now it's time to pay her back for it.

The whole car ride back to our apartment, I acted like a good boy and kept my hand on her thigh, not even trying to move it up just a smidge to find out the type of panties she was wearing. I kept myself in check. No matter how much she tried to throw me off course.

I had a game plan, and that game plan wasn't going to get thrown out the window, even when she leaned over the center console and teased me with her tongue.

I was able to make it to our apartment, though, so now it's time for my game plan to come out in full swing.

As soon as we walk into the apartment, Sophia swaying her hips in front of me, I close and lock the door behind us, and I pounce.

Sophia is turned away from me, so she doesn't see me coming up behind her, twisting her body and throwing her over my shoulder.

A gasp leaves her lips when I have her situated. "What are you doing?" she asks, sounding out of breath.

"Having my way with you," I state, walking us over to the master bedroom.

As soon as I deposit her on the bed, she lets out a huff and looks up at me with bright eyes.

God, she's so fucking gorgeous. And she's all mine.

Thank fucking hell.

"And how exactly are you going to be doing that?" She says, leaning up on her elbows and throwing me a smirk. I don't miss how her legs open up just the slightest bit.

I lick my lips at her as I answer.

"I was going to have you fall to your knees for me and take me in that pretty mouth of yours, but I have a better idea."

The vision before me is too much to take, and as much as my dick wants me to take him out so that I can fuck my girl right now, I want to take my time with her. So instead of Sophia falling to her knees, it's me, ready to have my second dessert of the night.

Placing my hands on the tops of her thighs, I drag her body closer to me, her little black dress riding up and exposing her barely covered pussy to me.

Not having the patience to wait a second longer, I tear apart the mesh-style panties and start devouring her.

One lick, or one taste, is never enough when it comes to Sophia. I always want fucking more.

I wanted more after our first time, and I wanted more during our second. I've always wanted more, and now I can get more whenever I want.

My fingers start to tease Sophia, and as one of my fingers starts to slide into her pussy, Sophia arches her body and slides her hands into my hair.

I fucking love when she does that.

"Oh my god, Blake," she moans, tightening her grip on my hair with every movement.

"You like my mouth on you?" I ask, already knowing the answer.

"Yes," she pants, her legs tightening around my head.

I hum against her, sucking on her clit and moving down to lick every inch of her pussy as if she was my last meal on earth.

"You're my favorite taste in the whole fucking world," I say, as I lift my head just enough to plant a kiss on her inner thigh. "I can never get enough."

One of her groans fills the room, and that delicious sound goes directly to my cock. I'm throbbing to slide into her and get wrapped in her warmth, but my concentration isn't on me right now. It's on her and giving her all the pleasure she deserves.

"Blake, I need more," Sophia states, bringing my face closer to her heat and grinding along my face.

A smirk forms on my face. I want to smell her everywhere.

"Take what you want, baby. Take it," I order, moving my fingers faster and circling my tongue around her bundle of nerves.

I pull my mouth away from her and blow on her exposed core. She squirms, and her legs start to shake when I take her clit and pinch it.

"Yes," Sophia pants out. "Oh my god, yes. Blake, please make me come. I'm right there," my girl pleads out, her legs starting to shake even more.

Who am I to deny her?

Whatever she wants, she will get.

I bring my face back to her pussy and give her what she wants. I hold nothing back. Not with my fingers, with my mouth, or my tongue. I take everything that she gives and am rewarded when she explodes and coats my tongue with her sweetness.

Sophia is a panting mess as I lick up her release, and her breathing still isn't controlled by the time I pull away and hover over her.

"I really love when you do that," she says, still breathless.

"Good," I say, leaning down and placing my lips against hers, giving her a taste of herself. "I'm not done with you yet, though. So I hope you are ready for part two of round one."

"I'm ready for everything you want to give me." She smiles up at me, wrapping her legs and arms around me, bringing her body close to mine.

"Good girl,"

I detach myself from her for a quick second to get rid of my clothes, then I'm right back in her arms and give her everything that I can.

Just like she wanted me to.

SOPHIA IS fast asleep right next to me, and I take in every single inch of her face. She is absolutely gorgeous, and I can't get over the fact that she is actually here with me. That she loves me just as much as I love her.

Instead of sleeping, especially since I have an early skate time in the morning, I just lay here and watch her. Memorizing every detail of her face, like I haven't done it a million times already.

As I lay here watching her, my mind goes back to earlier.

As I sat across the table from Sophia at her favorite Thai place tonight, I realized something.

This is probably something I've probably known for a while, but it was during one of the moments when she smiled like I was her favorite person in the whole damn world.

And it was that I wanted to give her everything.

Not just my heart, but my future, no matter where I may land if I ever get traded. I also want to give her my last name. I want to have Sophia at my side through thick and thin. I want her to be there for the rest of my hockey career, cheering me on and telling me how much I suck, no matter the win or the loss. I want to give her the house she deserves and the love story I know that she wants. I want to give her the kids who are exactly like her while they get their love for hockey from me. I want to give her absolutely everything.

We may be young, we may have just started dating, but I want to make this girl mine. Once and for all.

Hunter and Liam told me something a while ago. I may

have been fifteen and eighteen when I heard it, but it has stuck. Sophia can be my best friend and girlfriend at the same time.

At the time I just thought they were just talking out of their asses, that I couldn't have her as both, it had to be as one or their other, but now that I'm looking at her as she sleeps in my arms, in our bed, I know that I was wrong, and they were right.

Fuck.

That will be something I never tell either of them because if I do, I will never hear the end of it.

But they were right.

Sophia can be both things to me.

Even more so, she can be my wife and my best friend.

I *want* her to be my wife and best friend.

It may be time for me to start planning something special.

In the morning. I'll start planning in the morning. For now, I'm going to enjoy having my girl in my arms and getting lost in her body in every single way I can.

CHAPTER FORTY-NINE

BLAKE

Three months later

EVER SINCE WE WERE KIDS, Sophia has always told me she never knew what she wanted to be when we grew up.

Her first option was princess, but of course, that wasn't going to be feasible unless we randomly met someone who was connected to one of the many royal families the world had to offer. Which I doubted was ever going to happen, and I told that to her. The comment earned me a cupcake to the face because, according to her, I was telling her that she wasn't princess material. She was, and definitely still is now, in my eyes, but she didn't take it t way.

Thankfully, she moved away from the princess route.

For years, she kept throwing out ideas of what she wanted to do, never sticking to one thing for more than a day.

When we went to Montana State, she was the same way. Not really sure what she wanted to commit to. Then she randomly fell into nursing.

Well not randomly. I like to think that I helped her a bit with that choice. Especially since I've thought of her as a nurse ever since that party we went to after graduation, the first time we had sex, and she was fixing up my face after that fight with that douchebag Miller.

Since then, she has been helping me with every one of my injuries, no matter how minor it is. She'd helped before then, but I'd like to think that was the tipping point.

When she chose to go into nursing, I supported her the same way she supported me with hockey. With everything that I have.

I might not have been there for every study session, or every long shift she had at the hospital, but I still tried to support her in every single way that I could.

Today, I'm supporting her in the best way possible.

Cheering her on as she crosses the stage at her graduation.

My girl fucking did it, and I could not be prouder.

As soon as she steps foot on that stage, I'm going to be the loudest person in this stadium.

"Was he always this annoying as a kid? Or is that something that came about when he hit puberty three years ago?" Liam leans over and asks Isaac, as we sit in our seats waiting for the graduation ceremony to start.

That's the type of question I would expect from Christian, not my captain.

Isaac, who is sitting next to me, gives him a nod. "I would have him run drills when it got to be too much."

The audacity. The fucking audacity. You would think that being his daughter's best friend and boyfriend would make him love me more, but I guess not.

"How the fuck am I annoying?" I ask, looking at my team-mate and now ex-friend.

"You're bouncing up and down in your seat like you just ate a damn bag of candy," he answers.

"Shut up. I'm not annoying," I say back, flipping him off in the process. "If anyone is annoying, it's you."

"What the hell are you talking about? I'm not annoying," he throws back.

"Both of you are fucking annoying," Christian says, inserting himself into the conversation.

"How?" Both Liam and I ask at the same time.

Christian rolls his eyes at us, but answers anyway. "You," he starts, pointing at me. "You're like a little puppy. A hyperactive puppy, who needs attention all the time. And you," he says, pointing at Liam. "You use way too many punctuation marks when you text. A single period, exclamation point, or question mark is fucking enough. I don't need a damn text bubble filled with them."

Damn.

Why do I get the feeling he's been holding that in for a while?

"Oh my god," Chloe exclaims from the row in front of us, turning in her seat to look at us four men. "All of you are annoying. Now shut up, the ceremony is about to start, and I don't want to hear your voice again until they call Sophia's name. Got it?"

Mama Chloe means business.

She's even giving us the same look that my mom and Maya have given me more than a million times in my lifetime.

"Got it," the three of us answer, and she huffs and turns back to facing forward in her seat.

For a solid minute, Liam, Christian, and I sit there as if we are in timeout or something. We don't say a word, and we don't even move.

"Chloe, are you free to come to some practices back in Montana? I bet if you can shut up three professional hockey players, my kids will fear you," Isaac says, inserting himself into all of this.

The three of us narrow our eyes and look over at the old man, all the while the three women sitting in front of us, Maya, Eliana, and Chloe, start to laugh.

"I'll see if my schedule can allow it," Chloe answers him, the sweetest smile known to man. That smile is nothing but sweet.

Liam picked a good one, and I truly mean that.

Soon the women's laughing dies down when the music to signal graduation is starting begins.

All seven of us don't say a peep until someone spots Sophia in the crowd of graduates, and we all yell like it was our job.

As the ceremony moves through the speeches, and they begin calling out graduates' names and giving out diplomas, my mind starts to run through the plan for tonight.

Sophia thinks that we are going out to dinner with her parents and our friends as soon as we leave here. While that may be true, there is more to the night she doesn't know about.

I've been planning this night for weeks now.

For weeks, I've been both nervous and excited for tonight to come, and now that it finally has, I want this graduation to move faster so we can move on to the next step, and I can hopefully end the night with Sophia in my arms and getting lost in every single inch of her body and her heart.

Name after name is called, and as each passing graduate gets called, it seems like Sophia purposely positioned herself at the end of the line to torture me. I wouldn't put it past her either. The girl knows how to light a fire under my ass, and she enjoys every second of it.

A few more names get called when Maya points toward the crowd.

"There she is. The sixth in line," she says, and everyone scans to where she is pointing.

I have my eyes on my girl within seconds, and as soon as I do, a part of me relaxes.

She's almost there.

One step closer to getting to the rest of the night.

Five graduates cross the stage, then it is Sophia's turn.

As soon as she steps on the stairs to cross the stage, the seven of us stand up and the second she steps on the stage and her name gets called out, it's pure craziness.

All seven of us yell out in celebration as she gets handed her diploma and walks off. Even as she walks back to her seat, the yelling continues and doesn't quiet down until she is sitting down.

From there, the ceremony finishes off quickly.

And we all rush down to floor level to find our graduate.

It doesn't take long for me to find her, and within seconds of her catching my gaze, she is in my arms.

"I'm so damn proud of you," I say to her, before taking her in my arms and giving her a kiss.

Sophia beams up at me when we pull apart, and she is quickly pulled into her mom's arms, followed by her dad's.

As I watch her go from one person to the other, my heart pounds in my chest.

She went to Montana State not knowing what she wanted to do, and when she finally decided and was settled, I asked her to follow me to Chicago. I will be forever grateful she did. Coming to Chicago without Sophia was never an option, and I'm glad that she went along with the craziness and decided to come with me, because if she hadn't, I wouldn't have known what to do with myself.

Now two, almost three years later, here we are at her graduation for her nursing degree, as an official couple, and I'm hours away from making her mine forever.

Because just like I couldn't come to Chicago without her, I can't continue living life without her officially being mine in every single aspect of the word.

Like she told me when we were ten, always and always.

"WHAT ARE WE DOING HERE?" Sophia asks as I pull up to the Knights arena.

Hockey season is officially over for the Dark Knights. It has been for a few weeks now, so coming to the arena is a little out of the norm these days.

"I have a surprise," I answer her, pulling the car into the player's parking lot.

The security guard on duty tonight waves me right in which just confused Sophia even more, because usually I have to show my ID or something.

"A surprise?" she asks, shifting in her seat to look at me.

"Yes, a surprise," I confirm, pulling into the first parking spot I see.

"Is this some sort of secret concert I don't know about?" she asks after I get out of the car and circle around to open her door. "Oh my god, is it Taylor Swift?"

I roll my eyes at her as she takes the hand I offer, and she gets out of the car.

"Do you really think I have the kind of money to get Taylor Swift and have her play a secret concert just for you?"

I don't even want to calculate how big my next contract has to be for me to be able to afford that.

"No, but you could have asked your brother or even

Grayson Lane. You're always saying how he would do anything for his players, and his family is filthy rich. I'm sure if you'd asked him, he would have made that happen." She gives me a look like it's the simplest thing in the world.

"It's not Taylor Swift," I say, nailing it down.

"You suck. What kind of boyfriend doesn't want to surprise his girlfriend with her favorite artist?" she asks, a playful smirk forming on her lips.

"The kind who has other surprises," I say, guiding her out the parking area and into the arena.

"Can you just tell me what the surprise is then?" she asks as we start making our way through the corridor of the arena.

I shake my head at my girlfriend. "Nope, you are going to find out the old fashion way."

Soph lets out a small grunt that just makes me want to snort. The girl is pulling out all the stops tonight, and I'm loving it.

"Fine," she says with a slight whine. I know if I were to turn around right now, she would have a smile on her face right about now that would tell me how much she was enjoying herself.

If she is smiling, hopefully that smile is about to grow ten times over when she sees what I have planned.

Thankfully, I don't have to wonder what her expression is going to be for much longer because soon I reach the door I was directed to use and lead her through. As soon as she walks into the lit-up arena, she lets out a small gasp.

"Why is the ice up?" she asks as I close the door behind us and take her hand as she takes in the space a level down.

"Because I asked them to," I say to her, a smile forming on my face.

"Why would you do that?" She turns to me, a curious look on her face.

"Because I wanted to treat my girlfriend to an unforgettable night." I take her hands once more and guide her down to the ice.

This is all part of the plan.

A few weeks ago, I was thinking of how I wanted this night to go. I wanted it to be special and something the two of us would find special. I kept going back to how we first met all those years ago, and since we couldn't go to Montana for the night, I thought I would recreate it here.

Thankfully, Grayson was able to help me out with letting me use the place and having the ice set up with no questions asked.

As we make it down to the ice, Sophia's eyes grow a bit bigger as she takes in all the small little details that are in front of us.

The two pairs of skates—a hockey pair and a figure skating pair. Flowers of all kinds making a pathway to the ice and some more flowers at center ice.

It's like she is putting all the pieces together and trying to figure it all out in her head.

"An unforgettable night," she says, repeating my words, as I guide her to the nearest seat and go and grab the skates that are waiting for us.

I grab hers and hold them up.

"Can I help you tie your skates?" I ask, a smile forming on my face.

Sophia right away looks up at me, like she's remembering something.

If this is going to plan, she is remembering the first time we met.

"Do you even know how?" she asks, her own smile forming as she asks me the question her mom asked me all those years ago.

I give her a shrug. "I've been skating since I was two. I definitely know how to tie some laces."

She lets out a sweet laugh that is absolute music to my ears. "Then I wouldn't trust anyone else to tie my skates. Go right ahead."

My smile turns into a smirk as I fall to my knees in front of her and start sliding off the heels she is wearing and switching them for the skates.

She can tie her own skates. Sophia actually learned to do it before I even did, but no matter what stage we were at in our lives, or even in our friendship, she would always have me tie up her laces every time we went skating together.

As I do it now, she watches me the entire time, like she is in awe of what I'm doing.

When her skates are done, I quickly put mine on and don't hesitate in reaching for her hand again as soon as I'm finished.

She happily slides her hand into mine and walks onto the ice with me, her smile growing with every single second.

I skate us over to center ice and turn to face her, placing my hands on her hips and bringing her body closer to mine.

"What are you doing, Blake?" she asks, placing her hands around my neck as best she can with our new height difference, just as a soft melody starts playing through the speakers.

"Recreating the first time we met," I say, leaning down and placing a kiss against her lips.

"I don't remember us dancing." She smiles up at me, her eyes absolutely glowing.

"I made a few tweaks," I say, giving her a smile on her lips.

"Okay." Another one of her laughs fills my ears in the best way possible. "Better question, why are you doing all of this?" she asks.

I'm about to answer her, but she slides one of her hands into my hair, and I try not to get lost in the way her fingers move against my scalp. Trying, but definitely not succeeding.

"I wanted to give you a special night. One where it's just you and me while we relive a few key memories that brought us together." I lean down and press my forehead against hers, wanting to be as close to her as possible.

"Is this the surprise?" she asks, curiosity coating her voice.

"Part of it," I answer truthfully.

"What's the other part?"

"Dance with me for a bit longer, and I will show you."

She gives me a nod and we glide across the ice as one song turns into two and then three.

During the fourth song, I break our comfortable silence. "Do you remember what I promised you that first day? Right before we got on the ice?"

Sophia moves her head as it's still pressed against mine. "You told me not to worry, that you will protect me."

"I still stand by that. It doesn't matter if you're afraid of falling on the ice, or if I'm barging into a hotel room. I will always protect you, you will never have to worry about that."

"I know," she lets out, her breath shaking a bit.

"I will also stand by your side whenever you need me, and if you ever want to move to a different state because that's where work is, then I will follow you, just like you came to Chicago with me. Wherever you go, I'll go, too."

Tears start to form in her eyes, and I can tell that she is trying her hardest to keep them at bay, but she is having a hard time.

"Before we got together, before you officially became mine, I never wanted to lose you. I didn't want to tell you I was in love with you because I would have been beside myself if I ever hurt you and lost you completely. Now, I still don't want to lose you, but I'm going to tell you that I love you every single day for the rest of my life. Because I do love you, with everything that I am and have."

The tears she was trying to keep in finally make their way out, so I reach out ever so slightly and wipe them away with my thumbs. My fingers caress her skin as I touch her face.

"I have two things for you. One was supposed to be your Christmas gift this past year, and the other is something I hope you hold as dear as you hold the locket I gave you when I was fifteen. Do you want to see them?"

Sophia nods eagerly, not saying a thing.

With a smile, I slide a few inches away from her, letting both of our hands fall off each other as I reach for the box that I've had since December and have been waiting to give her.

In retrospect, I should have given her this a long time ago. There were plenty of moments to do so, but for some reason, this felt like the best time to do it.

I take the small box out of my pocket and open it before handing it to her.

Inside are two pictures of the two of us that fit perfectly in her locket. One from last year from when the Knights won the Cup, and the other from a few weeks ago. Originally, I had a picture of the two of us from my first NHL game, but when we officially got together, I wanted to use a more recent picture. One where we are in bed, and Sophia is cradled under my arm as I take the picture.

She lets out a small chuckle as she looks at the small circles, while the tears finally escape. "I love these so much," she says, looking up at me.

"I'm glad."

"Thank you, my love." She closes the distance between us and gives me a kiss.

"You're welcome," I say against her lips. "I have one more thing for you," I tell her. Taking the box from her hand and closing it again before sliding it into the pocket of my slacks. Can't go losing the pictures.

"What is it?" she asks, her voice barely a whisper.

I reach into my other pants pocket and cradle the box that's there with all the strength I have.

"I love you, Sophia. I've loved you for as long as I can remember, and I never want to let you go. You're going to tell me this is way too fast, that we just got together no more than five months ago, that there is no need to rush. But I'm not rushing. I've thought about this moment for years, and when it comes to us, it could never be too fast. We know each other in a way we will never know anyone else. We are two pieces of a locket that came together by chance, and now people will have to pry us open in order to separate us. You are my world, Sophia, and you have been since I was a kid who barely knew how to tie skates. So, I want to ask you this."

I put a bit of distance between us, and getting down on one knee as stable as I possibly can with skates on and pulling out the ring box I've had hidden in our apartment for three weeks now.

A gasp leaves her mouth accompanied by more tears.

Feeling tears of my own starting to spring, I try to keep myself controlled as much as I can to be able to ask the question I've been planning on asking for a long while.

"Sophia Martinez, will you marry me? Will you marry me and be by my side, always and always, from now to forever?"

Not an ounce of hesitation rolls through her as she answers my question not even ten seconds later.

"Yes. Oh my god, yes. Yes, I will marry you."

I'm not going to lie, there was a part of me that thought that she was going to say no. That she was going to fight me on this and tell me to wait a little bit longer because we are still young. I would have waited if she told me to, but thank fuck she didn't. Because now she is one step closer to being all mine.

"Yes?" I ask, just to clarify.

She nods eagerly. "Yes. A million times yes."

With a grin, I take the ring I had designed for her out of the box and slide it onto her finger. It fits effortlessly. It's fucking perfect.

I stand up to my full height and take her face between my hands and take a second to stare into her light brown eyes.

Earlier this year, I didn't think I would ever be getting this moment. I never thought I would tell Sophia that my heart beats for her and only her, let alone propose to her. I thought I was going to live the rest of my life, with memories of our two nights together and having to watch as she married someone else.

Never did I think this moment would ever come, yet here I am.

Flying high, with the woman who owns every single part of me, wearing my ring on her finger and my locket around her neck.

She's mine. She has been for years and will be for more years to come.

Sophia is my everything, and I am hers, and I can't see spending my life with a better person, a better woman.

This all started when we were five years old on a chance meeting, and now, almost nineteen years later, it's turning into this beautiful thing.

This woman is my best friend, the love of my life, my everything, and soon she will be my wife.

Thank fuck I got my head out of my stubborn ass.

"I love you so damn much, Sophia. I don't think I can ever explain just how deep my love for you goes," I say, leaning forward so that my lips are barely gliding over hers. I'm hungry for her, but at the same time I want to take my time exploring every inch of her and give her the sweetest type of pleasure.

"You don't have to explain because I feel the same way. I love you, Blake, so damn much."

Always and always.

That's all I need.

That's all I ever needed, and I'm finally getting it.

Hockey or no hockey, I will always have Sophia at my side no matter what.

From now to forever.

EPILOGUE
SOPHIA

One year later

I WALK DOWN THE AISLE, with flowers in my hand, and when I see him, I can't help but to smile.

At the end is the man who is my everything, meeting my gaze and giving me the brightest smile known to man. It's my favorite smile of his, one I will always love and cherish. The fact that it's even directed at me still blows my mind, even after everything we've been through.

I let my eyes move down from his face to admire him in a tux, and my smile can't help but to grow even more. This must be my favorite look on him, especially when his curls are gelled to perfection. I can't wait to mess them up later.

Seeing him in a suit, though, will never beat seeing him in full hockey gear.

The man may stink like a pair of dirty socks at the bottom of a hockey bag that haven't been washed in months half the time, but there is something hot about it.

My eyes travel back up to his face as I continue to walk

closer to the altar and hold onto his gaze the whole time until I take my spot with the other bridesmaids.

He mouths I love you, and I instantly feel a blush creep up my cheeks. Even if we've been a couple for an official year, I will never get tired of hearing him say that.

I mouth the words back, and our stares connect until the wedding march starts.

Both of us turn to watch as Selena walks down the aisle to Hunter.

After years, they are finally getting their happily ever after.

As I watch Selena walk down the aisle to Hunter, with her mom and her dad at her side, I can't help but feel so much love for her. She looks absolutely beautiful today, glowing in every single way.

I turn to Hunter for a quick second and see him wiping away a few tears as he watches his bride close the distance between us. Seeing him like that brings tears to my own eyes.

Blake better have tears on our wedding day, too, or I'm going to kick him.

All thoughts of violence go out the door as soon as Hunter takes Selena's hand in his, after shaking her dad's hand and placing a kiss against her mom's cheek, and the ceremony officially starts.

For fifteen minutes, close to a hundred people watch as these two people who are made for each other, come together as one, and there isn't a single dry eye in the house. Everything about the ceremony is perfect, even more so when the officiant tells everyone in attendance the two of them said their vows privately before the ceremony. Something that suits them both perfectly. I'm happy they were able to have that moment for themselves.

Right before the exchange of the rings, I look around the couple and catch a glimpse of Blake.

He's not looking in my direction, his whole concentration is on his brother and new sister, so I take the time to admire him.

For almost twenty years, we have been in each other's lives.

We have seen each other at our best and our worst. We have been there for each other when the other needed it most. Whether it was a shoulder to cry on, someone to laugh with, or just to hold someone's hand, we have been there for each other.

At five years old, I knew that Blake was going to be in my life for a very long time. I knew he was always going to be there for me, and I was going to be there for him. I knew that we were going to be best friends forever before I knew what forever meant.

And he is. We may be in a different type of relationship, but Blake will always be my best friend forever before anything else. And I wouldn't have it any other way.

There is no greater person I could have loved to go through life with than him. He has been my everything since I was five years old, and he will continue to be until the end of time.

Our love for each other has evolved into something unimaginable and unexpected. It makes me glad my mom wasn't able to tie my skates that day at the rink, because if she had, Blake and I wouldn't be here right now.

We wouldn't be engaged to be married. We wouldn't have had our nights together. We wouldn't have been able to move past everything to do with Elijah and the dropping the charges against him. I wouldn't be here, wearing the locket he gave me for my fifteenth birthday. So many things wouldn't be what they are now.

Her not being able to tie my skates was probably one of the best things that could have happened to me.

Next time that I see her, I will thank her. She'll think that I'm crazy, but I don't care. It's because of her, I'm so close to marrying my best friend.

My attention comes back to the wedding when the officiant announces that Hunter may kiss his bride.

Everyone erupts and doesn't hesitate to show their happiness for the couple. After years of being together, they are finally married.

Soon things shift to cocktail hour, to pictures for the families and the wedding party, and in a blink of an eye, dinner is done, and people are dancing like there's no tomorrow.

"Dance with me," Blake asks, after spending the last five minutes talking to his dad, while I talked to Jainie.

I give my fiancé a smile and place my hand in his outstretched one and let him lead me to the dance floor.

A slow song is playing, and couples are filling the space, getting lost in their little bubbles.

Blake and I get lost in each other, too. Because even though we've been within five feet of each other since the ceremony, it feels as if we haven't had a minute just the two of us.

"Have I told you that you look fucking beautiful tonight?" he asks, his hands molding themselves to my body.

"You might have, but I don't mind hearing it again," I say, throwing him a smile.

He lets out a chuckle before leaning down and placing a kiss against my lips.

"You look fucking beautiful," he says, his lips barely a whisper against mine.

"I can say the same thing about you," I say before stealing another kiss.

The laugh that he lets out is like music to my ears, and I wish my brain had a record button so I can hear it when he's gone for an away game, which is going to be a staple in our lives for plenty of more years to come.

Come September, Blake is entering his fifth year in the NHL, just signing on for another four years in Chicago, and he shows no signs of stopping. He's at the top of his game, and even though they didn't make it to the Cup Finals this year or even last year, I have a feeling they will get back to being that championship winning team in no time.

They might need some extra work, but they can get there. More so if Liam, Christian, Blake, and Logan are going to be Knights for a while.

While Blake signed on for another four years for the Knights. I signed a contract of my own with one of the top hospitals in Chicago. After getting my degree and license, I bounced around different departments around the city until I was able to find one that had a permanent opening.

I've officially been a pediatric nurse in one of the top departments in the state for five months now, and I couldn't be happier.

Things are working out. Things are better.

When I was with Elijah, I didn't think things would ever be like this. I thought I was going to continue to live with fear running through my veins. I'm glad I was wrong.

Because if I had continued to let fear dictate me, I wouldn't be in Blake's arms right now, with his ring on my finger, ready for whatever comes next.

As the music flows around us, and one slow song turns into another one, I get lost in Blake's arms, absolutely content with where I am.

If I could live life with his arms wrapped around me until I'm old and wrinkly, I would.

"Let's get married," Blake says low enough so that I can only hear, taking me out of my thoughts.

"Um, we are," I say, lifting my head from where it rests on his chest and giving him a confused look. "Or did you forget?"

The way he smiles at me, makes me want to melt right here in the middle of the dance floor.

"No, I didn't forget." He leans down and places another kiss against my lips, before pulling away all too quickly. "We should pick a date, though, because I don't know how much longer I can wait not having you as my wife and officially mine forever."

"Babe, I've been yours since we were teenagers," I say to him, threading my hand in his curls. And it's the truth. From the second he gave me my locket, I was his, even though neither one of us knew it at the time.

"True, but it's not official until we share the same last name. So, we should get on that." A smirk forms on his face as he speaks.

"Do you have a date in mind?" I ask the question, curious if he does or not.

We've just started talking about wedding planning, since things have been hectic because of my work schedule and getting ready for Hunter and Selena's wedding. Things are going to become crazier come September and hockey season starts back up again.

"I do," he tells me, with a curt nod.

Color me even more curious.

"And what date would that be?"

"September 1st," he answers without even thinking.

I let the date run through my head.

"Why does that day sound familiar?" I ask, trying to remember why that day is important.

"Because it's the day my parents announced they were getting a divorce."

I feel my eyebrows shoot up. "You want to get married on the day your parents told you they were getting a divorce?"

That's a little weird. I know his relationship with Roy is getting better with each passing day, but getting married on that day seems a little much.

"No," Blake says, reaching to run his thumb between my

eyebrows. "I want to get married on the day my best friend told me that she will love me always and always, hockey or no hockey."

A small gasp leaves me.

That night has always been a prominent moment between the two of us, and it's something I remember constantly. The fact that I do, makes me wonder how I forgot such an important date.

The more I think about it, the more I like the idea of getting married that day. It's a special one for us, and it fits our story so perfectly.

"Okay, let's get married September 1st," I say to him, giving him a grin.

"Fuck yeah." Instead of kissing me, he non-discretely places his hands against my ass and gives me a good squeeze.

I can't even reprimand him for groping me in public, especially where his parents and grandparents are, because I realize he never said which September he wants to get married. He just said the month, not the year, and currently we are in June, and September is less than three months away.

"Wait, September of this year or next?" I ask, crossing my fingers that he says next, because no way will we be able to pull off a wedding this September.

"Did you not hear me when I said that I don't want to wait any longer? Yes, September of this year." He rolls his eyes at me like I'm the crazy one.

Instantly panic runs through my body.

Two months.

He wants to plan a wedding in two months?!

"Are you insane?!" I ask, the dancing completely forgotten.

"Baby, when it comes to you, always," he says, throwing me a wink, bringing my body closer to his and continuing moving us.

Dancing is the last thing on my mind.

As Blake spins us, my mind starts to panic-create a list of everything we need to be able to do to pull this off.

I need a dress.

We need to find a caterer.

Fine tune the guest list.

Find him a tux.

Find a venue. Oh my god! We need to find a venue!

What is the possibility this venue has availability? It's nice. I'm sure they would be happy to have another Jacobi wedding. It's in California, though, and we have no ties to California.

But right now, I can't be picky.

Oh my god, is this how my parents felt when we were planning my quinceañera? Because this is stressful as fuck.

I'm in the middle of putting together color pallets in my head, when Blake places a finger under my chin and brings my face up so that I can look up into his icy blue eyes.

"Soph, baby, relax. We will handle everything tomorrow. For right now, let's just enjoy each other. Tomorrow we'll think about our future."

Tomorrow.

Right. We don't have to think about planning a wedding right in the middle of another one.

Tomorrow I will worry about everything. For right now, we just need to enjoy the moment.

"Tomorrow," I say, giving him a smile on my own.

Panic about planning a wedding in two months still rolls through me, but I try to forget about it as much as I can. At least for the next couple of hours.

Right now, I want to get lost in this moment with Blake and not think about anything else.

"Soph," Blake says, his hold on me growing tighter.

"Yeah?"

"You'll love me even when I stop playing hockey, right? You won't leave me?" he asks, and as soon as I hear the words, tears spring into my eyes.

For a minute, I'm taken back to that moment fifteen years ago, and I remember the hurt little boy who just wanted his dad to show him love in any way he could.

Like that night, I wrap my arms tightly around his head and bring his face closer to mine so that my lips can ghost against his.

"I will be by your side and love you for always and always. Hockey or no hockey."

"That's all that I want. I love you, Sophia. Always and always."

"I love you too, Blake. Always and always."

WANT TO STEP FURTHER INTO THE DARK KNIGHT WORLD?

Read the first 2 books in the series!

Read Liam and Chloe's story!
Grab Skating the Blue Line today and start reading!
Read it today!

Read Christian's and Eliana's story!
Grab Passing The Red Line today and start reading!
Read it today!

CHECK IT OUT!

Did you know that Blake's brother has his own book?
Check out Hunter and Selena's story in Worth Every Second!
Read it today!

WHAT'S COMING UP NEXT?

Are you wondering if Logan Volkov is getting his own book?
He is!
But before we get to Logan, we have to step into the darkness
a bit.
And why not start that by stepping into the world of the Lane
Family?
Book 1 of the Lane Family is coming Summer 2024! I hope you
are ready!
Pre-order now!

PLAYLIST

Little Do You Know - Alex & Sierra
Jealous (with Ella Mai) - Kiana Ledé
Nonsense - Sabrina Carpenter
To Be So Lonely - Harry Styles
Cruel Summer - Taylor Swift
I miss you, I'm sorry - Gracie Abrams
Best Friend - Rex Orange County
Dress - Taylor Swift
Anything 4 u - LANY
Friends - Ed Sheeran
Feelings - Lauv
You Are In Love (Taylor's Version) - Taylor Swift

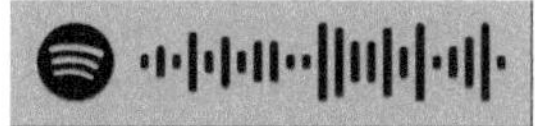

ACKNOWLEDGMENTS

Where do I start with this?

This book has been a long time coming. I for sure thought that it was going to be ready by the original release date that I had set up, but it wasn't. I cannot begin to tell you how much it hurt to see the date come and pass and not be able to give readers this book.

But Sophia and Blake needed time. They needed the fine tuning and that extra time to become something that I'm proud of.

These two were definitely a challenge, to say the least. They were both stubborn and so hard to get right but I think that I did it. I think I was able to capture them in the best way that I could.

At first this was supposed to a simple Friends to Lovers story. It was supposed to be overly steamy and get right to the point. That idea changed drastically. These two needed to tell their story from the very beginning. They needed to show people that the love that they have for each other has been there for day one. This book has taken so many different direction and I'm so happy this was the final one.

This one is a hard one, one that I didn't think I was ever going to finish, but here we are. With the words THE END finally written.

I couldn't have gotten here with out a few people.

To the readers - thank you for sticking by me as I got this book right. Thank you for your encouraging words and your patiences. I don't know what I would do without you.

Shauna and The Author Agency - Thank you for telling me it was okay, and for being there for the number of release date changes that I threw your way.

Becky - I truly appreciate you! I don't know if I could have gotten to the point of loving this book without your help. This book probably wouldn't have seen the light of day without you.

Ellie - I can't tell you how much I appreciate you for always dealing with my craziness of last minute deadlines.

Now it's time fore the next one.... But is it Logan?

I guess you're going to have to wait and see....

ABOUT THE AUTHOR

Jocelyne Soto is an independent author living in California. She loves reading romance and discovering new authors. She comes from a big Mexican family, and with it comes a love for all things family and food.

Jocelyne has a love for her mom's coffee and writing. In her free time, you can find her reading a romance novel on her kindle while writing heartwarming and chaotic romance stories in between. From sport romance to dark romance, there is no limit as to the type of stories that will come to Jocelyne's mind.

Check out her website for ways to connect with Jocelyne!
www.jocelynesoto.com

bookbub.com/authors/jocelyne-soto

goodreads.com/jocelynesotobooks

instagram.com/authorjocelynesoto

tiktok.com/@authorjocelynesoto

facebook.com/authorjocelynesoto

x.com/authorjocelynes

pinterest.com/authorjocelynesoto

threads.net/@authorjocelynesoto

JOIN MY READER GROUP

Join my ever-growing Facebook Group. You get first looks, sneak peeks and giveaways!

NEWSLETTER

Sign up for my Newsletter!
You will get notified when there are new
releases to look out for, giveaways and more!